Christmas
Dad '93

CITY OF LIGHT

CITY OF LIGHT

A NOVEL BY

MICHAEL DOANE

Alfred A. Knopf   New York   1992

A NOTE ON THE TYPE

The text of this book was composed in Melior, a typeface
designed by Hermann Zapf and issued in 1952. Born in Nu-
remberg, Germany, in 1918, Zapf has been a strong influence
in printing since 1939. Melior, like Times Roman, another
popular twentieth-century typeface, was created specifically
for use in newspaper composition. With this functional end
in mind, Zapf nonetheless chose to base the proportions of
its letterforms on those of the golden section. The result is a
face of unusual strength and surpassing subtlety.

Composed by Brevis Press, Bethany, Connecticut
Printed and bound by The Haddon Craftsmen,
Scranton, Pennsylvania
Designed by Irva Mandelbaum

For Claudine

ACKNOWLEDGMENTS

I am indebted to more people with each book, and this time I would like to thank my sister, Kitty Doane Byram, for her assistance with medicines and healing; my wife, Claudine, for her accurate French; Eric Ashworth, for his unswerving confidence; Gary Fisketjon, for helping me through the clumsy phases with humor and skill; Mark Rosenberg, for his belief in the story; and Bradley Aldern, faithful reader, who knows the language.

Contents

CITY OF LIGHT

ELEVEN GONE
TO BLUE

On a white-hot August morning in the City of Light, the second message comes in over the wires and Zane is there to transcode it:

ELEVEN GONE TO BLUE. LIGHT WATER.

The first message, identical, had arrived the previous night over the leased line, a public network more commonly used for press dispatches. It had been addressed to Zane if not the whole plugged-in universe. In theory, only Zane would be able to understand it, having devised that language himself and taught it to his rakers, each in his own dialect. It is their parallel language, slangs and idioms personal to Thomas Zane of ABRI rather than a system or code that might be cut down to size by a microcomputer and some clever technician. There is no way to solve it except through Zane. He is the only possible listener. When they speak, they speak to him and he is the unraveler of both their news and their loneliness.

Petitjean cuts a screen print to record the message, date, source, and time. He wonders whether or not Zane will tell Emelle. "I mean to say, now that we have the kicker."

The message in the night, coming over the leased line, had cut no ice. That line is known to traffic in strategic lies, plants and rumors, personal rumination, electric graffiti, and parasitic 16-bit hogwash; whatever God knows in his own tele-lingua. Now

5

and then, when scanning the prints, Zane has recognized love notes from homesick rakers coded as agricultural data or bogus flight reservations or a simple fuzzwah of garbled letters that only an intimate or a lover would understand. Some even drop the code altogether and send worded arrows into the network like personals in the *Village Voice*. Once there was this message: "Gloria sings me to sleep. This lullaby I heard all night. I awaken clean." The message was from Mozart, at the time in Afghanistan, who'd known it would get from print to eye to mouth to her ear, his mistress in London, the discreet wife of a Sir.

Zane is sick from the heat, from fear, from no sleep at all. He has waited ten hard hours for this kicker or its denial to appear. The man who sent the first message—and only Zane can identify him—must have been hurried and thus had grasped for the leased line; a warning shot through the public phones to get Zane's attention. Protocol calls for confirmation of such a message and it has come ten hours later over the dedicated line, a direct-dial numeric-letter equivalent that has shown up first in raw octal numbers: 65 6C 65 76 65 6E 20 67 6F 6E 65 20 74 6F 20 62 6C 75 65 2E . . . And then as a decode on the black screen:

ELEVEN GONE TO BLUE. LIGHT WATER.

Zane taps for a repeat and the same message appears.

He is running but he vomits on his shoes before hitting the toilet. Bends to remove these shoes and clean them in the sink. Rinses his mouth with warm water that tastes of metal. Spits and leans low to the porcelain and just breathes in and out.

Petitjean is behind him. "Must be the heat," he says. "It gets to all of us. The wind blows like this and it's worse. Makes you be crazy."

Zane wipes his shoes dry with a paper towel, checks his socks, and laces up. "Where's Emelle?"

"At the Lebanese embassy," Petitjean says. "On the rue Copernic. She won't be in till this afternoon. Do I put in a call?"

"It can wait."

"Rules say—"

"The rules can wait, too. They can wait forever. I'm waiting."

Returning to his desk, Zane takes keys, cigarettes, lighter, address book, and money from a drawer. The Air France calendar says it is *lundi, le 20 août*, and the moon is at three quarters. Until two weeks ago the weather was stunning and cold from Oslo to Madrid but now the temperature has risen and summer's gone to hell on them all. Eleven gone to blue.

Petitjean follows him to the front door. "If Emelle calls, what do I tell her?"

"Tell her Eleven has gone to blue. Tell her Light water."

"You're the only one who knows what it means."

Zane stops, turns, and leans his head back against the open door. His eyes are closed and he takes several deep breaths. "Light water means proof of purchase," he says. "It means he saw it with his own eyes."

"Who saw it? Zane, wait! What did he see?"

But Zane is already halfway down the rue des Martyrs, heading south, a sheet of paper with those same printed words in his shirt pocket. The morning has a chemical smell to it, a stink of diesel fuel and fish oil, and the sky has already gone white from the heat. Crossing the street, he dodges a green garbage truck manned by a team of Senegalese. The driver looks right through him and rumbles into the intersection while Zane imagines the alternative of his own corpse in disarray on the pavement. On the narrow walk, he dances over dogshit and a rolling empty bottle. A bus pausing at the corner blows a hot blast of exhaust at his midriff. When he touches a hand to his face he finds that both cheek and fingers are laced with sweat. He continues on for another six streets before realizing that he's walking aimlessly and to counter his lack of direction he heads for the nearest kiosk and buys the *Times* of London, *Libération, Le Monde*, and the *International Herald Tribune*, then he tucks them under his arm and walks another street before stopping to scan the headlines. But his eyes won't work for him—he registers nothing—and one street later he stuffs the pages into an overflowing trash can.

There is not a chance, not the least hope of rain or the sanity of a cool breeze. He feels the full weight of himself within his shoes and there is a rattle in his breath that hours of swallowing has not stilled. He would exchange day for night and proof of purchase for his money back. The sky is as empty as it has ever been and that is what he will long remember of that morning, the pure and powder-dry emptiness of that sky over the chaos of August. And this, he knows, will be the living out of his loss; to breathe it in, all of it; to breathe in all that sky and then to breathe it out again. He is already crossing the Pont des Arts when he remembers where it is he truly is heading. To tell a wife that she may be a widow. There is nothing whiter than this sky and he has forgotten his shades and he is going blind looking for the other side of this water.

Raker is Zanespeak for the writers, photographers, merchants, witnesses, and simple tourists who supply him with his text. Zane writes on dead leaves the stories they have to tell.

It is the work of amnesty, the search for that wider network of intersecting beams of the human face. Our candle and your mirror, these rumors for your eyewitness: The location of a construction site said to be a budding prison. Names of detainees and of first kin. Was it N'Kaunda or N'Karanda? Monday night or Tuesday dawn? Four hundred rifles, yes, but of what origin and make? Our needle to your thread, we stitch rags of evidence together, print it, file it, broadcast it. The ABRI historian died three years ago and has never been replaced. The task of weaving what they know into a coherent rendering of humanity is too staggering for any one employee.

Our candle to your mirror. Shining on the human face.

Twenty-six dead. I counted twice and wrote the number on my palm. All female. Some raped. Kalashnikov shells in the ashes of the village. Sick scene. Need drugs or worse to get to sleep here.

G. Honsou set free today. Right foot amputated. Authorities say infection from self-inflicted wound. G.H. not saying.

Forgive the silence. Laid up with pharaoh's curse. Quinine in lieu of gin. Solomon dead. Light water.

Stars everywhere and no juice. I hang my head. Send funny hats.

When the message is urgent and the heat is on, the words are transmitted in Zanespeak for those who can write it. Stars, he is the only one to know, are soldiers. Juice is a path of communication to the outside world—a phone, a telex, a telefax. If you're hanging your head, you're in hiding. Sending funny hats is a spin on a particular way of asking that the threat be published.

Stars erased the Hilton. Gone back to the bush to read paperbacks. Stay tuned.

When a message comes in Zanespeak, he has to treat it with care. He is the only one listening and so the next move is his alone. It is his own sector, Africa, which has sprung a leak, and for some time now Emelle has only tolerated him because of the quality of his data—and perhaps as well because of that look of rage showing through from just under his thin skin. He's been six years in the agency and to protect his sources he goes out of his way to look as though he might snap at any time.

But even if he were to ask it, the rakers would not break code. They've been burned too often in the past, sending messages in straight English and finding them either buried or reproduced in a flat journalese that has twisted the truth two or three degrees either way. Demi, Mozart, Snake Eyes, Full House, Postcard, Eleven. Zane protects their anonymity with gritted teeth. In the past few years he has had to dance around the mountain with Interpol, MI6, the IRS, the FBI, and French internal security CRS, always the constant *persuasion* to provide a glossary, a key, or a transcoder in the name of international cooperation. We are in this together, is a common refrain. East and West, North and South. So let's pitch in. Speak to me, Zane. Sing.

Eleven gone to blue, he is singing. Light water.

He finds that he hasn't yet walked to the ends of the earth. This is still Paris and there is still this white sky. He stops at the first brasserie that's open for business and orders a double whisky with ice. The French are stingy with ice and there is a single cube. He drinks the whisky down and orders another, but then his legs are carrying him back to the street and he continues to walk west until his feet are firmly on the rue de Babylone. The traffic has thinned and the morning has grown quiet. Number 17 is to his left. He buzzes for entry and pushes open the heavy door.

Plastic flowers decorate the entryway, and a framed Monet print that has yellowed from years of exposure. The concierge parts the curtains to see who's there and he looks at her until she shivers and goes away. He stands for a moment in front of the elevator, and decides on the stairs. He is buying time in minutes to slow his beating heart. Then he climbs the six floors a step at a time. A step at a time to her door.

She doesn't know the language. She is fluent in English, French, Spanish, Afrikaans, and Zulu. She has notions of Italian, Russian, and Arabic. She knows the language of paint on canvas and can express herself in black-and-white film. She has written haiku and cut elaborate origami dancers from paper of her own making. Her home is overcrowded with books which are classified not by language but in the order in which she has read them, a tracing of from then to now in alternating tongues. But she does not know the language, and when he has crossed the room and kissed her forehead and given her the printed message, he considers that she still has to be told.

She sits down, her thin hands covering the arms of a wicker chair. Those long black fingers. Her straight back and high forehead. That indelible gaze. Nothing, of course, is proved. That is what she tells him. "I don't know any Demi, Thomas. No one by that name ever comes here to dinner. Don't talk your funny words to me."

He admits there is room for doubt. He is unable to use the word *hope*. "Even the dedicated line can carry lies. Rumors and disinformation just to throw us into a tizzy. But not when they use the language. The language is usually reliable."

The surprise is that she isn't mourning. She trusts him or she doesn't. He has never known. She is always polite with him and her greetings are warm, but she is twice alien to him, female and African, and it has been months since he has been alone with her.

Rising from her chair, she takes the note from the low table where she's left it and folds it once before putting it back into Zane's shirt pocket. He searches her eyes for a glint of steel or the diamond drop of impending tears. But there is only wood in her gaze, oak or mahogany. "It is maybe only a distress signal," she says. "A call for help. What does Emelle think?"

"She doesn't know. I came here first."

"Why?"

He shakes his head. "The order of things. You first, then his wife in Northampton. Emelle comes after Abby. I have a heart."

"You have," she confirms. Then she astonishes him with a smile. "Have you been drinking, Zane?"

"Yes."

"For the courage to find the words. You had to tell me and now you have. And you are still thirsty."

He doesn't have an answer for this and stands mute, waiting.

"There is evidence," she says, "that you have a heart. What shall I pour for you?"

"Whisky."

"And?"

"Whisky."

She mixes it with water anyway and then goes into the small kitchen for ice. Zane is stock still in the sunlit room. He realizes he has interrupted her work. Papers and open books cover a desk where she has been translating Zulu chant-poetry into French and English simultaneously. There is no proper dictionary to work from, no reference except her own training and experience. Her handwriting, in black ink on yellow unruled paper, has the look of print, the letters even and measured, line by line, on the page.

"There is no word in Zulu for glass," she says, handing Zane his whisky. "No word for mirror. Nothing in Zulu is synthetic or concatenated. Each word is whole. I have to use *reflection* for words that don't quite mean that."

For herself she has poured orange juice and she drinks it down. "I can translate out of Zulu into almost any language but I cannot translate *in*. I can take away but cannot give back."

Precious little in that apartment reminds him of Harry Street. During his long walk through the city he had felt dread at the prospect of seeing a photograph, or a shirt on a hanger, or of hearing a record being played that would thrust Street's face onto the black screen of his thoughts. But M'Khlea fills the space. Her books cover two of the walls from floor to ceiling. Against another wall is a dining table piled high with magazines and newspapers. There is her writing desk with its yellow stacks and those southeast windows filled with light. African icons are jammed between books, and a wicker couch, and chairs are covered with bright red and blue cushions. It is M'Khlea's room, because Street is so seldom there. When he was home, he must have inhabited the bedroom or the kitchen. His absence is everywhere else.

Zane finishes his whisky, ice and all, and waits for her to refill the glass. They are standing together in the middle of the room. The white light comes in at a slant through the window and crosses M'Khlea's heart. She is wearing a blue skirt and a pink blouse open at the throat. A thin gold chain hangs to between her breasts, bearing a black stone teardrop. He is looking at that teardrop as if at her breasts. She breathes in and out, in and out. He gives in to the impulse and takes her in his arms. Pressing his face to her black hair, he can smell her perfume and his own sour breath. Whatever she smells of him he does not want to know. He is waiting for her to wail or to weep: One of us has to give in to the grief.

But it isn't M'Khlea. Moving away from him, she looks up at his face. "I thought," she says, "that you were about to cry on my shoulder. I was going to comfort you."

Once he thought he loved her. She had the serene look of someone who could fill in all his blanks with her simple presence. She would be the sudden green leaves to his barren white tree. She would take the whisky from his shaking hand and turn down the bed. And there she would swallow all the thorns and broken glass of him and in the morning he would be healed. For long months he carried a quiet torch for her while Street sent Zane-speak over the wire from Durban, Bamako, Brazzaville, Addis Ababa. A fledgling affair with the wife of a noted sculptor ended all at once and for a long time he spent his nights in Paris utterly alone and laid a curse on every other woman who crossed his path. None of them were her. His celibacy enraged him, but there was a welcome side-effect. He awoke one hundred mornings running with nothing special to regret. After nearly six months he realized he was only feeling envy; it was Street he was in love with. He wanted to touch what touched him and men touch only each other's hands.

"Is it comfort you want, Thomas? Or information?"

"I've got to find the man who sent the message."

"To see about this light water."

"It means he saw it with his own eyes."

"Where was he? I mean, when he sent this message?"

"The source wasn't noted. We put a trace-back on the transmission and lost it in a multiplexor in Abidjan."

She blinks. "Which signifies?"

"All it means is that the message could've come from anywhere in Africa. That's as precise as we could be. Do you know where he was?"

"He has been many places. It has now been two months since the last letter. He called me in late June and said he had been in Senegal, Mali, and the Ivory Coast. He talked about a drug that's said to cure river blindness."

"You haven't heard from him in two months?"

"This is nothing unusual. He was spending more and more time in Mali, helping the Touaregs, who are being wiped out. He was very busy gathering evidence and witnesses to expose a man who assists in torture. And he has met with Ambrose. That is the last I know."

Ambrose Okimbo is her legal husband. Once a Nigerian poet, a husband, a political prisoner, a torture victim with ABRI files that filled a dozen cardboard boxes. Now a terrorist or a revolutionary, depending upon one's point of view. Three years ago, both Zane and Street had been instrumental in springing him from a Nigerian prison and he had come to Paris to leave his wife in their care. But then M'Khlea asked for sanctuary from her own husband, and for nearly two years had been hiding from him in various addresses and in the arms of Harry Street. Only in the past year did they stop hiding altogether. The earth is a limited space and there is no place to hide from a man like Ambrose Okimbo. His watchdogs haunt the neighborhood. Zane steps to the window and looks down to the sidewalk to see if they are there now.

"I went to the shops this morning," M'Khlea tells him. "Only my own shadow followed me."

The marriage ceremony included a Zulu rite. They shall be forever bonded, even after death. When Okimbo dies, M'Khlea will have to follow.

"It is stupid of him. Harry. He wants to reason with Ambrose. To ask for a divorce." Her laughter is cheerless. "As if my husband would pay any respects to an English court."

She must know fifty words for sorrow. In six languages. Perhaps when he is gone she will recite the entire vocabulary and the room will be filled with rainclouds. He is wanting another whisky but is too spooked to ask for one. Without Street between them he doesn't know if he counts as a friend or an interloper. His sour breath already shames him and it is not yet noon. He will have to make an effort to stay sober in the daylight. He is not a drunk, but he has his moments. Numbered like the stars. He is today what has washed up on M'Khlea's shore to disturb her tranquillity with slurred speech.

"If he is with Ambrose," Zane says, "he is in danger."

"Ambrose would never harm Harry. Nor you. He owes his life to both of you. His hands and heart."

She opens a desk drawer and removes a bundle of letters, fat envelopes with various-colored postmarks. "If he is still in Mali, there is a reason I have had no letters. The postal service in that country is unreliable. I once received three letters from Harry in a single day, each written and mailed two weeks apart."

"Two months is a long time, M'Khlea."

"But the letter will come. There have been others." She hands the bundle to him. "None of these are love letters, Thomas. He isn't inclined that way, toward the literature. I know for certain that his letters to me are letters to his own self; for later, when he will want to remember. You may read them without invading our privacy. Perhaps you will understand the mistakes in your messages."

She slips the letters into a plastic shopping bag with a drawstring she tightens. He tries to slip the bundle into his breast pocket, but it's too large. "I'll return them as soon as possible," he says.

"This is the seventh address I have shared with Harry. In the past three years, I have learned not to have keepsakes or memorabilia. Anything that can be made to look like evidence. And the letters may be safer with you."

"What kind of evidence?"

She moves away from him, toward the window. "Of the man that Harry is looking for. The man you don't believe exists. Read the letters and keep them well hidden."

Street talked endlessly of this man, whose face he had never seen and whose name was an elusive set of syllables. Okimbo to the left of him and the unnamed man, his obsession, to the right.

Street said he first came across him in Southeast Asia in 1971, when his superiors had discovered that drugs and medicine destined for Laos had been diverted to Cambodia without their consent. Street was already in Vientiane and they asked him to investigate. He met nothing but resistance, except from a kindly old Frenchman who put him in touch with a CIA operative, his first contact with a Yank spook. British Medical had made three shipments to Vientiane but only two of them, with blood plasma, had arrived. The third, which included whole medicines, still unprocessed, like pure adrenaline. The CIA man said he didn't have any information concerning the diversion, but once Street heard what was missing, alarms began to ring. The CIA man pointed him in the direction of a man whose name began with the Bj sound. Either a Swede or a Dane, he said. There was no file, no photograph, no witnesses to interrogate. Some of the drugs were later found to have ended up with the Khmer Rouge. And some had been used as toxins during interrogations. This affair cast a very black shadow over British Medical Company but the man was never captured.

He reappeared to Street in 1978, in an article that Street read in a medical journal, a single paragraph relating how a Scandinavian said to be in the employ of Idi Amin had developed a torture toxin. Not six months later he read of the care of torture victims, a serum that brought on hallucinations that eased the pain of torture. When prisoners were at last liberated, there was nothing indelible that the Red Cross crew could put a finger on. For a long time he didn't know if it was one man or several but he knew he was looking for a doctor, or at least someone who knew medicine. The name stuck with him, as well as any derivative. Bjearn, Bjorn. The market seemed vast and Street was convinced that he had brushed up against him more than once. A torturer whose signature was medicine.

Zane put all this down to jungle fever, to Street's too many years in the fields of wanting. Every raker is a crackpot. One of Zane's rakers, code-named Mozart, is convinced that he has an incurable disease that never shows up in his blood tests. Demi refers to himself as an Arab, a black African, and a French count according to his seasonal moods. And through the years, Zane has felt himself obligated to humor Harry Street whenever the subject of Berne arises. A transmission that reads: "The Bj demon's fingerprints found on test tubes in Wollayta torture lab. Stink of euphoria and Molly's soliloquy." Street assumed he had found his man, or evidence of him. Calling from Addis Ababa, he added, "He is obviously a chemist and is giving counsel to interrogators. His victims are first tortured physically and then 'cured' by this man. Many of them describe their recoveries as euphoric. And nearly all of them remember having told their life stories in technicolor detail."

The torturers have their own language for the pain they deliver. In Brazil, they call it *the telephone*; in Vietnam, it was *the plane ride*. In one of the few instances in history in which torturers were put on public trial, in Greece in 1975, Amnesty International collated the transcripts. These transcripts were mandatory reading at ABRI. "Here, you will tell all," a torturer was quoted. "You are going to open out like a rose."

The dentist with the death grin. The doctor with the scar on his cheek and a foot-long syringe. The hokey cinematic image of the bearer of agony. Zane doesn't buy into it but has never had the courage to say as much to Harry. Light water, that's all that Zane has ever asked for. "I can't transmit anything until you've seen this bogeyman with your own eyes."

"Is there more?" he asks M'Khlea. "Evidence, I mean. Photographs? Documents?"

"Nothing but what is in the letters."

He senses dismissal in her voice, and a rejection of the man with the stinking news and the bad breath. Once, he remembers, he spent the night in that same apartment after a particularly intense bout of drinking with Street. He'd been put up in a make-shift cot bed in the living room and in the middle of the night had wandered naked, still drunk, in search of the toilet. The hall light had led him to a doorway which he thought led to the bath-room. Pushing it open, he found M'Khlea staring across the light at him. The look on her face was what he is now seeing. Impas-sive, expectant, nearly judgmental. It occurs to him that she has begun to believe what he's come to tell her.

"It is only your language," she says. "Something between the two of you, you and this Demi. Maybe it was stolen from him, your code. Maybe someone just sent along a stab in the dark to get your attention. Another lie on your network. You said yourself there are many of these."

"In English, yes. In French and German. Even in Latin. But not in this language."

She moves to her table and takes up a sheaf of papers. "Trans-lations," she says, and there is anger in her voice. "Every one of them imperfect, every one a lie. When you translate, you betray. This is a fact of my profession. *Traditore, traduttore.* I can find no word in Zulu for mirror so I write *tells-back-the-face.* I just make do, Zane. You, too. You just make do!"

She has moved closer to him and he understands he is meant to move away. But when he's at the opened door she kisses him, touching her lips to his and brushing his nose with her own. So he is her intimate brother again and not a drunken stranger stand-ing naked in the doorway. "I forgive you," she says. And then for a long while she cannot speak. He says her name and she looks away over his shoulder, though there is nothing there but the stairwell, the elevator, the blank wall. "I forgive you," she says again, "for coming here with your lies. Harry will call me soon and I will tell him you have lost faith in us."

"M'Khlea," he says, but at last her eyes are fierce with tears and she closes the door.

He descends the stairs and as he arrives at the second-floor landing he bumps a man who is coming up. "*Pardonnez-moi,*" he says and at the same moment the man mutters "Sorry," and continues up the stairs, another Englishman who never learned French. The city's full of them. Zane reaches the bottom of the stairs and pushes the heavy door open. On the street, the day is still white and oppressive. Street's letters are in his hand and he heads for the nearest brasserie for another whisky. He is the only customer. It is not yet noon and the owner is setting tables for the lunch hour. Zane orders a whisky and a beer and settles into a booth toward the back, away from the sunlight streaming through the front glass.

The letters are tied together with blue ribbon and the knot is difficult to solve, a series of loops that only patience or a knife could undo. There are forty-three letters all together; Zane doesn't know why he counts them but that's the total. Some are very thin, a page or two, whereas others, by their bulk, look to be ten or twelve pages long. The handwriting is careless, stabs of ink instead of a flow. And the envelopes are of every size and shape, as if Street has taken whatever was at hand in his various hotels. The oldest of the letters dates from three years ago and the most recent is two months old, with a postmark from Mali. At random, Zane chooses a fat letter written three years ago and begins to read. The writing paper is wrinkled, as though each page has been folded a number of times, and from page to page the penstrokes vary wildly, from small and cramped to large and elaborate. He wonders if this letter was written on the run or late in a Scotch-soaked night. Street begins by complaining about the Euro-African Uplift Agency and his fatigue, then drifts into details of his work. He was inspecting a Belgian project in an African nation where a lake was being restocked with larger fish than those already available. The villagers were being taught how to read the waters to find those new fish, how to dispose of the shed scales and heads to make fertilizer, and how to make simple medicines from the fish oil.

He stops reading at the end of the third page. He can hear Harry's voice in these words, and those ropes around his chest have grown tighter. He orders a second whisky, still without the courage to go on reading, when a man comes into the brasserie with a story to tell the owner. A crowd has formed across the street and he is gesturing in that direction.

Zane gathers the letters and puts them back into the shopping bag. Rising from his chair, he pays his bill, steps into the street, and crosses against the traffic. Someone is shouting to step back, make room. He merges with the mob and shoulders forward. From up there, someone says. The top floor.

Light water. With his own eyes. Zane is there before the press, before the ambulance. But already three policemen are on the scene. The day is white and the night will be no color at all. Her body is twisted into the sprawlstance of a scarecrow, her head askew and limbs scattered. She is wearing a blue skirt and a pink blouse. A gold chain hangs to between her breasts, a black stone teardrop.

The police are questioning the concierge who stands in front of the building. She looks bewildered and her eyes search the crowd. For a moment he imagines that she is looking in his direction and he remembers that she spied him through the door when he arrived. Turning slowly, he slips into the crowd that is gathered around M'Khlea's body. He clutches the shopping bag with both hands and moves along the street, a spook, until he is lost among the citizens.

NOTHING, DEAREST M'KHLEA, IS WHAT IT SHOULD BE. The roadmap tells us that the highway to hell is paved with good intentions. It doesn't take a Michelin guide to understand that your dark continent is being paved over daily with the consequences of enlightened incompetence. African day is giving way to European night, the forests are giving way to the desert, and as I write this, the Belgian-supplied lorries are being loaded with every man, woman, and child of my doomed fishing tribe. Van Kee is in his tent, no doubt staring down the barrel of his Colt and giving serious thought to pulling the trigger. Four hundred and some people are being moved for their own good to where fresh fields have been ploughed. They will leave their nets to rot by the lakeshore and take up shovels and hoes at dawn. The agency has built bamboo huts with tar and plywood roofs to keep the bitter rain from falling on their heads. The plywood sheeting is labelled EAUA Issue and includes the triangle of the agency's logo. I can imagine the tribesmen lying in their new beds a week from now contemplating the meaning of that hieroglyph.

Forgive the hand that writes this. Blame both fatigue and alcohol and consider the scrawled words one after another as in one of your translations and you might make sense of this. I hurt my hand this morning in a fit of pique. My guess is that I've cracked a metacarpal on my writing hand, which might explain to you my cramped and ungenerous penmanship.

Forgive the hand if not the man. I have had no news to lighten your heart, despite the usual enquiries during my visit to Libreville and my stopover at Nairobi. A Frenchman I met in the Abidjan Hilton pretended to have information that might lead me in your husband's direction but after his third gin and tonic I figured him to be a tourist who was amusing himself with talk of Africa. Or, if not a tourist, one of those representatives of a consulting firm, on triple fees as compensation for the hardships of working in Africa. On the whole, dear M'Khlea, I have had a time of it and am tonight mixing my Scotch with self-pity rather than with ice.

So I have landed in dusty Mali, where I am watching firsthand another blunder of an African relief agency, more of the usual techno-angels of scatterbrained mercy. The Euro-African Uplift Agency, a group that's come to help these people to join the century. Faithful to the usual reasoning that this century is a golf club that everyone aspires to. You remember the project I told you about a few years ago, on the shores of Lake T——. The tribesmen have been fishing here for centuries. They have gone out in long boats in the early morning and swung nets across the surface. Groups of two boats face to face. The net was weighted at one end and would drag towards the bottom and the men in one of the boats would then row with all they had into a circle, arriving alongside the second boat with a now-closed net. Or all of the boats would pull a series of nets towards the shallows near a sand bar and the women and children would wade into the water and snatch the fish in lattice baskets. The catch was never vast. These fish were small and difficult to net. But they were plentiful, especially in the rainy season. And the tribe was nowhere near the bottom of the misery index like any of the tribes in Somaliland or western Sudan. All in all this was a pretty upscale folk set, despite their persistent wars with another tribe across the lake and the occasional slaughter that resulted from it.

It was the size of those fish that got the attention of the Euro-African Uplift Agency. If the fish were larger, it was reasoned, the catch would be all the better. And the instances of malnutrition would be checked by at least a greater variety of fish. The villagers had of course heard all of the promises and if they were sceptical at least no one wrote any letters of protest to the agency chairmen. Three years ago the lake was stocked with a kind of bass that was considered well suited to the environs. After a year the hatchery was opened and the larger fish unleashed into the lake. Fish the Size of Men is how the locals referred to them.

I was interrupted by a visit from Van Kee. His supervisor, a Bruxellois who arrived last week, has come up with yet another idea for merging the two hostile tribes. They will be sharing adjacent acreage now that the lake is dead and a way has to be found to cease their hostilities. Their grudge goes way back, though its origins are murky. Nowadays if you put two of them in one room they go straight for each other's throats. The shots I've been administering to children have also been a source of irritation to them. If I jab the children of one tribe with a white fluid then those of the other will refuse my visits if I ask to do the same. We had to convince the chemist to sheathe the needles with blue-colored bands to make the shots look different. And then Van Kee and I took turns, each a doctor of a different set of spells. And the inoculation project, which should have been a two-day affair, took five.

The Bruxellois told us his idea just yesterday. He wants to arrange a marriage between the two tribes. To create a cultural synergy, he advised us, and thus put an end to their conflicts. We were asked to find a Romeo and a Juliet for the operation without, of course, recounting to them how the tale might end.

So we visited each of the villages in search of a male and female that we might match. The tribal leaders had to sanction our choices and we knew better than to expect the pick of the litter. In the first village we were led to a man who must be fifty years old, which in these parts is utterly ancient. His face was pitted from the pox and his hair and face had not been cleansed or cared for in years. Though he had only a few remaining teeth it was said that he often chased and bit young children. This man, we were told, would be allowed to take a wife from across the lake.

In the second village we were offered a girl of perhaps twelve who suffered from seizures which frightened away the boys. She surely wouldn't have had the strength or the courage for a union with the child-biter. I spent an evening with Van Kee and a bottle of his best while we made cruel, crude jokes about the situation and in the morning we simply reported to the Bruxellois that it was no dice. All the same the child-biter was presented to us late in the afternoon. His hair had been cleaned and rubbed with oil and there were two baskets of fish and dried seaweeds as an offering. Van Kee began to explain to the tribal leaders that the marriage was off but they interrupted him to point to the old man's mouth. In the interest of tribal peace—or of marital harmony?—they had removed the last of his teeth.

Yesterday, K brought a man to me, a Touareg who had been captured by the Malien soldiers. He was unable to speak and although I gave him a thorough examination I could not discover why. There were no marks from wounds and his vocal cords were intact. The only signs of mistreatment were tiny pinpricks in a semicircle around his skull, as though they'd made him wear a hat lined with thorns. He had not been beaten or cut.

We asked him if he'd been tortured and he answered both yes and no with his eyes. Other than treating his obvious exhaustion, I could do nothing for him.

K says there is an evil in the region. This man, he tells me, is not the first he has seen struck dumb. He has heard of at least a dozen others, two of whom later regained speech after washing their hands and throats in rainwater. I discount his superstitions but not his message. Until recently the Touaregs who've been captured were later found dead or were never seen again, but for the past five months there are fewer reports of atrocities and the Malien army has had great success in rounding up the Touareg insurgents. This news doesn't make it all the way to Europe. Beyond these borders, it is just another dirty secret and Z is as ever reluctant to relay my point of view. But he is here. Your husband's tormentor and my own. The man K brought to me suffered from lapses of memory but he clearly remembered a white doctor with "sky eyes." I have taken blood samples from the man and had them sent to Abidjan for tests. It has been ten days already and still no word has been sent to me, though we have a telephone as well as a telex machine and K has relayed money to the telegraph office to make certain that I receive incoming messages.

Z sometimes talks about the Frozen Snowball Theory. It is his antidote to the Repeating Slander Theory, which says that this kind of behaviour in Africa was well rehearsed with North American Indians and, before them, etc.

The Frozen Snowball Theory comes to mind at trying moments like these, when you have to remember that a million years from now the planet will be nothing but a frozen snowball whirling through a vacuum. So what does it matter what happens in a day or in a year or in a millennium? Even the cockroach is not immortal.

I told this to Van Kee not an hour ago and he looked at me as though I had leprosy. I thought for a moment that he might get aggressive, which he has been known to do when he's been drinking straight gin. I was alert to his foul temper and even had the passing idea to reach into my boot for a knife, but he just cursed and went back to his tent.

I don't think I would have used the knife, even if he'd jumped me. Our nerves are shot but I can recognise that he has a reason to be angry with me. I appear too flippant and he wants me to be on my knees with him howling at the African full moon. The Frozen Snowball Theory doesn't apply here. The notion that the world will be made of anything other than steam and sweat, mud and the scales of dead fish, is too difficult to envision. Tell that to Z if you see him. Tell him Eleven puts the pharaoh's curse to Frozen Snowballs.

There was an occurrence the other day, a major event in the history of these people. The arrival of a truck filled with slot machines. The driver had crossed up his travelling papers in K——and ended up here with his cargo. The farming equipment we were waiting for was apparently sent to the resort, which makes for a fair enough exchange if Van Kee and I can follow through with it. The tribesmen can become gamblers now that they are no longer fishermen. Instead of casting their nets they can swing the levers downwards and watch the fruit and the coin symbols flash before their eyes. And the residents of the resort near K——— will be put to work in a garden out by the tennis courts. This is what I call cultural synergy.

I have been to that resort. It was built about ten years ago and is several notches above those places that make book with the Club Mediterranée. Nearly all of the guests are white, mostly young Europeans sent along to stay out of harm's way. In a place so remote from Europe, all hell can break loose. There are certainly no policemen in the vicinity. There are three swimming pools, in- and outdoor tennis courts, sauna and massage, disco, game room, biweekly photo safaris, three restaurants, six bars, twenty-four-hour room service and, I suspect, a squadron of in-house prostitutes for those too busy to make the twenty-kilometre jaunt into town.

I spent two nights there some years ago. My company sent me there to see about beds that were being replaced. We wanted to know if the resort management would consider donating the old beds to a new hospital being built a hundred miles to the west. We were refused but it was no matter. The beds, it turned out, were too large for a hospital, either king or queen or fat-boy size. Some of them were perfectly round, none of them appropriate for the desperately thin patients to the west.

About fish the size of men. They were no ordinary fish. They were a result of years of cross-breeding and selective environmental conditioning. I am told that the oils that can be extracted from them are exceedingly rich in vitamin E as well as iron, which the villagers sadly lack. The bones are easily extracted and the white meat is both abundant and delicious. Twenty thousand of these lake bass, which the Belgians referred to as angels or angel bass, were loosed into the lake nearly five years ago. At the time the population of the perchlike fish that the villagers had been catching was estimated at two million. But the angel bass also reproduce with surprising alacrity and a computer printout that I have seen in Van Kee's files presumed that the twenty thousand would multiply with lightning speed. Twenty thousand begetting fifty thousand begetting one hundred fifty thousand begetting five hundred thousand begetting two million, with each generation taking only six months.

The misery of that statistic is that it almost happened. The fish have a lifespan of eighteen months and by the end of the second year the population was estimated at over one hundred thousand. The end of the third year, three hundred thousand. The locals cast their nets and caught these fish in great quantities. But the catch was too heavy; the nets were often torn and the fish could not be carried easily in the small boats. At the same time, the smaller fish were fast disappearing, as was the lake-bed vegetation, which was being devoured by the angel bass. Whereas the perch move in schools of fifty or so and roam the entire lake, these Belgian bass tended to move slowly and feed in a scorched-earth fashion. Overgrazing, as it were. They consume half their weight each day and the vegetation was systematically torn as a result of their feeding traits. In the past year, the shores have been stinking with dead fish, both perch and angel bass, and the water has changed in colour. The Euro-African Uplift Agency hired a group of ecology experts to examine the situation and it was determined that the lake was nearly dead. New vegetation will return, we are told, in five or ten years. And the lake will be restocked with the perch that once inhabited it. In the meantime the tribes will be relocated to the west, where they can make a living on a farm that has been prepared for them. And these fish the size of men, gathered from the dying shore, will be used as fertiliser instead of as food.

Tomorrow evening, a last truck will take me to K—— from where I have a plane back to Johannesburg via Abidjan. Besides growing impatient to see those blood tests, I have a rendezvous with a man in Abidjan who sells information. He's just returned from a conference of the West African Free States. I will only have twenty-four hours to find him. My employers are barking again

and it is time I gave them their money's worth. It occurs to me
that this is the fifth letter I've written to you since my last visit
to Paris and I have yet to apologise for our final night together.
But consider, M'Khlea: how am I to say *sorry* to you while shouting hallelujah to the ceiling? Love squeaks and sniggles too often
in the dark and I have a devil of a time remembering ancient
promises. I will find your husband in whatever village or city
houses him. And when I get you free of your vows I will get
myself free as well. And then I might live with you in more than
address. A man the size of a fish, swimming against the current
of your past.

Van Kee is making obscene noises in the tent next door and I
think I'd best calm him down before the locals come to sort him
out. I will mail this letter in a few days from the hotel in K——.
A page or two will be missing from what I've written tonight.
Those pages that are always missing. Whatever you can translate
in the dark.

THE OFFICE GETS BLACK WHEN HE IS ALONE. THE spook-looking gray screens are set to *Receive Only* and the thief lights leave blue shadows along the floor. The only sounds he can hear are electronic hums or the telex when it bursts into print. He sits in a pool of his own lamplight and just lets time pass. Night. He lets the night pass. After night comes morning and he'll be here then as well. Waiting on Zane.

The lies are piling up in the office around him, as the stones of facts are eroded into the sand of rumor. Strangers come and go with their own sets of keys, the place is going all to hell, this traffic of multiple sources, of names and AKAs, of alternate spellings, of dates, and cutting through the fat of rumor in search of the bone of fact. His raw materials are letters, photographs, telexes, microfilm, cables, bank statements, canceled checks, airline vouchers, travel receipts, cassette tapes, and human voices across telephone lines. Lies are information; hearsay is currency. As each day passes at ABRI, lines are forming behind the paper shredder.

Petitjean knows his English. Thinking back on it, he must have been waiting to meet Zane or to end up here at ABRI, where those words matter more than the weather or the rent. He knows all of the words now. He barters for them day and night. He dreams in English and Zaneslang and awakens to a woman, Sylvie, who only understands French. He tells her that makes nothing, *ça ne fait rien*, it is no matter, he can speak that, too.

28

His company tonight is a water bottle, coffee, cigarettes that taste of steel, two new German novels that he hasn't had the time to read, and these messages on Zane's screen and on his own saying *Receive Only*, blinking or ululating, he loves that word, you-you-lating. He could have gone home to Sylvie but he thought Zane would be back and that he'd be needed. God damn Zane. It is sometimes difficult for Petitjean to think of Zane as a partner. Though they share space and electricity and cigarettes, Zane wouldn't think of telling him what it meant, the message they received. Petitjean stood next to Zane and poured the coffee, black for Zane and sugar for himself. He lit Zane's cigarettes and offered a glass of water that he spilled all over his shirt front. Zane wouldn't drink the whisky that Petitjean sluiced into the coffee cup. He wanted, he said, a clear head and clean eyes. Clean to read the message and clean again to know what to do about it. Being with Zane then was like visiting the sick and maybe dying. When Petitjean called Sylvie, that's what he told her. I won't be home tonight, I am visiting with the sick and maybe dying.

She just said *oui*, like a pent-up word meaning more or less that she understood.

Petitjean supposes she went back to bed and listened to her girl moaning in the next room. And listened to her girl make that sound like she does in the night. Her girl, who is getting to be too much of a woman and doesn't have the sense to wear clothes in the daytime. Why he lives with these two is probably tied up in why he sat here all last night holding Zane's hand, so to speak. Because it kills the loneliness. Boredom kills the loneliness. Worry puts the loneliness into a drawer. The loneliness of a woman with a daughter almost twenty years old but soft on the brain and who barely speaks to him. Moaning like that at night, saying her words. And her mother knows that the girl is getting older, knows too Petitjean is listening for her and watching now. So Sylvie reaches for him with soft hands to get him to do some-thing to her, something to take his mind off her daughter. She can't accept that he is only an agent of mercy, sharing the rent on four small rooms and a bathroom with shower only because he once had nowhere to live and now he has somewhere. They live next to the railroad tracks that fan out like the bones of a hand above the Gare du Nord. The trains stop coming after eleven at night and it is as though time stops; he catches himself listening for train sounds that don't come anymore and then it's time for bed. The trains begin to move again at five in the morning. When Petitjean leaves the house for work, the woman sets up at a little table by the window and drinks coffee, ponders lottery numbers, and watches the trains come and go. She has it in her head that they are going somewhere fine, to great cities with colors far beyond the paleness of this one. He knows better. He knows they are only moving north, to Saint-Quentin, Lille, Brussels, Liège. You can't get to Italy from the north station, he tells her, and she just nods and says she knows but that one can imagine otherwise.

When he was a boy he stuttered and his mother offered a strange remedy. She placed a stone or two in his mouth and the discomfort of their clacking against his teeth induced him to speak more slowly. Each syllable was earned. He still relies on this remedy at those odd times when his tongue is knotted, and for years he has been seeking the perfect stone, perfect in size and roundness. Once his mother brought to him a pair of stones that had been found in a sow's belly during butchering. They were both the size of a large pea and had been worn as smooth as marble, but after a week of using them as speaking stones, he accidentally swallowed them.

He reaches into his pocket for the pair of stones he has been carrying of late. They are common pebbles that he picked up from the ground near the Place d'Anvers. Though he seldom stutters the way he once did, the stones relax him. He places first one and then the other on his tongue and then rolls them backward. What is left of his malady is an occasional repetition of a word, his inability to simply say one word right after the other. In times of anxiety. He reaches for one of the German novels and opens it to the first page, where he left off, but the words are too small, just tiny black points that he can't seem to focus upon. Maybe he needs glasses. Or he has forgotten his German in the space of a long week. *Ich bin, du bist, wir sind . . .*

Zane. His eleven is gone to blue, so now he's out the door again. They all lose people, that's a part of the deal at ABRI. Their job is to cut losses. Inevitable losses. They're supposed to subtract pain and death from Pain and Death; nothing is promised in that subtraction and the results are seldom visible. Anyway, Africa isn't Petitjean's sector. He's Eastern Europe and he has already got his hands full these days with this agitation in the Caucasus and the Baltic States and a new set of arrests in Romania, including a doctor he has on file, and no one in hell transmitting the news. The heat, they say. Nothing happens in the heat. Dogs die and not much more. He doesn't know. Old people die in bed just from the heat and his Romanian doctor with his name in ink dried and damning on a Helsinki Accord watchdog contract, *he* is feeling a different kind of heat altogether.

Out the window Petitjean can see the sun coming up like a hot flash over the rooftops. After any sleepless night, daytime is a drag. The sunlight reveals a crude and uneven street and shows up the dirt and trash that the night kept hidden. The trains will be moving again, heading north to places he never wants to see. The woman will be waiting for him in the bed and she will be short of breath even with the window opened wide to the train tracks. She will be lying there naked with the lamp turned on in the daylight and a stack of magazines and a water glass left over from last night with lipstick marks on it. She will be hot from bad sleep and angry that once again he hasn't turned up. Two nights in a row he's been here like a zombie waiting on words and waiting on Zane. She wants to go to the country and keeps asking why they can't, everyone goes to the country in August. They can take a train to Cabourg and be on the beach in the space of hours. He and the woman and her daughter, who wouldn't know well enough to stay close to the shore. He has this picture of her swimming out toward England and drowning and not even knowing she's done it. We'd have to tie her up, he tells her mother, we'd have to keep her on a leash and then there'd be a lot of people looking at us like we're freaks. He tells the woman to wait. He always tells her the same thing. Waiting is like that. No promises given, you just wait. Receive only.

There is a mattress in the archive room in the back. They sometimes sleep there during bad times, when leaving the screens is unbearable and they have to *be there*. He considers going and laying himself down but then the words are coming over the line. His line and Zane's, too. The Romanian doctor has been interrogated and let go. His house is being watched. A journalist from Prague sends the address of a detainee's wife and asks that Petitjean start up a letter campaign.

One of Zane's rakers is sending a cryptogram when all at once the line goes down, the cursor winking out like a dead star. Petitjean powers down Zane's micro and then kicks it back into dead start. Moments later a message begins to scroll across the screen but there is a line lag and the screen is splashed over with octal gibberish. On his own screen, Petitjean logs into the control library and types WHO, the command to identify current users. The modem settings for Zane's line are correct and no hardware malfunctions are flagged. The Receive function should be operational. There are six lines open through the night, two general lines, his own, and those addressed to Zane, Kirk, Nadine, and Nguyen. But the transmission queue lists seven users, only six of whom have a displayed ID. The seventh is the eavesdropper who has once again cracked into ABRI from an outside line.

The network, AMNET, is supposed to be an "open" system, transparent, the data flowing freely to whoever bends to drink of it. But "open" systems attract the telecom roamers and crackpots, C-boys and cowboys, government hackers and software saints who offer free, if nearly useless, programs to the various end-users. All it takes to get into the base network is the hundred U.S. dollars to lay out per computer hour of access from any of the six interfaced networks from around Europe and North America.

But open systems are like public swimming pools and the true data, or at least the *accurate* data, are commingled with communal input that leaves a scum along the surface; tainted, contaminated, polluted. The Romanian encyclopedias are rife with Ceaușescu's dental records, the sporting habits of one of his ministers, statistics on the price rises and falls of maize and soybeans, tourist tips, a graphic, lie-ridden history of immigration to Romania. And like any open system, parts of it are more open than others. Access to levels and sublevels often requires passwords or ID or both and locked doors never fail to attract the snatchers, locksmiths, serpents, blasters, and ice picks. In the name of security, the system thus includes smoke screens, barbed wire, access traps and labyrinths, and tracers. It is with great pleasure and surprise that Petitjean ever dips into AMNET files that he knows to be both accurate and secure. Like coming upon an artesian spring in the midst of an industrial suburb.

Switching out of the control library, Petitjean launches his stalker routine, a program he has written which will attach his screen to Zane's line and allow him to detect any intrusion. Every transaction leaves an electronic footprint. If he is given enough time he might be able to trace the source of the intrusion, the other end of the line, but at best he will be able to reroute Zane's incoming to his own disk and assure reception.

It is the first time in a week that he has detected the eavesdropper, who tends to lie low during working hours but prowls the byways of AMNET, and thus ABRI, by night. Petitjean first discovered him six months ago, when he'd launched a program, ARCDAT, that he'd written for Zane. ARCDAT would archive any of Zane's files from the ABRI computer to the AMNET. The file-search key was DATE $>=$ TODAY. Even when the archiving was heavy, the number of files exceeding two or three hundred, the program took ten to twelve minutes of run time. But one night in February, Petitjean had launched the program and noticed after twenty minutes that it was still running. The ABRI center in Paris connects through a PTT line to a mainframe just outside London. The mainframe is in turn connected to a network that includes Amnesty International, the Red Cross, and a few of the minis used by various United Nations agencies. Time spent on any computer outside the ABRI Paris center is accounted for and billed to ABRI, so Petitjean was especially sensitive to a run time that was nearly double the usual.

He logged into his own micro and immediately cut his way to the system management. Typing WHO, he received a list of user IDs, none of which had any special significance. When he typed JOBS, he received a list of all jobs running, including his own

ARCDAT. The run time was by now twenty-five minutes and he began to wonder if perhaps he'd mistyped his date at the beginning and was in fact archiving a year's worth of files instead of a single month. He was about to kill the program and start again when something in the JOBS list caught his eye. ARCDAT file size, the size of the program, was 37,000 bytes. But it was a simple enough routine, twenty or twenty-five lines of easy code that should have come to no more than 10,000 bytes, including the file addresses.

The run time exceeded twenty-six minutes.

Switching to his program library, Petitjean listed the ARCDAT program and found what he was looking for. Someone had tapped into his library and amended the program. Instead of merely searching for files within the date parameter given and copying them from the Paris installation to the English mainframe, the program was also copying to another address. That explained the excessive run time. Petitjean noted the additional destination on a notepad and also found that he'd been in luck. Whoever had grafted on the siphon to his program had also included a routine that would erase the code once the program had completed execution. Had he not listed the program while it was running he never would have detected the siphon.

He dialed Zane's home number but there was no answer. He had to make a decision on his own. If he simply killed the program, the intruder would know he had been detected. But if he didn't kill the program, all of Zane's files from the past month would be copied elsewhere. He decided to simulate an interference in transmission, line static or something on that order. The program would be interrupted and the intruder would assume it was merely due to a bad connection. Petitjean switched back to Zane's ID file and geared down his transmission speed from 4800 to 1200. Then he changed the parity setting from ODD to EVEN and when he logged back out the ARCDAT program abruptly ceased execution. The message on Zane's screen was *Transmission error; interrupt JOB ARCDAT; re-run Y/N*

Petitjean typed N and then quickly reset Zane's telecom settings back to their correct status, baud = 4800, parity ODD. Then, through his own screen, he watched as the intruder logged out. It was impossible to know which of the files had already been stolen. Out of curiosity, he relisted the program ARCDAT and found only his original routine. The siphon was erased.

Ever since, Zane has insisted on using the language for all transmissions to and from his rakers. And they have never let the intruder know that he has been discovered. Instead, Petitjean wrote the stalker routine and among other things they found that the intruder entered their system through a user account that should have long ago been retired. User name: ML. Password encrypted.

Each month, they have allowed the siphon routine to run un-interrupted, but the files being copied are of little consequence or bogus, memos and transmissions concocted by Zane to give the intruder the impression that he is removing the crown jewels instead of sand. Whenever either of them detects the intruder, they run the stalker routine, simply to know what he's up to. The program is an ABC right out of the operating system; all that is required is the ID to be followed and a line printer echoes any of the keystrokes made by the intruder. Though he has occasionally perused Kirk's libraries or even Petitjean's, his obvious interest is Africa. The intruder has even gone so far as to attempt a decode of Zanespeak, using raw commands from the operating system:

```
USER NAME: ML
PASSWORD: ********
WELCOME TO AMNET
FILESET IS SEEK
GETFILE TZ1001
GETFILE TZ1004
GETFILE TZ1090B
MERGE FILE SET/ALLGET
WHO IS "POSTCARD"
NO DATA
WHAT IS "STARS"
NO DATA
WHAT IS "IN THE CRADLE"
NO DATA.
```

Only Zane and the sender have the data. There is no decode to be found in any computer.

Tonight the stalker routine detects an obvious attempt to divert Zane's transmissions to a new destination so that not even Zane will receive a copy. This isn't the first time and Petitjean is prepared. He runs a program that reroutes all of Zane's transmissions back to source. If a message is coming through the Abidjan line, it will be saved in a mailbox there. If it is coming through the public lines, it will be loaded into a coded file and Zane will be able to pick up transmission at his leisure. Nothing will come all the way to ABRI; every transmission will be temporarily deposited elsewhere. The risk is that the intruder will suspect he's been discovered. But the greater risk is that Zane's rakers will assume that he's received their transmissions when instead they've been intercepted by the intruder.

This delta routine has been running for fifteen minutes when the intruder logs out. Petitjean waits ten minutes to make sure that he hasn't logged back in with a different ID, then disengages the delta routine. Zane's mail flows inward. From the Ivory Coast: SONATA ENDING. ARIA UNDERWAY. MOZART. From Ethiopia: STARS IN RETREAT. INTERNATIONAL HARVESTER ON THE HORIZON. No signature. From the Munich multiplexor: DOC IN THE CRADLE. KICKER AT HIGH SKY. POSTCARD. From New York: PHOTOS ON THE WAY. BLACK AND WHITE AND RED. SNAKE EYES. Petitjean can't decipher any of this.

The phone is ringing in Emelle's office. After the third ring, the answering machine turns on. The telex starts in and more messages arrive. It is morning and Kirk comes into the office with a thermos of coffee and the newspapers. He says Petitjean is early this morning and Petitjean replies he is late.

"Seen Zane yet?"

"No sign."

"He's bats again," Kirk says. "Over the top."

Petitjean doesn't answer him. No one other than Zane and himself is aware of the intruder or the fact that the intruder is using Emelle's old ID and password.

Then Nadine arrives and goes straight to her terminal at her desk behind Petitjean's to print and cut her mail. He can feel her eyes on him but when he turns she is reading a transmission as if it's a racing form. Emelle steps into her glass office and from where she sits she stares at Zane's empty chair. Petitjean catches himself looking at that chair and then at her. Then he doesn't know what he's looking at, his eyes are closing even as he tells himself to stay awake. He reaches for the coffee cup but his hand stops in mid-air and he has to put his head down just for a moment, to close his eyes for a minute, maybe two. Behind his lids he can see words coming across the screen. All of them are Zane's, the gibberish that causes him such pain. Petitjean feels tired to the center of his head and back again. From what seems like a distance he can hear Kirk telling him to take the mattress. But he can't answer, he is reading the words behind his lids, and then he doesn't see anything but black, words in black on a black screen, and he reads them over and over again.

WHEN SHE IS CERTAIN THAT FINGERS IS ASLEEP, HIS shining head motionless on the pillow, she reaches to pull the shade down low, leaving the window open to give him air. She places the money bag in her purse and snaps it shut. This evening the wine-and-beer man will be coming and there won't be enough to pay him. She will have to give him a token, a fraction of what he's owed, and a female smile. Whatever she can manage.

The old man breathes deeply and there is a wheeze when he exhales. The summer has been unkind to him and there will be no more easy breathing for another month. But the heat is good for his legs. His walking is improved, though he is hardly fit to dance. He tells her that's what he likes least about growing old, that he can no longer dance. *I still do dance inside a my skin but it's not the same thing.* His age is overtaking him now and each day he seems smaller to her, more diminished by the heat and the city's noise and the smoke in the jazz club. A year ago he still had some of his hair and could climb the stairs alone. He stayed awake all night and played his piano with few breaks and he slept in the day. He *took* his sleep, like a drink or a meal. Now, though, sleep is what takes him. It happens to him, like a seizure or a falling. A month ago he told her he was going to die soon and he wanted to be buried near the famous men at the Père Lachaise Cemetery. It is an obsession of his, a last eccentric fantasy. She has told him that he cannot; he is not French. He has answered: Don't kid with me, Marie, I have seen the gravestones of Gertrude

Stein and Oscar Wilde and even Jim Morrison in that cemetery. He asked would she please write a letter to ask permission. She has received an answer and they are saying no to him. He is neither French nor famous and the letter hints that he is probably without a stay permit as well.

This was five months ago, during the rainy weeks of March. He was having his evening meal before the club opened and she sat down next to him and took the letter from her purse.

"They said no, Fingers."

"No, what."

"No to you being buried in Père Lachaise."

He had a leaf of lettuce stuck on the roof of his mouth and was reaching for it with his tongue.

"So how come?" he finally asked.

"Because you're not French. And they don't seem to know who you are."

"Maybe," he suggested, "you could write another letter and this time send some of my news clippings."

She shook her head. "No good, Fingers. *C'est fini.* This answer is final."

"So there's no way around it?"

"I keep telling to you. If you want to be buried there, you have to be French."

"So how do I do that?"

She said she figured he could ask to change citizenship. "You can't stay both. You want to be French, you have to stop being American."

He argued that he was never American to begin with. "I'm of the black persuasion, Marie, and we're not all the way citizens of anywhere except parts a Africa. So what else?"

"It takes about a year. Maybe longer. There are forms to fill out and interviews at the prefecture and the Ministry of the Interior."

"A year?"

Just thinking about it almost put him on the nod again. She was afraid he would faint on her.

He told her that a year is a very long time to wait.

She reached across him for the wine bottle. Saint-Amour, it said. Like a name for a perfume. She poured herself a glass and drank it down. Then for a moment she forgot herself and simply said the words in French. He asked her to say it again.

"*Mariage à blanc*," she said. "A white marriage."

He didn't understand.

"A white marriage, Fingers. You marry a Frenchwoman and you get citizenship."

"Why do they call it white?"

"I don't know. Because it doesn't require love?"

He thought about this for some time. Nearly sixty years separate them, as well as race and nationality. "I have not been married since Alva. I have not even been conjugal in fifteen years." But he admitted he'd heard of dumber reasons to get married, though. "Lots dumber."

"How long's it take?" he wanted to know.

"Three months. Maybe faster in your case."

"Elopin won't do?"

Now she didn't understand.

"Just run away and do it."

She said running away first wouldn't change anything. "You must receive permission."

He remarked, "There's a whole lot a permissions that you need here in France. Do I have to live with her afterward?"

"Who?"

"This white wife."

"That's up to you and her."

"Her," he said back. Then he said, "Marie, we got a problem here. There's no her."

For a long moment there was no sound except Smith-y-Vega tuning his guitar in the front room.

Marie said to him, "Yes there is."

"There is what?"

"A her."

His tongue was working in his teeth again, searching out bits of lettuce or corn. "You are not so ugly as you think, Marie. You can do better than a old black rat man. What's in it for you?"

She hadn't known the words, either in French or in English.

Fingers could play her reasons on his piano, maybe. To answer him, she poured another glass of wine and smiled so he would know she was sincere and he said "Yes?" and she said "Yes." He looked at her and then looked away. And then he swallowed whatever was there to swallow.

The only part of him that is still young is his hands, those unnaturally long fingers, freakish almost, that she so envies. It is as though his fingers have grown to meet his desires, to span the distance from one note to the next, whatever the reach. Her own hands are fat, all palm and easy to cramp. After years of practice she can manage a finger fan just past an octave and even for that there is pain.

He is playing his "Last," he says, meaning his final composition, and each morning, after the club is closed, he sits down and adds to it. She listens and transcribes the music into notes, which he has never learned to write. When he is finished, she becomes his wings, helping him to stand, to walk, to climb the steps from the basement club to the room two floors up. The club, Chez Fingers, belongs to him and in August the take is slim. There are musicians to be paid—July, Smith-y-Vega, Darren L., and old Sing, who can barely get the wind to breathe let alone play his saxophone. Fingers says he's waiting for the faithful to come back from the beach. In the cool of autumn, he tells her. In the cool sane of autumn, business will pick up again.

And from day to day he casts his eyes in her direction, wondering how it is that she is serious about becoming the her. The civil ceremony will be the next day at 7:30 p.m. and they will have a reception at the jazz hall right afterward, just before opening the club for business.

From the hallway, she locks the door with her own key and descends the stairway. The chairs are all stacked on the tables but Leon hasn't finished sweeping up. He is sulking again, exhibiting his displeasure at not being asked to sit in with the others. He works all night as bar-back, and lugs ice crates and beer kegs in from the storeroom, washes glasses, and mops up spills while his trumpet case rests in a corner under the bar. Now and then, mostly on slow nights, Fingers will show him some mercy and let him join in for a brief set. Last night Fingers forgot and here is this broken glass, these cigarette butts, and the dust spelling his anger.

Moving behind the bar, she reaches down for the broom and dustpan and hears a voice at her back. She turns, startled, and sees it is the American. He is seated at the end of the bar, his head propped on his hand, with a full glass in front of him.

"*C'est toi?*" she says, forgetting her English; forgetting herself entirely and addressing him in the familiar.

"Ice," he says. "*Glaçons.* Have any?"

She is tempted to tell him they are closed. That is what she would say to anyone else. Closed, *fermé.* She is embarrassed to see him there, to have him see her. Her dress is wrinkled from the long hot night and there are stains from bar spills around her waist. There is make-up in her purse, lipstick and rouge and eyeliner, and she wishes for the time to paint her face over and cover her plainness. But there he is, looking at her naked face. He asks again for ice and she sets aside the broom and goes into the back room and opens the freezer. The freezer seems a luxury to her, here in such a small club. The French don't care much for ice but the Americans always insist on it, glasses of it, ice in everything, even sometimes in their wine. She fills a bucket and carries it back into the bar. When he sees this the American smiles briefly, his eyes upon hers, then he looks away.

She tells him she had thought he was gone. "Before, I mean. In the night."

"I left and came back again. For the ice." He reaches a hand into the bucket, takes out a cube, and runs it over his eyes and forehead. Drops of water slide down his cheek as the cube melts. Gazing at him, Marie can see there are tears mixed with the water. He weeps silently and when the ice cube is gone he reaches for another.

When he had come in the night before, sometime around midnight, he was clutching a shopping bag to his chest and his drinking was worse than ever. Fingers had said to Marie, "Look at him. He got some hell in his eyes." The American is a regular, one of Fingers' faithful. He comes at least three times a week, always alone, and sits politely at the bar or against the far wall. A whisky-ice man who never asks for credit and whose eyes seem to follow Marie, though when she looks at him he nearly always turns away.

The night before, he paid his bill with a stack of small bills. When she counted them, he was already gone, and she found a slip of paper folded among them with a typewritten message. She read it three times before handing it to Fingers.

"Jazz talk," he told her.

"Yes. This is what I am thinking."

"Like a poem."

"Poems have more than words," she answered.

The American runs the ice cube over his eyes, beneath them. "You have drink too much," she tells him.

The ice slips out of his hand and he reaches for the bucket. She doesn't know what more to say to him and then remembers the note. Was it for her? Poetry, or just jazz talk like Fingers said?

He is still clutching the shopping bag. "Take this," he tells her. "Keep it for me. Show it to no one."

"Eleven is at blue," she tells him and his eyes meet hers. "Ice water," she continues.

"Light," he corrects her. And then his head tips forward to the bar and he is motionless, the ice cube melting in his outstretched hand. Marie touches his shoulder and shakes him. He is out.

This isn't the first time. He has been drunk like this before and she has had to call a taxi to get him home. She knows the address and the security code for the front door. But he has never been quite this bad. He has never passed out before. And there is something else, a weight to him that is different, as though it is sorrow that has laid him out and not the whisky. She has been working in the club for years now and thought she'd seen every color of drunk. Suddenly she is afraid that he is dead, as if such a thing could happen just like that; his heart stopped short like a quarter note, his breath snuffed out with a last word—*light*—and his life all at once gone dry as dust and not quite in her arms. But no, he is still breathing. A mist below his nostrils shows up on the zinc bar.

The telephone is on the wall behind the bar. After dialing a four and seven sevens, she is told to wait five minutes. She hangs up, wishing she'd asked that the driver come inside to help her. They seldom do, even when you ask, even when you are prepared to pay extra. Not in Paris at least. In Paris the drivers can't be bothered.

There is a loose panel behind the bar where Fingers sometimes hides the cash. She places the shopping bag inside and replaces the panel. To revive the American, she takes another cube of ice and runs it over his neck and forehead. When he doesn't respond, she grasps him by the shoulders and shakes him. But he is dead to her, motionless. She considers leaving him there for the day, perhaps making a bed for him on the floor, then thinks better of it. She would have to lock him inside until evening and doesn't like the thought of him awakening and finding himself alone and captive. She knows practically nothing about the man, only that he comes often, drinks too much, and spends long hours watching Fingers' hands at the piano. She feels she has to waken him. He has to walk out on his own steam. She takes the bucket around the bar and throws the remaining cubes into a sink. An inch of ice water remains and she empties it over his head.

He stirs and raises his eyes to meet hers. "A taxi," she says. "You must walk." She lifts his arm around her neck and pulls. The American staggers off the barstool and follows her lead to the door. He leans into her, his face touching hers, and they nearly fall. When they are outside, she props him against the wall just long enough to lock the door.

"The letters," he says. She doesn't understand him.

"Are they hidden?" The taxi is already waiting, the driver at the wheel. Marie shouts at him to at least open the door and he leans backward and extends an arm to pull the handle.

"Your package is safe," Marie tells him. "Now count until three, and walk."

When he lunges, she aims him at the door and he falls face first across the back seat. Marie has written the address on a slip of paper but the driver tells her he's not taking charge of a dead man. Marie will have to ride along. She agrees and starts to move to the front but the driver wags a finger, citing insurance rules. No one up front but him. Cursing, Marie pushes the American from behind and makes just enough space for herself to sit, though one of her legs is draped over his. She gives the driver the address, 58 Avenue de Clichy. "*A La Fourche. Vous le connaissez?*"

The Fork. Yes, he knows the place. Not far from the Arab district, a part of Paris that is never on the postcards.

When they arrive, she offers the driver fifty francs to help her carry him up the stairs.

"How many flights?"

"I don't know."

"Make it a hundred."

She doesn't have that much. There is the money from the club but that belongs to Fingers. When she smiles at the driver he simply shrugs. She pays the fare and tells the man to drive himself to hell.

The ride has revived the American just enough to get him up. She presses the code buttons that spring the front door open and they enter the building. Marie is in luck; he lives only one floor up and they take the stairs one at a time. She has to reach into his various pockets for the keys and then they are inside his home. It is a single large room facing the street. An entire wall is filled with books in French and English and a table is covered with letters, file folders, news clippings, photographs, and envelopes. A narrow bed is pressed into a corner and she drops him there and seeks a chair so that she can catch her breath.

Other than the chaotic desk, the apartment is orderly and clean. It is, she thinks, the apartment of a man who has long lived alone and not at all like the littered bachelor quarters she has seen from time to time. At the foot of the wide front windows there are pots filled with ivy and alyssum, some geraniums, even a weeping fig. Clean windows are framed with white curtains. Opposite where she sits is a kitchenette. When she rises to pour herself a glass of water, she finds that the kitchenette is neat as a pin, dishes stacked and glasses laid out in rows, the cupboards impeccable. She is reminded of her own apartment two floors above the jazz club. Though it is small and short on light and the walls have forever been in need of paint she keeps it every bit as tidy and wonders if his reasons are the same. To kill time, to distract herself from periodic heartbreak; to have, at least, a home. In lieu of whatever else hasn't come along. She has never kept animals, but once she had a finch. She had purchased a bamboo cage for the bird and hung the cage close by her piano, thinking its presence would brighten the room. But the bird had died within a month.

"It was solitude," Fingers had told her. "You forgot to buy a mirror."

She moves to the bed, sits on the edge and turns him over. Twisting his torso one way and then another, she manages to remove his jacket and tie and shirt. Then she stands, takes off his shoes and socks, and gathers up the clothes, which she arranges neatly on the chair. They are cheap, the shirt of the type one can buy in a bin at the metro shops for fifty francs, and the jacket is frayed at the cuffs. Returning to the bed, she unbuttons his pants at the waist and tugs them off. He is wearing boxers and she is somehow relieved. When she is alone with men, she seldom watches them undress. They are awkward until they are naked, then they either strut or cower. She finds a towel and wets it under the sink, then washes his arms and chest and is surprised when he doesn't wake. Folding the towel, she wipes the sweat and tears from his face and expects him to open his eyes and ask how he got there and why and when. But he is oblivious to her, his chest rising and falling. It is as though he will sleep forever and never know she was there with him.

She leans close to him and watches his eyelids. Then she reaches carefully for the elastic at his waist and gently slides the material to his ankles. Here he is.

She draws a breath and lets it go.

For a long moment she simply observes him, curious at his nakedness and his stillness. She has never felt so peaceful looking at a naked man. And in the daylight rather than darkness. Her face. He could see her face. In the daylight rather than darkness. This face without bone, with its too-sudden chin, and a nose too large, and that hollow below her eyes that everyone takes for sleeplessness. She is the color of corn, neither pale nor tanned, but her body has been known to please. When it happens, when men take her, they do so in the dark, after drinking. Where seeing has no purpose. Erasing her face.

But the American is sleeping and there is nothing in his eyes to hurt her or to send her away. In daylight.

And then her hands are at her own buttons and she steps out of her skirt and underthings. Her hands reach behind to unclasp the brassiere and she remembers that she is unwashed since the day before. Her purse is on the table and she opens it and takes out a vaporizer of perfume. She bathes her throat, her shoulders, the gap between her breasts, her upper thighs. The spaces where men go with lips and tongue. Then she returns to the bed and chooses a place at his side, a narrow strip of mattress against the wall. After a brief hesitation, she lays herself down. If he awakens she will have nothing to say to him. If he touches her she will turn into either ice or fire.

Her head close to his, she places a finger to his lips and then kisses that finger, tasting salt. Though she closes her eyes and wishes for sleep, there is too much daylight and she sees red through her eyelids. One of her hands moves to her breast and the other between her legs. She shifts her hips but there is no pleasure in it, only lonesomeness, so she stops and lifts her hand to her face. The smell of swamp and salt, of whisky and perfume. The same smell from other times. But then the darkness gathers and she twines that hand in his. The day is night. The night is long.

She sleeps for a minute or an hour, maybe two hours, then comes awake to the sounds of someone at the door. A Frenchman speaking English through the wood. He is cursing the American, who doesn't awaken. A finger of sunlight crosses the floor toward the bed. The hand in hers is limp. She waits, still without the courage to wake him. One of the hard men she has known once told her to wake him in the morning with her tongue. When she had done it she felt shame. Memory of that shame makes her rise from the bed. The man at the door goes away and she lifts her feet from the bed and places them on the floor. She reaches for her skirt and then wavers. Men are said to dream of women doing just this, offering the surprise of sex in place of love. But she doesn't know this man and has no idea what his dreams are. In daylight and not in darkness.

When she is dressed in the same stained dress, she reaches for her purse and casts him a final look. For a long moment she wills him to awaken. To rise and stretch his arms in her direction. But he sleeps a dead sleep, like a man who will never be awake again. Or until sleep has healed him and made him forget about the night and the ice.

He moves his head and panic overcomes her. She is out the door and down the stairs and is almost to the street when she remembers that she left that door wide open. And so she returns, with feather-light steps, looks in to find him still asleep, and nudges the door gently closed.

DEAR GOD, HERE IS MY MORNING PRAYER. THAT THIS taste of shit on my tonguo is really honey and that the stink of me is only a sacred vapor You havc breathed upon me to remind me to be humble. That Street lives and M'Khlea will reincarnate in his loving arms. That we all will be granted amnesty from ourselves and from our brothers. That I am not damned to hell on earth but am merely paying this morning's steep rent on an acute whisky habit.

There were other prayers that came to him while he slept but his waking has erased them with the stars. He is naked and at first doesn't know how this could be. His clothes are arranged on a nearby chair and there is the smell of lavender in the room. He has to rctrace the night and can remember walking through Paris, afraid to rcturn home. The heat of the day was still running in his veins and he was walking to and from the river in search of ice. He came to the jazz club and couldn't walk anymore. There was music and there was ice. He gave the letters to the woman and then he slept. He slept a black sleep and was awakened by the noise of traffic. He thought he heard Petitjean's voice but was too weak to rise. "You are doing it again, Zane. Fucking royally up. However you say it. Christ we are sick of waiting on you."

He came a second time, when Zane was at last conscious, propped up in his bed like a bent cigar-store Indian, staring as they do into blankness. Petitjean repeated the messages and then slid some papers under the door. Pink slips, he was thinking.

Requests for bandages, insulin, whole blood. Or maybe it is hush money. There are things he can tell them they don't want to know.

He rises from the bed and his legs are stiff but no longer sore. Deep knee-bends would do more harm than good. He settles on stretching his arms outward and reaching his fingertips toward heaven and then takes several deep breaths to clear his lungs. Dear God, this morning prayer. When he is at last unraveled, he stoops and retrieves the papers. There are four telexes from the main office with the usual insults and an envelope addressed to him in Emelle's elegant hand. At the London bureau there are five staffers and transient uncounted volunteers whose chronic incompetence is one of the things that necessitate the language. They cannot be trusted. Though that bureau exists primarily for liaison with Amnesty International, the people working there have these illusions about the extent of their influence. Among other things, they try to give Zane orders.

He leaves the telexes unread on his desk and opens the sealed envelope from Emelle. A number of A4 printouts from the telecom line. A handwritten note is clipped to it. "More of your cursed doubletalk that we need to put into English. I have counted straws and this is the last of them. Are you a lunatic or is this poetry?"

This counting of straws has been going on ever since the Bartholomew incident. No one agrees on the facts, let alone their significance. Once their best and brightest in the African sector, Bartholomew disappeared from ABRI months ago, after a less-than-gentle push by Zane.

Nothing in the mail speaks of Harry Street; only updates of troop movements in Mali-Niger border towns and a request for a plane ticket from Snake Eyes. A note from Mozart: "Stars in their usual places. The moon is down. RAS." With this evidence, Zane could tell Emelle that the Libyans in Chad are stationary but the situation is hard to read. The moon is down. Beyond that, *rien à signaler*, nothing to report. Mozart, he could tell her, is fading. He is tired of it all and is thinking of going home for a while to listen to music and study his navel. This happens every six or eight months and Zane always wonders if he'll come back.

There is a letter from a married Frenchwoman who goes on writing to him despite four long years of separation. But there is nothing from Demi, and Zane assumes he'll turn up for a face-to-face in due time.

The last piece of mail bears U.S stamps, a typewritten letter from the state parole board. Dear Mr./Ms. Zane. "The attorney for your mother has requested parole. This request will be reviewed by the Stillwater board effective 10/3 of this year." He stares at the letter for a long moment, confusing the American date 10/3 for the tenth of March. The writer wants Zane to contact them. When the parole board meets, the attorney will require the name of a sponsor or guardian for a released convict. Though if such parole should be granted, his mother would almost certainly be transferred to a clinic up north. She will be needing medication, surveillance. He is her only surviving family.

This morning prayer.

In answer, there is no wind and no rain. The same white heat. The universal rent to pay. In the center of his head, a low bass hum of pain. She has been imprisoned for nearly twenty years for crimes that are no longer en vogue in the States. He hasn't had a letter from her in four years. The last of them was unreadable. "The medication," her lawyer had written in the margins. "She is drugged but she is well. She has her appetite and sleeps most nights."

Eleven gone to blue. He is all thumbs, a clumsy fisherman of captive men and women, and his nets are more tangled as the days go by. He casts threads into a dark water and gathers driftwood, kelp, and a single shell. He holds the shell to his ear, expectant. Lunacy or poetry? he asks.

He goes into the bathroom and shakes out two aspirin. As if merely a matter of faith, his headache begins to recede immediately. There is a better remedy, a spicy tomato concoction that Street once showed him, but he has no Tabasco and will have to settle on black coffee. He glides to the kitchenette, careful with his footfalls, and puts water on to boil. He clicks on the radio next to the sink but there is no reception. The tubes are shot and he hasn't got around to replacing them. He remembers how, one rainy night when he was young, his mother was fussing with the radio, trying desperately to tune in to a faraway frequency. The sound faded in and out and the radio voices seemed foreign and scratched. His mother held a cigarette between her lips and turned the dial a few degrees to the right and then to the left as though in search of a safe combination. They were hiding in a cabin near the Canadian border of Minnesota. Lightning preceded a roll of thunder and the lights blinked off and on again.

He put down his textbook and crossed the room toward the kitchen, where his cot was laid out next to the refrigerator. As he passed alongside his mother, the reception grew clear and then faded again.

"Tom, come here."

He obeyed whenever she spoke to him. She pointed to a spot on the floor and he moved to it.

"A foot to the right. Good. Yes."

She was listening for a message, a combination of words that would symbolize menace or shelter. She leaned and bent her ear to the radio and he stood for an hour, still as a sentry, with his left arm slightly upraised, her antenna.

He measures a spoonful of instant coffee and drops it into an immaculate cup. There is no sugar to be found and he mourns his lack of the essentials. Grocery shopping is a chore he seldom gets around to. He is more often in restaurants with an unread book and his hunger and rising thirst and lonesomeness. By the time he gets home from work, the shops have long since closed; even the corner grocers, usually Algerians or Moroccans, pull down their steel shutters by eight or eight-thirty. So he sips at bitter coffee and makes a note to buy what he needs.

He goes to the window and looks out on the street. He half expects to find men in gray suits across the street, pretending to read *Le Figaro*. The French use the same word for *foreigner* and *stranger*. But there are no gray suits, only the usual pedestrians, the dirty pigeons, loitering Arabs. Strangers that he is seeing with the distrustful eyes of Harry Street.

In polite French company, when he is asked where he lives, his answer is usually met with uneasy silence. He is too far north, above the Place Clichy, by a crucial two hundred yards. La Fourche, it is called, where the Avenue de Clichy splits into a continuation of itself to one angle and the Avenue de Saint-Ouen to another. The Arab zone, some say, though in fact the North Africans are definitely in the minority. It just seems otherwise to those who get jumpy when they see an Arab face. You have to go east, to the other side of the Montmartre Cemetery, to Barbès-Rochechouart, to find the center. Though he admits the smell of *méchoui* and *merguez* is in the air, particularly on mornings that are stale from a night of no wind and too much heat.

Not a poor neighborhood, it's just a trifle down in the dumps. At street level, below his first-floor apartment, second-floor to the Americans, there is a cut-rate clothing store where three-piece nylon suits go for five hundred francs, 60-percent silk ties for eighty or three for two hundred, and factory-rejected Arrow shirts are cheaper by the dozen. In a back room, behind the tailor's quarters, the owner's son cuts thick mounds of black hashish into even bars and wraps them in tin foil. Zane avoids the stuff. He is too much of this earth nowadays, held fast by the gravity of alcohol and anxiety. Anyway, the boy's dope is too strong for him. The last time he smoked he ended up weeping into his forearms and swearing he'd go back to America on the next plane out. The following morning he couldn't for the life of him remember why.

At the extreme south of the avenue is the Place de Clichy, a busy circle around a ten-ton statue of Danton. Where Paris, the Paris of postcards and honeymoons and Yves Saint-Laurent, truly begins. Zane lives in Zola's forgotten Paris, almost as if in a suburb. Paris is the woman he loves who isn't there. Instead, it is the evidence of her. He is never at ease here, never at rest. His concierge calls out to Zane on his way to work and tells him to wear a hat: the rain is falling and his head is bare. He has no hat and his concierge mourns.

There is a knock at his door and he rises to answer it. He has to undo both the normal locks and the double bolt. Of course it is his concierge. She is from Portugal and despite her twenty years in Paris she has yet to master the accent, those swallowed consonants and crushed diphthongs. She has recently returned from a month back home and is deeply tanned. It will soon be the first of September, *la rentrée*. In a week Paris will again be overcrowded.

"You are alone?" She says of course, so he pulls the last bolt backward and opens the door just slightly. His concierge speaks softly and he has to ask her to repeat herself. His rent is late, she reminds him. By nearly a month. He can tell by the look in her eyes that she is suffering from the chore of having climbed the stairs to ask him for money. It is what she likes least, she has told him, collecting the rent. So much to pay for so little space and poor light. In Covilhã you can buy a house for what we pay in a month of Paris rent. A house without plumbing but with a garden, a few trees, and windows filled with the sun. He writes out a check for both August and September rent and hands it her with his apologies. Not for being late but for making her come to ask. She inquires about his health. Having noticed that he is home rather than at work. Does he need medicines?

He assures her that his health is the same. He makes no mention of the shakes, headaches from staring at his screen, or the after-effects of emptied bottles in the dead of night. His eyes must say it all. "If you see anyone," he says, "if anyone comes asking about me, tell them I no longer live here."

She doesn't ask him why. She is a rare concierge and never meddles. She says she will tell her husband to remove Zane's name from the mailbox below. And to notify the post office that he is no longer a resident.

Then she is abruptly gone and the space in front of his door saddens him. He will not be going back to ABRI. The registered letter telling him so has not yet arrived. And now it will be returned to sender along with his severance pay.

He stares at the space before his door and is tempted to call back the concierge, to ask her if she enjoyed her vacation in Covilhã, to glean news of her family, her brother who is a carpenter with six children and her mother, once a waitress, then a dancer, then a wife and mother, and now a bedridden widow with a window that looks out on a grove of olive trees. To ask her if perhaps she has a niece, unmarried, who would like to meet an American gentleman of humble means. So many times she has offered this news and he has been too busy or too preoccupied to truly listen. So many times he has nodded and moved inches at a time away from the door to encourage her to disappear so that he might return to his book or his bottle or, in years past, to whatever woman was sharing his room and warmth for the evening.

He wants to call back his concierge to ask if the olive trees are barren or if they bear fruit and who gathers the olives and will she bring some back to him the next time she goes there.

He finishes the last of his coffee and heads to the mirror to see about the day's beard. He rinses in the water of salvation and is as clean as any newborn but for those eyes in the mirror. This is a fact: you cannot wash your eyes with soap and water. Staring back at you must be your own unwashed self. He keeps harping on this but it's inescapable: Street is dead and he didn't save him. M'Khlea took a leap into oblivion and he was the last man on earth to speak to her. He bore her the news of her loss as if he had opened that window wide, given her a leg-up to the ledge, and whispered Do it, baby, and take what's eating at me with you. He had forgotten that Zulu women tended to follow their husbands and masters into the hereafter. Faithful to Street where she was not to Okimbo. He loved them both and now they're dead; he does not love himself and here he is in the mirror.

He hasn't had time to read the letters. Grief and alcohol poisoning blurred his vision and now he is anxious to be sober again, to retrieve the letters and to read them with care.

He fills his palms with cold water and runs it over his open eyes. There is no cleansing in the sting and his eyes, already red, are blown to scarlet. This just won't do, he decides. Whipping a tie from the rack, he makes a wide knot, knowing he will fidget it into a clenched baby's fist before the night is done. Meanwhile, he will have the appearance of a man who means business. Gray slacks and blue blazer, summer-weight. A clean pressed shirt with a missing button he chooses to overlook. Black shoes with rubber heels worn at the outside, because he has this way of walking that his mother never corrected. He inspects himself in that same mirror and searches for a smile of bravery or any image that might invoke respect or fear or wariness. He sees an amnesty agent posing as a shoe salesman.

There are things he can tell them that they don't want to know. Where the bones are buried is one of them.

It was the Bartholomew affair, on top of Emelle's increasing annoyance regarding Zanespeak, that first cast him into a shadow as far as ABRI was concerned. Bartholomew was a bright young man from a troubled West African quasi-democracy who came to ABRI to volunteer his services. He had the look of a victim, with haunted eyes, and his frail body was pocked with tiny scars which they assumed were the leftovers of some childhood malady having to do with parasites. Because of his languages and the state he was in, they took him in and gave him a small salary as a translator and contact with his homeland. ABRI was monitoring his country's budding civil war, the abuses on either side, and Emelle dispensed with her customary political interrogation.

In the beginning, Bartholomew seemed to be a godsend. His translations were impeccable and his contacts brought data that chimed with the rest. Pressure from ABRI was credited with the liberation of half a dozen civilians who'd been arrested by the government for unspecified crimes, and the ensuing publicity was a shot in the arm for the entire organization. Success leads to visibility, which leads to a rise in contributions, which will often lead to more success. In dollars and cents, the liberation of a high-profile prisoner of conscience is almost measurable. They never speak of this in so many words, not even among one another. But the equation is there all the same, a distraction and a wound to their pride. They are made mercenaries by the need to pay the rent.

A few months after their initial breakthroughs with Bartholomew, Zane noticed that the African's absences grew more frequent and more lengthy. He said he was working his contacts with heightened discretion and his situation had become more delicate with passing weeks. Some mornings he would arrive early, read his telexes, jot a few notes, and then wander outside, not to return until sometime in the afternoon, if at all. At the same time, information from his country was becoming more sporadic and uneven. Phone calls were missed, transmissions garbled, and confirmations of previous reports were slow in arriving. This sort of situation was characterized as *The moon is down.* Emelle chalked it up to the escalation of the war, but Zane had his doubts. Though Mozart reported a second massacre in an obscure village, Zane had no record, not even from Bartholomew, of a first massacre.

Once an agency is spooked, it is useless. Suspicion of infiltration or bias, grounded or not, can put everything in the can for months. Whenever Amnesty International releases a report on political prisoners in the United States or in England or in France, the familiar chorus is that the agency is funded by the East Bloc countries, by the Cubans, by the KGB. This, despite the fatter and more condemning reports of abuses in Eastern Europe. Nevertheless, there will follow a significant drop in contributions and the agency has to spend significant time demonstrating its neutrality. And despite persistent denials from Emelle and her equals, many of the members of the amnesty circuit are agents, in the shadows, dealing raw data to the CIA or to MI5 or 6, to political parties or to various elected governments. No screening process is flawless and Zane himself has been approached on a regular basis by a man named Smith who has a tendency to re mind him of his country of birth. Credibility therefore requires continual vigilance, and if the agents are ever suspected of blinking they might as well be blind.

So Zane kept watch over Bartholomew. And he waited.

During the worst weeks of the civil war, Emelle tugged firmly on her political strings and Bartholomew was awarded a peace prize from a French medical committee. His award and name were featured during a fall cash drive and he had become one of ABRI's icons, a survivor and symbol of ABRI itself. Emelle had never wielded so much influence in what she referred to as "the circle." But Zane added up his data, and the evidence was mounting that something was askew. According to Bartholomew's input, the worst of the atrocities, the massacres and torture, were by and large attributed to the government. Lesser abuses, the burning of homes, detentions, and occasional pillage, were blamed upon the rebels. Mozart said otherwise, in the language, and Zane asked Eleven to provide a second opinion. Within ten days, Mozart and Eleven separately reported the assassination of a prominent missionary by a band of rebel mercenaries. In Bartholomew's version the priest had been killed in a cross-fire.

One November morning, when Bartholomew slipped out for coffee, Zane pulled on Petitjean's gray overcoat and followed him out the door. A heavy rain was falling and Bartholomew covered his head with a thick folder and crossed the rue Lafayette against the light. He was a tall man and a swift walker and Zane had to run to stay up with him. A parked car was waiting behind the Opéra. Passing his folder to someone inside, Bartholomew retrieved a green binder. Then he circled the Opéra to the metro station and ducked inside. Zane lost him in the crowd.

That night, during ABRI's weekly coordination meeting, Bartholomew produced that green binder. Inside were detailed accounts of torture on the part of the government. Names, dates, and places of detention. Locations of hidden gravesites. Eyewitness narrative accounts. Zane copied the information and shipped it to the drop box where Mozart would find it. A week later his response came over the dedicated line: Science fiction. To the letter of the law.

So, a lie based on truths. A turning of the imaginative screws to tell a story of what might be. Zane took his files and went to see Emelle, telling her it was time they were alone. "I think our boy is a plant, Emelle. I think we're being had."

She denied it, which wasn't unexpected.

"*We* are the mercenaries," she told him. "Bartholomew has lived these wars. He has survived what we can only report upon."

"His information is too neat, too complete. And it's at variance with what my rakers have to say. I've sent two of them in to verify his findings and they're telling me they smell a rat."

"He was tortured back in his country, Thomas. You heard yourself and you believed him."

"There are two sets of people who can describe torture in detail. The tormentor and the tormented."

"Is this envy I'm hearing? Not from you, Thomas."

He produced his counterdata, a file of telexes from Mozart and a handwritten letter from Eleven. She glanced at them and told him that they were written in his infernal code and were therefore useless to her. "Send these men to speak to me. In a language I can decipher without assistance."

"The peeling of an onion, you once said. All we can do is peel away one skin to find another below. One after another, Emelle, and there will never be a clear truth beneath that skin, never. Why do you take his word for these things? Look around you."

She begged to differ. Emelle reflects, always. Reflects and genu-
flects and will not be hurried into unhappy decisions. Zane began
to suspect that she cared less about the work of amnesty than she
did about the flattering attention that ABRI was receiving. Two
weeks later, with Petitjean as his witness, Zane caught Bartholomew red-handed shredding a telex that had just come in. Pulling the plug on the shredder, he was able to salvage the last two
lines. Mozart, in Morocco, begging for acknowledgment. Zane
told Bartholomew his name was poison. "Birds will eat your
bones and die."

Bartholomew disappeared and Emelle blamed Zane. Zane had
spooked him, she said. He was always frail and timid, particularly after what he'd had to survive back there. Perhaps Zane was
simply jealous of his success. Perhaps he was a racist. Perhaps
his rakers were telling lies. Zane had his first inkling that Emelle
was living an illusion. ABRI had never been entirely accepted
into the international circle of the Red Cross, Amnesty International, Doctors Without Borders. An important financial backer
was dismayed at their loss. His confidence, he wrote, was wav-
ering. Emelle was not invited to a routine conference of corre-
sponding agency directors.

Within a month, Bartholomew had surfaced back in his country
with the title of colonel in his rebel army. Mozart faxed a photograph of him in his uniform and Zane taped it to the wall over
his desk. Emelle came by and tore it down with a look on her
face like a knife to the sternum. In the months that have followed,
ABRI has slipped back into its peripheral role in the world stage
of mercy mongering. Zane peels another of those onion skins and
there is grief but no forgiveness.

Bartholomew was not the last of the intruders. Three months
after his disappearance, Petitjean found the hacker in the computer system. When Zane took a printout from the stalker routine
and presented it to Emelle, she rejected his claims as more of the
same. His job, she reminded him, was data collection, not security. Her eyes, once a source of warmth, had gone cold.

So the civil war continues. In ABRI and in Africa and around
the globe. It has gone on for years, hand to hand and eyeball to
eyeball. It is still going on. Zane's mother once told him that all

men were born with pen in hand and an ominous dotted line awaiting their signature. The human contract. The universal deal that says we are all of us responsible for everyone else on the trek from cradle to grave. When our blue jeans, djellabas, kimonos, dashikis fall away and we are uniformly naked and recognizable. A nipple, a navel, fingers, toes, lips. The same word on the tips of our tongues. The human form in one of Darwin's crowded centuries. Zane keeps meaning to sign his name but it won't happen. Not all at once, with a satisfied flourish.

M'Khlea says I just make do.

Among her last words, this message to me that I just make do.

CHEKHOV TELLS HIM THAT THE WAY TO FREEDOM IS TO squeeze the slave out of himself drop by drop. What he doesn't say is the trick is in knowing where to squeeze.

It is five in the evening and the crowds are leaving the rue des Martyrs. The street market is closing down and men in blue jumpers are dismantling the stalls, loading fruit and vegetable trucks, and packing unsold fish into ice. Near the office, a team of Senegalese are water-sweeping the street, hosing bits of vegetable, fish scales, and cigarette butts into the gutter and sweeping the wash water to the corner drain. The water smells of the Seine and of various kinds of fish. Cats will follow and will go mad.

Stopping at a phone booth one street from the office, he dials a number. The woman answers on the third ring and for a moment he struggles to remember her name. "Marie?"

"Yes?"

"This is Thomas Zane. The man you helped last night."

There is a pause on the other end. Then she says, "I never knew your name. Are you well?"

"Yes." There is another man waiting to use the phone and the door of the booth is broken. Unable to close it, he speaks more softly. "I left some things with you last night."

She says not to worry. "I have kept them hidden."

He says he'll be by this evening. "No, later. Near closing time."

She says she will be there and he hangs up, forgetting to thank her.

6 1

I barely know her.

Kirk is waiting for him when he comes in the door. Glancing at his bare wrist, he means to tell Zane that he is late. He has already called the airport to see if Zane was on the flight, and when Zane asks him what flight, he just shakes his head. "London wanted you," he says. "You were invited to explain yourself."

"Where's Petitjean?"

"On the mattress. He waited all night for you and then passed out at his desk. When I woke him he was all in a fever and went out looking for you like it was life or death. I thought he'd go home but he came back. What's on, Zane? Or is this none of my business?"

"What about Emelle?"

"In her office. She's been asking about you."

The office Zane shares with Petitjean has a desk for each of them, and for Zane a microcomputer with graphics card, matrix printer, and telecom functions that reach to 9600 baud. Though the budget is getting thinned monthly, he still has privileged connection to the Amnesty International data base in London and the AMNET lines that allow him to share data in the disks that are fed from twenty various agencies. Though Petitjean is the superior programmer, Zane has the juice.

At his desk, he traces out translations of the day's messages. There is nothing of any great interest and nothing whatsoever from Demi. He prints and cuts the messages and archives the transmission files, then turns to the keyboard to tap out the telecom addresses for the Abidjan and Johannesburg drops. Reference *Eleven.*

DETAILS NEEDED. SHIT IN THE FAN. LIGHT WATER INSUFFICIENT. ZANE.

Petitjean has left a set of files on his desk, all marked *Eleven,* dispatches from Street from past years. Zane knows Petitjean has been walking on glass. The African waters are polluted and although Petitjean is Eastern Europe, he has sided with Zane against Emelle's eccentricities. And ever since the Bartholomew incident he's been riding shotgun to cover Zane's failures at the wheel.

Nguyen brings him a cup of coffee, smiles as though he's in need of pity, and goes back to her desk. Her sector is Southeast Asia. She came over in 1979 with half of her family, boat people who settled in the thirteenth arrondissement, Paris-Saigon, and opened restaurants. She is twenty-five years old and thinks that all communists should die the death of a thousand cuts. Emelle has to keep an eye on her outgoing mail to make sure that this point of view is not too evident.

The office duties are divided into geographical sectors with five administrative assistants and occasional volunteers to be shared by the sector-desk agents. Mr. Li was in charge of Asia before the arrival of Nguyen but he's getting on, well past sixty now, and seldom has the strength to make it into the office. The electronics have always been a cipher to him and when he needs to send a telex he will write it out longhand and give it to Nguyen for transmission. Nguyen has taken the lead in his old sector. Raymond Li is reduced to organizing letter campaigns or tapping into ancient contacts for the odd donation. Emelle keeps him on the payroll out of loyalty for his years of service both out of the office and in the field. From the dark days of Vietnam and, later, of Kampuchea.

Kirk, who runs North and South America, is forty-six, divorced, balding, a chain smoker who has no luck with the ladies. He has on occasion made attempts to befriend Zane on the basis of their common nationality. "Your parentage," he explains, "is of no import to me. I was practically an orphan myself." Zane continues to dodge this bullet; something about Kirk, he senses, is not on the up and up. His past connections, for example. Zane has sometimes suspected that part of the pressure he gets from the CIA is due possibly to a leak in the office, and conceivably, to Kirk.

Nadine is a former Carmelite nun from Ohio whose faith slowly eroded to nothing during twelve years of missionary work in South America. Manning the Middle East desk has done nothing to resuscitate her belief in a single merciful God. The rest of the staffers are younger than these three, sometimes too young. The hours and pay ensure that anyone at ABRI will be without family, the emotional and economic strain of children.

His telephone is ringing and when he picks it up he hears the flat voice of the American, Smith, who calls from time to time. "You've heard your mother is up for parole," he says.

"I got a letter."

"This makes, how many, three tries? Maybe this time she'll have a friend in her corner."

"Her friends are all dead or locked up. Don't you read your mail?"

"I was thinking of the company."

"You don't know my mother, that much is clear."

"She doesn't have to know, Tom. We can keep it between us."

"Don't bother finishing. I know what you want and it's not for sale."

There is a pause in which Zane listens for the sounds of other voices in the background. A conference call?

The man continues. "We've already appealed to your patriotism and gotten nowhere. Consensus around here is that you're a sleazeball if not an outright pinko."

"That's a mighty old-fashioned word, pinko. Getting moldy on the CIA vine, wouldn't you say?"

"And this time we wanted to see if you had any love for your own poor mother locked up all these years. You must be itching to take her for a walk in the park or a run down to Mexico."

"You could start by giving her paper and a pen," he says. "As a sign of faith."

"That can be arranged. In return, we have a list of code names we'd like deciphered. Mozart is one that really gets us up in the morning."

"Wolfgang Amadeus. Austrian national. Look him up in the Vienna phone book."

"Don't you have any fucking idea how to cut a proper deal?"

Zane, acting on instinct, hangs up. Then he waits for a full minute with his hand on the phone in case Smith tries to call back. This haggling has gone on for years and it's the first time they've brought his mother's freedom to the table. In return for

Mozart's fingernails or a layer of his tanned skin. No, Zane reflects, he doesn't know how to cut a proper deal.

Emelle's office has a clear glass door and two glass walls and Zane has never known if this is so that she can see them or so that they can see her. These things go one way or the other and he has long since stopped believing in two-way streets. From across the office, he can see she's on the telephone. She is looking through the glass at him as she speaks and he is at once fascinated by her moving lips and the heartbreaking look in her eyes. A typed quote is in a small frame on the wall behind her desk: "A lie gets halfway around the world before the truth puts its boots on."—Winston Churchill. If she takes away his rakers, the fraying threads that bind him to this job will be cut. He will feel like a mouthpiece or a liar repeating credible lies.

He swallows coffee with his three aspirin.

The Eleven files are cluttered with news clippings and random notes relative to Street's specter, Bj. A world map with circles and dates around Algiers (1962), Vientiane (1971), Phnom Penh (1973), Bucharest (1979), Wollayta (1984), Lagos (Sept 1986), Port Harcourt (Feb 1987), Bamako (Mar 1988). The dates describe a proximity that is illusory. In the past few years, desperate for an ally in his search, Street has turned over more and more of his "evidence" to Zane: A Red Cross coroner's report listing a Nigerian prisoner's cause of death as "unidentifiable poison." A similar report, filed by Amnesty International in Chad in 1981. Photographs of corpses uncovered from a mass grave in Wollayta. None of the corpses show bullet holes or knife wounds or bruises or any other external sign that might identify the cause of death, though all of them are without hands. Zane sees no connection whatsoever between any two of the incidents but Street persists in his weird hope to put a human name to evil that might be erased with a single stroke. Zane's own Wollayta casebook from the famine wars of 1984 includes a rumor, passed on by Mozart, of a fair-haired man who was said to have provided "scientific consulting" to the Marxist soldiers who had stolen a British Medical shipment straight from a guarded warehouse outside of town.

Thin, Harry. Thin as onion skin.

Zane first met Street in Geneva in August of 1983 during a hunger
conference sponsored by the World Health Organization. A director in an English-based medical-supplies company, he had for-
merly been a salesman in the Southeast Asia region. They were
chosen as random panelmates on a logistics forum. There were
twenty representatives all together, nearly all of them from either
Europe or Africa, and the question put to them for the day had
to do with the imminent famine in Ethiopia. There were conflict-
ing reports on the level of hunger and various arguments pertain-
ing to methods of addressing this touchy political situation.
Street was wearing tan slacks and a beige safari jacket over a
colorful Hawaiian shirt. His name tag bore the logo of his company and the conference ID assigned to him: Eleven. He didn't
look the part of a company director, but Zane found that his
credentials filled five paragraphs in the printed program. He
carried weight. He was thirty-eight, badly shaven, in need of
a haircut, and quite clearly unhappy with the forum. He was
stone silent through the first few hours and sat calmly in the
chair next to Zane's, sometimes gazing toward the ceiling and
at other times into his water glass. His face was taut with boredom. Near the end of the morning, in reply to a question concerning his opinion on the matter, he said simply, "Trains, boats,
planes, lorries, helicopters, piggyback, bicycle, sampan, camel-
back, horseback. But first the Yanks and Europeans have to give
it all away."

Logistics. Street knew they meant Third World politics and
North American economics. Storage and transport costs in excess
of production overheads. The poor shelf life of Midwestern American strains of wheat. African microparasites that could turn the
wheat to dust or to poison. Marxists manning the ports of entry
and their politics of starvation. The usual bottom line of push
coming to shove.

Someone ventured that perhaps Mr. Street was being simplis-
tic. There was a general agreement that the resulting mass defla-
tion of grain prices would devastate a good part of middle
America, closed-down farms and unemployment as far as the eye

could see. "If we start giving away grain in massive doses, won't we be making these people aid-dependent?"

Street replied that he was not suggesting they send *all* of the Western surplus to Ethiopia. "We are looking at one hundred thousand tonnes and supplementary supplies of butter oil and milk powder. The cost alone of storing the European grain mountain is comparable to the cost of giving it away."

"But the European strains of grain are incompatible with African bellies."

"If the alternative," Street said, "to that incompatibility is starvation . . ."

"And what about self-reliance?" he was asked. "The creation of another aid-dependent state . . ."

Street figured the Yanks could absorb the blow. "The Can Do approach. The New Deal. These people are more elastic than the Ethiopians."

He was reminded that the subject was logistics, not pie-in-the-sky.

Street rose from his chair in the third of three circles and leaned his weight on the seat before him. Zane's guess at the time was gin but Street later told him no, it was red wine that had given him those tiny eyes. His Hawaiian shirt was unbuttoned and there was a film of sweat along his brow.

"Three quarters of the blackest, richest, most arable land on the planet," he began, "is found in that sweetpot triangle between the Ohio River, the Missouri River, and the Mississippi Delta. In 1964, the state of Iowa alone had a crop of one billion bushels of corn. Please check your matrices for the nourishment equivalency, in years, for a population of one million. We are now twenty years later and the annual harvest has doubled. Three percent of Americans live on farms and these three percent could damn near feed the world. Not to mention the grain mountains, the butter mountains, and the citrus mountains of the European Common Market." He paused to reach for his water glass, then changed his mind. "There is more to do besides giving away our surplus. We can stop dumping water into treeless lands. That may wash our conscience but the end result is saline pools, no insects, no wood, no leaching of the soil. Send trees and shovels, build rain spouts, sand filters, solar and wind pumps. Teach crop rotation and terracing. Distribute grass seeds to discourage erosions. Plant fuelwood trees where these people can find them, so they won't cut down the fruit trees when they're cold."

"But the Ethiopian war—"

"Send tanks to accompany the grain. Soldiers of the earth. Logistics are meant to apply logic. Logic says give it away. Grow it and give it away in truckloads. That's *my* logistic."

"But you are suggesting making these people forever dependent on aid!"

"The problem is not a dependence upon aid," Street replied. "The problem, dear man, is that these people are totally, hopelessly, irrevocably addicted to *food*."

There was an uneasy silence in the room. Half the panelists were embarrassed for him and others were checking their earphones for translator malfunctions. Then he turned to Zane. Later he admitted it was only because he was seated closest to him, no other reason. "You agree," he said coolly, "I'm sure."

Zane squirmed. He didn't have Street's balls. He had his own pains and bruises and had come along to the forum with all intentions of nursing his way toward lunch while taking a few worthwhile notes.

"Do . . . you . . . bloody . . . agree?"

He was the second of Zane's rakers. He already had Demi, the Algerian Frenchman. Their language was wrought over the usual workbench, empty glasses and bottles, piled ashtrays and a sleep that wouldn't come easily. Their first phrase together was *paying the rent*. This meant putting up with inefficient relief agencies and mull-it-over groups which nevertheless gave them the wherewithal to do what they did. Mengistu, Marcos, Pol Pot, and Baby Doc were not the only arm of the enemy; logistics galled them as well. So Zane admitted that he agreed with him and during lunch they were each taken aside and asked not to join the afternoon session. Their presence, they were told, was disruptive.

Zane learned that night that Street had it in for Americans, too. Listening to him, Zane found himself wondering at which of the Englishman's stanzas he would be forced to lay him out. These things happen to him from time to time. He will stoke up on alcohol and some Frenchman or Dane or Englishman will start in on the Americans and in no time he'll be hearing "The Battle Hymn of the Republic." When you live overseas, he learned years ago, everyone takes you for either an ambassador or a target. Street included.

"You treat us in England like we're your fucking cousins when we have long since disinherited the lot of you. The sorrow is that because we speak the same language you all seem to think we mean the same thing."

The only bars they knew of closed early, so they bought a bottle over the counter, Street picking up the outrageous Swiss tab. Then they sat on a bench near the shore of the lake and passed the bottle back and forth. As it emptied the conversation accelerated. Street regretted his outburst during the conference. "The logistics *are* a nightmare and these people who come to meet are in earnest. But it seems that the *fact* of a conference is enough for most governments. They are *represented* and have therefore participated. But to what end?"

After a third whisky, Street described how he rose up in the company after his Asian experiences. His natural salesmanship returned to him and over the years he'd won his prizes and promotions and in time had become "a muck, as it were, a gold-plated ambassador of good medical will," and was given freedom to roam Africa as a diplomat of his company. His role at the time was to kibitz with officials from the International Red Cross, Doctors Without Borders, the United Nations Committee for Refugees, Zero Population, and the like. "I inspect war fronts, drought-stricken regions, villages plagued with spreading maladies, and I report back to the company any commercial or public-image opportunities that those may suggest to me. I make parallel reports on what I've witnessed to all and sundry. Sometimes my reports are published in magazines or journals, but I am a very poor writer. Editors are forever striking out my underlining and exclamation points. It is difficult to shout in print. I never use my own name, of course. If I did, I'd have a hell of a time getting visas for any of a dozen countries. I have an open budget for travel and my calendar is largely my own affair. The company will also provide me with product sample cases, something to pass out like chocolates in the name of goodwill.''

Zane had stories to tell, but few that could match Street's many years of selling medical supplies in Saigon, Singapore, Hong Kong, and Manila.

"Can you imagine how ridiculous it was? I sold *machines*, full-scale *systems*. Respirators, cardiac monitors, suction devices. These things will cost you a whole hospital wing plus maintenance. I'd roll into Saigon with pamphlets and charts, a whiz-bang slide show on the merits of two-track inhalation monitors, and these frazzled doctors would just stare at me and nod and send me down the hall to fill out some inventory clerk's wish list. The place I got to know best, the client that tore a hole in my heart forever, had this very tired young woman in charge of purchasing and inventories. She would sit in this steaming office and shuffle little pink and yellow slips around on her desk, trying to match them up like a hand of gin rummy. Pink for a supplies request and yellow for supplies available. And me saying all cheery, 'Take your order, miss?' So she passes over a big stack of those pink slips and they're all requests for bandages, dressing, disinfectant, syringes, rubber gloves, aspirin, surgical needles, cotton swabs. That was *not* my product line. She wanted spare parts, trinkets, consumables, and was not in the least interested to learn that I was in the Critical Care Division. The know-how I'd gathered over six months of training in Swindon and the three months' refresher course in Sydney were of no use whatsoever to this woman. 'Pansement,' she was telling me in French. '*Gants, adhésifs, masques hygiéniques.*' With this clipped accent which annoyed me, no asky why. When I didn't respond to this little speech, she made a gesture, putting her thumb between her fingers to mime a syringe, and when I shook my head again and said I didn't have any she lifted that mock syringe to her temple and squeezed.

"I left her my sample kit, which included one of just about everything from the goodwill bag—*one* surgical mask, *one* syringe of each size, *one* roll of surgical thread, and *one* roll of gauze—and she wrote everything down on those yellow chits and started matching them to pink ones. Still doing my business of course, I left her the color pamphlets and charts describing our famous cardiac monitors and she just put them to one side. When I rose to leave she was still sorting out chits and didn't even raise her head to say goodbye.

"I was only twenty-six at the time and already had a wife and a two-year-old boy. I had ambitions of climbing the company ladder; my gaze was turned wistfully to a post in South America and later a directorship out of the U.K. But I soon realized that, other than for the Hong Kong and Malaysian and Thai markets, I was in the wrong territory or the wrong sales division. There was no end of hospitals, mind you, but let's just say that my clientele's enthusiasm was a bit thin when the subject turned to high-tech items when there were so many other pressing needs. So I started packing extra sample kits, like ten and fifteen at a hike. Or filling out these sales reports that said such-and-such clinic might be enticed by our products if maybe we could first send along fifty dozen sample cases of triple-weave gauze for massive hemorrhaging. I was doling out whole product lines under the guise of client relations and whatever commercial instincts I'd once developed were soon forgotten.

"After a while my superiors got wise to it. Of course they did. There are statistics to these things, cost of sales, market-penetration scatter graphs, visit/turnover ratios, and the like. The spreading pollution of statistics is another of those sins I blame on you Yanks, but no matter. Considering that I wasn't doing a booming business in multistation self-regulating respirators, one thing just led to another and I was transferred to a New Zealand office just about the time your brave boys were pulling out of the war for keeps.

"I got back to Saigon for one last visit and went straight to the same hospital to see that woman. Her desk was covered with pink slips and she was just sitting there gazing at them, not even stacking them or sorting them into categories. There were hundreds and hundreds of pink slips and only a few scattered yellows to mate with. I made ten trips back to my station wagon and hauled in forty sample cases and stacked them on the floor next to her desk. She didn't react. 'Here you are, love,' I told her. 'Let's get cracking.' She didn't so much as wink at me. All right, I was

thinking. I didn't insist. Those pink chits were like a lake between her and me and I went round back of her desk and found
a stack of blank yellow sheets and began filling them out myself,
in English. Rubber gloves, forty pair. Number-sixteen stainless-
steel tweezers, forty. Hundred-millimeter butterfly syringe, forty.
Extra-wide tongue depressor in plastic sheath, forty. It took me
the better part of an afternoon to do the unloading and the forms
writing and the whole time this woman sat watching me, letting
me have at it on my own. It was pathetic and I didn't care whether
or not she *knew* I was aware of it. I still had this belief in *symbols*,
you see. It was a *gesture*. And when I was finished, I went about
rummaging through the *pink* slips to find matches for my yellow
ones. By this time I was a mess, weeping and sniveling, in a panic
because my French wasn't so good, not at all what it is today,
and I didn't know whether or not my matches were precise. *Gaz,
ampoule, cicatrice.* I swear in that afternoon I became an old man.
And when it was done, when my yellow slips had been matched
with at least a dozen pink slips each, I stood and said there
wasn't anything more I could do. For me the war was over and I
wished her luck with her own.

"The woman looked up at me and made that gesture again with
her fingers, that mock syringe. But this time she aimed it at her
heart and I didn't wait to watch her squeeze."

The first time Street sent a cable in Zanespeak, his dateline included only the country name, Iran.

"Pink slips everywhere," he cabled. "More than I can count."
The name of a valley where boys had run the minefield to clear
the way for tanks. The date and then his signature, Eleven.

Pink slips thereafter meant corpses. The dead for whom no
sample case would suffice.

With a deep breath he begins to sift through the oldest of Street's
files and dispatches and is not surprised to find them filled with
references to Ambrose Okimbo.

Ambrose Okimbo, Poet, Playwright. Port Harcourt Nigeria.
Born 1942.

Ambrose Okimbo, the killer poet.

M'Khlea Kane, spouse.

Interpol has files. So does France Presse, Amnesty International, Africa Watch, and the *International Herald Tribune*. For a monthly fee or the right personal contacts, you can access parts of them freely from remote stations. Cutting screen prints, Zane has twenty pages on Ambrose Okimbo in the space of half an hour. The laser printer even reproduces a photo in 300x300 resolution and the face in his paper tray is oddly familiar. A dark and open mouth saying words that aren't repeated in the caption and eyes that could start fires in dry grass. Seeing the photo, he remembers what it was like to meet the man three years ago, to shake his hand and to feel for a fleeting moment the end of all bloodshed and mayhem. When Okimbo was a man of all tribes and of no tribe whatsoever. Before he turned. And now the entire world, Zane included, has been on the lookout for him. He is a man who will never die of old age.

Born in Iwo, Nigeria, Okimbo had divided his childhood between Lagos and Port Harcourt. Educated at the University of Ibadan and then postgraduate work at the University of Manchester. Twin subjects: European literature and astronomy. Zane was once puzzled over this fact for long minutes, having never imagined the existence of a black African astronomer and wondering to himself why not. Okimbo had remained in England for a number of years while making his living as a journalist and playwright, though few of his plays were ever produced and his skills as a journalist were thought to be limited. He returned to Nigeria in 1972 at the age of thirty and took up a position as a writer-in-residence at a budding university in Lagos. To this point his only publications were in English, mostly in small journals and one thin volume of poetry. Turning his full attention to his writing, he quickly made a name for himself with a series of long poems that were championed in the English press as stellar examples of the New African Literature. The poems were written in English and have since been translated into thirty African and European languages. They were later bundled into a *Collected Works* and from this single publication Okimbo was turned into a spokesman for West Africa.

In Africa, as in Eastern Europe, poetry and politics tend to mingle like sulphur and potassium chlorate. The Nigerian civil war provided the spark that lit the match. Okimbo was forced to flee and he became one of the planet's more famous exiles. Amnesty International circulated petitions. *Newsweek* wrote an article. ABRI opened a file.

Traveling extensively over the next few years, Okimbo learned Arabic, Bantu, Swahili, Zulu, and French and gave readings in a variety of languages, attracting followers who began to look upon him as something more than a poet. Returning to Lagos in 1978, he was imprisoned but his case was never tried. He was released nineteen months later. No charges were ever made public, nor was it known whether or not he had *confessed*. In his interviews after being liberated, he often mentioned how the general public, the untortured, confuse the issue by being obsessed with the torturer's tools. This is natural, he observed. The torturer's first act is to show his victim his array of tools; his blades, canes, clubs, and rods. The first pain is in the imagination. But he added that the worst of the tortures are not physical.

"You begin to take heart when the pain is associated with a question. At least then you have a chance at providing an 'answer' and thus stilling the pain. When the pain comes without a question, it is a lonely, hopeless agony. In such instances, the only two options left to you are to resist or to die."

The book he wrote, based upon his months in prison, was widely translated and he was said to be discussed among the Nobel Committee in 1982. That same year he married a South African, M'Khlea Kane, in a private ceremony in Soweto and returned to Nigeria to take up a position as writer-in-residence at the University of Lagos. In public statements he made it known he meant to retire from politics but his notoriety made that impossible, as did the fact that a great number of his countrymen, many of them writers, were in and out of prison. Early in 1984, he helped to found a *free* newspaper and in a very short time was being hounded by the police. His files and manuscripts were seized; his house was watched. It was at this point that Zane first learned the details of his life. He had recently taken over the African desk at ABRI and the Okimbo file was in the high-profile collection, along with the files on Mengistu, Doe, Mandela, Qad-

dafi, and Tutu. Villains and heroes, everyone was being moni-
tored.

At the time, Nigerian law included a pair of decrees that were
cited by Amnesty International as the underpinning of most arrests. Decree 2 specifically empowered the authorities to detain
anyone suspected as "concerned in acts prejudicial to state security." The duration of the detention was unspecified. Decree 4
prescribed stiff sentences for people criticizing even the *previous*
military government.

When Okimbo was arrested by the Nigerian Security Organization, both of these decrees were invoked. Zane was prepared,
with an extensive mailing list specific to Okimbo's case and a
costly letter-writing campaign that resulted in a flood of over
twenty thousand letters sent to the Nigerian authorities in the
space of a single month. When the French television station An-
tenne 2 offered a half-hour documentary on a Sunday afternoon,
much of the documentation was supplied by ABRI (duly credited
at the end of the show).

Street, under cover of his British Medical job, haunted Lagos
and Port Harcourt for three full months and his dispatches back
to ABRI included details as to the number and names of detainees
as well as sketchy secondhand reports on prison conditions. Amnesty estimated four hundred detainees but Street pointed out
that fifty or so from the Lagos area had been released and another
eighty rounded up in Port Harcourt. Though Okimbo was moved
from cell to cell and prison to prison, Street was always able to
locate him anew. Rumors of torture and of marathon interrogations were unsubstantiated and then a series of muddy photographs were smuggled out of the prison and relayed to Street.
When the fax arrived at ABRI, Emelle was skeptical. One of the
photographs was simply a picture of hands without fingernails,
impossible to identify as belonging to Okimbo. A picture of his
face showed no marks whatsoever, except for an empty gaze that
might have simply been the result of poor focus.

Emelle released the photographs to the European press, then
asked Zane for clearer evidence. He used the dedicated line
through the Abidjan drop: *Face of God illegible. Shroud of Turin.*

An urgent appeal to the Nigerian government was made by Amnesty International but Okimbo's plight was linked with ABRI in the public mind and Zane found himself fielding queries from the Associated Press, Interpol, Human Rights Watch, and numerous callers who refused to identify themselves. Donations to ABRI were on the rise. Though he hadn't asked for anything, Zane was given upgraded computer equipment and a faster transmission line to AMNET. A letter arrived from his mother in prison. She had read of his involvement in the affair and offered an old slogan: *Venceremos*.

Zane received a number of phone calls from the Nigerian ambassador to France, whose speeches bore an imprint of steadfast denial laced with unspecifiable menace. These calls were exhilarating; he had struck a nerve. In early 1985, the Nigerian Security Organization (NSO), pressed to answer various charges, admitted that it had lost count of the number of detainees. A week later, a more relaxed interpretation of Decree 2 was declared and three of Okimbo's friends were discreetly freed. But Okimbo's international profile put the Nigerian authorities in a bind. Word was passed to Zane that he should lower the volume. Emelle concurred and all activities except for the letter-writing campaign were suspended. Through Zane's influence, a mercy visit to Lagos planned by an American group of Baptist ministers was canceled. Okimbo's case slipped into the back channels and the Nigerian minister of the interior met twice with Street to discuss "new arrangements."

Finally, in late February of 1985, after nearly a year in various prison cells, Ambrose Okimbo was given a suit of clothes and an empty suitcase and expelled from the country. No official statement was made. Okimbo was reunited with M'Khlea in Abidjan and was able to duck the press entirely. After refusing all interviews, he was flown by the French government to an unnamed destination. His only public utterance was to the effect that he was not yet free.

For the next three weeks, Zane worked his rakers overtime in an attempt to locate him. His disappearance was a letdown after the euphoria of his liberation. Zane had expected something more, and felt disappointment in himself when he realized that he merely wanted recognition; the cousin to glory. While imprisoned, Okimbo had served as a reminder to the world that there were others like him in prisons everywhere. A free Okimbo was now invisible and silent. And Zane longed to hear him speak. In mid-March, he received a message over his line from Street. He was in town, he wrote, and needed skin on skin, a meeting. He requested that they meet at a small hotel in a rundown section of the city, near the Jaurès metro stop. It was past midnight and a black rain had been falling for hours when they met outside the hotel. Street wanted to know if Zane had been followed.

"Not that I know of."

"They want us to be sure. Come this way."

Zane followed him into the hotel, but instead of taking the tiny elevator they followed the hallway to the back of the building and out a service door into a narrow wet alley. At the extreme right were steps leading into another building. The ground floor was an abandoned bakery and Street paused for a moment in front of three large ovens. "Are we lost?" Zane asked him. In reply, Street opened the door of the oven on the left. It was not an oven at all but a door. There was no light and they had to crouch to pass through. "Put your hand on my shoulder and follow," Street said. They advanced forty feet and then stopped. Zane heard a rustle of metal and then Street tapped against the wall. A door opened in front of them and they stepped into a wide closet. Yet another door opened and they found themselves in the lobby of another hotel. A young man with Arabic features was waiting for them. After looking long and hard at Zane, he glanced at a photograph he was carrying. "Mr. Street," he said. "Mr. Zane. Come this way."

He led them up a worn stairway to the third floor, room 36, and knocked twice. Zane heard a voice answer from the other side, in a language he didn't know. Then the door was pushed open to reveal Ambrose Okimbo. The flesh and blood and bone of him. He was tall, nearly six three, and wore a simple white dress shirt and tan slacks. The lone window of his hotel room looked into a blank wall, and though it was past midnight he left only a single weak lamp lit. Whatever emptiness had shown in the faxed photographs of his face was no longer there. He was unsmiling but in good health. His handshake was neither firm nor gentle, a simple grasp of the palm.

A woman rose from her chair in a dark corner of the room. She wore a blue wraparound dress and her throat was encircled by a bone necklace. "My wife, M'Khlea."

Weeks later, Zane would wonder how it was that he took so little notice of her. Perhaps because of the surprise of her and the dwarfing shadow of her husband. It was she who expressed their mutual gratitude and, after having done so, left the room. They did not see her again for the remainder of their stay.

Okimbo directed them to a pair of wooden chairs next to the bed. A bottle of J & B Scotch whisky and two glasses were arranged on the nightstand to Zane's left.

"My friends tell me that you are fond of this brand. Please, serve yourselves." He took his place on the edge of the mattress and refused with a slight head movement the glass that Zane offered him.

"Why the stagecraft?" Street wanted to know. "Labyrinths and secret doors."

"Paris," said Okimbo, "is just another African capital."

"But surely you aren't in any danger."

"Not at this moment, no. I am in your care. I have read many versions of how it was that I was liberated and few of them reproduce a truth that I can trust. My wife informs me that it was through your persistent efforts that I am no longer behind bars."

What he wanted, to their amazement, was to hide M'Khlea. Zane, he pointed out, was in the business of sanctuary. Obviously, he could arrange for a safe house.

"ABRI doesn't have any Holiday Inns," Zane said. "Slang, Mr. Okimbo, for the kind of place you're looking for."

Okimbo pondered this for a moment. He knitted the long fingers of both hands into a single fist. His nails had not yet grown back and the tips of those fingers were the color of pale roses. "I am asking you because of that fact. You are not in the business of harboring fugitives and therefore no one would suspect you."

There was a long silence during which Zane thought of the kitchen in which he had slept one Minnesota winter, the green linoleum floor and the open oven that warmed him while his mother tied knots around explosives.

"Something can be arranged," Street said. He turned to Zane

and there was a word in that look. He was asking a question that he felt only Zane could answer. "We aren't without resources," he added with a smile.

"For how long?" Zane wanted to know.

Okimbo answered, "Months rather than weeks."

"And where will you be?"

Okimbo unlaced his fingers and described a circle with his hands. "On my continent," he said. "Doing my work."

It was not a sufficient response for either of them but neither was ready to press the matter. For the next hour they discussed various possibilities for M'Khlea's safety and fashioned a set of code words that would be broadcast over a small French radio station. These code words would be meant for Okimbo, so that he would have news of her. He would not promise them, however, that they would hear from him. "Perhaps," he commented, with his only smile of the night, "you will read of me in the news-papers."

Zane wanted details of his imprisonment and torture, any in-formation that could be used by ABRI to help the others, and Okimbo was able to provide a few names, sketchy physical de-scriptions of his tormentors and interrogators, and only cursory accounts of the actual interrogations. He spoke extremely slowly, as if each word had to be grasped and tested in his memory. "At first," he said, "I was beaten, and of course, this." He showed his bald fingers. "But later I was fed drugs. Sodium pentathol, I was thinking. You know, the talk-talk medicine. I did not suffer pain. I was light-headed. Weightless. My head was shaved and I wore a halo. I remember seeing clouds."

This made little sense to Zane but soon he would understand why Street grew suddenly so agitated.

Okimbo continued. "For a long time, I could not speak clearly. Perhaps only a poet can understand this. I could not make a metaphor. I could make no comparisons in words. When I opened my mouth, I heard myself singing. I was not heroic." For a long moment he was staring into empty space. Then Zane realized he was gazing at the door that led to the room that held his wife. "Though I do not remember distinctly," he finally continued, "I am sure that I named names. The slaughter that followed my interrogations can only confirm as much. I confessed, though I cannot remember the words I used. I am only now beginning to rediscover a familiar vocabulary.''

Street asked, ''Were any of your jailers white?''

Okimbo found this to be a curious question. He answered by quoting himself from his book: ''All jailers are without color. They are ghosts and not men.''

Street continued. Could he describe his torturers? Their faces or mannerisms? What were their uniform insignias? Did they speak Bambara? French? English?

Okimbo glanced at Zane and then at his hands. Street abruptly dropped the line of questioning and they returned to the subject of a safe house for Madame Okimbo. Zane sensed that there was some sort of bond between the two of them and felt strangely excluded.

It was nearly dawn when Okimbo rose to signify that their meeting was ended. Again he shook hands with each of them, but now there was a vacancy to his eyes and his grip was more indifferent still. Zane followed the same young man down the stairway before noticing that Street had lingered with Okimbo. He felt a surprising flash of anger mingled with envy. He waited long minutes at the closet door before Street finally appeared. ''There's something wrong,'' Street said.

''What?''

''I don't know. He's not right in the head. This halo business and seeing clouds. I told him we'd be back tonight.''

But the following evening, when they returned to the hotel, Okimbo was already gone. M'Khlea greeted them and offered whisky from the same bottle, apologizing for the lack of ice. ''Where is he?'' Street asked.

She shrugged. ''In Africa.''

''Lagos? Abidjan?''

''Or London, or Geneva, or Copenhagen,'' she said. ''Wherever Ambrose is, is Africa.''

She fell silent while Zane and Street stared into their whiskies, embarrassed at their ignorance. It was clear that there was something she wanted to say. And equally clear that the two disheveled amnesty agents would not be her confessors. They drank up, stood, and touched her hand in parting.

Street told her to pack her things. He would call for her the next day.

The following week, Zane was busy at ABRI, updating his files with the information Okimbo had supplied, so it was Street who made the arrangements for M'Khlea. First he rented a two-room apartment in lower Montparnasse, signing the lease with a fake name. When he learned of her experience with languages, he was able to find translation work for her through a third party in London. The material to be translated would be forwarded to a post-office box in Paris, and because Street could not always be in Paris, it was up to Zane to fetch it for M'Khlea. Once she'd completed her translations, she was to contact Zane, who would see that they reached Street for relay to London. Zane was surprised to find how easily Street had obtained false papers for her, so that she was relatively free to circulate within the city. She had a Kenyan passport and residence and work permits for France, an international driver's license, and, the crowning touch, a library card for the American Library in Paris.

The first time Zane visited her with a package, he was surprised to hear music coming from the other side of the door. When she opened to him, her first reaction on seeing him was joyous laughter. "A friend," she said, and urged him to enter. "I have not seen a friend since Mr. Street returned to Africa."

He had expected to hand her the package, inquire as to her comfort and safety, and leave. But she insisted that he linger, "If only for a few moments. I should be very happy to speak English with you."

She opened the parcel and smiled at the sight of her new project. "The poems of Rilke," she told him. "Do you know his work?"

Zane admitted that he knew little about poetry.

"'Loneliness is like the rain. From out the sea it comes to meet the evening; And from the far-off plain ascends again . . .' A very moody poet, very European, very sad to read. I am always reminded of watching flowers slowly rot." She returned the pages to their envelope. "There has been some mistake, however. Rilke wrote in German and these are translations to the English. I shouldn't translate a translation. A grievous sin, that, don't you think?"

In place of the bone necklace she had worn the night they met was the gold chain with the black stone teardrop. She noticed him looking at it and told him it was a gift, mailed to her just last week from Senegal. "From Mr. Street."

Though there was work awaiting him at ABRI, he spent the remainder of the morning in her living room, listening to her stories of life in Africa. She had been raised near Capetown, where her father had worked as a journalist for a newspaper that was shut down or suspended on a regular basis. "They crossed out the word *blacks* and replaced it with *nonwhites*. My father was once arrested for including the term *chocolate bunnies* in one of his editorials."

This, too, made her laugh. As did her stories of how Street had been so helpful in finding her the stereo and the records, and how he called her often, or sent packages to her, addressed to her new pseudonym. It was her frequent laughter that Zane found most surprising. That and the fact that not once in nearly two hours did she betray the least concern for her husband.

"When do you expect to hear from him?" Zane finally asked and the smile disappeared from her face. Without it, she appeared suddenly older if no less beautiful. "Not ever," she replied.

"Translation?"

"There is none. I have no expectations of hearing from him. He is no longer a man who expresses himself to me."

"What kind of man is he?"

The smile returned to her face. "Is this for ABRI or for a book you're writing, Mr. Zane?"

"Thomas."

"Thomas, then. The Doubting Disciple. Well, *Thomas*, there is nothing to say except that, contrary to rumor and your own dispatches, my husband is no longer master of himself and his peacemaking."

"Do you miss him?" he asked.

"No," she answered. "When he was imprisoned I missed him. Now I only mourn him."

When Zane admitted that he didn't understand, she asked if he had ever read the poems of Charles Wright. "He is American."

Zane had never heard of him.

"'The danger of what's-to-come is not in its distance,'" she quoted. "'Two inches can break the heart.'"

She saw in his eyes that he understood nothing. Her gaze, so tranquil, made him uneasy. He could not look long at her face without turning away.

"Do not frown," she said to him. "You have the look of a man in a lifeboat, combing the sea for survivors. And here I am, in your boat at your side. I have not drowned."

"I was thinking of your husband."

"Do not worry. He is a very strong swimmer. He will never drown."

The next morning, in fulfillment of the arrangement he'd made with Ambrose Okimbo, Zane forwarded a news item to his contact at the radio station. Embedded in that item were the words that would signal to Okimbo that M'Khlea was safe. And her guardian angels as well.

There is nothing in Zane's files to suggest what befell Ambrose Okimbo. Zane reads what he can between the lines and can only imagine rage, though the source of that rage, at least in his documentation, is obscure. Zane has never been in prison and he has never been to Africa. He has never been tortured, he has never been so hungry as to eat soap or bugs, nor has he seen those explosions of butterflies in the deep Southern Hemisphere that Street often spoke of. From a distance he has watched Mozart and Snake Eyes and then Street grow jungle-drunk, unable to tear themselves away from the continent for longer than a month at a time. Like the colonial fever that could overtake the French and the English in Southeast Asia. But he is on the other side of the screen and has only the words to work with. Someone else's memories. He has to stick to the facts rather than his imagination. And why anyone puts down a pen and picks up a gun is never easy to explain. Wherever Ambrose is, is Africa.

Okimbo already knew what he was going to do the night he left M'Khlea behind. They had assumed he would recuperate for a time and then return to writing. That was once his action, but now action was to be his action. This is what he wrote in a warning-shot article that appeared on the editorial pages of *Le Monde*, the *Times* of London, and *The New York Times*. Pan-Africanism was in at the center of his operation; that much is in the file and his declarations. His past poetry reflected a continuing obsession over the clash of European and Yoruba cultures and now, from his various hiding places, he began to call for the overthrow of nearly every governing body on the continent. To some he was a liberator and to others a murderer. The European and American press was unable to make up its collective mind. Ambrose Okimbo was a revolutionary. Ambrose Okimbo was a terrorist. The easy logic quoted by nitwits: revolutionaries are merely terrorists who succeed.

Less than two months after their meeting in Paris he was arrested while boarding a plane in Lusaka. A handgun was found in his luggage—the same handgun, it was claimed, used in the recent assassination of a Nigerian colonel. He stated to the press that he'd been framed and his claim of innocence was echoed by Zane and ABRI as well as Amnesty International and Africa Watch. Street flew to Lusaka but by the time he arrived Okimbo had already been expelled and had disappeared just as quickly. The gun was cold, according to the wire reports. It had not been fired. A mistake had been made and Okimbo was free. On the loose.

After a six-week absence during which Zane visited M'Khlea twice more, Street returned from the Sahel and the two of them went on their usual Paris rounds. He was wired, overwrought, though on the face of it, other than his rapid-fire visit to Lusaka on behalf of Okimbo, this had been one of the less stressful of his tours. He had barely taken the time to change clothes and was drinking even more than usual. "He's hopped the fence," Street said, referring to Okimbo. "Bloody ju-ju in his blood. Violence. The latest rumor is that he's middled with the Syrians for a cache of arms."

Zane said he hadn't received any such data.

"There's more to be had and we'll have to stay in contact. It might just be that someone is trying to make him look bad. Can you put me onto Mozart? He has some informants amongst the Syrians who do business in West Africa. He might be able to confirm or deny."

Zane said he would run up a flag. "But Mozart's moody, hard to locate on short notice. I'm not sure where he is just now."

That night Street asked for the check earlier than usual, confessing exhaustion. When Zane offered to accompany him back to the hotel, Street said not to bother. "I could use a short stroll before sleep. The nerves. Alcohol poisoning." When they parted, Street headed off in a direction away from the hotel. Zane began to walk toward home and after a moment turned around and saw Street flag down a taxi. The next day he returned to Africa and within a week had sent a half dozen transmissions to Zane reporting various rumors as to Okimbo's newfound nastiness.

Zane's files show that, one month after his release in Lusaka, Okimbo was identified as the man who took a pot shot at Mengistu in Addis Ababa, but by the time the witnesses came forward he was safely in London, attending a conference on hunger in the sub-Saharan belt. Street missed him there as well and flew directly to Paris. But he didn't have time to see Zane, he said over the phone. "Visits to make. Amends to British Medical, whose directors assume I'm neglecting them. I'll catch up with you next month."

It was more than two months before they saw each other again. Street arrived in Paris from Abidjan and said he was due in London in two days. Though pale, he was calmer than during his previous visit. They met at a Vietnamese restaurant near the Place de Clichy and consumed their habitual quantities of whisky and rosé. It was the first time since Okimbo had been jailed in Nigeria that Zane didn't feel oddly distant from his friend.

"Did you agree with me the day we met?" Street wanted to know. "That conference in Geneva. Or was I simply a successful bully?"

Zane didn't know. "What I agreed with was the boredom. I'm no good in conferences or groups of any kind. I don't have your experience or background. I'm an office boy."

"Dealing in information."

"Rumors. Sometimes facts. Occasionally even the truth."

Street sighed: "If only I could knot my tie just so and say the words, like your Emelle. Just say the words and be done with it. I tend to shout when a whisper would do more good. The proverbial loose . . . Now, where's that bleeding bottle?"

Zane lifted the wine bottle from its bucket and poured for him.

"The proverbial loose cannon."

When the wine was gone, they ordered coffee and cognac and Street allowed himself a rare cigarette before launching into another of his many stories.

"This last trip I helped a desert soldier unload a lorry filled with blood bottles in the middle of the Sahara. He was a Moroccan and was fighting the Algerians over a patch of fucking *sand*. His homeland, he had me know. He copped the lorry in Algiers and drove it through some hefty roadblocks before meeting up with me in the middle of Allah-knows-where. And right off he trained a pistol on me while I drove to his camp. His brother was dying there. He'd stepped on a mine and was bleeding all over the holy ground. I spent a long hour saying over and over that I could not *guess* the man's blood type and would *not* stick a needle of those blood bottles into his veins. You do it, I told him. I am not a bleeding doctor. As it happened, I *did* stick him in the arm while three rifles were aimed at my head. The transfusion took. Jesus bloody wept, as we say where I come from. A hero with the toss of a coin. Type O won out."

This night there was a single obscene flaw, a recurring skip in the playback of his winding narrative. Zane caught the thread of it in slow degrees. Street spoke with respect for every race and tribe of man, Oriental, Hindi, American Indian, Slav, Celt, Mongol, Jew, and Latin. Arabs, in his speech, were Arabs and the Chinese were Chinese. Never chinks or wops or frogs or nips. Only the blacks. In his discourse they were variously treated as jungle bunnies, burrheads, niggers, and tam-tams. From Alabama to the Ivory Coast to the tenth arrondissement of Paris. These racial tics showed up at odd moments and Zane began to wonder if he was for some reason being provoked. The way Street would pause after saying sambo or darkie. As though Zane were meant to fill in some hideous blank and would be graded on either his assent or his silence.

"A few years ago I was in Gabon and this spade told me unload the serum right there on the beach and when I balked he prodded me with his walking stick and I had to give in. I was bloody surrounded by this sambo army going hoogaboo at the sight of my cargo. They thought it was fire water, I'm sure, and I was just the white-fuck bartender come to serve them up their glory. There was no moon, insects feeding on me, and I couldn't even get their outline good and proper. You know what I mean?"

He queried Zane about his origins and Zane told him he didn't really know. Something Mediterranean on his mother's side. He never knew fact one about his father.

Street was all English, through and through. "To the Cromwellian core," he admitted. "A born-and-bred islander. Doesn't it bloody show?"

He had his wife and two children back in Northampton. "Think of it. Divorced now, almost five years. Abby didn't take so well to travel, not like me. All those foreign voices troubled her sleep. You know what foreign means to the English, don't you? *Foreign* is whatever is not English. When we lived in Malta for those six months I mentioned, there were Italians, French, Egyptians, Lebanese, every manner of jigaboo. And they were mostly citizens of the place, real live Maltese. But to Abby, *they* were the foreigners. They were not, definitely not, English folk."

Zane finally asked him why in hell he said jigaboo instead of black.

He answered that a color could not define a race. "I am laying down irony, Zane, like rails of track from what I believe to what you believe. For example, could you love a black woman? I don't mean one of your coffee-colored quadroons, I mean midnight smoking ebony. Don't they smell so God awful differently to you than do white women? That infamous musky fragrance of loam."

"I don't have the least idea what you're talking about."

"And their bodies are quite different to the touch. Harder in some spots and softer in others."

"What are you telling me? That you have a mistress in Abidjan?"

"Trust me." And then he changed the subject again.

They were evicted from the restaurant at one in the morning

and carried on their conversation in a brasserie at the foot of Montmartre. To drink all night with Harry Street was nothing unusual. The brasserie closed at three and they had to move on, this time south to Châtelet, where one of the bars stayed open all hours. When the sun had risen and put a sudden stop to the conversation, Zane found himself touching his face, as if to measure the damage, but there was only a thin stubble of beard and the first intimations of a headache.

Street then stunned Zane by admitting that he had recently met a woman and set up housekeeping. "Common law, as it were. I'm still financially bound to Abby, of course, and will pay her marital taxes such as they are."

"So where is this woman?"

"Back at her apartment, no doubt wondering what's become of me. Shall we go round for breakfast? I know this American concoction, a Bloody Mary with a great splash of Tabasco and a palmful of ground black pepper. Wakes up your nervous system and opens the pores."

So they crossed the Seine to the Left Bank at Saint-Michel and walked two blocks in the wrong direction before Street righted himself, crossed Luxembourg Gardens, and emerged at the Boulevard Montparnasse. The rising sun was full in their faces, blinding them, and the leaves on the thin trees were shining with dew. Shielding his eyes, Zane suffered through that sordid flash—the realization that he'd been drinking for ten solid hours and now was on the way to meet his friend's new woman. Riding the cramped elevator to the fourth floor, Street made a last boozy remark about the Black Muslim Brotherhood, something about designer genes, but Zane let it pass while Street simply stared at him. They stood before the door and weaved to and from each other while Street searched his pockets for keys. Finding none, he rapped on the wood with his fist. After a short time they heard footsteps on the other side. Street gazed at Zane with unbearable sadness. "We just moved here," he said. "I had no other way of telling you."

The door opened and her brown eyes fixed on his bloodshot blues. Perfect teeth parted in a smile. A simple blue wraparound revealed delicate bones at the shoulder. And, as Street had promised with his provocation and his five-and-dime jokes, M'Khlea's skin was as black as the ace of spades, and more beautiful, and more luminous.

A safe house, Street explained, more for M'Khlea's benefit than Zane's. A bed and dresser and table and chairs, books to read and the curtains to be pulled tight even in broad daylight. You count how many times the telephone rings. One ring followed by two will be Zane. One ring followed by three, myself. You answer to nothing else. You keep the bolts and police locks in place at all times and open the door to me or to Zane and to no one else, not even the concierge. If Zane calls you and uses words you don't understand, write them down. I'll know his meaning.

For a time, Zane had to keep up the radio transmissions to Okimbo, to give him the impression that nothing had changed. M'Khlea at a new address is all. No other news to report. But Okimbo, through his lieutenants, finally asked for details. Pseudonym, address, phone number. For a few weeks, Zane stalled, begging discretion and the security of new codes. He transmitted through the radio station that he didn't know these lieutenants. Couldn't Okimbo show himself directly?

They never knew how he discovered the truth. And although they kept a close watch on his movements, they could not determine whether or not his increased activities had any connection to M'Khlea's abandonment of him. Street said it would take more than a battery of attorneys to determine who had abandoned whom, but he chose the path of care and found yet another apartment, this time in the ninth arrondissement, closer to Zane's office. "We have to stay in the city," he explained. "The suburbs are like villages, prying neighbors everywhere. The concierge in the new building is eighty if she's a day and probably hasn't even realized M'Khlea is black."

Okimbo never showed. Only his lieutenants, who called Zane from time to time to remind him they were in the neighborhood. Okimbo himself was busy with his own mayhem. In the following year his name was linked with a dozen killings or attempts but each time he eluded the authorities and emerged somewhere else in the continent, or in Europe, or in Asia. Early in 1986 he dropped out of sight. From this point on the file is slim. He was rumored to have paid a visit to Cuba. His name was erroneously linked to the fanatic set within the African National Congress. He was seen in a funeral crowd in Soweto. He had converted once and for all to Islam. For the past year there is nothing new in Zane's computer file. Not a single electronic word.

EMELLE IS FINISHED WITH HER CALL AND TAPS THE glass to get his attention. When he looks up from the screen, she is waving him in, so he takes the most recent Eleven folder like a shield in his arm and crosses to her office. Without looking at him she tells him to close the door. "This might get personal."

Her desk is nearly bare. No papers whatsoever, no file cabinet, no terminal or telefax, and no books. There is only a lamp, a crystal ashtray, a digital clock, a pen and pad. On a side table is a white telephone with a multifunction keypad, a speaker for conference calls, and her own double-spaced numbers list. She has no interest whatsoever in the telecom systems, but she can dial anyone on the planet if you ask her to.

At the height of the French-Algerian crisis of 1962, her husband died, leaving behind a Paris office, telex, files, Smith-Corona manual typewriter with the French AZERTY keyboard and no accent keys, and two lists: names and addresses of donors and code names and numbers of informers. He was a pioneer in the world of amnesty and is revered by those in the profession. His widow has carried on his work and has the annoying habit of invoking his name at regular intervals, intimating that no distinction should be made between the man and his wife. She was born Marguerrita Luisa to a Spanish father and an English mother, became Margaret Louise as she was raised in England, but signed her publications with the neutered M.L. to avoid sexist stereotyping. The initials have, in years since, become her name. Emelle. Only intimates ever refer to her as Margaret.

"You've been drinking?" she asks him.

"When?"

"Today. This evening."

"Not yet."

"That's an odd answer. As though it's inevitable."

"It is. Inevitable. Like the sun going down."

She is a striking woman who in her twenties must have been a heart-stomper, a burning flame in her thirties, and silk and smoke in her forties. Her hair is still red and her skin is naturally taut, smooth, and clear. She never tans but isn't pale. As though the fluorescent lamp or the wind alone gives her her color. Nearly sixty, she is one of those women still embarrassed by her breasts. She hides them behind layers of scarves, high-buttoned blouses, and loose-fitting dresses and she tends to walk with her shoulders pressed forward to mask the jutting. He agreed to join the agency because he admired her. Now he merely craves her patience and has given up trying to resuscitate her affection for him.

"Are you an alcoholic, Thomas?"

"Not according to the universal definition, no."

"But you drink daily."

"Not true. Days go by when I am high and dry. I have these moments."

"A craving?"

"A drowning."

She leans forward and reaches for her pen. "Now we're splitting hairs again."

You started this, he's thinking, but he knows what she means. For weeks now if she says red he will answer scarlet or cadmium or coral. If she says evening, he tends to say late afternoon. His cynical paraphrasing of vague dispatches frazzles her nerves.

There is a pause. Emelle has a way of holding her breath between sentences, as though the words are forming in the wind. She is still gripping the pen as if about to write something down, but there is no paper in front of her. Then she says he should clear out his desk. "I think you know why."

The crystal ashtray is for show. No one ever smokes in her office.

So when he lights a cigarette she is almost surprised by the blue smoke that hangs over her desk.

"I must have offended someone in the donors' network."

"You have offended everyone."

"That goes with the territory. I'm doing my job."

"*Your* job, not ours. These men you call rakers, they—"

"Free agents, if you prefer."

"We are all free agents, Thomas. You, Kirk, Nadine, Nguyen, Petitjean, the others. Floating and without gravity. What holds us together is cooperation. You know my meaning. This is a family. We work together, we coordinate. Your endless coming and going I can put up with. Your odd hours and even that bottle you keep in your drawer. But these codes you use—"

"I pass along everything that comes across my line. I translate the messages into clear English. Nothing's hidden but the original transmission and the source name. And the data have always proved reliable."

The smoke is bothering her, turning her office into a fishbowl of fumes. Like the black plumes that precede a fire. He didn't mean to be rude and so stubs out the cigarette, then rises to open the door to clear the air.

"The trouble," Emelle is saying, "is that we have to trust you. You insist on being a filter instead of a helper. As though we work for you. I sometimes get the impression you have lost patience with us. As though you no longer have faith in the process and prefer to take matters into your own hands. As if your mother—"

"Let's leave my mother out of this."

"I'm not going to cross myself, Thomas. I'm not going to shut up just because you're unable to face . . ."

"What is it you want?" he snaps. "Their names? Addresses? Photographs?"

"That might've helped. But now we're running late. The sun is going down, Thomas. Time is running short. I have made inquiries about you that I should have made long ago, and have come to this decision with distaste."

"This agency has swamp rot, Emelle. You open the door and all manner of lowlife just crawls right in."

"You are referring to Bartholomew. Since that incident, I have tightened security. I suspect that your absence will do us all some good in that area."

"I'm not the leak, Emelle. There are termites in every wall. We're being listened to. Can't you feel the stethoscope at your chest when you sleep at night?"

"We are concerned about your neutrality. Your point of view is beginning to show through."

"Did you know that someone's tapped in to my telecom line? He's been listening in on me for weeks on end. When I pick up the phone I hear choirs of mosquitoes in the background."

"Now you're being paranoid, Thomas."

He stands and leans over her desk. "Come into my office and I'll show you my evidence."

She is unmoved. "I do not need to hold a wet finger in the air to know which way the wind blows. These codes, Thomas. Secret languages and disappearing ink." Her voice grows hot. "Skulduggery! We are not spies!"

"No, but we are spied *upon*. We have what they want. Or they imagine we have it."

"This is intolerable. You are sounding like those men with neat haircuts and gray suits who always want us to take sides. Don't you understand? There is only one language that will work for us. A human language, a common language. When you mimic the CIA you *are* the CIA."

"The language protects us. *Abri*, Emelle. Isn't that still French for sanctuary?"

"There is no sanctuary in secrets, Thomas. Codes corrupt and cryptograms attract the malevolent."

"So it's off to the firing squad?"

She shakes her head. "Talk sense, if just this once. I intended to suspend you. One month minimum, though now I'm thinking two or three might be a better idea. I'm hoping your absence will make my heart grow fonder."

"I'd love to oblige but in the meantime there's a last matter I need to settle. Let me clear this up and then I'll go quietly. You won't even have to listen for slamming doors."

"Your Mr. Eleven?"

He nods. "He's a friend and he's missing, maybe worse."

"We deal in names, Thomas. We *reveal* rather than conceal. If you'd let us know his name we might be able to help you."

"That's what you want? Is that all?"

"I want to know that ABRI is a neutral site, a window and not a labyrinth. I want to know who it is that feeds you and caresses your forehead. Africa is becoming an embarrassment to the agency. I am convinced that your Eleven and these others are at the source of it."

"What I need for now is my juice, an open line. To be here when the messages come."

"What I want from you is the identity of this Eleven. As a token, shall we say, of your trust in me?"

"I can't do that, Margaret."

"And why not, since we're being so familiar? Is this man that you're hiding a criminal?"

"He doesn't want to know ABRI. He understands how muddy our waters have become."

"Is that your last word on the subject?"

"Yes."

There is a silence that is broken only by the sudden staccato of a telex down the hall.

"You will have to leave the building, Thomas. If forced to, I will change the locks. And I'd suggest you get out of the city. Go somewhere else, where there's no telephone and no electricity. Take along some cheap novels and try to stop drinking. Come back to us whole."

Shadows fill her office and she reaches toward the lamp, then changes her mind. He has risen to leave and is standing by the door when she says, "You must have known I once had you pegged for my successor."

He nods slowly. "Before that business with Bartholomew."

"We've been through this before." Changing her mind again, she snaps on the light and in that instant her face is enlarged and her eyes bore into his. This is the look she gives to rich men and politicos when she's trying to shake them down for help or contributions—a look that seeks out the territory behind the eyes and has a peeling quality to it. "That first year you were here, I'd never seen anyone so white hot. You were incredible, a godsend. That case in Gdańsk, the man you saved."

"I passed on underground hearsay. And he's still in prison, our man."

"He's been in and out a dozen times. At least he's not dead. And they wouldn't dare torture him. You were his life support for so long. I loved your soul."

The word jars him.

"Doesn't anyone love you, Thomas? Even Petitjean goes home to something. In six years I've never seen you with anyone. I have never heard you speak of what happened to your mother. I have seldom known you to be with a woman. As though you have no life outside of this place. No one to love, no one to miss."

"I think my Portuguese concierge loves me, but—"

She waves a hand as if to slice the words into pieces. "Don't be breezy with me. Not now, Thomas. The fact of the matter is, we believe in the same God, you and I. We just say different prayers these days."

Mine in my own language, he is thinking. Then he realizes she is whispering. "I loved your soul," she says again, very softly. The door is open and she is getting personal. Then she lifts her head and says, "Think hard about giving up the language, Thomas. Speak to us like a human being. Tell us about your Eleven and we will welcome you back with open arms."

Their movements are random, their locations varying according to the rhythms of their lives. Snake Eyes, Full House, Eleven. Mozart is independently rich, a perpetual tourist looking past the postcards. January is a precious-metals speculator. Demi, the only one known to the others by name, is a poet, an importer of African art, and, on occasion, Zane suspects, a drug dealer. He uses a variety of signatures: Zebra, Nun, Pinstripe, Penguin, any reference to black and white that he can conjure.

One of the few things the rakers have in common is the nasty habit of risking their lives for no reason at all; at least, they seem to say, none that they can think of when the smoke has cleared.

Postcard may have been headed to Giza to ruminate over the geometry of tombs, but inevitably he directed his taxi driver to some dark corner of Cairo to see what the brotherhood was up to on that same moonless night. Attracted, no doubt, by the glint of metal among djellabas or some uncorroborated rumor of the massacre of children. Or Snake Eyes was off to Peru to taste the snow and found instead a wealth of mythology amid a crush of colonels arguing over elbow space, loose change, and the blood of Indian peasants. After a stint with the Peace Corps, Mozart was lounging on a West African beach. The sun was high and white, straight up in the great blue beyond, and the waves were writing and rewriting the surface of the shore; a list of names of those to be shot in the morning.

A raker lives on handouts or on luck or on some inheritance he is always a bit vague about. Laser-printed paychecks arrive from Time-Life or Knight-Ridder or Reuters. Brown hands pass a bowl of *semoule* or black hands scale fish for him, leaving the eyes intact. Some eat what they can see. Or no longer look at what they eat. And each of them, at one time or another, confesses to Zane that he never meant to go on so long with all of this. It just seemed like a good idea at the time, to have a quick look-see into the inferno and then head back to the beach, the sand, the cool blue water. But it has its perverse charms, this life of reporting on a human swamp of one damned thing after another. Detention, kidnapping, car bombs, rape, a coup d'état with a popular backlash. Flooding or drought or acts of God. Or reporting on the torture of a suspect, the forced bleeding of a man in search of his confession, those justifying words: I did it, I did, now kill me, kill me now.

Stars did him in last night. Molly's soliloquy.

They have long since lost their detachment, the rakers, that cool sense of gazing into the arena of mayhem and making sense of it. Finding no sense whatsoever, they turn nevertheless to wordcraft. Zane listens and passes on their stories. From their language to yours.

Through Zane they share their directions to far-flung oases where one can find Cutty Sark, ice, a jukebox, newspapers, a shower, a telex, a telephone, a post office, succor, and forgetfulness. Raking can never be a full-time job. Space is often required, small gaps in time when a healing might occur. No one mentions good health; each of them reports on varying states of illness. There are occupational hazards too numerous to catalogue: the boredom of spending nights in police stations or in hiding or awaiting a contact on an empty street corner filled with rain; arrests, threats, occasional beatings or worse; and of course that impending madness, not unlike the madness that might overcome the night-shift nurse on the emergency ward on a night of the full moon. Eleven once wrote: It isn't true that when you've seen one slit throat you've seen them all. It isn't true at all.

With donated money from petty cash, and sometimes from his own pocket, Zane sends clothing, airfare, addresses of contacts, or simply fresh film. Only Emelle's three hired observers ever wire for cash. Zane's rakers want wheels, cassette tapes, Polaroid, waterproofed pens, and the juice to get it all back to him in English or in French or in Zanespeak, the language they have taught each other in European bars and during night-long walks through the Paris streets. Through thick and thin. And when a raker comes home to cool his feet for a spell, the only way to tell of what he's seen is in oblique word jabs, stammering, or flat-out sobbing. And late at night, or near dawn, when all the news that Emelle can fit into print has been *raked* from the mass of pain and confusion, then they will tell the rest of it in whisky talk or drug talk or whatever talk comes to mind. And together they will melt it down into another scrap of Zanespeak they will still remember in the morning, a phrase or two that might show up weeks later on the dedicated line.

Laid up with pharaoh's curse = I got too close and looked directly at the face of it. Molly's soliloquy = a confession. And I said yes I did, yes yes yes yes yes yes.

Emelle will dine at the Nigerian embassy and over coffee and cognac will tap her glass and declare her dissatisfaction with the ruling government's record of rights abuses. A raker will risk his life to tell Zane where the bones are buried. So that no one on the face of the earth has to die alone.

· · ·

To all rakers:

ELEVEN DOWN AND MAYBE OUT. CALL HOME.
THE SHOP IS CLOSING.

He goes to the back of the building to the mattress room. Petitjean is stretched out on the floor and sleeps with a forearm covering his eyes, his mouth open wide and his breathing labored. Zane knows that he still doesn't know the meaning of the message but is already in a state of parallel mourning. Bending low, he touches his shoulder and shakes him; Petitjean only shifts his arm. Zane shakes him until at last he opens his eyes, his face lined with fatigue and a film of sweat. The room is stifling. It takes him long seconds to focus on Zane's face. "You shit," he says.

"Angel face."

"I waited all *night* for you."

"And here I am."

Years before he came to the agency, Petitjean stole cars. That much came out in the fourth and final interview, back when Emelle hired him. He did his first hot-wire job at sixteen and spent his twenty-first birthday in a prison near Orléans. But on his own he has mastered English and German and has a surprising grasp of simple transmissions in a dozen other languages. He always carries a book with him—to lunch, on the metro, to the men's room—as though the time he might spend staring at his own hands might otherwise be spent absorbing words. He is also the only one besides Zane and Nadine who fully understands the telecom network, the line switches and multiplexor settings and protocols, when to use the dedicated lines and when to ride the public-transport lines. He is twenty-eight now and still has his black leather jacket and is skilled with a knife; he tells this with a smile meant to alarm whoever's listening. When he leaves the office, he goes home to a woman older by fifteen years who has a retarded teenage daughter. He has lived with these women for the past year but seldom mentions either of them by name. Maybe he will marry the mother, he once said; or maybe he will marry the daughter.

Zane offers him a towel and extends a hand to help him to his feet. "It's late. You should go home."

Instead he takes the towel into the bathroom and runs water into the sink. He strips off his shirt and when the water is warm enough he splashes it over his chest and shoulders. His jet-black hair is prematurely thinned along his temples; his eyes are the color of wood smoke with a perpetual look of worry; his words are often surrounded by awkward parentheses of silence, his swallowed stutter. He washes his hands with care, like a surgeon.

"We had, had company last night. Your line again. I followed them as best I could with the stalker routine. It was a straight grab this time, not just a copy."

Zane nods. "I need a police report," he says.

Petitjean glares at him.

"Suicide or murder? I need to know how they read it."

"Where's your kit?" Petitjean asks and Zane reaches into a cupboard for his overnight bag. There is shaving foam, a blade, soap, and aftershave. "You owe me," Petitjean says.

It takes Zane until ten in the evening to sort through the correspondence left in his box. Besides the transmissions, there are letters and news clippings. Nguyen needs a precise translation of the word *décapité* and when he tells her *beheaded*, "B, e, h . . . ," the look on her face makes a snapshot that will come back to him before the night is out. He also has to update status files for detainee reports from a dozen countries in Africa. Petitjean, working next to him, does the same for Eastern Europe.

One of Zane's transmissions is meant for Petitjean. "Your doctor is safe," Zane tells him.

"How do you know?"

"Postcard. In the cradle, he says. Came through Munich via the Leipzig drop."

Petitjean says that's too far north.

"Not for a telecom send."

"When is the kicker due?"

"Any time now."

"I'll sleep better, Zane, if you pass it on to me."

"Of course. When it comes."

When they finish entering data, they cross-check each other's updates for accuracy. Petitjean's Polish sources, it appears to Zane, are getting desperate. For weeks on end they've been sending trash, as though any news is information and any information has value; as though it's better to send even sports scores or weather reports than to let the line go silent. A little past eleven, Zane tells him again to go home.

"They're asleep by now," Petitjean tells him. "They won't miss me."

He never talks about the woman and her daughter except to mention that they exist, that when he does go home he is not alone. Though he seems to crave loneliness and can find it only at night, in front of his screen. Zane once was like that. He kept a row of paperbacks next to the mattress which had his name on it and the dent in the pillow fit his head just so. He toed the dotted line between dedication and insanity. The week Israel invaded Lebanon, he was asked to give Nadine a hand with the Middle East desk. Without knowing it, he grew a beard. Sunup to sundown he stood watch at his screen. Emelle loved his soul. When finally he shaved, he was the same man he'd always been and had no idea what he'd done in the preceding three weeks. The news that reached him wasn't history, but was biography of the worst sort. Nothing could be traced from back to front and everyone at Sabra and Chatila was still dead.

While Petitjean struggles on, Zane logs out, putting his transmission on *Interrupt* for the first time since it's been installed. He cuts his way into the operating system on the England mainframe and is face to face with a prompt for his ID. When he types in what he hopes 'to be a back-door code, he is rejected; he types another and is still locked out. Back-door codes are programming oversights, easy-access codes programmers create for their own use and later forget to erase—usually simple things like TEST, GO, or a birth date. Zane is beginning to wonder if the system has been swept of them when he finally gains access with ABC. Once inside, he retrieves the initial directory, the routing files for the transmission network. He is not authorized for this, nor to know what to do once he gets in. The network is driven by a mainframe west of London and, in theory, all you need is a modem and the right access codes. But there are some barbed-wire routines, verifying programs that search and eject intruding captors. These are the programs he seeks out, and when he finds the one relevant to his sector it is written in Pascal. Taking out his manuals, he goes to work. Though the language isn't foreign to him, he lacks experience and it takes him a full hour to analyze the flow of commands. A familiar headache looms upward from the base of his neck and fans out across his forehead. The program was purposefully written without structure or clarity, full of meaningless and inefficient branches and loops meant to confound a probing hacker such as himself. Just as he is obtaining a clean compile, his revisions yielding zero errors, he senses Petitjean looking over his shoulder.

"Why always is it crime with you? Why can't I ever look at your screen without seeing prison bars?"

"You haven't seen anything. Static from a bad transmission. Just look the other way for a second while I tidy this up."

"There's a tracer, Zane. Or maybe you haven't heard. They can trace that kind of access to the screen source. It takes only a few hours."

Zane tells him he's written his cuts with a nomad routine plugged to the internal clock. Every two minutes, the program will copy itself to a new address in a different library and erase itself from its previous location. "It isn't foolproof, but no one will start tracing until morning anyway. And by then I'll be long gone."

"Gone where?"

"To another line. I'm history here. Emelle just gave me the word."

Petitjean is silent for a long moment. "History?" he says.

"I'm the victim of slander, Petitjean. The squeeze is on and I don't know why. Emelle has it in her pretty head that I've thrown in my lot with the spooks."

Petitjean is doing his best to wise up. His mastery of the language has never entirely included Zane's English. It is one of the thorny points of their working relationship. "What can I do?" he asks.

"I'm going to have to work from home for a while. If this cut stands up I can still get my transmissions. But that doesn't help me with the mail or the telex or fax machine. Can you handle that for me?"

"Watching you break into unauthorized files is one thing, Zane. You ask a lot."

"I just want my mail. Whatever's addressed to me."

"I'll do as much as I can. At least until you've got this Eleven business cleared up. Whatever *gone to blue* means."

Zane wastes a few minutes searching for an empty box to put his things into, then realizes there isn't much that needs to be taken with him. Pens, pencils, calendar, a dozen files with telecom prints, telephone numbers, and address book. A spare box of blank diskettes. It all fits nicely into a plastic shopping bag.

"We're out of whisky," Petitjean says. "I killed the last of it waiting for you." Then he stands, reaches for his Gauloises, and stuffs them into his shirt pocket. "So I'm going home now."

"Sweet dreams."

"I don't, don't dream, Zane. I just sleep. Leave a message on my box if you get the kicker."

When he is gone Zane doesn't have any ideas of what to do. He had merely meant to be the last one out the door, as if to make up for all of Petitjean's waiting. A nod to the days when Zane was, de facto, the last one out the door. When he grew beards without noticing and Emelle loved his soul. So he wanders the halls, looking in on darkened rooms where ghostly stacks of paper are piled on every desk, the cathode gray of screens awaiting telecom, and the ammonia smell of cleanser left over from the cleaning crew. There is a stack of unopened mail on Raymond Li's desk and half of a ham sandwich that looks to be days old. He considers tossing it into the waste bin, reaches out his hand, then changes his mind. Mr. Li is said to have nearly starved to death as a child, in a prison camp north of Hanoi. One of his office habits is to hoard the others' leftovers, though Zane has yet to see him consume any of it.

In Kirk's office Zane finds an incoming from Peru, the story of another of the disappeared, a man from the Unión Democrática del Pueblo. No charges published. Taken by the Guardia Civil, according to street talk. Prisoners in Brazil have continued their death lottery to publicize terrible living conditions. They just

killed the third of their cellmates with a losing number. Stran-
gulation. Kirk will have his hands full in the morning.

Though Kirk's files are locked behind passwords, Zane sits in
front of the screen and runs a locksmith program that is child's
play compared to others he's had to use. For years, Zane has tried
to convince the man to secure his files. Zane taps the access codes
for North American files, then POLDET for political detainees.
His mother's file, ZANE.DAT, is alphabetically the last one listed
on the directory.

ABRI NA943226; FILE OPENED JUNE 1968, CASEWORKER: ML

LAST UPDATE: 06 SEP 86

NAME:	JEAN ZANE
MAIDEN NAME:	SAME
BIRTH DATE:	AUGUST 3, 1930
RELATIVE(S):	THOMAS ZANE (SON)
DATE OF INCARCERATION:	AUGUST 14, 1969
PLACE(S) OF INCARCERATION:	SHAKOPEE, MN
CAUSE OF ARREST:	INCITEMENT TO RIOT, MPLS, MN 1968, MADISON, WIS, 1968, 1969 GRAND THEFT AUTO, DES MOINES, IA, 1969, OMAHA, NEB, 1969 POSSESSION AND INTERSTATE TRANSPORT OF ILLEGAL FIREARMS, POSSESSION OF EXPLOSIVES 1969 HOMICIDE, 3RD DEGREE, OMAHA, 1969 ATTEMPTED HOMICIDE, DENVER, 1969 RESISTING OF LAWFUL

ARREST 1969, LAKE OF
THE WOODS, MN
SEDITION; ACTS OF SABO-
TAGE, OMAHA, 1967–1969

PREVIOUS ARRESTS:

VANDALISM PUB PROPTY,
DULUTH, MN, 1961
PUBLIC NUISANCE, MPLS,
MN, 1963
DISORDERLY CONDUCT,
CHICAGO, 1964, RELEASED
WITHOUT BAIL
OBSTRUCTION OF JUSTICE,
DENVER, CO, 1965
VANDALISM PUB PROPTY,
MPLS, MN, 1969

JUDICIAL NOTES:

TRIAL, STATE OF MINNE-
SOTA, FALL 1969 TO
SPRING 1970; FEDERAL
CHARGES INCL MURDER
OF FEDERAL EMPLOYEE,
DESTRUCTION OF GOV'T
PROPERTY/ASSETS, IN-
TERSTATE FLIGHT (SEE
RICO)
DETAINEE REFUSED COUN-
SEL; FEDERAL APP'T
COUNSEL (JAN 70); NOT
GUILTY PLEA TO ALL
COUNTS REVERSED; GLTY
PLEA FILED FEB 70; CON-
TEMPT OF COURT CITAT.
MAR 70; PROSECUTION
LINKED SUBJECT TO SDS,
WTHRMEN, BLK PANTH,
IRA; NO CONNECTION
PROVEN.
SENTENCE = 25 YRS.

APPEAL DEC 70 DENIED
MAY 71

CASE NOTES   SEE BLUE FILE FOR PRIOR TO 1982

PAROLE DENIED "UNRULY
BEHAVIOR" APR 82, ISO-
LATION JUL–OCT 82 FOR
CITED "VANDALISM,
THEFT OF OFFICE SUP-
PLIES"; ATTY BRIEF FILED
DEC 82 CLAIMING CLIENT
ABUSE, DENIAL OF PUBLI-
CATIONS, WRITING
MAT.—"7TH SUCH COM-
PLAINT SINCE INITIAL
ARREST" (REF BLUE FILE
SAME REFERENCE)

ABRI STANCE:

ANTIWAR ACTIVIST, "SELF
PROCL REVOLUTION-
ARY"; CLAIMED ACCID
DEATH IN FIRE BOMB—
OMAHA, MAY 69. GUILT
PROVEN BY LEGAL
MEANS; DETAINEE ABUSE
DUE TO POLITICAL AF-
FIL.; PAROLE DENIALS
DEEMED AUTOMATIC
RATHER THAN JUSTIFIA-
BLE. NO GROUNDS FOR
HOPE IN LETTER CAM-
PAIGN. ANNUAL POL
DET LISTING 1970–1982
BASED ON DENIAL OF BA-
SIC HUMANE TREAT-
MENT—ML;

PAROLE REVIEW MOTION
DENIED SEP 86—L. KIRK

The blue files are the paper files used before ABRI was computerized. Kirk showed these to Zane a month after he'd begun working there. "We've done very little on her behalf," Kirk told him, "and none of it has been effective. I took over the casebook from Emelle last year. We haven't done a letter campaign because it seemed pointless. There's no press interest anymore. She's old news in America, and even the Democrats still remember her as something rabid. I mean, she doesn't exactly have Mandela's profile."

She was condemned for having blown up an ROTC office in Omaha and killing an old man in the process, the night watchman, who died of smoke inhalation. Before her capture, she fired a rifle at a Minnesota trooper. Her friends escaped and were never seen again. Zane is the only reliable witness.

He updates the file himself, including a last line: "Parole request filed Aug 88." Then he switches Kirk's screen back to *Receive Only*.

He checks back to his own screen for the kicker from Postcard, but nothing has come in via the Munich drop. There are two messages off the leased line, copies of AP transmissions forwarded to him by a friend in Brussels, neither of which he bothers to read in full. Remembering that Demi has on occasion addressed his messages to Petitjean's screen as a ruse, he leans to log over to that address and finds that Petitjean has switched his screen off telecom transmission and left the stalker routine running. It has been running for over an hour and the eavesdropper is still on-line. Long minutes pass, marked only by the blinking of the cursor, and then all at once the screen fills with a response display, terminal coordinates grabbed by the stalker routine. Zane runs a screen refresh to be certain there has been no mistake and then cuts a screen print.

The eavesdropper is working from a remote terminal, no surprise, through a dial-up line at 4800 baud. The send number is untraceable but the system-assigned ID is on the printout. Within five minutes, Zane has written a program for the control library that will jam the ID line and terminate reception. But before running the job, he reconsiders. The eavesdropper might not know he's been discovered, and the ejection would simply alert him.

Any block works only temporarily, and whoever has tapped in can slither back inside with a different protocol that the stalker routine might miss. So, instead, Zane sets an echo against the ID to ensure that every keystroke will be recorded onto one of his own files; a little something he will able to read in the morning.

He runs his routine and then logs his system out. Then, casting a look at the blank screen, he heads for the door. There are three locks and an alarm to be set. Every now and then, crazies from various countries try to break into the place, assuming that ABRI is a branch of the CIA or the French secret service. There is no guard in the budget and the alarms have more than once been set off by the wind, birds, and electrical lags.

As he is about to leave the office, he hears his phone ringing. Each of the phones has a different tone and his resembles a French police siren. He switches the alarms back off and crosses back to his desk.

But when he lifts the receiver, no one is on the line. Moments after he hangs up the phone, it's ringing again. This time he lets it ring.

They already know where to find me.

Though it's past midnight the heat is intense. The breeze coming from the south seems only to bring dry air. Carrying the shopping bag with his printouts and diskettes and address books, he feels a familiar wanting coming from his blood and skin and lips all at once. *A craving? A drowning.* He imagines that he is not alone and stops often to turn around and look. The street is empty. A taxi without passengers cruises past. So he walks south to the Seine and pauses on the Pont au Change. The water moves soundlessly beneath him, lit by the city into floating points of light. For a brief moment he thinks he sees something, or someone, floating on the water. A tree branch or a reaching hand. But whatever he's seen is lost in the shimmering lights and the black motion.

Notre-Dame, still floodlit, rises out of the shadows to his left, and he traverses the Ile de la Cité until he stands in front of it. A row of statues of saints and Judean kings runs across the front, high above the massive doors. During the revolution, they were torn down by peasants who mistook them as icons of the kings of France. These same mistakes are repeated from time to time, the confusion of kings and holy men and tyrants. There is no amnesty from ignorance. But two hundred years have passed and the statues have been replaced or repaired and almost no one's the wiser.

The bridge is en route to the jazz club, Chez Fingers, on the rue de la Montagne Sainte-Geneviève. He goes there often, alone, for the music and the Scotch and ice. It is a place without language, of no country and no prisoners, where no one knows his profession. He has been there countless times for the music but tonight he is anxious only to retrieve the letters.

Below the bridge is a wooden catwalk built by workmen restoring the bridge. Through the summer, he has noticed, bums gather here on rainy evenings, and though the sky is clear, he bends to see if the catwalk is occupied. As he does so, he can hear the sounds of an approaching motorbike. Paris is full of these bikes, *mobilettes* with tiny engines that make a ripping noise. The driver approaches with the headlight off and Zane moves slightly away from the rail. The bag he is carrying is similar to the one that M'Khlea gave him, and he loosens his grip so that he won't be dragged away with it. At the last moment he turns to see the face on the rider but it is covered by a black helmet and visor. The *mobilette* veers toward him and the driver reaches out and sweeps the bag from Zane's grip. He pretends surprise and shouts as the biker turns left at the end of the bridge and disappears along the quai. Zane runs in the opposite direction and can hear another *mobilette* at his back. Over his shoulder he sees it at the other end of the bridge, so he leaps over the railing and swings his body underneath to the catwalk. A man sleeps with his head resting on newspaper and Zane steps over him to where a knapsack rests against a beam. He flings the knapsack into the water and to his relief it sinks instantly. The man awakens and Zane grasps him by the throat to keep him silent. He is weak and drunk and his eyes are tiny circles of panic. Two *mobilettes* come to a stop just above his head and he can hear the drivers hurry to the railing. They are speaking a language he doesn't know. Though it sounds African, he can't hear them clearly enough to be sure. The man struggles under his grip and he realizes he is strangling him and relaxes his hands. The man coughs, but is otherwise obediently silent.

The address book is harmless, containing numbers and addresses that could be obtained in a phone book. The diskettes are old, with ancient data that no longer apply, and the printouts are trash from Kirk's recycling bin. He regrets that he didn't take more time to make the package more interesting, to make them spend useless hours decoding the material. The decoy is too obvious and they'll know soon enough that they still don't have the letters.

The men above him wait a long time, obviously watching the water. He doesn't know whether they were fooled by the splash but they are unaware of the catwalk beneath them. The water moves soundlessly beneath him and he can hear the men move back to their bikes, the cough of the engines kicked back to life. He waits until long after the sounds have gone away and then lets go of the drunk, who coughs and spits and rolls to one side.

I almost killed this man.

He takes a few bills from his pockets and offers them to him. Both of them are trembling. In the dim light, he can see that the man is young, younger than Petitjean. A criminal, perhaps. A man without luck. In Paris, the men who are released from prison tend to write their stories in chalk on the sidewalk. People stop to read these stories, *I just got out of jail I have no money no job no home just the clothes on my back and a good heart please help me.* The ebb and flow of centimes.

The man takes the money and stares at it as if unable to count it. Zane turns away, lifts his arms, and pulls himself upward to the bridge. When he bends to look back at the man, he is still staring at the money.

HE TELLS THE TAXI DRIVER TO STOP AT THE PLACE DE Clichy, where the oyster bars and cinemas are closed but the corner brasserie is brightly lit and crowded with Algerians and German tourists. As he walks north on the Avenue de Clichy, a dark-skinned prostitute steps out of the shadows and, when she recognizes him, retreats to the wall. She is always there, it seems, and he always walks past. But this time he stops, turns in his tracks, and approaches her. Her eyes widen with surprise and curiosity or fear. He asks her to come with him and she quotes a price.

"No," he says. He tells her he wants a favor. He gives her the key to his apartment and tells her to go ahead of him. She is to watch the avenue on both sides for two men on *mobilettes*. He says they are probably African. "Come back to me here and tell me what you've seen."

His apartment is a hundred yards away and he waits, smoking three cigarettes, in the shadows with the prostitutes. When twenty minutes have passed, he grows agitated and begins to walk swiftly in the direction of La Fourche. After a dozen steps, he can see the woman running toward him. *Walk*, he is thinking. But she hurries to his side and struggles to catch her breath. She has taken her knife from her purse and for a moment he thinks she intends to use it on him.

"*Il n'y a personne*," she tells him. "*Mais ton appartement . . .*"

He gives her another hundred francs and she vanishes. He had meant to buy the knife from her but realizes he wouldn't know what to do with it.

He continues north, past the Tunisian bakery and the clothing shop. An unpleasant-smelling breeze is blowing from the north.

He buzzes the downstairs door open and presses the button next to it; light fills the stairwell. Here are the steps, he says to himself, so just walk. He arrives at the landing and his first thought is to turn and run. His door is resting on its hinges and inside his apartment is a shambles.

He turns the door to the side and steps in. The chaos is complete and it is not the work of someone who knew his habits. A thief would have slipped in and out in search of what Zane doesn't have: jewels, cash, art. This is an upside-down job, including willful destruction; the bookcase has been pulled down, books and magazines scattered, the refrigerator opened and emptied, and the drawers ransacked of shirts and underwear.

His concierge appears in the doorway. "I heard the noise," she tells him. "I thought it was you." As if by habit she begins to straighten the room but he tells her to leave it be. "I should have called the police," she says. "When I heard all that banging. You drink too much some nights and I . . ." The sentence completes itself in his mind. She says she'll go get her husband and he tells her not to bother. Her husband is an old man and no one can repair what's gone on here. "If he can just fix this door in the morning," Zane says.

She says of course, they have tools.

"Did you notice anyone?" he asks. "Two men? African?"

She shakes her head. "There are always noises. I am sorry."

When she is gone Zane tries to close that door but it merely hangs on a single hinge and the best he can do is to prop it across the doorway. He searches through the ruin and then wades through books until he finds *The Complete Works of William Shakespeare*. Five thousand francs are hidden among the pages of the *The Tempest*; there's another ten thousand or so in his checking account. His bottle of J & B is intact, though almost empty, and he straightens a lamp and switches on the light. Never was there anything that needed taking. All of his files are under lock and key at ABRI and the letters, he assumes, are safe with

Marie. Nothing in his apartment linked Eleven to Harry Street of the British Medical Company.

He extracts his empty suitcase from under a pile of paperbacks and begins packing. The footsteps on the stairs are those of the old man from one flight up with a bundle of newspapers in his hand. The building is hardly secure. The buzzer system on the ground floor is ancient and can be opened with a butter knife. He moves to the stair rail and looks down to the ground floor. For a brief moment he thinks he sees a moving shoe. Then he can see a shadow against the floor. The shadow moves backward and disappears.

He folds the money into his pocket and treads to the front window. A car is double-parked on the Avenue de Clichy with a driver at the wheel. Though this isn't uncommon, his nerves are shot and he takes it for a sign. He wants to call Petitjean, but the telephone has been torn out by the root.

He leaves the suitcase where it is. It would only slow him down. Then he descends the stairway to the foyer. The concierge has left her door open to let in the night air and he can see both her and her husband in front of the television. They are watching CNN on cable, following the images with the volume turned low. He has five thousand francs, his passport, and his checkbook. His only weapons are his teeth and a ballpoint pen. When he steps out the front door, the man in the car slips down in his seat. Zane glances in his direction but can't tell if he's black or white. There are a number of men on the street, though none who seem to be watching.

He turns into the Impasse des Deux Nèthes, where the Algerians deal dope and play their numbers game on cardboard boxes. Two men in an unlit corner stare at him as though he were expected. One of them bares a blade and Zane holds up his hands to show that he is no one, he is harmless, he is invisible. The wall at the end of the impasse is twenty feet high but the Algerians have long since carved out a hole through which they can pass when the police cruise by. He hears steps at his back and rushes to the gap. A scrap of wire net has been pulled across its face and he tears it away with his hands. To the other side is the back of an apartment building. The court is strewn with garbage and broken glass and a narrow passage leads to the front. He emerges on the rue Cavallotti and is bleached yellow by a street-light directly above him. Ahead of him, at the end of the rue Tahan, is the cemetery. He runs in that direction as the two *mobi-lettes* pull onto the rue Cavallotti and head straight for him.

Upright shards of glass are embedded across the top of the cemetery wall and he measures his leap to get a grasp on solid stone and carefully lift his legs to the top. Dropping to the other side, he crouches low and moves crablike through the gravestones toward the bridge which passes overhead at the rue Caulaincourt. When he has covered fifty yards he pauses behind a black stone and can hear one of the motorbikes at his back. The driver is maneuvering among the gravestones, approaching Zane in a zig-zag fashion to the left of him, so he lights out, up an alley that leads north toward the rue Joseph. Cats howl and scatter in his wake and he regrets ever having fed the filthy beasts. At the bridge, he climbs the stone steps, considers and rejects the idea of seeking refuge in the nearby brasserie, and then runs down the rue Maistre until he comes to the Abbesses metro station. He pays for a ticket and descends before realizing his mistake: this is a line that runs from Montmartre toward the south and the station is empty. He peers up both sides of the tunnel and can't see any train. It has been years since he has run so far and he presses his back against the wall of the station and fights to catch his breath. A moment later he hears someone coming down the steps and he slides laterally until he's half hidden behind a firebox. A man steps onto the platform and looks in his direction, then reaches into his pocket for a cigarette, lights it, and turns away. He glances at his watch and Zane can hear the train approaching. Twenty, thirty seconds later it brakes. He can hear the rasp of a motorbike and he lurches forward, snaps open the door, and jumps inside the front car. Through the window, he sees the man crushing his cigarette under his shoe.

A motorbike with a black-helmeted driver jounces down the stairway and crashes into the train just as it begins to pull away. The train slams to a halt. Zane's car is half in the station and half in the tunnel. The driver has risen from the station floor and limps in his direction. Zane swings the lever that opens the doors and slips out of the car to the tracks. Wedging himself between the train and the tunnel wall, he shimmies sideways to the front of the train and runs down the tunnel, his feet slapping water and oil. The helmeted man is pushing the train operator out of the front compartment. The beam of the train lights his way for the first fifty yards but then the tunnel veers right and downward and only occasional bulbs relieve the darkness. Every twenty steps, the tunnel widens slightly and there are corners meant for workmen to stand in to avoid the oncoming trains. After another hundred yards, the tunnel suddenly fills with light. Turning, he sees the train coming for him and he sprints in search of a crevice. As the train nears, the light is blinding but to his right he finds an opening and he leaps into it as the train rumbles past. He stands and finds himself in another tunnel and the train slows to a stop. He moves ahead with his hands outstretched, feeling for the wall. The train begins to back up, but after another twenty yards or so, Zane can see lights ahead of him. He hurries forward and realizes he has come to the next station, Pigalle. As he emerges onto the platform, he finds at least fifty people to either side of him. This is an east-west line whereas the other went from north to south. A black woman stares at him, amazed. He ignores her and moves across to the other side of the platform, seeking to hide himself, and leans against the back wall near a posted map of Paris, thinking what in hell what in hell what in hell. His clothes are covered with oil and water and there is blood on his hands. Three minutes later, a train pulls into the metro stop and he pushes himself forward into a half-filled car. Grasping an overhead bar, he wedges himself into a corner and then sinks to the floor below the window.

He changes at the first stop, in the direction of Nation. Two stops later, he changes again at Barbès-Rochechouart and rides as far as Gare de l'Est. For the next hour he changes lines from station to station, from Réaumur-Sébastopol to Jaurès, Belleville, République, Châtelet. The last trains depart from their stations at 1:00 a.m. and at 1:15 he emerges from the network at Pont Neuf. He is alone on the quai du Louvre. In front of him is the Samaritaine, an enormous department store, and to his back is the Seine. A wave of headlights approaches and he ducks into the doorway to avoid them. A half-dozen cars pass on the quai, heading for Châtelet, and a single *mobilette*. When they are gone, he crosses the street to a phone booth and dials Petitjean's number. It is late so he lets it ring a long time. It is Petitjean who answers. "At this ungodly hour it can only be Zane, I am saying to myself."

"They're on to me, Petitjean. My ass is in a sling."

"Who, Zane?"

"I don't know. Emelle. Maybe Okimbo."

"Talk sense."

"That police report I asked about. The woman who died was Okimbo's wife."

"Tell me everything or don't say a word."

Zane tells him about the motorbikes and the ransacking of his apartment. He adds, "If they know anything about me, they might be on to you next."

There is a pause at the other end of the line. "I was thinking of quitting anyway," Petitjean says.

"Stay away from the office for a few days. This might be cleared up soon. There seems to have been a misunderstanding."

"No misunderstanding, Zane. You play with fire, you—"

"Cut the homilies, Petitjean. This is a friendly call. I wanted to warn you." Zane can hear Petitjean's breathing on the other end of the line.

"If you need a place to stay," Petitjean says.

"Can't do it. They know we're partners, *complices*. I expect you'll get a visit from someone with slutty connections anyway."

"Where will I find you?"

"If I don't tell you, there's nothing to confess when they put the bamboo to your fingernails."

"You're right, Zane. Trust no one, especially me."

"That's not what I meant."

"I'll take tomorrow off and go to the office the next day like nothing's happened. See what I can see. Try to stay sober long enough to get out of the city."

"I will do," Zane tells him, "whatever comes to mind." And the first thing that comes to mind is to hang up.

. . .

Pont Neuf means new bridge but it is the oldest bridge in the city. This isn't much as ironies go though at the moment it seems crucial. Details matter when the subject is life or death. But he doesn't know what the subject is. It's hard to hide, he's thinking, when you don't know what's chasing you.

The last of the night's tourist boats cruises past and he ducks to avoid the floodlights that cover the bridge.

M'Khlea is dead. Street is either dead or being hunted. In another three hours the sun will rise over Paris and if he is still on the streets he will be an easy mark for whoever wants him. There is only one place left to go, and he has to retrieve the letters in any case. He is the last of the Zanes and the night isn't getting any younger. Crossing the oldest bridge in the city, he heads west.

NORMANDY

THE WEDDING DRESS IS THE COLOR OF LOSS, OF SI-
lence, and of being without sin. God the Father, she reasons, will
allow her to wear it this once. This once, on the day of her wedding. Black man in black to white woman in white.

Rising from her bath, she dries herself with a clean towel and
bends to the mirror. Her skin is pale and there are blue shadows
below her eyes from lack of sleep. She hardly resembles a bride,
she decides. She is not from any magazine she knows of. The
repeating slander of her face in the mirror. There are those who
assume that an ugly woman working in a jazz hall must be a
whore. Jazz, after all, is human heat and it mixes into sex with
alcohol and, late in the night, ugliness takes what it can get.
Marie is nothing to look at but she is clean. She wears nice underwear and pressed skirts and the perfume on her neck costs
more than they would think. She isn't waiting for flowers. Neither
flowers nor money. She is waiting for a song on the radio or a
rainy day. When she was sixteen she couldn't bear the sight of
her own face, the weak chin and listless eyes. She cut her wrists
but they were girlish cuts, scratches. The wounds healed and she
was no longer at the Sorbonne. To pay her mother's rent, she gave
lessons at fifty francs an hour and suffered brats with fat fingers
or adolescents hopelessly plonging through "Für Elise." Her
mother said there would be other men. We make these mistakes
but they don't have to last for life. Look at my face. I am hardly
Brigitte Bardot yet I have your father.

After a year had passed, she studied music theory at the University of Orléans until, four months later, she noticed her professors averting their eyes. Or what she imagined to be an avoidance. She never knew if she was being seen or not. There was a definite shortage of human contact, eyeball to eyeball. Her mother said she made too much of it and wrote to her that she should come home. And if a man will love you all he will see is your soul. There, past all the anger of your face. The face we gave you.

She reaches for the creams and mascara.

They have agreed as to how the marriage will work. "Nothing's different," Fingers has said. "Nothing changes except we might sleep side by side on Sunday noons. If you can stand a man in my condition."

"I can. I will."

"And when I'm gone," he's told her, "you just keep up the place for a time. Like a home for old jazz men and with no cover charge for the faithful. Keep July and Darren L. and Smith-y-Vega out a the rain as long as you can make a go of it. Then you sell it for what you can and make a new life."

Meaning, the same life with a bit a money.

In the meantime she will go on living in these two rooms; her wide bed and slim bookcase stuffed with music and compositions from her childhood, the black Steinway, comfortable chairs, Moroccan throw rugs, and dangling plants. Three floors above the noise of the street, where men and women tread their way to and from the Seine, to and from work, to and from the restaurants on the other side of the Place de la Contrescarpe. Where the sunlight is hers between nine and eleven in the morning and, coming home from the club, she refuses to sleep if there is light on her bed. Will stretch herself nude across the mattress and watch the light move across her belly toward the near wall. She is three floors from the club and one floor from Fingers' room. He can call her on the telephone or shout up the stairwell and tell her to come be his wings. Day in and day out.

Before putting on the dress, she sits at her piano to finish transcribing "The Last." There are four movements all together, though Fingers has never composed in any classical sense. He

123

refers to the four parts as The Finding Out, The Rumble, Mad Times, and Stop Breathing Here. While working on it, he played it differently each time, but for the past week he has always played it the same. And though he hasn't said so, she can gather that means it is finished. Her wedding present to him will be the sheet music.

She will marry him because it is the only marriage she can imagine. To forever after be Madame rather than Mademoiselle. The marriage permit will be delayed but they will go ahead with the ceremony anyway. Permission will come after the promise, as always.

Before meeting Fingers she wanted to sell herself to blind men who would pay for her with their gratitude and not their money. She didn't have the courage to choose a doorway on the rue Saint-Denis and make it hers. She dressed herself for the part and made of her face a cartoon of red lips and blue eyebrows, and took the metro to Strasbourg Saint-Denis. It was ten in the evening and the men were parading up and down while the women stood in crooked rows. She chose the rue Blondel, near the top, but the harshness of the women on the street repelled her and she quickly lost heart. One man asked how much and she said two hundred francs. Though he said he might be back, she wasn't there to meet him. She went home to her room, where the bird was dead for lack of a mirror. Still wearing her garters, she sat down at the piano and played until she was tired enough to sleep. To play Chopin is to search the ceiling of a sleepless night.

In her ancient building on the rue du Temple there was a blind man who lived with his mother. She made a point of passing him on the street when he was out for his morning walks. That way she could talk to him alone, without his mother to come between them. He was in his early thirties and always by himself in his darkness. One winter afternoon he came tapping up the stairs to visit her. He had heard the music from the stairwell and followed it to her door.

"Are you alone? Or is your husband with you?"

"I thought you knew."

"I am being polite. Tell me to go away."

"There is a chair to your right. What can I serve you?"

They became friends and she would play for him on Saturday afternoons while his mother did the shopping and visited friends. Afterward she would sit close to him and hope that he would catch her scent, her heavy perfume. He remarked that she had a lovely voice, that she spoke an excellent French. Blind men hear these little things, he said. The wood and grain of speech instead of the wind of gestures. You don't, he asked, have any wine? A glass of Burgundy?

He drank too much but was good about covering it up. Pawning it off as another facet of his blindness, his occasional lack of balance. Or he would sit back in his chair with crossed arms and pretend that he was listening intently to the music or to the sounds of midday traffic, his head moving as blind people's heads move, a perpetual nodding. On his third visit, she had him sit in the corner chair and then excused herself for a moment, going to her bedroom. She took off her clothes and returned naked to the large room. He turned his blind eyes in her direction and looked beyond her. She was both naked and invisible.

When he next visited, she finished playing quickly and then poured him the wine he asked for. She opened her blouse and sat near to him, placing herself between him and his wine bottle. When he reached out, his hand found her flesh and he stopped and withdrew. So she reached for his hand again and laid it to her breast. A part of her men covet. His mouth followed his hand and he tasted perfume. She corrupted him that day with the windows opened wide. He was her first sober man in three years. A light rain began to fall and some of it fell inward, reaching the foot of the bed and wetting their legs. And when it was over she confessed to him the sin of her face. He only laughed, telling her he'd thought his mother had asked her to have him. He was not a virgin, he told her. I know my way around a woman. Once a year for the past ten years, whenever my birthday approaches, my mother buys me a prostitute and leaves me alone for a night. I will be thirty-three next week. I thought this year was you.

She was his with neither fee nor the least gift and it lasted five months. She was waiting to become pregnant, to have a boy or a

girl, someone to wear his face through life. She took warm baths
to heat her belly before he arrived and made him love her twice
or three times, whatever he could manage. She held him in her
long after he'd stopped and then waited for what never would
happen. Of course it couldn't last. As the weeks wore on, he was
more and more unkind to her. His drinking was uncontrollable
and he sometimes came lurching up the stairs with his pants
already unhitched, his hair unkempt, in no mood for music. A
last month, she told herself. And then it will happen. But when
she had bled, she lost heart. In bed she confessed to him that she
hadn't been protecting herself. No pills and no IUD. He said it
was no matter, that his mother had had him fixed. "This new
surgery, Marie. A precautionary measure for the congenitally
sightless like myself. Any child of mine would almost certainly
be blind."

Lipsticks, eye shadows, eyeliners, rouges and powders.

A brown suitcase with six dresses and the underthings I wear
as skin.

A box of sheet music for pieces I will never play.

I left behind an empty bird cage and the lint that I'd swept out
from under the bed.

As I was leaving the building the blind man appeared on the
front step. My hand left a mark like a flower on his face.

She found another apartment, in the fifth arrondissement. A jazz
club in a basement was looking for a barmaid. The pay was as
bad as the hours but she needed work and the job included a
room and bath three floors above the club with a window that
gave a wide triangle of sunlight in the late morning. She thought
at first that the music was a scandal. She heard only chaos and
wanted to scrub the notes clean or to sand the noise down into
melody. It was a music without a map, a getting lost nightly, an
endless stumbling. Her heart ached for the sound of a violin or a
flute and she leaned into that music as if into the wind. Once she
broke a shot glass on the floor and the explosion of it was part of
that music. But the musicians paid no attention to her insults and
her obvious scorn. She poured whisky and beer and gin and

vodka and much of it ended up on her blouse or skirt or soaked into her hands. Later, in bed, if she moved her hands to her face she could smell the tobacco and alcohol. So she doused herself with cologne and someone said she smelled like a fire about to go out.

Then one night Fingers chased everyone away and played a sonata. It was fractured but immaculate, a sequence of movements that kept tipping over some edge but always came back to a refrain that might have been called *faithful*. The haunting. She didn't hear anything else, had gone deaf to everyone in the place. The pleas for drink that went over her head, around her head. *La vie tient à quoi?* A thread, a gust of wind, his eyes on my face.

When he hired her, Fingers said to pour generous and be polite. No drug taking or getting juiced on the job, please, and would she mind making coffee for the boys? "Not to make a nigger out a you," he said. And he waited for her to laugh, so she did.

"What's wrong with being a nigger?" she asked.

The ceremony at the *mairie* of the fifth arrondissement lasts less than the usual twenty minutes, during which the city official makes no attempt to hide his disdain. Fingers, a full head shorter than Marie, lifts himself on tiptoes as she bends to receive her kiss. There is no music, no hail of rice. They and the musicians who have joined them break up into various taxis and return to the club and open up for business. Marie climbs the stairs and exchanges the wedding dress for her work clothes. A fifty-franc ring of copper and brass on her finger.

By midnight the club is crowded and her dress is stained with champagne and spilled beer. The American said he would come before closing and she doesn't want him to see her like this. Her wedding night. Fingers' friends from the other clubs have come along to join him and at times there are more than ten musicians and the music is not good but no one is complaining. At the two o'clock break, Fingers stands up to announce that he has been married that afternoon and mingled with the applause is an undercurrent of shock. When eyes turn in her direction, she wears the smile that she has practiced for the occasion.

She is pouring whisky and smiling like that when he comes in the door. She can no longer hear the jazz being played or the drink orders being shouted at her. His eyes are wild and he stumbles to the bar.

"The letters," he says. "You still have them."

He is not drunk. He smells of sweat and oil. She moves from behind the bar and he leans his weight against her.

"The letters."

"Hidden," she says. His hand is on her arm and when he removes it she sees blood.

The musicians are playing furiously and all eyes are upon them. Marie leads him to the far wall, where a stairway leads upward. But he is unable to climb those stairs, his legs no longer work for him. He is as helpless as Fingers, she thinks.

When his legs failed I became his wings.

And carried him up the stairs.

WHEN HE AWAKENS THERE IS NO WAY TO KNOW THE time. No clock, no radio. And the room is strange to him so he can't tell the hour by the shadows. His right leg is stiff and pains him just below the knee, where he'd stumbled into a low gravestone, and his right palm throbs from a deep cut.

Sitting up in bed, he surveys the room. The furnishings are all in wood from other centuries. An oval rosewood table is pushed against one wall and a stick chair is folded beneath it. Opposite the bed is an enormous oak armoire with white-and-pink lilies painted on the lacquered face. A steel sink is fastened to a corner beyond the door and next to it is a square pine cabinet with a botched stain job. Shaving lather, toothpaste, water glass, and lotion are lined along the top.

Next to the bed is a night table with a black telephone, various medicines, a thermometer, a teaspoon, coffee cup, and thermos. He touches the thermos, finds it warm, and so pours himself a cup. There is also a new package of Winstons; he cracks it open, but doesn't have a lighter. When he stands the leg aches anew and he lifts the knee and stretches. Then he notices the wall behind the bed.

Every spare inch from ceiling to headboard is filled with photographs or postcards or news clippings. Some of the photographs are framed but others have been pinned to the wall and most of the news clippings are yellowed to brown. JAZZ STORM HITS PHILLY Fingers Mink at the Soft Shoe Alvin Little's Big

Sound featuring Lester "Fingers" Mink on Ivories MOVE OVER COUNT BASIE at the Jingo Bar thru Tuesday Slow Jazz on a Hot Night September 12, 1931 March 11, 1954 Chicago Tribune August 9, 1961 NY Times May 3, 1951 LA Free Press November 14, 1968 The music you've listened to and never heard before . . .

Some of the faces in the photographs are recognizable, Thelonious Monk, Dizzy Gillespie, Bird Parker. In one picture Erroll Garner and Fingers stand with their palms pressed together, comparing finger spans, and in another Fingers leans to the keyboard with closed eyes, but the sheet music in front of him is "Sentimental Journey," a tune Zane thinks that he would never have played even if he could read the notes. Fats Waller, Lennie Tristano, Charlie Mingus. But most of the people on the wall are strangers, the populace of a far country belonging solely to Fingers. This man with his arm around Fingers and a laughing young woman in a low-cut dress. This skinny girl, fifteen at most, singing into an oversized microphone and smiling across the piano to the top of Fingers' head. A portrait in black and white of a young woman staring almost angrily into the camera. There are even a few pictures from the Paris club with Smith-y-Vega, Bobby Sing, the saxophonist who just died, Marie behind the bar. With a shock he recognizes himself in the audience, his tie knotted low and an unsurprising whisky in his upraised hand.

I was here, too. I am a part of this wall.

Once he has examined every inch of that wall, peered into every flat frame of someone else's memories, noted the names and dates of articles and reviews, and looked into the newsprint eyes of twenty Lester Minks, he feels as if he has just been told a long story with a confused order of events. The chronology is lost, though not the moral; or a life story is only marginally more valid than a laundry list. The music you've listened to and never heard before. And what of Zane with his wrecked home and dissected computer? No dream is lost for him, because he hasn't yet dreamed. His feet are nailed to the ground and he always imagined less of his life than what could fill a wall with photographs.

He notices for the first time that he is naked. Did she do this or did I? He had stumbled into the bar without knowing he was bleeding. His torn hand had spilled blood on his shirt and pants

and it all looked worse than it really was. Those clothes are nowhere in sight but on the table are his possessions, checkbook,
cash, passport, and Street's letters. Also a pair of clean trousers,
boxer shorts, and a folded shirt. A note is pinned to the shirt:
*Portes ces choses pour le moment. J'ai pris tes chaussures pour que
tu reste.* I have taken your shoes so that you'll stay. He notices the
tu and remembers that it's always been the familiar with Marie.
This familiarity is either her own doing or part and parcel of the
jazz tradition. The trousers must belong to Fingers and he has his
doubts. But when he slips his weary legs into them he finds they
fit.

The bed, the sink, the window looking out on trash bins. The
paper mosaic. He walks in barefoot circles and doesn't know the
time. Then he stops and looks again at the picture that contains
him.

So I know that I am here.

She awakens in her clothes and can smell Fingers next to her, the
sweat of his body. His breathing is still labored, each intake forming a syllable of a question. Twice in the night he had awakened
to ask her to open the window and twice she had told him it was
already open. It is the first time they have ever slept together,
their wedding night. They had planned to remain in their separate rooms but Fingers insisted they give his room to the American. One of the truest of the faithful, Madame Mink.

Madame Mink. When he calls her that it brings a smile to her
face. The French say Meenk. *Vison*, a word of luxury. He doesn't
even know that she is descended from nobility, a family with a
coat of arms. Roots and branches that no longer matter, the leaf
has fled the tree. When he started talking in his sleep she wanted
not to listen. A sigh, a sung note, his daughter's name in vain.

"The window, Marie. I got no air here."

"It's opened wide, Fingers."

She lifts herself from the bed and goes to the far wall to start
the coffee. It is Sunday, nine in the morning, and she has only
slept four hours. Leon helped her carry the American up the stairs
and she stayed to clean his cuts and wash his face. When he'd

come in the door she'd thought he was drunk but he was only frightened. He'd refused her offer of whisky up to the last minute and then had drained a tumbler in one go.

"You don't know my name," he'd said.

"You are Thomas Zane."

"You don't know my name," he'd repeated. And had fallen to sleep.

Downstairs she'd spread the word and then Fingers had gone into the night's last set. Smith-y-Vega on bass and July on sax with Fingers just playing riffs according to his mood. Darren L. kept an eye on the door. At four o'clock they came in the door and wanted to talk to Fingers.

"He's busy now."

"We'll wait."

When he'd called for his wings she'd whispered to him to play dumb and he'd pretended senility until they gave up and left.

"They weren't the law, Marie."

"How do you know?"

"I'm an American Negro. I know."

After the club was closed and the last guest hustled out the door, she had climbed the stairs to check up on him. Had undressed him and left his things on the table, examined Fingers' wardrobe for what might do, and then brewed coffee and left it in a thermos. Smith-y-Vega, she remembered, smoked the same brand of cigarettes and she'd asked him for a pack and left it next to the coffee.

She runs bathwater and shrugs out of the nightdress, which is nothing more than a long stretched tee shirt. She wore it for Fingers' sake. Though he smiles often about her body he is uncomfortable if she is naked, so she has slept in clothes for the first time in years. The American's clothes are draped over the tub. The shirt is torn at the rib and soaked through with sweat. The trousers are bloodstained and ripped across the knee. There is a folded letter in the shirt pocket and she sets it to one side. She tests the water, finds it too hot, and turns on more cold. Taking up the clothes, she copies the sizes on a Chez Fingers matchbook.

She steps into the bath and sinks to her neck in hot water. When she relaxes she is almost floating, her body giving off steam. The

marriage has been consummated with a kiss. Fingers says it's all
there need be: We know what we're about, you and I. She had
acted the disappointed bride but he'd known better. "Don't go
pout on me, Madame Mink. Anyway, I need my sleep." She
reaches for the soap and washes their smell from her arms. She
could smell his age in that bed and had been surprised. Maybe
you only know a man when you've slept at his side, his scent in
slumber. He is almost ninety years old and I am thirty-one. My
mother called an hour before the ceremony and asked was I
drugged, was I mad? Fingers forgot the flowers but Smith-y-Vega
handed me a bouquet of irises and a copper ring and said they
all chipped in.

When the water goes cold she rises and dries herself. The day
is already warm and she chooses a blue cotton dress that she
imagines suits her mood. Fingers will sleep another few hours
unless being in a strange bed perturbs him. She takes her purse
and closes the door behind her, then descends the stairs to the
club. Leon has left the place in a mess with a promise that he'll
drop by early on Monday. The room stinks of cold ash and spilled
beer and when she steps outside the air is fresh with a breeze
from the north. The first sanity of autumn. She descends the
street to the Place Maubert, where only the heathen shops are
open, the Vietnamese and Algerian markets selling rice, white
beans, semoule, green tea, and dried duck. The sky grows dark
and then light again as clouds race over the city from north to
south. She crosses Ile de la Cité in front of Notre-Dame, where a
mass is letting out and the parvis is filled with old people and
no children. She once went to one of those masses and was struck
by how forlorn it was, only two dozen people in a cathedral of
that size, survivors of a dying culture. The bronze Christ on His
mahogany cross gazing down on the empty pews. The priest's
knees cracking whenever he bent his body. She had gone there
during a particularly lonesome winter to see if a man was there.
Any man, a man looking for her. If he'd been there he could have
held me in the palm of his hand like a hypnotized bird. The
genuflection.

Walking more swiftly, she crosses over the Pont Arcole and
notices that the Seine is shallow after a dry summer and the

current is slow. Along the quai the flower and seed vendors are already open for business. Not far from here is where she bought that bird that died. She doesn't think that she will buy another.

At Châtelet she descends into the metro and feeds her ticket into the turnstile. The train takes her north to Les Halles, Etienne-Marcel, Château d'Eau. Opening her purse, she takes out the matchbook. Chemise 39–40 : Pantalons 49. The dimensions of the clothes and not the man.

At noon she is with him.

"There were two men," she says.

"White or black?"

"A white man with a black man. The black man I think was French and the other spoke with an accent, English or Nordic. They asked for Fingers and wanted to know if he'd seen you. He said not lately and they said they'd be back."

"They always say that when they don't get what they want."

Marie asks if he knows them.

"Tell me about the white guy."

Marie shrugs. "He was taller than you. Blue eyes and yellow hair. Not gold, like straw. He was without a gun."

"How do you know?"

"Fingers said. He says he can read the way men walk. If they have guns."

"And the black man."

"I don't know. It was the white man who spoke with me." She hands him a plastic shopping bag. Inside are two pairs of gray slacks and three shirts of the type he usually wears, those out-of-fashion button-down collars.

While he changes into the new clothes she neither stares nor turns away. She watches his face and glances at his cuffs and collar to measure the fit. Then she hands him his shoes, which have been cleaned and buffed.

"I am making lunch in one hour. For the three of us. Do you want a bath?"

"Need *and* want."

Something about the phrase confuses her. After a moment she

says to follow her upstairs and she will bring him a razor and a clean towel.

In her wake he recognizes the perfume.

While he washes the blood and sweat from his arms, Fingers leans his ass on the edge of the sink to talk to him.

"You got troubles I wouldn't give to a snake," he says.

Zane is surprised to hear himself laughing. "Not that bad," he says. "Some unscheduled mayhem."

"Marie checked out your place this morning and says it looks like the south end a Bed Stuy. Course she said it different."

"I had to leave town anyway. I'll pull through."

The old man nods his head. "Years I been seein your face in the crowd. You stay here with us as long as you need."

Zane says he'll be going that same night.

"Tell that to Marie if you want to see some waterworks."

At sundown she finds him in the club fixing himself a whisky.

"I would have asked," he says, "but I didn't want to bother you any further."

"Stay on this side of the bar," she advises. "They could see you from the sidewalk window."

He holds the glass in his hand for a long moment before taking a swallow. "I don't know what's happened," he says, "but this stuff has lost its magic."

She is silent but he gets the impression she has something to say. The way her eyes move over him from forehead to chest to his hands and back again.

"I should be going," he says. "There is no moon tonight and the streets are empty."

"Even a black night will not hide you as well as we can."

"They've come once. They'll come back."

"Are you a criminal, Thomas Zane?"

"Just running. You've seen my apartment."

"Where will you go?"

"To the ends of the south suburbs. Catch a train from there. After that I can make my way out of France."

"To go where? To America?"

"Haven't decided. Choose a country for me?"

"One night will make so much difference? Look at you, you can barely walk."

"I walk just fine."

But that is not what she means and he knows it. He finishes the first whisky and pours another but then her hand closes over the glass. "That isn't what you need."

"What do I need?" he asks. "Does it show that clearly?"

He walks away from the full glass and follows her up the back stairway. The light is out and the stairs are pitch dark. Her dress is like a ghost above him on the steps.

At the door she loses her nerve. "Fingers will be waiting," she says. "On Sunday nights I take him for a walk. A stroll, he calls it. These night hours he sleeps so little."

When he leans to her she holds his head in her hands and the kiss is like biting. They touch lips, tongue, teeth, but when he reaches his hands to pull her into him she resists.

"His walk," she says. "He is waiting for his walk."

Zane's mouth tingles. Next he will be tasting blood. When she has disappeared up the stairs, he goes back down to the club. The telephone is on a shelf behind the bar.

He dials Petitjean's number and while it rings he reaches for his whisky and finds that the ice has melted.

HE AWAKENS TO THE STEEL-AND-IRON CLASHES OF
railway cars being coupled and the low shuddering of a locomo-
tive from below the window. Closing his eyes, he tries to sleep
again, to return to that blessed ether of wordlessness, but it won't
take. The spark and hum of moving trains has his blood moving
and he is captive to another day of smoke and sunlight.

He opens his eyes and can see the woman at her dressing table.
She is taking pins from her hair and brushing that hair into yellow
waves that fall to her shoulders. She is already dressed and her
bowl of *café au lait* is empty. The clock at her elbow says it is
just past eight in the morning.

He lifts himself in the bed, plumps the pillow at his back, and
leans his head against the headboard. A bowl of black coffee is
on the nightstand and he finds it is still hot. He lights a cigarette
and blows blue smoke into the room.

"First thing," Sylvie says. "First thing every morning, it's a
cigarette instead of a kiss." She is watching him through the
mirror and he sees both sides of her, back and front. She is transparent to him. He is relieved that she is already dressed.

He knows that he will not be going to work. His sleep has
changed his thinking, pacified him, and he is counting on the
heat that blankets Europe to give him a day of rest. His Romanian
doctor is free for the moment. Zane, in his own way, is free. So,
says Petitjean to himself, is he.

The girl comes to the bedroom door and smiles across the air

to him. She is holding the coffeepot and he just shakes his head
no. "*Non?*" she repeats. Her face is unwashed and her dark hair
is in tangles. She is dressed in old jeans but has put on her pret-
tiest blouse, blue with lace at the collar, though the buttons are
badly done. She has tried to dress herself this morning. Sylvie
tends to neglect her in the morning, preparing first herself and
then Catherine.

"Come here."

When she is near to him, he takes the coffeepot from her hand
and places it on the nightstand. He reaches to her and undoes the
buttons, then refastens the lower button. "Monday with Monday,"
he says. "And Tuesday with Tuesday. Do you understand?"

She does not. He buttons the rest and smooths the blouse at
the waist. From the mirror, Sylvie watches them and strokes her
hair with the brush.

"Another scorcher," she says. "I heard on the radio it will only
get hotter."

He doesn't have to call in sick. He has vacation time coming
to him, weeks upon weeks that he has never taken. Though
Emelle prefers that he tell her in advance. But can one day make
a difference? One? He knows in his heart that it can. When the
heat is on and the lines are alive with mayhem. Yesterday made
a difference to his Romanian doctor.

He waits for Catherine to leave the room then rises from the
bed and pulls on his jeans. His speaking stones are on the night
table next to the bed and he places them in his mouth. Zane won't
be there, so Kirk will already be doubling on the lines. If things
get busy, maybe the new girl will give him a hand. She's fresh
from England and her eagerness hasn't yet turned to what it turns
for them all, to exasperation, cynicism, and the pernicious, dry
fatigue that expresses itself in black humor: Auschwitz jokes, and
ethnic slurs, Zane calling his screen a filthy murdering nigger or
Kirk saying that pizzas don't scream in the ovens but Jews do.
Despite these outbursts, the others look upon Petitjean as a hot-
head, a perpetually short fuse; he tends to seriously lose his mind
from time to time, usually in reaction to the news of a death in
his files. At times like these, Emelle will call him into her office
for a talking to. A trip to the woodshed, Kirk calls it, but Emelle

is never scolding. She tends to purr, which gets on his nerves. She wants him to be steadier, she says. To be stoic, patient, *collected.* Our work, she tells him, is not unlike raising palmfuls of sand and watching them slip between our fingers. That sand is the question we are asking and those grains that remain are our answer.

Poetry, he is thinking. She tries to comfort me with poetry.

He goes into the living room and finds Catherine on the floor in front of the couch. She is reading the travel brochure that he gave her months ago, something he picked up on Kirk's desk and brought home to her. A Club Méditerranée catalogue, with photos of winter resort spots in Sicily, Tunisia, Morocco, Senegal, and the Ivory Coast. Now it is summer and the pages are worn from hours of her gazing at the pictures of beaches and palm trees, azure pools, golf greens, and tennis courts. He has since brought her real books, color-photo albums of faraway places, but it is the travel catalogue that she returns to always and it has taken him as if forever to understand that it is the people in the pictures that fascinate her. The books he bought have no people in them, only sand and sea, exotic trees and weird birds, mountains and lakes, sunrises and sunsets. She has lived her entire life in Paris and has seldom left the city. And in Paris there is no sunrise or sunset that can be seen, no full or half moon unless you climb to the rooftop to seek it out.

He kneels down next to her and she points out her favorites. A man in American shorts and a golf shirt is holding a pineapple cocktail with the straw to his lips while a woman in a strapless silk dress smiles in his direction. They are seated in a ballroom of some sort and couples dance fuzzily and unfocused around them. In another, children are playing on a white beach, half in and half out of the surf. One girl has fallen into shallow water and has a look on her face that makes Catherine laugh. Her favorite of all is of a woman in a glowing pool, swimming alone at night while others look on from surrounding tables.

"I know," he says to her, "what we will do today."

Catherine looks up from her catalogue and is again what she is becoming more and more. Not a half-wit but a woman. With shining eyes that strain the muscles round his heart.

"One word," he says. "A word you haven't learned yet."

She is waiting for the word as if for a lump of sugar. Her look is enough to send him howling into the day, but he only smiles. Sylvie comes into the room and says "What word, Alain?" but he ignores her. Taking the catalogue from Catherine's lap, he turns the pages until he comes to the photo of a wide beach with dark water in the distance. He points at the picture. "See?" he says to Catherine.

But she is looking at him and not the picture.

"Normandy," he says.

Within an hour they are at the Gare Saint-Lazare, weighted down with beach blankets and two bulging bags that Sylvie has packed for the lunch.

"Three, second class, round trip." Petitjean pays for the tickets and they hurry to track 16, arriving a full minute before the train pulls out. There is no room in Smoking, so Petitjean suffers through the two hours north by northwest, through the flat green reaches, while Sylvie does the crossword in *Paris Match* and Catherine sits with her face to the window, seeing everything while her hands clench into fists as though she is trying to touch the vision or to slow the moving train. It is nearly noon when they arrive in Cabourg. The beach is bare blocks away and the moment they touch sand Catherine is on her knees, grasping it, smoothing it with her palms, lifting it high above her head and letting it run through her fingers. The sky is overcast and a strong wind is blowing in from the sea, making the waves black and white. Sylvie bends and whispers something in Catherine's ear and the two touch cheeks and laugh. Then Petitjean leans to take Catherine by the elbow, telling her to follow, and they advance toward the ocean.

The beach extends a mile in either direction and with a low tide there are pools and rivulets a full fifty yards from the shoreline. Despite the clouds the beach is crowded, but Sylvie finds a dry spot, an island between two pools, and spreads the blankets side by side. The moment they are settled, Catherine wants to go into the water.

Petitjean looks to Sylvie, who has removed her shirt and jeans and has already stretched out on her blanket. She has not removed her top. This topless business happens more in the south, though here and there are women who haven't heard the word. Petitjean silently takes offense at this, their indifference to him, to his eyes upon them. If he sees one of them, he looks away.

"Swim, Sylvie?"

She says not now. "The clouds don't matter. It's in the rays, the tanning. I need some color."

So Petitjean tells Catherine to come with him.

She struggles out of her jeans and blouse, folds them neatly, and leaves them on her blanket. Her suit is badly cut, a blue two-piece with a high waist that covers her navel but a top that is too tight. It pinches her breasts and back and he can see that she is uncomfortable. Her skin is pale against the blue, the color of an eggshell. She has spent the spring and summer in shadows, as has Petitjean, whose face and forearms have color but whose legs are alabaster. A ghost and a half. He looks around them to see if anyone is staring, then gestures in the direction of the sea for her to follow him.

When they come to the water she insists on taking his hand and her grip is tight. For the first ten yards the water only comes to their ankles and then there is a sudden drop and they are up to their knees. She screams once, stops still, and then laughs aloud. Further out, there is little undertow and they come to where the water is waist deep and rises to their chests, then falls in gentle swells. She lets go of his hand and dips up and down in the water, riding the swells. Woman, half-wit, woman. She is by turns hysterical or placid. Then a high wave slaps against her face and she stops stone still, and then turns and looks furiously out to the western horizon. Her gaze sweeps the expanse of water in search of an explanation. The sun burns a hole through the cloud cover and the color of the sea goes from steel gray to blue.

Catherine's eyes are walnut, ebony, or the color of wet sand; her mother's eyes are porcelain blue. Catherine's father was from Latvia. Sylvie could never quite pronounce his names and took to calling him by his initials, C.Z. *Say zed.* He had jumped ship in Copenhagen in 1967 and made his way to Paris, where he'd obtained a stay permit on the premise of *réfugié politique.* She'd met him in the restaurant where she waited tables and he was hired as a dishwasher, and he'd left her well before Catherine was born.

Come and gone. Back to Latvia to face the music. He couldn't find work that suited him here.

Once he'd left, Sylvie wanted an abortion. A fatherless child would be a burden. She was still only twenty-one and had no family, no parents or aunts or uncles to whom she could turn over a baby. Lacking the necessary money, she'd taken drugs that a friend said would do the trick. When nothing happened, she'd taken more, but still Catherine was born. "In the spring of 1968, during all that trouble in Paris." He wonders if Sylvie understands that those drugs might have caused Catherine's condition, the mood swings and slurred speech, that nocturnal moaning. It had taken him a year to realize that she is not an idiot. She is capable of speech, of reasoning, of learning. When he speaks to her she listens and understands him, though she is slow to respond in words he can comprehend. He is convinced that much of her pain and fitfulness is due to the fact that she has never been to school or had friends or been given treatment of any kind. According to Sylvie she was diagnosed at the age of three as retarded and has spent the better part of her life in those same three rooms watching trains come and go, alone with Sylvie or with the other fathers.

C.Z. wrote letters from Latvia that hinted at his return. This lasted five years and then there were no more letters. In 1974, Sylvie gave in to loneliness and a need for money and took on a Spaniard as a boarder. He worked for the city, sweeping the metro, and stayed for three full years without ever paying her rent. When he was short of cash he would fill the gaps with petty thievery, breaking into apartments in the neighborhood where he knew the habits of the occupants. When he was arrested, he plea-bargained his way out of the country, back to Seville, where it turned out he had a wife and two teenage sons. After him there was a German graduate student, then a Greek who drove a taxi, then a Dane who wanted to blow up the world. She once said to Petitjean that he is her first French husband. And when he has reminded her that they are in no way married she has winced and withdrawn.

Contractors were tearing down the building in the tenth arrondissement where he lived and had given him a check for a thousand francs and two weeks' notice. So he answered an ad for a room to rent. It was pinned to the bulletin board in the post office on the rue du Faubourg Saint-Denis, just across the street. *Room to offer, man, 25–50 yrs, nonsmoker, rent free.* Certain there had been a mistake, no room in Paris was ever free, he had nevertheless taken the note from the board and gone knocking. Before admitting him, she wanted to know about his past, what kind of man he was. "I am alone except for my daughter who is not right in the head. I have to be sure of who I let stay here. You understand." So he'd sucked in his breath and admitted who he was and wasn't. Then he asked if she could take in a *taulard*, an ex-con, and she said it would depend upon the crime. Crime of greed or crime of passion? When he'd answered crime of joy, he was in.

No room in Paris is ever free. After two days he was allowed to smoke and on the third night she slipped wordlessly into his bed and covered him with her body. Then he was made to know that her bed was wider and more suitable. She was kind to him and her demands did not go past those of the mattress. He saw her as a good woman who didn't see the fault in her method of killing lonesomeness. It was her fashion for finding husbands, offering space in return for body heat. But Petitjean was already yearning for a room of his own, where he could sleep and awaken alone, where he could bring the women *he* chose, at those moments when desire would speak more urgently than a simple itch. He would line his books, French and German and American, along the wall next to his bed and he would read through the night, and mark passages for memory, and in the mornings over coffee he would write letters to someone, though as yet he didn't know to whom.

The first night he heard the daughter moaning he thought it was his own nightmare. The sound of something wanting out of its own body, the sound of himself in the prison near Orléans. He had risen from the bed and gone to her room, expecting to find her awake and in pain. But the moaning had turned to a humming, a kind of song. Something she sang while still asleep. Thereafter, each night he lay awake listening for it. Sometimes she was silent the whole night through and other times she started in early and kept it up until dawn. The more he listened, the more he realized that it wasn't only a lonely sound; there was at times a crooning of joy, almost laughter, and at other times the moaning was like a drawn-out question to which he was certain he had the answer.

He had his job at ABRI and after two weeks he told Sylvie he'd prefer to pay his rent in the usual fashion. She wanted to know what he meant by that and he said he felt stupid not giving her any money. He added that he wasn't comfortable in bed with her. That the sex was an expectation and nothing much from the heart. "I'd probably do it better if I didn't think of it as an obligation." This part of the argument swayed her and she accepted his offer of a thousand francs a month. He decided that after three or four more weeks he would leave but he didn't get around to it and reset the date for the end of the next month. But when the date had passed he was still there, listening through the night to Catherine's voicings, following carefully each rise and fall. After a time he knew that he wasn't going anywhere. He had left one space for another, and though it was Sylvie's bed that his body occupied, the rest of him had begun to wander.

He rises from under the surface and blinks the water from his eyes. Squinting in the sudden sunlight, he searches for Catherine. She is nowhere in sight and he suffers a few panicky moments before she bobs her head out of the water and laughs in his direction. When she stands her breasts are bare. There are red marks from where the bikini top has pinched her. She is holding the material in one hand and reaches the other to rub herself. He tells her to put the top back on but she shakes her head.

"Too tight?"

She nods and says the word back to him.

He swims the distance to her and helps her snap it back on. "We'll buy you a new one," he tells her. "One that won't hurt you."

"Red," she says. "Red, please."

Then they head in toward the shore, her hand in his, but before they arrive at the beach she stops him and leads him back into the waves. Then she lets go of his hand, turns her head in the other direction, and lowers herself into the water to pee. "Okay," she says when she is finished. And he can see that she is blushing, which he doesn't think he's ever seen her do.

When they return to the beach blankets, Sylvie has already laid out the packed lunch. Bayonne ham and *saucisson*, a pair of baguettes, Gruyère, pickles, mustard, butter, a plastic bottle of water, and two bottles of Côte de Buzet that she's buried in the sand so the wine won't sour in the sun. He would prefer rosé but doesn't complain when red is all there is. Anyway, you can't keep the rosé cold without ice. He opens the bottle with his pocket-knife and pours a glass for Sylvie and one for himself. Catherine is watching him and seems to be waiting for something. "Wine?" he asks, and she nods in return. He doesn't remember ever seeing her drink wine. "She's old enough," he says aloud, more to himself than to Sylvie. And passes his glass to Catherine, adding that he can drink straight from the bottle. She takes the glass with both hands and lifts it to her nose. A sound escapes her lips, maybe even a word, but he can't make it out. She closes her eyes, tips the glass, and drinks. Then she sits back on the sand and a smile covers her face. "Old enough," she says.

Petitjean reaches across the blanket for his shirt and tells her to put it on. "Instead of that horrible top. Go on. It won't hurt so bad."

Sylvie helps her undo the clasp in back and she shrugs out of the top. When her breasts are again bare he catches himself looking and can feel the heat of Sylvie's gaze. He goes on looking anyway, until Catherine has donned his shirt and tied it at the waist.

"Better," Catherine tells him.

He slices the *saucisson* and the ham and they eat in silence. Then Sylvie stretches out on the blanket and closes her eyes. "In a single day," she says, "I can have a tan like two weeks. It always happens. I have Mediterranean skin. Not like you, Alain. You're from the north and without your shirt I'll just bet you get burned easily."

He notices that Catherine's eyes have again gone dull. Like the Normandy sunlight, she is in and out, always in and out. There are moments, even days at a time, when he can forget she is a half-wit, when her speech is relatively unfettered and her eyes are lit from the inside. She knows a thousand words and can often make sentences. He has heard her converse with the television, though she always turns the volume too high and Sylvie shouts at her to turn it down for the love of God. Her hearing is impaired as well, Sylvie says. Though to Petitjean's knowledge she hasn't been to a doctor in years. Whenever he brings up the subject, Sylvie just shrugs and says they've seen them all and what's the use? She is what she is, and after almost twenty years what more can be discovered? Pondering this, he drinks from the bottle and is surprised to find that it is nearly empty. He has been drinking wine from thirst, which is never a good idea. Water is for thirst and wine is for something else. He wishes he'd worn a hat to shade his head. He tells Sylvie he is taking a nap.

"Then who will keep an eye on Catherine?"

"She can take care of herself. Can't you, Catherine? Just so you don't wander off."

He brushes sand from his blanket and lies down. The sun is red through his eyelids. The wine has gone to his head and he feels as though the earth is pulling him downward, pinning him to that spot. He can hear Sylvie and Catherine speaking to each other, but the sounds of the sea cover their words. He listens only for the rush and pull of the waves and after a time he can hear nothing else.

He remembers exercises from his English workbook. The book he kept with him the whole time he was in prison. There were phrases to be repeated to teach himself correct pronunciation. Th: The thin thistle thickens. R: Rare red roses. The aspirated H: Hot head Harry hurts here. Aspiration; breath and hope. He rolls the speaking stones to his right cheek and sleeps.

When he awakens the sun is lower in the horizon and the beach is nearly deserted.

"So," Sylvie says to him. "You're back with us." She leans across the blanket to kiss him.

"What time is it?" he asks.

"Nearly seven. We should be going, is what you will say next."

He feels a tug at his ankle and, looking down, finds that a cord has been tied to it. The other end is knotted round Catherine's waist.

"Sylvie, for the love of God."

"What else was I supposed to do? I wanted to sleep, too. And if she'd wandered off and been lost you'd have never forgiven me."

He unties first his ankle and then Catherine's knot. "I wouldn't have gone," she tells him. "I wouldn't have left you."

Her eyes are red from crying. This wasn't in the pictures, he's thinking. At Club Med they don't tie you up. "I'm sorry, Catherine."

Catherine bites her lip and looks away.

She's embarrassed because of me.

She is seeing herself in a color picture at the beach and now her mother's tied her up.

He wishes there were more of that wine. He could drink it all, could drink the ocean in, and not get rid of the taste in his mouth.

"We'll come again soon," he says to Catherine. "And next time we'll bring the right clothes."

During the train ride back to Paris he considers how long now since he's last driven a car. More than ten years. He no longer has a driver's license but that is unimportant. The first time he'd been arrested for stealing, at sixteen, they'd taken his permit away from him and never returned it. A fake permit had been seized a year later, when he'd been sent to the prison near Orléans. He has the right to another, having completed his rehabilitation, but hasn't taken the time to get it. Sometimes, though, he looks with longing at cars parked along the street. A tan Audi, a white Renault 12, a metallic-silver Mercedes or a scarlet Alfa Romeo. He can remember the fit of a driving glove, like skin, the leather tight across his knuckles, and the sweet counterpressure of the clutch and accelerator. When he'd first stolen cars it was for money and later it was for pleasure. He'd meant to keep the last car he stole forever, but the police had found it parked in front of a brasserie in Auxerre where he had a job washing dishes.

And then they'd found him, too, crouched in a corner of the men's room. And since that time he has not driven a car. He has never even been inside one except for an occasional taxi ride. He has done his time in the prison they've chosen for him, learned his English, chattered with the warden in the evening, and let his thoughts drift easily with the drifting of the sun. And if ever he feels a wheel beneath his hands, he knows what he will do.

I will drive and I will keep on driving. In any direction. Until the gas tank is past empty.

When they are home, Sylvie strips, draws a bath, and settles into the water with a satisfied sigh. Catherine goes to her bedroom and closes the door behind her and for a long moment Petitjean stands in the middle of the living room with a picnic basket in one hand and a rolled-up blanket in the other. The last of the evening trains are pulling out of the station and the passengers are lit with a gold light, so close that he can almost see their faces.

He puts the picnic basket in the kitchen and keeps the blanket. Then he goes to the closet in the bedroom and takes down his clothes. There are a dozen hangers with shirts and trousers and two worn jackets. His few ties are hung on a long hook attached to the door. Taking everything in a bundle, he goes into the spare bedroom and begins clearing boxes off the old bed. The mattress is ancient and a number of the springs are broken and protrude from the surface. He has only slept once on this bed, that first night. But it will be softer than the street and he has slept there, too. In the street and in alfalfa fields, in doorways and hallways, and once in a field of corn. Though the corn was meant for pigs, he found it edible and had lived a week in that field. When the bed is cleared of boxes and books, he tosses the beach blanket over it and tucks it into the sides. There is another blanket in the hall closet and he folds it over the first and turns down the corner. In prison he learned to make a bed like this, with squared corners and tucked sides. He learned for the first time how to still his own fear with minute activities, folding clothes, shining shoes, scrubbing pots, sweeping the walk, or writing his name fifty times and each time writing it differently. He is afraid right now and doesn't know why, so he makes up the bed as best he can. He knows he can face down Sylvie's anger. It is her sorrow that terrifies him. And if she puts him into the street he will not be in a panic. He could always go to Zane's place. Zane might be crazy but he's still a friend.

He undresses and considers that he needs a bath as well. His skin smells of brine and sand and sweat. But he would have to join Sylvie and then she might get the wrong idea. So he turns out the light, climbs into the bed, and pulls the blanket over himself. It is a thin blanket and he is comfortable despite the heat. If he lies still, the loose springs to either side of him are of no consequence. He tells himself to learn to sleep without moving.

Some minutes later he hears Catherine go from her bedroom to the toilet. Then he hears Sylvie getting out of her bath, the rush of water down the drain. "Alain?"

He can hear her moving from room to room, first the living room and then the kitchen and then the water closet. "No," she says, and he can hear her going to Catherine's bedroom. Then, "He's not in here? Alain?" She comes to the bedroom and hesitates before entering.

"Don't turn on the light," he tells her.

"What are you doing in here?"

"I'm going to sleep here. Tonight and tomorrow. From now on."

There is a long silence. He can see her face in the hall light but knows he is in shadows. She is wearing a short bathrobe and her legs are thin and pale in the dim light. For a moment she reminds him of her daughter and he considers that, all in all, she has given far more than she's taken. She has cooked his lamb and his carrots, his *lapin à la moutarde*, poured him wine from her own cellar, and later done the dishes while singing to the wall. She has washed and pressed his shirts, chosen his ties and shoes to match, fed him aspirin and whisky in the evening, and rubbed the knots from his neck when he's returned home. "Behind the eyes," he would say, and she massaged his hot temples with her cool fingers. She has moved toward him in the bed and sometimes she has smelled of vinegar and other times of lemon tea. And now he's going to do her some dirt. This is my thanks to her. *Le grand merci.* Because I've found myself straight downwind from her idiot daughter and would become an idiot myself to give symmetry to the misfortune of loving her.

Sylvie stares into the shadows, to a spot to the left of him. She says she doesn't understand.

"Hot head Harry hurts here," he tells her.

An hour later the phone is ringing. It is the first sound he has heard other than Sylvie's pacing and sniffling. He knows by the hour that the call is for him so he rises and goes naked into the living room. Sylvie is there before him. She has lifted the receiver and holds it between her breasts. Then Catherine, too, is with them. They are all naked and the room is lit from the lights over the tracks outside. The surprise is that he's surprised. For a long moment he contemplates the anatomies before him, Sylvie's cartography, slim shoulders with sharp bones, long breasts that swing when she walks, a flat belly, and the legs of a young girl, Catherine all shining, rounder and paler, her skin blue in the gray darkness. She is looking down at him and when he follows her gaze he finds he is erect. Bursting into tears, Sylvie holds the receiver out to him.

It is Zane. He wants his mail.

ON THE RUE CAULAINCOURT, JUST ABOVE THE PLACE de Clichy, is a bridge that crosses over the Cimitière du Nord, better known as the Cimitière de Montmartre. To one side of the bridge is Paris proper and on the other side the hill rises steeply into the remote environs of Montmartre, where the sudden tranquillity and abundant trees and even houses are a surprise; the higher up you go, the less you are in the city. It is a village that overlooks Paris, a place for walking aimlessly and alone, and the metro stops are few and far between.

With time on his hands, Zane climbs to the top and moves swiftly into the tourist crush at the Place du Tertre. The dogshit factory-made artwork is out on display, *affordable* French art, and although it is nearly ten in the evening, the square is packed. Pushing his way forward, Zane crosses toward the basilica of Sacré-Coeur and then circles back the way he came. Emerging on the east edge of the square, he turns briefly to be sure that no one has been able to follow him. Spooks, assassins. No use telling anyone that his mother thinks of him as a noncombatant.

On the rue Norvins, he freezes in the street as a young woman crosses his path. Her hair is black and wild and there are cosmetic smears across her cheeks and blades of anger in her eyes. For a moment he thinks the anger is directed at him and his heart stops still. But she hurries past him and disappears into a numberless doorway, one of the millions of numberless doorways in the secret streets of Paris, streets with no name and doorways,

150

passageways, arches that might or might not lead to the rooms of troubled beauties. Zane has been seven months without a woman and six years without loving anyone, and the sight of that woman, the fleeting sensation that *he* had been the object of her rage, has taken his breath away. That's what it's come to. He can only go on for so long forgetting that he has a lifetime to live out and then a woman crosses the street in front of him and disappears into a doorway and he is alive again and without a companion or an alibi.

Walking more swiftly, he comes to the bridge that passes over the cemetery and looks down into the yard. The streetlamp casts a flat light across the gravestones and he can see a pair of cats moving among the shadows. Lonesome old Frenchwomen often come during the day with rosaries and novels and bags filled with horsemeat, flounder, tripes, and pâté to feed the cats and then stop to pray over strangers' headstones. The cats fatten and multiply and stay close by. There are no cars and no dogs, an abundance of birds despite the lack of trees, and more to eat than anywhere else in the city. It is the same in all of the Paris cemeteries: fields of marble with scratched names, saints and angels and praying hands carved from stone, the peace of no traffic whatsoever, no machines, only the wind in the trees and the cats and birds and old women walking the alleyways up and down.

At the south end of the bridge is a modest bar run by Algerians and frequented mainly by other Algerians or Moroccans or Italians or Portuguese. Zane has been here many times. It is a place with worn wooden chairs and chipped Formica tables on an uneven floor littered with Gitane butts, metro tickets, and scraps of Arabic newsprint. The whisky is cheap and no one will talk to Zane except Malik, the bartender, so he has no one to answer to but himself. He steps to the counter and orders a whisky with ice. Malik says good evening and gives him a glass with a single cube and a splash of J & B. Arab music is coming from the jukebox and Zane turns his back to it and drinks down the whisky. Such music, the ululating Moroccan melodies and bells and strings, always puts him into a bad frame of mind. He asks Malik for another whisky and to turn down the sound. The Algerian glares at him, then turns his back and reaches for the J & B. Zane is on his third when the music finally ends and the only sounds are the grinding of the espresso machine, the rattle of ice in glasses, and the guttural murmuring of quarreling Arabs at a table nearby. For a long moment he bows his head to the zinc counter and considers that from now on he will have the rest of his life to live. His life after ABRI, now that he is outside those comforting walls. When he finds out what happened to Street there will be nothing more he can do. His rakers are dispersing, losing their way. Without him they will find another ear into which they can whisper their confessions. Emelle may or may not take him back but that is of no concern to him. The world will spin the same as always, without his watching, will spin out sunrise and sunset, and he will have more time to kill. And whatever is memory to him, whatever he remembers of his own life, his mother and her ancient crimes, will come crowding back into his thoughts and he will have to find some other way to distract himself. Amnesty, amnesia. One or the other.

He reaches into his breast pocket for his cigarettes and finds instead the letter from the prison. Dear Mr./Ms. Zane. He hasn't received a letter from his mother since the note that included the postscript *Venceremos*. He hasn't seen her face in more than six years. The last time he visited, she barely spoke to him. She treated him as always like a civilian and wanted only to know if he had a girlfriend. There was a bruise on her face, just below an eye, that one of the policewomen told him was self-inflicted. "When she gets out of here, you'll have to keep her tied up."

For the first ten years of her imprisonment, she had written regularly and the letters were all the same: essays, more or less, that described an impending American cataclysm, the experiment blowing up in our faces, a house collapsing wall by wall, cockroaches taking the wheel of the Cadillac and driving it to hell. What her lawyer referred to as diatribes. She wrote similar letters to the governor, to the policeman who arrested her, to the prosecutor, the judge. She forgave them, she wrote, but they were still on thin ice with history. These letters were used as evidence against her whenever parole was mentioned. Dear Mr./Ms. Zane. Her phrases remained rooted in the decade in which she learned them: Up against the wall, off the pigs, running dogs one and all.

She stopped writing letters years ago and they rewarded her with a job in the stitching room. For a tranquil month she worked next to a black woman who was doing three to five for child abuse. The woman could neither read nor write but she did teach Zane's mother how to thread the machine, the settings for straight stitching, crossing, and hatching. But one morning all of the machines were found to be broken. His mother had opened the covers and stuck pins into the works and switched on the juice.

Nowadays Eldridge Cleaver is writing cookbooks and Tom Hayden hitched himself to Hollywood. Jean Zane is denied sunlight and moonlight and writes *venceremos* every chance she gets.

During his second year at ABRI, Zane went to a human-rights conference in Stockholm. One night, after the last sessions, he went bar-hopping and ran into a small colony of Americans, whole families living and hanging out around Stockholm and the suburbs. Most of the men were COs, conscientious objectors, in exile because of the war. Now Viking-like hippies, working as bricklayers, carpenters, bartenders, waiters, bellhops. Many feigned contentment and extolled the virtues of Scandinavian neutrality, the clean air, the tranquil atmosphere. One of these men, originally from upstate New York, drank shots of Wild Turkey and chased them with Heineken. He seemed especially pleased to make Zane's acquaintance. "There were more of us here before Carter's amnesty," he explained. "But after years of being aware of every horrid detail in that shit war and following the news of the pullout in the *International Herald Tribune* or on the radio or in the Swedish press, some of us couldn't see the point in going back." He added, "I read about your mother a few weeks before coming here. She was a real inspiration for me."

"She was behind bars. Still is."

"Yeah," the man said. "I guess you see all that from a whole different angle."

Zane ordered more shots of whisky and decided to join in.

"I guess you didn't have to worry about going. To Nam, that is. Would you have gone—if you'd had to—or would you be sitting here with me as a neighbor instead of a tourist?"

Zane said he didn't know. When his mother was imprisoned there were people in the movement who tried to enlist him and make use of his name. For a few months he played along but once he'd gone along with a girlfriend to an antiwar rally and watched the woman who'd made love to him the night before shrieking and spitting like a crazed alley cat in the direction of a policeman. Thereafter, he sat the fence.

"When I was still in America," the man said, "I felt a part of the underground. Like my country was being taken from me by fat white men in blue suits and red ties. Like I had to hide out in the sleeves and pockets and bide my time. I hated the flag wavers and the rednecks, plus I was afraid of them. Once I got busted at a rally in Albany. Twenty or thirty of us sitting on campus, high as Chinese kites, gathered up matches and gasoline and set fire to the highest flag in sight. Not much of a statement, really, and it's something I regret." He poured himself another Wild Turkey, looked at it for a long time, and knocked it back. "I was thinking about protest, you know, in a foggy cannabis way, saying something loud and damn clear about what I felt. And it got translated by Dick and Jane and John Doe into something else entirely, like what I was doing was burning them and theirs and the constitution and Abe Lincoln before their watching eyes. I took a beating even before getting into the back seat of the cruiser. Not from the cops, man, from *the people*. And it's not the flag burning I regret most. It was getting beat up by people who acted as if I was un-American, like I was some kind of evil foreigner. Even while this one guy stood over me and kicked my ribs, all I could think about was how badly I wanted to wipe that self-satisfied, snotty, *righteous* look off his face. But way before my ribs healed I knew that I'd never be able to, and that's what brought me to this shitty, boring ice box of a nation. I'm still as American as anybody—but whenever I remember that man's face, I get out my razor and think terrible thoughts."

Nearly all of the men Zane met that night had a hangdog look that smacked of guilt. Not for having missed out on the killing. That was a drawn line that would stay drawn. But for having checked out so entirely, so irrevocably, from the American upheaval while their friends were still back there fending for themselves.

.   .   .

"How did I know I'd find you here?"

He turns to find Petitjean, burdened with ABRI files, a plastic box of diskettes, and a stack of mail. He is dressed in jeans and a blue cotton shirt and his face is cherry red.

"Were you followed?"

He shrugs. "No one ever follows me. I have my own set of tricks."

"Anyone outside your door?"

"Only neighbors. I went to the cemetery first. When you weren't there I said to myself, Zane is thirsty again. Are you dead drunk or can we talk?"

"Your face looks—"

"Sun blows. Burn. However you say it. I told you, I went to the beach."

He sets the files on the counter and gestures to Malik. "*Eau minérale et un whisky à côté. Sec.*" Then he says, "The only one at the office was Nguyen." Malik delivers the whisky with a side glass of water and he reaches first for the water and drinks it down. "She was still in the office when I went in. Eleven o'clock at night and she's sitting in front of her screen crying her heart up."

"Out."

"Bad mail, she kept saying. There is bad heart black mail in my window today. Her English is no better than mine when she's, when she's upset like that. I told her to go home but she's taking the mattress. I think it's the first time."

"What have you brought for me?"

"Let me finish my drink first. You've had yours."

"It shows?"

"It never shows. You hold it so well, your whisky. That's the problem with you. You're a dignified drunk. And because you don't fall down or vomit you think you're all right."

"It's not that bad, Alain. It really isn't." Zane's calling him Alain startles both of them. They've always been Zane and Petitjean, holding each other at the arm's length of surnames. As if to show Petitjean something new, Zane leaves the last of his drink on the counter, flips a bill to Malik, and takes up the files in his arms. "Out of curiosity," he asks, "what were you doing when I called? Was it the wrong time?"

"I wasn't doing anything, Zane. Reading, reading a book."

They step out into the street and the night air is thick with chemicals and exhaust mingled with the dust in the trees. Down the street are a number of Senegalese with their wares arranged on blankets along the sidewalk. Ivory carvings, brass bracelets, plastic mechanical birds, Day-Glo necklaces, and earrings of bronze, ivory, bone, and mahogany. As Okimbo had said the night they met, Paris is just another African capital. At just that moment a gray police van crosses the bridge from the north and cruises in their direction. The Senegalese bend and lift the blankets by the four corners, then swoop into the shadows; it takes only a few seconds and the street is bare. When the police van turns left onto the Boulevard de Rochechouart, the men emerge from the shadows, kneel to the sidewalk, and go about displaying their stock. It is a scene that Zane has witnessed a hundred times, an African immigrant dance to which the French police call the tune. Depending upon their mood and the heat of the night, confrontations can grow nasty. Cursing and threats and the nervy plucking at the sleeves of djellabas. The police have the law and the handguns. Fraternity, at these moments, is just a slogan on the franc piece. And the only thing that could save the street vendors are papers that they don't have.

Next to the bar is a stone stairway that leads into the crowded cemetery. Zane and Petitjean pick their way past gravestones and markers to a remote corner where various members of the Famille Tarquin have been laid to rest. Zane can see the tracks of the motorbike that chased him the night before. There are a pair of stone benches in front of the mausoleum, and a patch of grass and potted geraniums. Setting the files and boxes onto one of the benches, Petitjean stretches out on the grass, folds his hands behind his head, and stares up into the clouds that glow red and alabaster in the city light.

The first document that Petitjean has brought to him is the police report he's requested. Petitjean, being French, has better relations at the prefectures than does Zane.

The report is a single typed paragraph: *Lucinda Niasse, Sénégalaise, 33 ans, célibataire, profession inconnue. Cause du décès: suicide, défenestration. 20 août 1988.*

"Who was she?"

Défenestration is jumping out a high window. A swan dive through cursory sky. What kills is the impact. Was it a broken neck or spine or crushed torso? He had not seen blood and she was not disfigured. The report ends without an endorsement for an investigation.

Declining to answer Petitjean's question, he thanks him for the report. Then he sorts through his mail and finds nothing of great interest and so turns to the box of diskettes.

"Archives from your own hard disk. For this whoever you call Eleven. When I didn't find anything on the central disk, I checked out Kirk's drawers and found these."

"What in hell was he doing with my files? He should have kept them under lock and key."

He reaches to his bag for a pack of Gauloises. "You're not the only one who knows how to break and enter. I used to hot-wire cars, remember? All day long I had the feeling I was being watched. Now that you're gone, it's obvious we're nothing but spies."

"That's all we've ever been, Petitjean, no matter what we might've thought. What's in the folders?"

"Hard copy. Same subject. Anything, anything that smelled of Eleven. That's still your, your obsession isn't it?"

Zane doesn't answer.

Petitjean reaches outward and lifts a round pebble from the ground. After a second's hesitation, he places it in his mouth. "Imagine," he says slowly, "how much better off we'd be if you trusted me."

"I do," Zane tells him. "I do, but there's nothing more to ask you." He pauses while a black cat slinks out of the shadows of the family plot and approaches them with caution. "Eleven is a friend. More. I don't know what he is or was but he wasn't only a raker."

The cat wants food and since they have none to offer it wanders back into the shadows and is gone.

"Have you ever heard of M'Khlea Kane?" Zane asks.

"Yes, but only from you. About two years ago you didn't shut up about her. I once caught you writing her name over and over on a telex pad."

"You never heard about her from anyone else? Never read anything?"

Petitjean considers for a while. "No. But I went through Emelle's files before coming here and found a casebook on Ambrose Okimbo."

"What was in it?"

"I didn't read it."

"Why the hell not?"

"Listen, Zane, I don't know. I'm Poland, I'm Romania, Czechoslovakia, Hungary, and Bulgaria. When I hear names that don't fit those places I just let them fall out my ears. Okimbo's in your patch."

"I want that casebook."

"You like to keep secrets but you never allow us to keep any. I've got a man in, in Prague, a source I've never mentioned to anyone. ABRI is a nuthouse and not too secure. If I ever write his name, or even mention it in my sleep, this poor bastard may wind up dead, dead. You've had your secrets, too. These rakers of yours, this private little club."

"There's a connection, Petitjean."

"Okimbo to Eleven?"

Zane takes the cigarette from Petitjean and drags from it. He realizes it is his first cigarette of the night. He didn't know he was quitting. "Okimbo, Eleven, the eavesdropper. Maybe even Emelle. I don't know what it is, but it's there. That's why I need the new addresses."

"Almost forgot." Petitjean sits up and rummages in his bag for a slip of paper. When he does, a paperback slips out and falls to the ground. "I didn't have time to test it through. These were issued today and, like I said, I was at the beach."

"*Merci* all the same."

"So I imagine it will be more breaking and entering before the night is through. I can already hear the glass breaking."

Zane just nods.

"Do you ever consider just quitting?" he asks. "Taking Emelle's advice and going on a cruise somewhere?"

"Do you?"

"More and more. Emelle is going to fire me anyway. I've taken your side too many times."

His hand rises from the ground with yet another stone, smooth and black. He puts it in his mouth and rolls it backward with his tongue. For a moment his lips move but no words emerge. Then he speaks slowly, fighting the stutter. "I get tired," he says, "tired of breathing air that is ten percent cigarette smoke. And I get headaches from watching the screens."

"You can find other work, Petitjean. You have your languages. And your talents on the systems."

He nods. "I know that. I'm not at the end of my hope."

"Rope."

"I was turning the phrase. Irony, Zane. It's very French."

Zane reaches for the book on the ground and reads the title. *Discours sur la Maladie d'Esprit.*

Petitjean snatches it away. "Now you're reading *my* mail."

"It's an old habit."

Petitjean puts the book back into his bag and rises from the grass. "I thought we'd be getting drunk or something. What we usually get up to when we come here. I assume you've got a bottle in your possession."

"Of course."

"But I'm not up to it tonight. Might be the sunburn. I'm feeling dead and you look worse."

Zane rises as well and they cross the cemetery to the stone stairway. When they have climbed to the street, Petitjean reminds Zane to cover his tracks. "There's a 'snowfall' routine I left for you on the file server. In the directory marked with your name. Use it."

Then he heads down the path toward the rue Caulaincourt, on his way to Blanche, the underground. His home with mother and daughter. When Zane is alone, the cat returns to his side and nuzzles his leg, begging, but there is nothing to feed her but the paper in his hands and the sour drops of whisky that have dried on his fingertips.

"IF THEY ARE NOT GUILTY, BEAT THEM UNTIL THEY are."

This was a favorite slogan of South Vietnamese interrogators. It is the only wall clipping Zane has salvaged from his former office at ABRI. He contemplates the logic for the millionth time while a transmission from Mozart unscrolls across his screen: *Dead dead dead dead tired. I will be in Italy until October, so leave me be. Mozart.* He's read this before. Mozart is always tired, always at the end of his existential rope. His complaints are his version of drinking his way into oblivion, his letters to the editor, his release. He has had a miserable summer in the cruel sand gardens of Chad and has been desperate for news from Europe. Though this is the third such message Zane has received in a month, he imagines that if he is still on the line he will soon receive another hot cable from Dakar or Lagos or Addis Ababa with news that isn't fit to print.

Marie has taken his scribbled paper and ordered his equipment in the name of the club. His new telecom kit—386 processor, VGA screen, 80-megabyte disk, high-speed modem, telefax card, and laser printer—has cost him most of his savings. Fingers has told him to stay as long as he likes and he has said he will be gone in three days, maybe four. "I don't count so good," Fingers replied. And Zane, grateful, turned back to his screen.

After installing the machines, he'd spent two hours cutting through access-control files to link his previous hacking to the new computer address and number. Taking inspiration from the intruder, he has placed an eavesdrop on his own ABRI line. Whoever Emelle assigns to replace him will continue to receive Zanespeak but the same transmissions will copy to his home line. He has also put in an eavesdrop on any incoming addressed to EMLX but as a precaution he has run the intercept from keyboard command. It will only activate when he runs the program manually.

Early on, he finds that, in addition to his South American desk, Kirk has been assigned Africa in Zane's absence. Two of his messages are queries from Snake Eyes and January: WHO ARE YOU? They only know Zane and Zane is in limbo. So he checks their mailbox numbers and answers them himself:

HE IS KIRK. IGNORE HIM. SPEAK TO ME AS ALWAYS. CAUTION.

Then he takes their news and relays it to Petitjean with instructions to send it on to France Presse, to Reuters, to the AP, to the Red Cross, or to Amnesty International. Whatever can be clearly stated to whoever can make a difference. He has been working for two hours before he realizes he is in business for himself.

The room is secure, but he is worried about the single stairway. He is three floors up and the window provides no safe exit. No one but Fingers and Marie know he is there and he keeps the door bolted and feels himself a prisoner. "Venceremos, Mother."

Just past noon, he finally has the time to dump the files made by the echo routine that he attached to the intruder at ABRI. Every keystroke made by the intruder has been recorded and the printout comes to nearly thirty pages. The intruder was reaching for file names related to Eleven. The printout reveals that he tried Eleven, eleven, onze, elf, 11, 10 + 1, as well as contractions such as Elvn and Elevn. No dice, Zane already knows. His archives of Street have scrambled labels. TRSTEE or ESRTET, any of the nearly fifty thousand combinations of the letters of his last name. He had set the echo routine at 11:47 and the intruder had logged out only eight minutes later. He had logged back in at half past twelve and tried a second set of file-access codes. But this time he'd used a multiple-try program which automatically tested four-letter combinations, beginning with ABCD, ACBD, ADBC. The program ran for nearly four hours, as far as HXYZ, and then was terminated. Near 6:00 a.m., the intruder was back and this time made a grab into Petitjean's libraries, from which he copied a number of programs, among them the ARCDAT routine and the stalker program. Half an hour after his last log-in, he terminated.

So the quarry is Street and the intruder has deduced that Zane and Petitjean are working together. But none of the facts interlink and there is no chain to pull.

By early afternoon, Africa has gone dark on the screen. He holds the seashell to his ear but the continent is no longer speaking to him. Messages come in over the line and the laser printer hums forth pages, but it isn't Africa that announces itself. Only the Baltic States or Patagonia, the Levant or Oceania. His room smells of electricity and he stares uneasily at the cathode shadows of his screen.

January has written: *Queries to friends and lovers across the beach. No sign of Eleven. Ghost man. Never was.*

The beach is the West African coast. Friends are trustworthy police or military personnel. Lovers are the owners of safe houses. And never was is the blankest of pages.

Mozart has answered the same. As has Snake Eyes. Zane has heard from everyone but Demi, who sent the original message. Eleven gone to blue. Light water. Zane has had nothing from him and has begun to wonder if he has gone to blue as well. There is enough blue to harbor all of them, endless blue, the blue of the sea or of the sky, take your pick.

He sits in the shadows beyond his window and stares into the alley. There is no one there to be seen. On the street outside his apartment at La Fourche, there were always the strolling Algerians, solitary men, no two together, hands at their sides. He saw them as poorly dressed figures from a painting by Magritte, each of them seemingly identical and anonymous. Whenever he passed these men on the street their eyes looked through him as if to a distant wall, as if even in the city they have eyes only for the desert's expanse. Late one night, while walking through the Tuileries in front of the Louvre, he came upon the sculpture garden that borders the rue de Rivoli. In the blue darkness, the statues were also blue, the gods and poets and ere-world figures. And suddenly, it seemed, they were moving. Almost imperceptibly, they emerged from their stillness and walked silently among each other. And slowly he realized that he was surrounded by living men, a score of Algerians and Moroccans cruising the garden. The lonesomeness of the place had him by the throat. No one spoke, not even to whisper. The men threaded each other's paths without making contact, there among the trees and statues, and the only light was the glow of a cigarette or a disembodied grin.

In Paris, the Algerian men outnumber the women three to one. The sex that results is less a point of culture or desire than of desperation. Loneliness is one sweet alibi for almost any kind of diversion. Try the east slope of Montmartre or the boulevard between Anvers and Pigalle. Or head up to the flea market at the Porte de Clignancourt on a Saturday and find them with their found objects spread on plastic mats, everything on sale, just name a price. A paperback, worn socks, plastic earrings, an empty water bottle, and, surprisingly often, one shoe.

There are footsteps on the stairs. The carpet over those wooden steps is worn and he has heard all the coming and going in the building from where he sits. The footfalls stop in front of his door and there is a tapping. Three taps, a pause, and then another. Marie.

He opens the door and she asks him if he needs anything. "Water," he tells her.

"Not whisky?"

"And I'll need keys to the building. In case I have to go out."

She tells him she'll have copies made.

She turns and descends the stairs and he pauses while his eyes follow her. From just that angle, fifteen feet up, the back of her stirs him. Her long hair and tight skirt and a walk that would ignite dry wood. When she is ten steps below him she stops, turns, and gazes up at him. Their eyes meet and for the first time he is looking at her face and forgetting its geometry. Even from the distance he can see the smoke in her eyes. She raises a hand as if to wave but the hand covers half her face and is like clothing over a naked body. Then she turns her back to him and continues down the stairs and in embarrassment he shuts the door.

He binds the letters into three flat bundles and ties them around his chest and armpits and despite the heat he covers himself with a sweater. When he is certain there is no one in the back alley, he slips out and crosses to the street behind the building. A few streets south, at the corner of the Sorbonne, is a Crédit du Nord. After filling out the necessary forms, he pays in cash and is led down the stairs to a basement chamber. The bank officer hands him a key.

"*Avez vous un photocopieur?*" Zane asks.

"*Bien sûr. Par ici.*"

Tyranny versus the photocopier. A standoff. It takes Zane close to two hours to copy the letters and then he locks the originals into his personal vault and then, his eyes used to the dim light, he steps blind onto the sunny sidewalk. Clutching the photocopies to his chest, he returns to the club in a zigzag fashion and pounds on the back door. It is the musician, Smith-y-Vega, who comes to open for him. The black eyes him with suspicion but reluctantly allows him to enter.

"Marie's been lookin for you," he says.

Zane hurries up the stairs and finds his room has been cleaned and dusted but his papers have not been touched.

Noting the postmarks, he has already created a base file of Street's movements, leaving a partition of memory active for incoming transmissions. Using his Street computer archive as a counter to the postmarks, he tracks the dates, names of cities, and key words from his coded messages. Kinshasa to Libreville to Nairobi to Lusaka. Abidjan, Accra, Lomé. Bamako, Dakar, Monrovia. Street's base of operations shifted from Johannesburg to Nairobi in 1986, when his medical company pulled out of South Africa, but he continued to visit Capetown, Durban, and Pretoria at regular intervals. When the file is complete, Zane tries sorting it, first by city, and finds that in the past year Street was most often in West Africa, in the triangle between Senegal, Nigeria, and Mali. Zane sorts the file into ascending dates and finds that there were consecutive round trips from Dakar to Lagos in January of 1988 followed by a rapid-fire tour of six cities in the space of ten days. Though there isn't a single message for the month of March, in April, Street's movements accelerated again, but now the triangle had narrowed to encompass only Mali, Sierra Leone, and the Ivory Coast. Zane last saw him in Paris in the spring, late March or early April, and can reconstruct with his file the fact that he had only been in town for two days before returning to Abidjan.

As he reaches for a bottle of Scotch that isn't there, the printer hums with new incoming, but it is only an intercept of a message to Kirk from somewhere in Bolivia.

Setting the photocopies next to the screen, he begins to enter the text, one letter after another, an exhausting task. There are close to three hundred pages and the handwriting is not always legible. Worse, many of the letters were written in blue ink that doesn't photocopy well. He is often tempted to go back to the bank and retrieve the originals but decides against it.

Late in the afternoon, having keyed in close to fifty pages of text, he weakens and shuts down the word processor and burns the photocopies of the pages he has entered. Switching to telecom, he taps out the mailbox code for Demi, who has been silent since the confirmation of Eleven gone to blue. As opposed to direct transmissions, mailbox sends are stored in numbered files on the AMNET mainframe west of London. They can be picked up at any time and any such retrieval includes an automatic acknowledgment of receipt. There are already three of his messages in Demi's mailbox with no acknowledgment. All the same, he keys in:

DESPERATE FOR NEWS OF ELEVEN. JUICE BACK ASAP.
LIP SERVICE INSUFFICIENT. REQUEST SKIN ON SKIN.
ZANE.

Demi isn't the most reliable of the rakers. He is only a part-timer, alternating his art dealing with drug running with raking and God knows what else. He disappears for weeks at a time and then will flood the lines with horror stories from the North African swath. His transmissions usually mean overtime because of the gravity of his messages and the shortage of verifiable facts. Had it been Mozart or Snake Eyes or January who'd sent the message there would be details by now. Zane is asking for skin on skin; in this sense, that Demi show his face. But there is no guarantee that he'll read the message let alone respond to it.

Following a hunch, he dials the number of an African embassy and asks for Mr. Munango. After a brief delay, there is a voice on the line:

"*Ici Munango.*"

"*Ici Monsieur Zed.* I am looking for a doctor."

"This line is secure, Mr. Zane. You may speak freely."

"A white doctor, specializing in mercy."

"Can you be more specific?"

"No. I am also fishing for a native. Ambrose Okimbo."

"You may have been misdirected. I am a cultural attaché. Perhaps I could connect you to our military rep. Have you a name for your doctor?"

Munango is trustworthy, a proven contact, but Zane knows that the phone is not as secure as advertised. "Without a name," Munango continues, "I can do little. Send you *les pages jaunes*." The Yellow Pages is a list of foreigners in Munango's country. It is supposed to be kept up on a regular basis, and of course is about as reliable as rain in the Sahara.

"Who do you suppose is listening to us, Munango?"

"Who is your doctor?"

Zane hangs up. Next he tests his other contacts along the diplomatic circuit, consuls, vice consuls, administrative assistants, secretaries, and the catchall cultural attachés. None of them speak the language and he cannot risk offering either Okimbo or Street in the raw form of a name. A white doctor specializing in mercy. A medical-supplies salesman. What does he sell? Respirators, cardiac monitors, salt pills, resuscitation. Or an African poet, hard to read and harder to find. What sort of poetry? Loud. Unwilling to offer specifics, he is offered less than roadmaps. Two of his sources refuse to take his call and a third tells him bluntly that ABRI is no longer on the white list. "Despite our continual affection for your person." The only thread offered him comes from a nervous secretary in the Nigerian embassy, who admits to knowing a number of whites who deal in medical supplies but has no knowledge of any of them disappearing recently. Her phone number is not in Zane's files but in his memory. She was offered to him by Demi and he has only turned to her at crucial times and has to be tender, careful not to spook her. Her line is perhaps the least secure of any diplomatic telephone line in Paris. After a long pause, he decides to risk a word group. His signal is to ask the date and she answers the twelfth of the month. Over the next few minutes, he engages her in a rambling conversation during which he mentions cities, streets, or names of persons. Key words. The twelfth key word is Stroot and after changing subjects a few times, he mentions the weather and she remarks that there isn't a hint of rain. She knows nothing. He hangs up, waits five minutes, and calls again. She is angry and he immediately tells her that he is *doubly* sorry and this will be his *last* call if she can spare him *two* seconds. A second name to ask about, first name and last, with the first name being the last key word uttered. In the midst of an otherwise innocuous apology for bothering her, he slips the name Okimbo. There is no way for him to codify it. OK. I'm. Beau. Followed by rapid-fire smoke about cultural events in Paris during August, who is expected to attend, who he has heard from, who has written postcards from the south of France, including his good friend Ambrose. Then he lets a few long seconds pass as the end mark. She tells him she is swamped with work and must ring off. He says of course, thanks her, and hangs up.

Half an hour passes before she calls him back. By the sounds around her voice, she is calling from a payphone. She asks him if he plans to attend the conference that evening. The World Commission on the Environment and Development.

He has an invitation, he says, and can hear her coughing at the other end of the line. He has never seen her face but has long assumed her to be a chain smoker. When she comes back to the phone, she tells him that at the end of the conference he should read the sports pages. "In your own language. Across the street in front of the building. And don't call again."

His credentials are still in his pocket. Emelle took away only his paycheck. Checking his mailbox archive, he scans the agenda. Noon luncheon, followed by an address by the Norwegian prime minister. Discussion and debate beginning at 18:00 and scheduled to last until 20:00. Dinner at 21:00 in the dining hall.

He considers that Emelle might send a replacement. All the same, he has his entry card and, if pressed, can still provide ABRI credentials. The suspension is only a day old and news doesn't travel that fast.

In Paris, the streets are named for saints or poets or composers, the odd king or colonel, or are sentences. There is, for example, the rue du Chat Qui Peche. Along the Left Bank of the Seine, jutting in from the quai, it is more or less a blind alley with two small, dim doorways shielded by trash barrels. The verb *pecher,* depending upon the accent, can mean either to sin or to fish. Sharp accent: to sin. Circumflex: to fish. But there is no accent whatsoever on the street marker. He chooses to translate the name as the Street of the Cat That Sins. The nature of the sin has yet to be determined.

He is late for the conference but he stops for a moment on the other side of the river to look again into the street with the name he has never understood. At his back, he hears the rasping of a *mobilette,* but when he turns the street is empty.

He came to Paris in search of an address. Where to sign on that dotted line and maybe to decide why he should have to after all. He is an only child and his mother was always up against a wall. He grew up in twenty cities and countless apartments. They slept on floors or sofas. He has little memory of beds. His mother went to jail and stayed there. She signed that dotted line in a way he never plans to.

In the beginning he stayed in Paris out of heartbreak, and then he stayed to read the letters on his screen. He will stay a while more and then he will go back. This is what he's been telling himself for nearly seven years now. He will stay a while more and then he will go back. He will speak a secret language with men who have signed their names. When they leave him he will wait with his heart in his throat to hear the words they have to say. And in the meantime he will visit the Street of the Cat That Sins, and he will tempt him with milk to his side.

THE
TROJAN HORSE

THE WORLD COMMISSION ON ENVIRONMENT AND DE-velopment issued a report in 1987 that called for economic expansion "within the planet's ecological means." Though this recommendation has not been universally ignored, it is in no way being heeded. One conference leads to another while economics get in the way and the heads of government move like wounded snails whenever the subject of the planet comes into view. Zane can sympathize with Ambrose Okimbo, if it is true that he has turned to assassination, though killing one head of government, or several, is shortsighted at the least; the process of elimination is no guarantee that the sinner's replacement will be the awaited saint. In fact, the dictator who profits from an assassination will often tend to be worse. And the satisfaction of pulling a trigger and seeing bullet striking brain can last only a minute or two. Then the usual chaos falls down from the sky and citizens are dragged from their beds and murdered for reasons that can never be adequately documented.

A Tunisian coral diver has come all the way from Sfax to ask why the coral is disappearing from the local bay. There are one hundred and forty representatives from sixty countries, most of them environmentalists. The Tunisian has come to the source. Holding up a withered branch of coral, he asks what is happening to the beauty of the sea and the single source of his income. "The reefs are dying and we are all going to starve."

A marine biologist suggests parasites, microorganisms sent by a shift in the Mediterranean flow: natural causes, in other words. A Spaniard suspects the dumping of toxic waste; the bay, after all, faces Libya and its vast petrochemical complexes near the sea. An Italian reminds the coral diver of the locust plague that has recently swept Tunisia and the tons of insecticide that have been unleashed into the atmosphere. But the educated speculation is cut short by the interruptions of others with their own nightmares. Mudslides in Thailand caused by maverick loggers, the lightning cancer of the expanding Sahara, the rape and burning of the Amazon rain forest, the aftereffects of the Chernobyl disaster, ozone depletion and the greenhouse effect, the plundering of Antarctica, continued whale hunting on the part of the obstinate Japanese, countless oil spills off the coasts of Norway, California, the Gulf of Mexico, and the Mediterranean. The recent discovery of used syringes and other medical garbage washed ashore on Long Island. The Japanese continue to make islands out of garbage, and they give these *gomi* islands names like Paradise, Sweet Harbor, *New* Sweet Harbor, despite a widespread objection to filling the Pacific with the refuse of Tokyo.

Zane listens to two hours of despair and rage from one speaker after another, and the pounding of a gavel by the conference chairman. Sometime early in the evening the coral diver slips out of the room and, though Zane watches the doors for him, does not return.

From habit, he keeps notes for all the continents. Both the Sudanese and the Algerians have stepped up the forced relocation of nomads although the nomads are the only people who know how to make a living from the Saharan fringe without destroying it. Soviet workers in an experimental semiconductors laboratory have failed to wear masks and now suffer silicon poisoning. Note to Kirk: the Sandinistas have resumed the burning of Mesquite villages to force the Indians inland.

During the break, he shares a corner of the lobby with a man from the American Civil Liberties Union. This isn't his subject, the man admits, but he was in town anyway and figured why not. He is in Paris to drum up international support for a retarded man condemned to die in Texas for the rape and murder of a twenty-two-year-old woman. "He has the mind of a six-year-old and the strength of a man. So who are we executing, an adult or a child?"

Zane is already aware of the case. Kirk has assisted in gathering four thousand French signatures on a letter demanding mercy and common sense from the American chief justices. He hands the man one of his cards and tells him to call and ask for Kirk. "The one with the high blood pressure."

When the man invites him to dinner, Zane says he has another appointment.

Outside, the sky is a smear of yellow on gray. The conference has given him a headache and an overpowering thirst. They all mean well, he considers, all these dismal failures. Their livelihood is to cry wolf when the wolf is ever at the door, but they can slip from righteous to foolish to maudlin with the turn of a phrase. The trading of tragic stories will advance no pawns in the defense of the ecology.

As one of those pawns, Zane is easily defeated. He crosses the street and finds the man he is looking for, a West African agronomist he'd once met who is attending the conference. He is wearing a white polo shirt and tan slacks and carries his *International Herald Tribune* folded open to the sports page.

They recognize each other but do not shake hands. The man passes the newspaper to Zane and stares at him through tinted glasses. "I am advised not to speak with you. I am sorry to hear you are in difficulty."

"Is this common knowledge? I hoped we might share dinner, catch up on old times."

"Unfortunately, yes. Have you been followed? No? I was told that you have to watch your back."

"There's been some exaggeration of the facts."

"No," the man says. "There has not. I would love to have dinner with you, but I am told you are no longer on the mailing list. I am very sorry."

Zane ducks into a brasserie on the rue Bellechasse, orders a beer at the counter, and carries it to a table near the back. It is dinner hour and the place is crowded. The bartender, annoyed that Zane has not ordered a meal, tosses a menu to the middle of the table. Zane pushes it aside and bends to the newspaper. He will have to read every article word for word. On the front page, a tiny red dot follows the letter o buried in an article about impending star-vation in Ethiopia. On page two, a red dot near the k in the word *fallback*. The system is simple enough. Names are found in the news articles, addresses or body counts or phone numbers in the financial pages, and advice in the classified ads. Demi has taught the system to Zane and, apparently, to the embassy secretary. The waiter returns and tells him he has to order food or get out, so he asks for a salad, hard-boiled eggs, cheese, and a whisky with four ice cubes, *merci*. Through a long hour of squinting, Zane gathers a letter from each of the first eight pages and on the back page are a flurry of marks disguised as idle doodling.

Okb, she tells him; her advice is to *bake a cake*.

But in the financial pages, where he has read every letter and figure, every stock quotation, the market diary, the currency rates, the interest rates, NASDAQ, AMEX, and International Funds, she offers no address, no phone number, and no recipe for the cake that will pay the entry fee to Okimbo's good graces.

He scales a high wall from the back street and crosses the narrow alley. With his new key, he unlocks the back door and steps into a dark hallway. It is early and the club is nearly empty. Fingers is playing without accompaniment.

He climbs the stairs and enters his room. His micro is set to *Receive Only* but there are no telecom messages awaiting him. Sitting at his chair, he runs a WHO and finds that only Kirk is still on-line back at ABRI. He switches to a dial-up of the England mainframe and finds that his slice into the operating system has been detected. After trying his ID and password three times, he is kicked out of the system. The nomad routine has failed him.

There are two print messages waiting for him in the paper tray that slips from the laser printer. The most recent, timed at 20:12, is from January, in Durban: TALK OF MANDELA RELEASE = HOG-WASH. AP INK UNFOUNDED. SAVE YOUR BREATH.

The second is an intercept from EMLX and, his gaze attuned to single letters, he finds a pair of them that seem to leap from the page. TZ HIGHJACK CONFIRMED. EVIDENCE OVERWHELMING. INTERPOL RELAY IN PROCESS.

It is signed BB, an acronym that has appeared from time to time in various forms. B or BB or BX. Out of London. The transmission is addressed to Emelle.

There is a disk archive of all transmissions on the mainframe in England. He taps again for access and finds the addresses have been changed. This might be a random event; the numbers are changed at irregular intervals and are issued new codes at ABRI; or it might be in reaction to his intrusions from two nights ago. He tries meaningful dates, initials, key words, but the file remains locked. The file server in the Paris office is empty, the day's backup having already been transferred to the mainframe. If there is an Okimbo file in Emelle's past, it is either on paper in her office or spinning on a disk west of London.

He taps for access to Petitjean's initialed directory and finds the promised routine in a file named ZAN.COM. Snowfall is a program that will set markers at the beginnings and ends of computer transactions. The routine will then erase from the system log every transaction that was made; covering tracks. He admires the work. Petitjean is a smooth technician and the program appears foolproof.

Cutting over to the England mainframe, he requests access to the ABRI archives. At the prompt for ID and password, he keys in the codes that Petitjean has given him. The cursor blinks twice and a second prompt appears: CROSSCODE?

Checking Petitjean's note, he taps in three letters and three digits, and waits. The cursor pulses, but there is no response; he repeats the crosscode but there is still no answer. On his third attempt, the message is: ACCESS DENIED. HANG-UP. A second later his screen goes blank.

A woman answers on the seventh ring and tells him that Petitjean is sleeping. "Est-ce urgent?"

"Dites-lui que c'est Zane."

"*Zane? Donc, c'est toujours urgent.*"

A full minute later Petitjean is cursing into the phone.

"The crosscode. It failed."

"BTC742, Zane. That's what I wrote. And if you—"

"Try it yourself, Petitjean. The system hangs up."

There is a pause. The sound of switching lines, that electronic breathing. "Tomorrow, Zane. We'll get to the bottom of it. Not now. Tomorrow."

"What's happened?"

"Perhaps they know you're trying to get in. They may, may know I'm helping you. They might have found you in the tracer. You're not so clever at these things."

"Call me in the morning. I'll be here."

"You can always try the Trojan Horse."

"The what?"

"*Le cheval de Troyes.* Everybody uses it, it's a shitty world. It's on the same diskette as the snowfall routine."

"What's it do?"

"Read it yourself. One of the oldest tricks in the book." He hangs up.

It is a program that promises access to nonexistent but attractively named files. A gift. These will appear on a menu of file inquiries, and any user who wants to look inside will be asked ID and password; the program will then store these in a separate file. Once the user enters into the program, he will find nothing very interesting and will exit. But in the meantime, Zane will have recorded a usable ID and password with which he can gain access to the ABRI archives as well as any number of useful libraries.

A note from Petitjean in a README file warns him not to run the Trojan Horse for more than an hour or two at a time, to get one or two passwords and then disengage.

It is past eleven and only four users, all of them in England, are on the system. Zane places the program into the root library and attaches it to the main-file inquiry menu with a label EURO-DOSSIER/SEX-PROFILES. Then the waiting begins. Waiting for someone to find this titillating marvel of a gift and to drag it inside the gates of the castle for a closer look. While waiting, he pours himself a whisky and continues to enter the text of Street's letters. By the time he has finished one hundred pages, he is convinced that M'Khlea lied to him. Though these are not love letters, love is expressed. He is both embarrassed and heartbroken to read. Though he has only a third of the letters in the computer, he runs a word-count program and finds that the words most employed in the letters are *love* and *mercy.* There is nothing in the language of love that he can translate to Zanespeak.

But there is evidence: menace and love and roses the color of fresh blood. He wonders now if she is not dead because of what's in those letters. And that he might die because of them as well.

DEAREST M'KHLEA, I HAVE SPENT THE BETTER PART of the day helping the locals rope off the racing routes through town and with the help of an interpreter I lectured several groups of children against crossing that street from the time they can hear the engines in the distance. The latest radio report says the advance caravan will be arriving at noon and the first drivers, the leaders, will follow by twenty-four hours. Even as I write this, the petrol vendors are in an uproar because the word has passed amongst them that a consortium from Bamako is sending advance trucks to the north and setting up makeshift pumps. There will be enough business for all concerned but the rates will have to come down to something resembling market price. I feel their pain. Two years ago, a man with a large enough truck and sturdy barrels could make a year's living in three days selling petrol and motor oil to the racers for five times its value. The same still applies for the sale of fruits and vegetables, a shower rental, beer and whisky, shampoo, and especially ice. When the Paris-Dakar comes to town, it isn't so much a clash of cultures as a feeding frenzy. A three-day whirlwind of dirt-faced Europeans with wrenches and lanterns and foreign currency, at the end of which Gao will be as desolate as always and somehow sadder.

This year, the field is larger than ever and is said to be unman-ageable. There is talk of eliminating the lorry division next year, leaving only the motorbikes and cars. The radio reports a number of injuries and already three deaths. That is why we have been spending so much time with the children this week, in an effort to make them understand the danger. They are like small animals along the English motorway and their mortality seems heightened as the caravan approaches and their eyes grow progressively wider. They look upon the Europeans as supermen with bulging pockets and several of them are intent upon selling candies and water bottles or bits of jewelry they have fashioned from green wood.

I am on my own here. British Medical Co. didn't see fit to underwrite the visit because of recent MUAC readings that put Gao on the yellow list, not in dangerous enough straits to qualify for assistance. I don't remember if I've told you, but MUAC stands for Mid-Upper Arm Circumference and is a "scientific" method we have for measuring how underweight a child is. In times of famine, decisions have to be made quickly, without time for weight-height calculations to determine who is the most malnourished. So we measure the mid-upper arm with our bare hands. It is as unreliable as it is cruel but BMC is short on resources and these methods are devised in rooms far from here. So I am officially on leave until the end of the month. My host, K, has put me up in a back room that looks out on a dry field of stones. Two years ago it was a garden and there are still a few breaks from the irrigation network. The garden failed first for lack of water and then from too much of it. You know the story. As I write this letter, a mangy Alsatian dog is sniffing through that field in search of mice. They often come out at night in search of food and the dog has been running himself ragged trying to catch them.

What is striking, when I stop to think about it, is that there are practically no birds here. Few trees and no food. To the northwest or to the southeast, trailing along the Niger, are birds and more than occasional green. But K's house is up the rise, where the poorer people live. It is safer in the rainy season but a longer trek for water or anything else. Here the night is soundless and I am used to the racket of the central continent. If I listen I can hear only God with his usual vocabulary of silence or wind. I can hear my heartbeat and my breathing. Now and then the dog in the field barks at shadows or a car passes on the road down the rise. Last night the winds were strong and I had to close the window to keep the dust out. All the same I awoke this morning covered in sub-Saharan dust and had to go to the river before breakfast to clear it from my eyelids.

Trees, M'Khlea. The solution to the ills of Gao. The cooling of the earth and the aeration of the soil. Trees as shade, trees as windbreaks, trees as defense against erosion, trees bearing fruit and fuel and the insects that will feed the birds that will feed the game that will feed the villagers. Nowhere that I've been, not even the Sudan, has filled me with such longing for the sight of a long-standing forest. It may just be my English background, nostalgia for that humid isle that housed me for so many years. But I don't miss the lawns or hedges or ivies or mosses. Only the trees. And it could be want of trees that brings me home.

While in Abidjan two weeks ago, I received the blood tests for the Touareg I told you about, the man who's lost his speech. I admit that I couldn't make heads or tails of it. I had to look up a man from the BMC labs for help and his analysis was both vague and alarming. Apparently there were traces of sodium pentathol (the *truth* drug, you remember) as well as Versed, an extremely powerful form of Valium. Large doses of Versed render a patient euphoric and it is frequently used during surgery in which the patient must remain conscious. The combination of sodium pentathol and Versed would make just about anyone feel right at home, singing, humming, or just shooting the bloody breeze. But my friend tells me that there were also a number of inoculations that effectively masked a proper analysis. Alphabet soup, he called it. When I asked about long-term effects, he told me that, after a brief period of relief, the victim would suffer from exhaustion and would, in effect, go mute. Whether or not the condition would be permanent depends upon the length of time the stimulants were administered. Without my asking, he has already sent the remainder of the sample and his own report to London for further tests. He is the first man I have ever found who shared my belief in the existence of this man with the sky eyes. My loneliness is dispersing.

K has been in contact with a number of Touaregs. They are naturally suspicious of him but he was able to locate two other men who have been captured and released. One of them is still quite capable of speech, though his memory is deficient. His blood tests show the same traces of Versed and sodium pentathol but also there were obscene amounts of an antilirium known as lorazepam still in his bloodstream. Lorazepam is mostly used in operations to create a loss of memory in patients who undergo surgery while conscious. It spares patients from traumatic memories of the surgery.

Needless to say, this man also has a circle of tiny scars around his skull. I asked him if he'd worn a hat with spikes and he said yes. With his hands, he traced a halo and then, M'Khlea, he *smiled*. He could also remember having needles in his arm, which may have been the Versed, since that drug is often administered intravenously. It took a week of treatment to counteract the lorazepam and restore, where possible, his memory functions. The effects were almost disastrous. The restoration of his memory was followed by intense shame and self-loathing. For the first time since he'd been released, the man could remember moments during his interrogation in which he gave away information. As for his interrogators, he vaguely recalls a Malien colonel and another man in a uniform he didn't recognise. I waited patiently to ask him the question I wanted answered most. And only when he was becalmed and at ease did I dare ask about the doctor with the sky eyes. He remembers him. He even remembers that the man spoke a language like my own. A white man with round eyeglasses that enlarged his eyes. I asked if he could identify him if he saw him again and he was certain that he could.

My friend in Abidjan has answered my queries about the cranial scars. The size and spacing of those scars allowed him to identify the source as a surgical halo. The X-form is still a cipher but he suspects that these people were given either electrical shocks or chemical injections to trigger memory.

He and the doctor in Abidjan are my first witnesses but there will be others. Touareg raiders north of Gao recently freed a dozen of their own who'd been taken prisoner four months ago. K has gone north to meet them and return within the next few days.

Prior to returning here from Abidjan I was in Bamako in search of your husband. Every scrap of news I've received suggests that he is there. By chance I met up with a reporter from the *Guardian* whom I'd worked with in Ethiopia in 1985. No names, M'Khlea. I will tell you about him when I get to Paris. He was astounded by my questions, certain that your husband was right there, in Bamako, and had been for quite a while. All of the time I have spent along the western coast has been for nothing. He has apparently ceased traveling and has been holed up here for over six months, maybe longer. The lingering hostility between the governments of Mali and Nigeria may be his best defence. With the reporter's help, I tracked down the few local contacts I have and in each case found that your husband had been seen in the area within the past three months. It is rumoured that he was under the protection of the sultan de Sokoto in Nigeria. It is also rumoured that he has just purchased light artillery. The local police are of no help whatsoever. They are difficult to bribe and at any rate I didn't have the funds for a chase into blind alleys. Everyone is currently suffering from rally fever and when the races are ended I will return to Bamako for another look into the black hole. As much as I tell myself not to hope, I can hear the drums in my chest when I lie down at night. He is here and I will be face to face with him. And when that time comes we will have to pray I find the words and the courage to do the deed.

There is always the chance, M'Khlea, that he will insist upon your bondage. He has a history of intolerance and in his current state I do not expect him to be reasonable when it comes to surrendering his vows. There is no court of law he will recognise and I doubt that appealing to his kinder nature will succeed either. I cannot offer him money and through third parties I have been made to understand that his supply of arms is unriven. I am at a loss as to what to offer him in exchange for your freedom and your life. My words, my sincerity, a talisman to protect him from stray bullets. This vow of yours to follow him to death undoes us all and I rage daily at the idea of a wife resigned to follow her husband into the afterlife. He has to call off his dogs. These men who follow you to the metro and to the market and whose eyes are forever on your windows to be certain that you are there. I remember the night you told me about them, when I rose from the bed, undressed, and reached to pull open the shades. That panic in your eyes over what I took for the simplest of gestures. Had I opened those curtains would I have been struck dead? Or would death have come more slowly, as slowly as to a tree in a field outside Gao? When the day comes that we are face to face. His watchdogs must have taken note of me in the past two years. Naked at your window or clothed in your arms. When I leave your building I feel their eyes upon me and I know I am wearing your face on my own.

A letter from Abby caught up with me in Bamako. It was four months old and informed me that my eldest son, Paul, has been accepted at Oxford. Am I that old, M'Khlea? I have not seen a mirror in three days and have to remember my face in order to take inventory. He intends to read medicine, Paul does, and I have written a long and guilt-ridden letter to wish him luck and to promise my help. From me, a medical-school dropout who once measured children's upper arms to determine whether or not they were in danger of death.

It is late in the night and I cannot sleep. The wind has awakened me and my thirst is outrageous. The dog in the field is feeding on something but in the darkness I cannot tell if it is a field mouse or a snake or a bird. The first supply trucks from the rally caravan came rumbling in from Timbuktoo an hour ago and some of the townspeople went out to help set up the tents. It is hard going with all the wind and the dust in the air but already there are half a dozen canvas rooftops across the flats above the rise. Someone has set up a boombox and despite the hour we are being treated to some French rock and roll that only makes the teeth of my headache all the sharper.

There is nothing to drink in this house. If I want water I have to go down the road to the well. Or I can meet up with the rally workers and barter for a bottle to help me sleep. But to do so I would have to be even closer to that music and might have to pretend interest in their ridiculous event. Raging thirst is a minor discomfort compared to such an ordeal.

In the past I have asked you to destroy my letters and out of misplaced sentiment you have refused. This time I ask that you save this letter and keep it well hidden in case anything should happen to me. The Touareg is named Katango and he is being watched over by K, whose name you already know. In Abidjan, Dr. Philippe Renault has his blood tests under lock and key. I will be using Z as a conduit toward Interpol or whoever he feels we can trust. I am counting on Z believing that I am not a lunatic. Light water, he asked. That I see this man with my own eyes. Katango can lead me to him. In Bamako, where he has been performing his wretched work.

So I am sealing this letter, half in the hopes that in doing so I will cease to think of words for either you or your husband or this man with the sky eyes and that these conversations I am having with the night will end at once. By mid-morning the dirt roads around Gao will be treacherous and I will be wearing a white arm band that will identify me to the children as a guardian angel. Picture that, M'Khlea, when you see those men in the street before your door. And by the time this reaches you the winds will have died down and the roads may be clear. Another night in the insomnia of Africa. And love for you in every sleepless moment.

By ELEVEN-THIRTY THERE HAVE BEEN TWO USERS WHO have logged into the Trojan horse. Zane retrieves the file that has copied their IDs and passwords, destroys the Trojan horse and the output file, and logs on using the first of his new IDs.

ID: JAMES
PASSWORD: SEMAJ

Within fifteen minutes he has displayed and printed the entire list of archive files. Although ABRI staff is required to follow a standard file-naming procedure, few of the file names listed can be easily interpreted. The convention requires an alpha initial by staff member—Z for Zane, P for Petitjean—followed by a two-digit numeric for country and five digits for file identification. When the file concerns something other than a country, it is supposed to be tagged as 00. There are nearly six thousand files in the root directory of the archive, a rat's nest that would take weeks to sort out. But beneath the root are dozens of subdirectories, and to obtain a map Zane runs a TREE routine that will show the root and all of the branch and subbranch names and obtains a chart on his screen. The chart overflows the screen, so he requests a print and then traces down the branches. When you run into a messy files tree, usually there are only two possible reasons: either the users are slovenly or they are purposefully hiding information. Throughout her career, Emelle has been guilty of both. After nearly an hour, Zane has begun to probe the subbranch directories and there are two that attract his eye: ML and BB, both filed under a main branch named SEC. The files in these directories, altogether four levels down, include a series L0001 through L0321 and another series B0001 through B0017. L is Emelle's system designate. B is an unknown.

He is in the midst of dumping these files across to his own hard disk when suddenly his screen shows an interrupt: WHO ARE YOU? An operator has discovered his entry and has tabbed him across the wires.

He types JUST JAMES HERE.

A few seconds later, the letters come across his screen. I AM JAMES. GOODBYE.

And his screen goes blank.

He works quickly, entering the second ID and password that he has stolen with the Trojan Horse. James, obviously the system manager, will have full network capacity, tracers, barbed wire, ice. Before he can be slapped a second time, Zane goes straight through the ABRI archives into the subdirectory AOU and dumps any file that includes the letters AO in the file name. The system responds that there are forty-six such files and when thirty-one of them have been successfully transmitted, James is back.

WHO ARE YOU?

Zane decides not to respond, hoping that James will simply go away. And ten seconds later, his screen again goes blank.

He spends fifteen minutes trying to break into the system all over again, but the IDs and passwords are no longer valid. Using the reliable back door into the operating system, he considers using the Trojan Horse to fetch the remaining files, but decides to first take a look at those that he has successfully copied.

His name is on nearly every one of them. In the files beginning with B, he is TZ. In the files beginning with L, he is Thomas. In all of the B files is an ongoing fiction of T. Zane's secret collaboration with various organizations, none of them on the ABRI white list. His name is associated with bared and sharpened teeth. Eleven, Demi, Mozart, January, Snake Eyes, Postcard, all a part of his profane network. The sender of these transmissions pretends to possess a key to the language and has twisted it into a new vocabulary, one that reads like a shopping list for murder weapons.

Emelle, the high priestess, has given him a thumbs-down. Next thing he knows the witch hunters will be gathering kindling.

IT WAS HIS MOTHER'S HABIT TO MOVE AND KEEP MOV-
ing. A trailer park near Racine, Wisconsin, a South Dakota farm-
house, apartments in Chicago, Duluth, Denver, and Sioux Falls.
He remembers sleeping on the back seats of many cars or on many
strangers' sofas. One winter he had a cot in a kitchen with green
linoleum and the oven left open so he wouldn't freeze.

She took full responsibility for his education and he was tutored
by her friends, whom he only knew as monosyllabic AKAs: John,
Jim, Joe, Jack. One summer he called a man David and the following
winter he addressed the same man as Darren. Tom was a civilian,
they told him, and as such was safe. The less one knows . . .

Besides teaching him English, mathematics, French, and her
own homemade version of American history, she occasionally
passed on aspects of stagecraft. He resisted these lessons but she
was adamant. While she didn't seem to care if he ever joined her
cause or approved of her actions, she did want him to know how
to proceed should he come late to the revolution.

Among other things, she was good with knots. Slip knots,
square knots, bows, and what she called forevers. One morning
when he was twelve he watched her cut a dozen strings of twine
to equal size. The twine was black and thin, almost like wire.
Then she took out the red and gold sticks and grouped them, one
gold to four red, and began to wrap them in that twine.

"You might not follow me, Tom. I sometimes talk over your
head and I don't mean to. Do you understand what this is?"

Tom nodded. He was watching his mother's hands, the way she gripped the twine between her forefinger and ringfinger and only used her thumb for the looping.

"Say the word, then."

"Dynamite."

"That's the old-time word for it. Now we just say explosive. These gold ones are incendiaries. They make fire. The red ones mostly make noise, impact. If all you want is noise and rubble, stick to the red. If it's burning you want, take gold."

Tom nodded again and saw that his mother was tying forevers.

"Sometimes," his mother said, "you have to do things you can't count on working out." She continued knotting for a moment, as though she'd forgotten he was even there. Four bundles were finished, and she was starting on a fifth. "These explosives," she said. "They're like fireworks, really. Meant to get someone's attention."

"Whose?"

She finished a knot and reached for the spool of twine. Then she couldn't find the scissors and Tom had to pass them to her.

"You're too young to know them. Men with faces you just can't read. White men who fuck things up for the red and the black and the yellow."

"Indians," Tom said. "And Negroes and Chinese."

His mother was silent for another few minutes while her fingers twisted the fuses into braids. "This is something I feel I have to do. Can you understand that?"

"No. I don't."

"These are spark charges," his mother said, "with powdered iron like in the Westerns. Light this end and you've got two seconds per inch. This one here"—she held forth a wound knot—"measures out to nine and a half minutes."

Tom wanted to ask her where she would be for those nine and a half minutes. Where they all would be, his mother and the others and himself. His mother asked him for the pliers, and though his hand closed around them, he didn't feel like passing them over.

"Tom, the *pliers.*" His mother twisted the end of the five fuses into a tight ball and then packed the charges carefully into a wooden box that was lined with aluminum. "When this is over we'll head up to Canada. In the winter we'll stay in a cabin with a fireplace. Go ice fishing, I don't know. Mother-and-son stuff."

When Tom didn't react, his mother's eyes welled up with tears. This was the last thing Tom wanted to see, but it went on for a long time. Then her arms reached out and she was squeezing the breath out of him. "If we're afraid," she said, releasing him but clinging to his wrists, "fear is the fuel of tyranny."

"Someone else said that. Not you."

His mother was calmer but the tears were still rolling down her cheeks. Tom thought of wiping them away but kept his hands to himself. "Sometimes," she said, "all you know is how to begin. It's up to luck how it all works out."

"Luck doesn't go with dynamite," he told her. "Or explosives either."

She held him at arm's length and stared into his eyes. "Maybe you're right, Tom. Maybe we've outgrown luck and taken this all too far."

Tom thought he'd scored a point but already his mother had returned to work.

While he still lived in America, Thomas Zane drove once each month south of Minneapolis to visit his mother. The glass that separated their faces held the mist of her breathing. When she spoke to him, he heard metal in her voice. Her hair was seldom brushed and she almost never looked him in the eye. She had written a book that no one would publish; he had been too embarrassed to read more than the first ten pages. Power to the people. There was no longer a calendar and she clung to her ideology, there within those gray walls, as though in self-protection. She had a succession of lawyers and one of them had urged him to use the book as evidence of her insanity, so that she could be moved from the prison to a psychiatric ward. But the book was all she had, the written word of an American saint and martyr. To use it against her would amount to betrayal.

.   .   .

In the visiting room, his mother would always ask him for a cigarette. She would carefully sift out the tobacco, tear away the filter, and with a fingernail she would slice the paper tube until she had a small white sheet in front of her. The paper, he knew. The lawyer had already told Zane that he'd been receiving letters from her written on scrap paper, toilet paper, the white backs of soup-can labels. She was convinced that the paper supplied to her by the prison would not hold ink, that the words she wrote on it would disappear. It wasn't until he'd read Kirk's file that he knew she was telling the truth. For months at a time, she had been denied pen and paper as well as reading material. At the time he said that her vision of America was laced with menace that he couldn't see; in answer to her reply that he was myopic, he told her at least he wasn't locked up. She couldn't slap his face through the visitor's window. Or she would have.

The year before he left, she hired a new lawyer, a young woman who mistook his quietness for indifference. She made him face it again, which both attracted and repelled him. To look into the mirror and remember that he has his mother's long chin and her mournful eyes. The blood habit of doing himself harm.

"Why haven't you tried to clear her name?"

"What for?"

"Insist on a retrial. The war is over now. People are being given amnesty."

"There is no amnesty. She was guilty."

"Of what?"

"Of a lack of patience, a lack of imagination. Of arrogance. Child neglect. Murder."

"Do you really believe that?"

"With all my heart."

His last winter in America came early and spoke itself in high winds and record cold. A woman on the radio announced the time, the temperature, the wind-chill factor, and an estimate of how many minutes you could stay outdoors before delirium would set in. That is the danger: mistaking comfort for warmth. When, as if you are sleepwalking, you no longer feel the cold and could walk forever. But when this happens to you, when that delirium sets in, you must be dying, the woman says on the radio.

"You have no memory," the lawyer said to him as she stood naked at the foot of his bed. "Forgetting comes easily to you. That's why you cling to that boring job of yours and let your education fall through the holes in your heart. Pretty soon, your whole life will be one big eraser mark."

When he didn't reply, she took him in her hand and began to stroke him. "You will remember nothing of me in years to come. Not even what we're about to do with each other."

The Chinese box of his past had been scratched, sniffed, rubbed, cracked, and clawed, but never pierced. And she was wrong. He remembered her urgency and her excitement, the way she put the boot to his heart to kick-start him, to revive him, to bleed him. And she was right. He could replay the coupling, could envision the twisting and turning and shortness of breath. He could remember the look of her above him in the watery darkness just before dawn. The smell of wood smoke from the last of the fire. But the sex itself, the sex itself was something he had entirely and eternally forgotten.

He watched his mother through the glass. He asked her to look at him but she refused.

"I am going away," he told her.

"You will come back."

"From America," he said. "I am leaving the country."

"You will come back."

"I'm not like you."

"No," she said. And then she looked straight at him for the first time in many months. "No, you are a citizen. You sleep and eat. Eat and sleep. You write letters to the editor and you watch the evening news without seeing yourself in the pictures. You could never do the things I've done."

"I would never want to, not the things you've done."

"What *do* you want?"

"I'm looking for a job," he said. "Something I can do that might be useful."

"Why not help me escape? Your own mother and you've never even offered."

"Where would we go?"

"Canada! Then to Sweden. I've already thought this through. I have friends in Stockholm, people who are engaged in the struggle."

"I was thinking about France." He meant to surprise her and surprised, instead, himself.

"You don't know the language," she reminded him. "I only taught you a few words."

"I'll manage. I'll learn."

"What about your girlfriend?"

"I'm going alone."

"Good. I don't want to be a grandmother to your children."

He took Icelandair from Chicago to Luxembourg and the first train to the Gare de l'Est. His ticket—round trip with an open return— was a waste of money. From the beginning, he sensed he would never go back.

During his first week in Paris, very early in the morning, he crossed the Seine to go into Notre-Dame. He was surprised to find no one else there and that he was alone with a very old God. He sat in a pew, breathing in the damp air of centuries, and re- membered there were tombs in every corner, bishops turned to dust under his feet and dukes gone to potash. And he considered that it took more than four hundred years to build this place, generations of families cutting and placing the stones according to a plan written in goat's blood on sheepskin. That the glass was cut and stained and laid into mosaic to catch the light of a watch- ing God. Expectant, Stern, Loving, Forgiving. Though he had only come in to escape the rain, keeping dry is a form of prayer, and he was surrounded by flickering candles lit for the poor and the infirm. Lit for him, he knew, by people he would never meet. But then he heard a murmuring off to one side. Sitting up in the pew, he adjusted his gaze to the oily light and could see an old lady kneeling before a statue of the Blessed Virgin. Her fingers wore the stones of a rosary to sand.

When he stepped outside, the rain had ended and the sunlight was a shock to him. He closed his eyes and drew back to himself

his heartbreak—of being unmarried, childless, a foreigner, a fail-
ure, and still wet with rain and a vapor of misery that the light
of those candles could not disperse. The only act of love that his
mother would believe in was the lighting of a fuse or the loading
of a gun. With me or against me. *Venceremos.*

But when he reopened his eyes there was the Seine. The Seine
and the *parvis*, the ivy and the equestrian statue of Charlemagne.
To his right was a man selling African trinkets of brass and ivory
and to his left schoolchildren were being led like chicks to the
bridge. The rain had ended and he was standing in the postcard
that was taped to the wall over his desk back home.

It was April and he had written ahead to half a dozen agencies.
Paris was full of these halfway houses, Third World aid organizations, societies for the prevention of whatever needed preventing.
His résumé, which proved he knew nothing, was distinguished
only by the measured earnestness of his cover letter. The larger
agencies—Amnesty International, Europe Watch, and the Bureau
des Droits Humains—had answered with polite photocopied re-
fusals but Emelle had realized who he was and this seemed to
make a difference. ABRI was a place that harbored misfit em-
ployees and asked them to sign their names on that dotted line.
She told him she believed he had the makings of a signee. He
filled out the forms, including an oath of fidelity to the agency
principles. He was fingerprinted, photographed, and given reams
of background documentation to study.

On his first day at work, Emelle solemnly provided him a copy
of "the book" and told him to commit it to memory.

1. Shed light. 2. Take no sides. 3. Express no opinions. 4. Avoid
compromise.

These four chapters were followed by a last chapter giving pro-
cedural guidelines for memos, press releases, and, to Zane's surprise, phone courtesy.

In his first position, as trainee/office boy, he was asked to gather
news clippings, file and cross-reference telexes and correspondence, and to type whatever was placed in his In box within three
hours. For years now in America, being a cog in the wheel had

been his most comfortable role. But he had not come to Paris to fulfill menial tasks. Kirk showed him the file on his mother, and a fuse was lit that would burn its way to his heart. Paper and pen. Indelible ink. After three months he complained to Emelle of boredom. She said she had expected as much, and after keeping him in the dark for another week, she relented. Given a screen and telecom line, he would help her monitor events in Eastern Europe.

The first meaningful news he received was of a midnight arrest in Poland. The message had a tag to it—TML, "to Emelle"—and she instructed Zane to search for a kicker.

"A what?"

"Confirmation. A second opinion. Without a second source, we could get burned. Disinformation, Thomas."

He called the Polish embassy and received his first official "no comment." Then he tapped into his European telephone directory, requested access to Varsovie/Warsaw and was surprised to find a phone number for the man who'd been arrested. He dialed the number and a woman answered on the third ring. She did not speak English and passed the phone to a friend. After three minutes of broken English, he had his kicker.

"From whom?" Emelle demanded.

"His wife."

He passed his news on to the Western press. The next day there was an article on page three of Le Monde and he remembered how his mother had once used him as an antenna. But now he was gathering messages from a frequency of shelter and of mercy. He compiled files on Ceauşescu, Honecker, Hodja, and a dozen other tyrants and began to write a monthly column in the ABRI newsletter. Versions of his mother appeared on the screens, in the Red Brigade, in Action Directe, in the Irish Republican Army. In Europe, he learned, violence is political. In America it was only too personal. He worked overtime and soon began to take to the mattress.

In his second year, Emelle asked him to wear a tie and to represent ABRI at various human-rights conferences. He suffered empty evenings in hotel rooms in the Northern cities, Copenhagen, Hamburg, Amsterdam, Helsinki, and London. Long nights with a paperback, a bottle, and a television show in Italian with Swedish subtitles. At the conferences, he listened to English spoken by people for whom it was a second or third or fourth language. So that he would be understood, he learned to speak more slowly and to use fewer words. His Midwestern accent was hammered into an international hum on the anvil of necessity. An Englishman told him he spoke quite well for an American.

Though he asked her more than once, Emelle refused to let him cross over to the other side of the barbed wire. She already had three of her observers on the payroll, men who were capable of watching firing squads and beatings and arrests without intervening. She told Zane that he was lacking the proper profile. His blood ran too hot, for one thing. "You don't have the bland look, the smell, the demeanor," Emelle said, "of a common and harmless civilian."

His passport grew black with entry and exit stamps and he stared at his face in the mirror, in search of evidence. The countries he preferred to visit were along the Mediterranean and Adriatic. Greece, Spain, Italy, Yugoslavia, even Lebanon. His mother's grandmother was from somewhere touching the Mediterranean; that is all his mother could remember and therefore all that he knew. His great-grandmother was a dark-skinned woman who didn't give out autobiography, but who spoke English with a thick accent. If he were to hear that accent today, perhaps he could place her origins. If his mother could mimic that accent he would recognize it. He has been gone for years and now knows the thousand versions of the same tongue.

EMELLE HAS BEEN LIVING AT THE PLACE VICTOR HUGO for thirty years. The place is swamped with photos of an English family, nephews and cousins and grandchildren she never sees. He has visited here before, in better times, for dinner and brandy and long talks deep into the night. When she loved his soul. He knows the layout of her rooms, the kitchen, the salon, her office. Five rooms for one woman whose past seems to embrace all of the middle half of the century. He has never seen her bedroom and has often wondered who has.

Third floor up. He avoids the elevator. It is past midnight and she might well be in, though he has dialed her number from a nearby pay phone and let it ring twelve times to assure himself that she isn't.

The door is ancient and there are two locks. One, an old skeleton lock, slips easily out of place with a bent nail. He heats a strip of copper with his lighter, slides it into the modern bolt lock, and turns it with his wrist. When he retrieves the strip he notes the dent marks where the teeth of the lock have held and he cuts away these pieces with a pair of scissors. Petitjean taught him everything months ago. Showing off his skills. It takes three tries until the copper strip, now fashioned into a crude key, un-snaps the lock.

The front hallway is dark, but the salon is lit from the street outside. The luminous face of a clock reads 12:17 and he considers himself an idiot for having come so late. There is a small table next to the door, upon which is a pair of leather gloves. The sight of those gloves gives him a start, as though he has seen her outstretched hands.

He steps into the salon and slides past the sofa and coffee table. The room is as always filled with magazines and newspapers. She seldom throws anything away. He opens a *National Geographic* and finds penned notations in the margins of an article about ozone depletion. Pages have been torn from a *Paris Match* that is eight months old, a series of color photos of the Paris-Dakar road rally that ABRI is always so ambivalent about: rich adventurers riding the waves of dust through the waste of sub-Saharan Africa, a weird kind of tourism. Zane is surprised to find an ashtray filled with butts on the coffee table. Emelle is definitely a nonsmoker, so she has had a visitor earlier, tonight or yesterday.

A pair of floor-to-ceiling windows give onto the Place Victor Hugo, where a simple fountain is floodlit and the water is white. The city is empty and hot and there is no one on the street except for a lone taxi parked at the stand, the driver dozing at the wheel.

Two wide doors lead from the salon to the study. The curtains are closed and the room is black. He walks slowly with his hands in front of him until he bumps against the desk, then waves his hands in slow semicircles until his fingers brush the lamp. The light is yellow from a bulb of low wattage. She has sensitive eyes and is often seen bathing them after the pain of contact lenses.

He begins with the desk, atop which are her notebooks, spiral pads with page after page of random notes and scrawls, phone numbers, dates, addresses. Circled comments and endless exclamation marks, as though the words could be spoken as well as read. There are a half-dozen of these notebooks and he finds nothing of Eleven or Bamako or Okimbo. The bookshelves are overstuffed and covered with a layer of dust. Photographs of people he's never seen are placed willy-nilly among gaps in the shelves. On a lower level is a dusty collection of records: Cole Porter, Judy Garland, Nat King Cole, George Gershwin, a boxed set of Mahler, Chopin, Stravinsky. There is no record player in sight.

Her library is dominated by modern history, politics, and economics, has a few novels and little poetry or drama; the only art book is a catalogue of a Matisse exhibit from 1973. On one of the shelves, at eye level, is a black-and-white photograph of her dead husband, Peter. He is wearing khaki shorts and a short-sleeved shirt; with one hand shielding his eyes, he stares into an unidentifiable distance. She married him when he was forty-five and she was twenty. He has been dead for more than twenty-five years and she has never remarried. "There isn't time," she once told Zane. "For companionship, there are nights. That has to suffice. I can't imagine waking to a man who has claims on my *hours* or who calls me to ask what time I'll be home. It's the mercenary in me that always wins out. Besides, I was already married once. Why should events have to repeat themselves?"

There is no terminal and no telefax. The telephone has a single line without an answering machine. He rummages through the side drawers of her desk but finds only pens and paperclips, phone and rent receipts, telephone directories, and torn envelopes with notes scribbled on the backs. One of the notes catches his eye: *Deliver, deliver, deliver. We'll make a run of it up the steep and stony hill.* If it is a quote, it is unattributed. Zane takes the envelope and folds it into his breast pocket, turns off the light, and abandons the study.

It is difficult to enter her bedroom. The door is wide open but there is a barrier of the heart that makes him hesitate. When she loved his soul. When the word was on the tip of his tongue. When she took the pen from his hand and rewrote the angry message he was sending to himself. The large bed is unmade and the chair next to it is covered with laundry. He switches on a lamp and finds that the pillow is smeared with make-up and smells of her perfume. On the nightstand is an alarm clock, an empty wine glass, a pencil, a bottle of eyewash, and a notepad with the top page blank. Taking the pencil, he lightly scribbles over that page, but this grade-school trick reveals nothing. All the same, he slips the paper into his pocket and moves away from the bed.

On the wall facing the bed is an armoire. Inside are her dresses and skirts and coats, all of which he has seen over the years. There is a white silk nightdress to one side that has the appear-

ance of never having been worn. The sight of it fills him with
shame and he closes the door, takes a few deep breaths, and
plunges into the chest of drawers.

In the third of six drawers, he finds what he is looking for.
Tapes, photographs, maps, letters. Files on every ABRI employee,
each of them marked *Confidence* in Emelle's hand. Like medical
checkups, there is a separate report for each of them for each year
of service. Three years ago, Kirk's unwitting friendship with a
CIA operative nearly cost him his job. Nguyen, Nadine, Raymond
Li, Petitjean, even the young secretary from England . . . all of
them have been shadowed at one time or another. The files include names and addresses of known acquaintances, profiles on
living habits (drinking, drugs, speculation of romantic linkings),
financial positions, family profiles (political leanings, parental
illnesses, background of siblings), and typewritten comments. In
attachment to the reports are photographs, bank statements, and
a surprising number of photocopied letters of a personal nature.
The conclusion of each report is a security rating, scored from
one to ten. In recent reports, the ratings vary from Raymond Li's
9.5 to Petitjean's 6.0. Emelle's three roaming observers are given
9.0. Zane has a zero.

There are four files that bear his initials, only one of which
contains the routine annual reports. In the other three he finds
the work of the intruder, including prints from the files that he
discovered at the bottom of the ABRI archives. The remainder of
the files provide supporting evidence: telexes that he, Zane, never
sent but which bear his ID at the bottom, photocopies of canceled
checks written out to T. Zane, a concocted Crédit Suisse statement, photos of himself on the street with passing strangers
meaningfully circled in red. The list of personal acquaintances
is tragically short. The only name that appears is N. Ribeiro, his
concierge. The bullets of accusation are fired on every falsified
page; death by documentation. One of the telefaxes even shows a
photo of Zane crouching over a case of rifles.

He can barely recognize himself, then realizes this is an old
picture of his mother. It ran in a number of magazines nearly
twenty years ago, and here has been doctored so his own face
appears in her place.

He can smell her perfume before he hears her voice. That mix of lavender and rose.

"One drawer to the right and you will find my underwear and a collection of brassieres, size 36D. In the drawer below, underneath the sweaters, is a bundle of love letters from a man whose face I've never seen. He hasn't written in over five months. Do you suppose he's forgotten about me?"

He stands and holds the dossier out to her. "If half of this is true," he tells her, "I should be behind bars by now."

She looks at the pages and then at Zane. "So you found it. That doesn't mean you know what it is." She unwraps the scarf from around her neck. The flesh below is pale and her breathing is heavy.

"We've been sold down the river, Emelle. Both of us in the same leaky canoe."

She approaches him and her nearness is unsettling, as though it is her underwear that he is holding to his chest and not the pages. She takes the papers from his hands and puts them back in the drawer. "It is normal to keep a watch on security. You know this as well as I do. I was lax when it came to Bartholomew, I admit. Stars in my eyes, perhaps. I had the illusion that we were joining the international circle. And when at first you exposed him, I couldn't trust you. How could I? You had your Demi and your Mozart and your Eleven. All of your code words and your nasty little secrets."

"And he's come back, Bartholomew. Or another sleazy version of him. He goes by the initial B. Sometimes BB or BX."

"My agent," she says. "Someone I can trust. Among other things, he has been observing you for six months."

"His files are creative but they are also science fiction. If you knew anything about the telecom lines, you'd see it clearly."

"You have betrayed ABRI, Thomas. You have betrayed all of us with these actions of yours."

"There has been no action. This is nothing but an elaborate electronic setup."

She moves away from him, to the side of the unmade bed, and seems to examine it for signs of his snooping. Abruptly she says, "Have you found him?"

For a moment he's uncertain: Okimbo or Eleven?

"No," he answers.

"I wanted to help you," she says. "In times past you would've had the run of the agency, no stone unturned, all that. But you have continually broken the most important of all of our rules. You have taken matters into your own hands."

"I could teach you the language," he says. "Provide you with the glossary. You could understand what's fiction and what's the truth."

"Early on I had my doubts about the transmissions. Stars, juice, Molly's soliloquy. References everywhere to alcohol abuse. I even doubted the telefaxes, though I had the originals traced to your dot matrix printer and they are genuine. One of the pins in your printer was purposely broken. You were right about Bartholomew, I grant you. But ever since you exposed him you've been emulating him. And anyone who does not use this code of yours is your enemy—our own people, ABRI, even me."

"That photograph of me with the guns. Have you ever seen a negative?"

"The most damning of all. Arms for money."

"It was in *Newsweek*," he tells her. "My mother had that picture taken by a friend named Jack in July of 1968 with a cheap Polaroid. Her lawyer sold it two years later for five hundred dollars. Take a closer look at those rifles and you'll find that they're as old as ABRI and those trees in the background are northern-Minnesota pine."

He notices that her face has lost its color. She is transparent. She turns and strides from the room. He follows her to the study, where she lifts the receiver and dials nine. The police. Calmly she repeats her address, saying there is a burglar. Then she sets down the receiver. "The commissariat is six streets from here. If you hurry, you might get away."

She follows him through the salon to the front door. Before leaving, he turns to face her.

"You've confused me with my mother."

"I know the story, Thomas. I have seen it played out more than you know. From dedication to impatience. It isn't enough to be a witness after a while. It happened to your mother, it happened to Okimbo, and now you. We all want to kill the wolves to save the sheep. Isn't that what you've been up to, you and your dirty little group?''

He has no way to answer her. He would have to teach her the language and there isn't time.

"Now run," she tells him, "before they come to hunt you down."

THE SCENT OF GASOLINE AND OF ETHER. A THROBBING at his temples that may or not be the white bloom of a migraine. He finishes his sour glass and holds the empty in his hand like a torch gone out. Plumes of smoke encircle him and he leans his head against the cool stone of the basement wall. The music comes in through his pores and settles into the wet wood of his brain.

When he opens his eyes, he finds the woman adjusting his tie. She is still wearing her cotton dress and though the hour is late the club is full, drinks half price and all five musicians working through the night. Over Marie's shoulder he can see the top of Fingers' bald black head as he bends to the keys.

Marie reminds him that he should be upstairs. He could be spotted. She takes the empty glass from his hand and asks him if he can walk.

"Through hell and high water," he says. "Wild horses."

"You have drink too much. Again. Go upstairs."

She has a face with words in it. Something there to be read and more evident than one of Demi's coded newspapers. Christ, she's married now. He's come to her too late and has drunk too much to see properly. He sees two of her, herself and her other self.

The eyes, he tells himself. Concentrate on the eyes and forget the botched features. There is hope in those eyes. Or love. Or fear. Or all three.

WHITE
MARRIAGES

SHE HAS DONE HER DRAWING ON THE BACKS OF ABRI letterhead, wastepaper that he brings home to her for just that purpose. Catherine's art. She draws what she sees, not what she can imagine. A bed, a sofa, a lamp on a table. Flowers growing pale in a white vase. Before dinner, she shows him her work. The first drawing she hands him is her hundredth version of the rail lines, crisscrossings of track, her recurring motif. This one is unique. The detail is unexpected, the patient, fine lines in multicolored pen, the shading and the surprise of perspective. In this version, the tracks are curved and colored, like rainbows leading from nowhere to somewhere. Whatever she sees when she looks left to right out the window of her room.

It is three nights since he began sleeping in his own room. Last night, for the first time, Sylvie didn't come to tap on the door. As though she has understood that it would be like the first few nights, Petitjean out there, in the lonesome free cold of his own space, unanswering. She isn't speaking to him but neither has he seen her weeping; she spends more time than ever away from the apartment, leaving the two of them to fend for themselves. This is the calm he has been waiting for and he is still here, though he has expected at any time to be cast out, exiled, cursed. No one is saying what rent he shall heretofore have to pay.

After a day of working with one eye on Emelle's glass office, he has come home early, leaving Eastern Europe to run its course without him. The routine of ABRI has altered in Zane's absence and it seems that the phone rings less often and there are fewer bursts of incoming telexes. He reminds himself that it is still late August and that Europe is under a tent of hot cloud. The warmth and airlessness of the office makes everyone surly and no one's drinking coffee but Kirk. Early in the morning, he saw Kirk rummaging through his desk drawers and then stride directly to Emelle's office. Their conversation was a cipher. Kirk's back was to Emelle and Petitjean couldn't read her lips. She saw him watching, though, and her eyes bored into him. Zane's files, he knows. And Emelle is aware that Petitjean is the one man at ABRI who can pick locks. His fingers themselves are like skeleton keys.

At home he has knots of his own to unravel. It was eight in the evening when he understood that Sylvie wouldn't be there. Catherine has made his dinner and he cannot complain. She has a way with water and vegetables, steamed carrots and boiled fish. The flavor is gone but, given her presence, the food is delicious. A touch of salt and pepper and a squeezed lemon; Catherine and he alone in the kitchen. Her eyes travel the length of the tablecloth and rest on his folded hands. Once the dinner is finished, he crosses his knife and fork across the plate. Visibly pleased, Catherine rises to pour coffee and then reaches into the cupboard for the cognac he keeps there. The snifter is cracked at the lip and she pours too much, enough to put him to sleep. When he laughs she looks wounded, but all the same he pours half of the glass back into the bottle and replaces the cork. Not fifty words have passed between them in two evenings. He tells her that dinner was wonderful but she doesn't hear him so he has to say it again.

"The dinner was lovely. Very good."

"Yes," she says. "Fish. Turbot."

He drinks the cognac and leaves the coffee to cool, then lights a cigarette and smokes it as though it were a cigar, which makes Catherine smile. Making Catherine smile, he thinks, is an ambition more pressing than the salvation of distant Poland.

They rise and together wash the dishes. Elbow to elbow, they dry and put them carefully away, plate to plate and fork to fork. Then, for a long time, they stand in the yellow kitchen light and just look at each other. She is not an idiot. She knows that she has taken her mother's place. Her mother is gone and only Catherine is with Petitjean, with Alain. Him.

He suggests that they go for a walk and her first reaction is terror. "Just up and down the street," he explains. "Take some air."

He knows that she has warmed to the idea when she insists on returning to her room to put on her lipstick. It is a female trick she mastered long ago, coloring her lips just so, with a shade of red that makes it look as though she's just bitten her lower lip; a swelling and a blush. He is always surprised at what women do to be more of what they already are.

She holds the door so that he might pass and they descend the stairs to the sidewalk. It is nine in the evening and the only places that are open are the corner brasserie with its Kronenbourg awning and amber light and the épicerie run by the Moroccan couple, who almost never close up.

They walk to the corner and she steers him leftward, back toward the cul de sac that ends at a high fence overlooking the rail yard. The last trains are pulling out, crossing from left to right, moving in the direction of Clichy and Saint-Ouen. Catherine links her arm in his and they stand there for a long time, looking at exactly what she can see from her bedroom window or from the window of the living room. The difference is that there is no glass, only the bars of the fence. The difference is that her arm is linked in his and her breast is touching his elbow. He grows hard inside of his pants and is surprised that it doesn't make a racket, that she doesn't hear the pandemonium of his blood and his heart. But she is watching the trains like waves coming one after another. There is a flickering in her eyes. Her lids close and open. "I want to know," she says, "a word."

"What word?"

"To say to you."

When his next breath comes it is a drug, the hot night air, the cognac running with his blood like silk. The speaking stones are in his pocket. He is trying to think of the word to give her when her arm lifts upward and she turns into his embrace, encircled, small, turbulent. The ropes around his chest burst loose and he is saying her name as if it were a verb of wanting, to want, to have wanted.

When he was young his father beat him and through life he has carried the impression that his skin is harder than others', more elastic and insensate, as though his flesh would resist a blade. His father was a workman in a shoe factory and had lost a hand in Algeria. He would hold Petitjean down with his good hand and strike him across the face and head with his stump; it was like a wooden club or a hammer. Petitjean still doesn't know why his father beat him, though there were explanations for paternal cruelty in countless books or on the smug lips of the prison psychologist. Petitjean consoles himself with the belief that his father's cruelty was disinterested, that it wasn't specifically *Alain* he was bludgeoning. Were he a butterfly, his father might have torn away his wings. He assumes that as a child he was a burden, an open mouth, a wailing noise in the night smelling of piss and shit. Petitjean's father drank and struggled with himself, with his poverty and the missing hand. He never said how he lost that hand and Petitjean has always imagined a battle in the desert, an explosion, his father shrieking to God, the severed hand like a crab in the dust.

His father also beat his mother, though she had the wit to die when he was seven and thus escape further beatings. Petitjean forgave her instantly and made a vow to follow her. When he was ten he spent every waking moment intent on dying, a cool ride down the river or a walk in the park with his mother waiting on the other side. When his father, in a rage, broke his ribs, Petitjean missed two months of school. Not because of the pain but because of the humiliation. He learned that to go to school was to put himself into the light, where they could stare at his bruises, gawk at his scuffed shoes and mismatched socks and the tattered pants, and know too well how unloved he was. This much he understood from their bowed heads or averted eyes. So he learned to teach himself, to read the newspapers he found in the trash and the magazines with women in them that his father brought home. When he learned something, that was love enough. Loving himself and what was in his thoughts. They didn't have a television or a radio. His mother had left behind a few books and he read one word after another, strung like pearls from the speaking stones into long sentences that he wrapped around his throat and repeated aloud. When he was alone. If not alone, he was mute. And the words he learned were soundless. No one ever spoke them to him, and through life he has mispronounced many words and is sometimes taken for a fool.

When he was fifteen he fought back. When that handless arm came down over his head he caught it and held it in his fist. His father's lack of surprise was his undoing. His mouth opened into something like a smile, a wet red flower. There was smoke in his gray eyes. While Petitjean beat him he hardly resisted, almost as if he expected his son to kill him and had been waiting for years. Petitjean left him moaning into the rug and took all of his money to the train station. The first train was heading south and he sat in the second-class smoking car and calmly counted the fields, kilometer after kilometer, until night fell. It was the first time he had ever been on a train. The blue earth moved from right to left and the stars and moon stood still.

His work was picking grapes in a vineyard north of Nîmes. That first week there were thirty of them in the fields and then they were forty and the foreman was screaming at them to hurry. One morning the frost was on the vines and the foreman wept and cursed and bid *adieu* to his bonus. When the sun burned through the dawn clouds and the vineyards were bathed in light they found that only a small part of the harvest was lost, a few rows of bitter black grapes across a north slope that they tore from the vines and stomped into the gold, hard earth. They were paid one hundred francs cash and three liters of table wine at the end of each workday. They could keep the wine or sell it back for three francs a bottle. Petitjean sold his. If he drank then, he was sick. Thinking of his father. The workers slept in three large rooms in a converted barn, where the owners had put rows of mattresses and bedding and little boxes with soap and old towels. Bed and board and sanitation were provided by the owner of the château.

The workers were itinerant Portuguese, Algerians, Moroccans, poor French, and Italians. For the first time in his life, Petitjean heard words that he couldn't understand, strange tongues surrounding him like vines and branches. He felt mocked, as though the language he'd mastered was known only to him, all his reading come to nothing. One night a young girl, the daughter of a Portuguese foreman, came and sat next to his mattress. She lit a cigarette and blew the smoke over his head. He couldn't understand her French, her accent was too strong, but he understood that she wanted twenty francs. "For what?" She lifted her work shirt to display her breasts, but he was unimpressed. He had seen better in magazines and the nearness of the others sleeping close by was unsettling. "We're not alone," he told her. "Not here." She reached across the dark for his hand and put it to her breast; though cold, it burned his hand.

He followed her out to the vineyard, to a place between the rows where the ground was black, softened from the spill of grape. Naked, they both looked silver in the darkness. Her face was pale and when she closed her eyes he didn't want her anymore. Her hands reached to his shoulders and trailed downward. When she touched him he began to tremble. He closed his eyes. He had never looked at her until this night. Not these parts of her, her secrets. She leaned forward and he could feel the heat of her. After, when she was on top of him, he opened his eyes and looked through her hair to the stars.

After the *récolte* was ended most of the workers were let go and they scattered in all directions. Petitjean was paid less than the others and was without family, so he was kept on. By day, he helped with the bottling and labeling from a previous harvest, and at night he slept in the same large room where now there were only five of them, four men and himself. The wind came from the north and they tore up dead vine stumps and roots and tied them into bundles for firewood. They gathered the remaining sticks and leaves and trash into three high mounds and Petitjean spent a whole night tending the fires. His pockets bulged with franc notes and he warmed his hands within them while the flames threw sparks into the sky.

When winter came, he was out of work. He drifted south, to

Montpellier, and then west to Narbonne. Because of his accent, he was taken for a Parisian and had a hard time getting along. His money lasted three months and then his pockets held only change. When he was out of money, he slept in churches and read his books in the smoky candlelight.

He met Jean-Luc in a brasserie along the banks of the river. Jean-Luc was forty-five and wore a short-sleeved shirt despite the cold; a broken heart was tattooed to his forearm. He wanted to know if Petitjean was looking for work, and Petitjean wondered if he'd read this in his eyes. Later, Jean-Luc lent Petitjean his *Figaro* and bought him a meal of white sausages and potatoes. When Petitjean declined the wine, Jean-Luc drank it himself.

The next day, Jean-Luc taught him how to pop a tiny hole in a car window with a fat lead club wrapped in wool. The glass would fall inward, soundlessly. Or if the window was partially open one could use a string and hook and snare the lock like a metal fish. Once Petitjean was skilled at glass breaking, Jean-Luc showed him how to spark a car into ignition with the touching of hot-wires, with a screwdriver in one hand and a pair of pliers in the other. He knew a man who would drive the cars across the Pyrenees to Spain for new paint and serial numbers.

He also showed him the rudiments of using a knife. He poked the point of the knife at Petitjean's heart. "Never this, always this," he said, bringing the blade across on a diagonal from ear to breast. "The blade," Jean-Luc told him, "is for slicing, not stabbing."

Jean-Luc chose the cars and told Petitjean where to take them. He paid Petitjean a thousand francs for every car and they had to move around, from Narbonne to Beziers to Montpellier, sometimes as far away as Marseille. For a time, Petitjean stole one a day and kept most of his money in a steel box that he buried in the dirt alley behind Jean-Luc's place. This arrangement lasted through the summer. Tourist cars were always the safest, as the police paid less attention to the German and English and Dutch who came screaming into the prefectures demanding justice. But when the fall season was over, they spent the winter lying low and spending their money in restaurants and brasseries. Petitjean bought books and continued to read. He didn't know how to select books. He chose them by their covers, the color or the pictures on the front. Sometimes he ended up with a mystery or a porno story; other times the novel was too thick with words he didn't know, or stuffed and knotted with elaborate ideas that he couldn't fit into his head. Books that made him feel stupid and angry then sad.

One winter evening, Petitjean came home to find that the police had come and gone and taken Jean-Luc with them. In the back alley he discovered that his box had been dug up; it lay empty in the dirt. A neighbor told him that Jean-Luc had tried to bribe the police, who'd taken the money and arrested him anyway.

Fifty thousand francs, a fortune he might have lived on forever. It was the first time he wanted to kill someone. Someone with a broken heart on his forearm. He had a fold of bills in his pocket, enough to get away before the police came back for him. Since then he has kept his money on his body, all of it, always. He has heard men speaking of where they put their money. One man puts his in stocks, another in bonds, another in real estate. He puts his money in his pocket. You would have to remove his flesh to have any of it.

In Toulouse he read an ad asking for a secretary to a journalist and historian. He spent money on a jacket and tie and a new shirt. He cut and combed his hair and saw in the mirror that he looked older than seventeen. The journalist was an aging man named Jules who could no longer travel and so was writing his memoirs. He wanted to know Petitjean's ambitions and Petitjean replied that he wanted to become a writer. Stupid, Jules said, no one *wants* to be writer; it simply happens, like the sunrise or the high tide. All the same, he asked if he could spell. Petitjean said of course and then Jules tested him, asking him words that he'd never heard of. Petitjean wrote out the letters on paper and Jules nodded. Then he asked if Petitjean knew how to use a typewriter. Luckily he didn't insist on a test and in the space of a week the lie was made true. Typing was easy. He only had to know where the letters were, three to each finger. How words are made of a key, a hammer, and ink on wood. He had to take the yellow handwritten pages of Jules's memoirs and type them double-spaced onto white sheets. He was to number and date each page and keep a carbon in a separate room of the house in case of fire. The memoirs were terrible. Jules's writing revealed an excessive vanity; he took too many pages to savage his critics or puff up his own accomplishments. The parts that interested Petitjean most were either cut short or polluted with ideas. Jules had lived through four wars—the Great One, the Second War, Algeria, Vietnam—and had never carried a gun. Petitjean learned from the cleaning lady that his wife had given birth to children not his own and then, twenty years before, had left him.

Jules paid only a small salary, but Petitjean had the run of his library. Sometimes Jules asked him to do some research, to check the spelling of names or to verify his dates. The work was easy and Petitjean didn't complain, even though the hours were irregular, morning or noon or night, depending upon the old man's whims and health. Now and then, at the end of a long evening, Jules poured himself a cognac and talked at length about his work and his travels, his famous friends. He never asked anything about Petitjean. There were things Jules wanted to relate, he sometimes said, but he knew that Petitjean would never understand because he wasn't educated. He didn't even have his *baccalauréat*, did he? As though, like his father, he was missing a hand. One thing Jules told him that he never forgot; said in passing, it was more important and wiser than anything in his memoirs. "You can never leave France," Jules said, "if you cannot speak another language. If all you have in your head is French you will take France with you wherever you go."

Petitjean's first attempt was Russian but he was stumped by the Cyrillic alphabet. He turned to Dutch and had begun to make progress when Jules caught him with one of his grammars. "English," he said. "English will help you travel. No one speaks Dutch anymore, not even the Dutch."

When the job was finished and he was let go, Petitjean stole three books from the old man's library. A yellowed reader from the American third grade, a French-English dictionary, and

Thackeray's *Vanity Fair*, which he has never read but which still occupies a place on his bookshelf and seems to symbolize the tenacity of his ignorance.

At the river's edge was a silver Mercedes with Dutch plates and the NL sticker on the back hood. Jean-Luc had said to avoid parking lots. Shop first, he had said, then steal. Take your time and never, ever take a car from a crowded lot. With so many cars in the same place, the chances of being seen are that much greater. Better to choose a rusted Renault on an empty side street than a Cadillac in a busy carpark. Because of the heat, the passenger window was lowered by three or four centimeters and he would be able to use a line and hook. Two men were crossing to their car and Petitjean knelt next to the Mercedes and waited for them to drive away. Then he dropped the weighted hook into the window, jiggled it until it was caught in the lock, and yanked upward. Once inside, he made fast work of the ignition, backed out of the slot, and headed for the exit. The policeman was standing at the pay gate, his motorcycle parked nearby. He had appeared as if from nowhere. Petitjean slowed down and pressed the button to lower his window.

The policeman saluted. *"Bon soir. Je peux voir vos papiers?"*

After a brief hesitation, Petitjean answered that he didn't have his papers with him. It was his father's car, he added. He realized his mistake immediately: the Dutch plates.

The policeman raised an eyebrow and moved to the front of the car to look again. Then he returned to the window. *"Sortez de la voiture,"* he ordered.

Petitjean's right hand was on the steering wheel and his left hand held the knife that he had used to cut the ignition. The policeman was still bent to the window. He had brown eyes and long lashes for a man. Those eyes bored into Petitjean's. In years to come, those eyes would follow him everywhere. *"Sortez."*

Compact, swift, clean. A gesture not unlike that of throwing a cigarette out the window. The blood was a surprise. When he'd practiced with his knife there had only been air at the end of his blade. The policeman was screaming and with his hand he clawed at the holster for his gun.

Petitjean drove away.

He was caught with a stolen car the following winter while driving toward the Pyrenees with vague plans of selling it on the other side of the border. Because of his age and the sorrow in his face, he was given a suspended sentence. The following spring he took another car, an ice-blue Audi, from the parking lot of a supermarket in Orléans. This one time he didn't even think of selling; he was too far north and wanted to keep the car for himself. For three days he drove it everywhere, on country roads, down highways, along the banks of the lower Seine. One spring morning he took the autoroute north to Paris, where he'd never been. All day long he was in that car, not daring to stop anywhere. He entered the city from the south and navigated north through Montparnasse. He crossed the Seine at the Pont au Change, cruised around the Place de la Concorde, then glided up and down the Champs-Elysées with his arm resting out the open window and one hand guiding the wheel. When darkness fell, all of the lights were white, the shopfronts blazed, and the leaves of the trees were lit like emeralds. At stoplights he didn't even look at the drivers on either side of him. The air smelled of lilacs and chestnut blossoms and there was the perfume of gasoline and exhaust. Late in the night he drove out of the city and stopped at a petrol station in the western suburbs. It cost half of his remaining money to fill the tank. He bought a ham-and-cheese sandwich and a cup of coffee and felt as though he had driven to the moon. The car was dirty and he paid the attendant ten francs for a bucket of soapy water and the use of his hose. When the car was all shining steel and chrome he took a handful of mud and obscured the license plates, then he took the wheel and cruised south again, toward Auxerre, where he had a job washing dishes in a restaurant.

Going to prison was like going home. They let him keep his books and the laundry was always fresh. Two years, they told him, but they kept him only eighteen months. Next time, he was told, he would spend five years. He should keep his hands off other people's wheels. Take the train. Or use his feet.

Mornings at the prison, he worked in the bakery and in the afternoons he helped out in the infirmary. At night, the only time he really had to himself, he read his third-grade American book. I speak, you speak, he speaks. We speak, you speak, they speak. To have spoken. He read Prévert and found the prayer that he had forever been reciting to himself: "Our Father who art in heaven, stay there."

His warden found a collection of Byron's poems and he read them until they were his own. "She walks in beauty like the night of cloudless climes and starry skies." The warden was a married man with three children. It was in his company that Petitjean started smoking cigarettes, those black Gauloises that the warden would pass to him as a way of saying hello. Petitjean could have escaped with ease but he would have had to kill the warden first, or at least do him serious harm. He didn't give it a second thought. He was haunted by the sight of that torn eye and how he had driven a hundred kilometers while blood had turned from red to brown on the windshield. When he reached the Pyrenees and was ten miles from the Spanish border, he had stopped the car by the roadside and wiped at the blood with his fingers. A mountain stream flowed from south to north alongside, and he wetted his hands and smeared the blood across the glass until there was only dust. For days thereafter his hands felt dirty at the wheel and he drove with his fists clenched, afraid of what was inside of them.

They are standing near the fence that looks out on the tracks. She is still wearing the shawl and her forehead is beaded with sweat. He thinks of taking her back to his room and turning out the light, but he is frozen by indecision.

"Merci," she says.

"For what?"

"Merci. The walk. To look at my face. To eat my fish and the carrots I burned."

His venality vanishes, and everything melts in the wake of the longest phrase he has ever heard come from her lips.

"My mother will be home. If she finds us she will die. In your room. Sleep when she comes in the door."

But when they return to the apartment, it has been altered in their absence. Petitjean at first assumes it was Sylvie expressing her outrage. But the rooms have not been torn apart from rage, merely disturbed. In Sylvie's room, the bed is askew as though someone had been searching between the mattress and the box spring. The kitchen cupboards are open. In the living room a lamp has been tipped over, the sofa cushions have been removed, and the rugs pushed to the side. Catherine begins straightening the sofa but Petitjean stops her, holding a finger to his lips. He moves quietly from room to room while she waits in the living room. When he is certain no one is still in the apartment, he checks the telephone for bugs, doesn't find any, and goes about straightening it up. He refuses to let Catherine help. He wants to know what has been searched and what, if anything, has been taken. Zane will want to know.

Half an hour later, the apartment is as it was, threadbare but clean. Nothing is missing, which does not surprise him. Unlike Zane, he leaves his work at the office. Sylvie long ago insisted on it.

In his room, he lights the lamp and opens the book to where he's left the marker. *Discours sur la Maladie de l'Esprit.* He has already read three essays on epilepsy and a fourth on the various methods of treating melancholia. Not one of the pages has Catherine's name or face in it. She is in her own room, perhaps sleeping by now, though when she kissed him good night she said she might never sleep again in her life.

Near midnight he rises and goes into the kitchen for more cognac. The bottle is half empty. For over two hours he has stood his moral ground and not broken through the wood of Catherine's door. And Sylvie is still out somewhere in Paris—with friends, he imagines—putting together and taking apart the geometry of herself, her daughter, and him. Doing whatever he is doing with his glass of cognac and his bewilderment. He is in his bed with the cognac at the nightstand and a lit cigarette in one hand when he hears the front door open and close. In no time Sylvie is at his door, tapping, asking if he's sleeping.

He tells her no, he can hear her. She says she's thought it over and he is not to worry. Life has its funny turns, she says. Is a river and then is a desert. She has been drinking and has to repeat herself to finish a sentence. Her speech sounds memorized, as though she has been honing it for hours on end, as if she has practiced the perfect balance between sorrow and anger and final wisdom. My life, too, she says. My life has its moments.

Then, for a moment or two, he hears nothing more. And finally the sound of her bedsprings, one body on the mattress he has shared with her both as rent and as sustenance. Dead silence. Slumber. Ether. Night.

An hour later the phone is ringing and, assuming it is Zane, he leaps from bed and answers it before the third ring. But the voice at the other end is that of a stranger; faultless English with an accent that he cannot place. The voice is asking to speak to Zane.

"Try calling where he lives."

"Mr. Zane has no home. We assumed you would know where to locate him."

"You'd better update your files. He doesn't work at ABRI anymore. He says he's history."

There is a pause and he listens carefully to the static to judge whether the phone had, in fact, been wired.

"Perhaps," the voice suggests, "you could forward a message to him."

He doesn't have his speaking stones and for a moment his tongue fails him. He reaches across the table for a pen. "I have already told you. Call him at his home."

The voice delivers the message anyway and Petitjean, without paper nearby, writes it directly onto the tablecloth.

He continues his reading. *Discours sur la Maladie d'Esprit.* He learns that epileptics have nervous systems like watchsprings too tightly wound. The bursting is inevitable and the end of one attack will set the alarm for the next. That lobotomy is still common practice the world over, an alternative cheaper than therapy or secure confinement. That certain birds can be driven certifiably mad if made to listen to distorted music for three months at a stretch. Rising from bed, he walks naked to the kitchen, pours cognac into a glass, and then stands for a long time in the darkness before going back to his room. Women are sleeping to either side of him; only walls separate them, but the room is alive with radio waves, wind, the exhaust of dreams. He lights a cigarette and the smoke forms a blue cloud above the bed. The cognac is warm and tastes of wood. He drinks it down and returns to his book. He reads that phenylketonurics might start walking on a given morning and go on walking for up to three days if there is nothing or no one to stop them. Then he can hear her through the wall, a small sound, barely audible. Catherine's moaning. Sylvie is up and crossing the hall to the bathroom. The sound of water pouring into the tub. All at once, the night is filled with noise. The klaxon of a siren in the street and Catherine's chant and the rush of water. He turns the page and begins to read another chapter. Halfway down the page are the words: *Ceux qui ne sont pas du métier confondent la sourdité et la débilité.* Those who are not professionals confuse deafness with mental deficiency.

For a moment he feels what he felt as a child, a dream of his father reaching into him with his stump, in search of his hand. His hand in me. He closes the book and folds it over his chest like a shield. And in the shelter of those words, Petitjean finds sleep.

When he rises at dawn, Catherine is already in the kitchen. Her blouse is badly buttoned and she is wearing one shoe. Her back is to him as she butters her toast.

"Good morning," he whispers, but she doesn't move. "Good morning," he says more loudly.

She lifts the toast to her teeth. He claps his hands and she swallows.

Sylvie is at his side, looking up at him with red eyes. "We have to talk," she says. "You have to listen to me."

"I know. Not now."

"Tonight. When you come home."

When he is dressed and seated at the kitchen table, Catherine sits across from him with a magazine in front of her. Lifting his spoon, he taps it against his water glass three times. She doesn't look up. He taps again and Sylvie glares at him.

Sweeping his hand leftward, he knocks the water glass onto the floor and it shatters.

"Is this a game?" Sylvie asks. Then she throws her coffee cup against the wall above his shoulder. Bits of porcelain fall onto Catherine's page and she brushes them away with her hand.

SUNDAY EVENING. MARIE HAS TAKEN FINGERS FOR his walk and the club is empty. Setting his screen to *Receive Only*, Zane descends the stairs in search of ice, and at precisely 8:00 p.m., he dials Petitjean's number.

"What have you got for me?"

"I've had a visitor."

"Did you see anyone?"

"Not a soul. They came and left while I was out for a walk. They were delicate about it, at least. No bedlam."

It's a word Zane has taught to Petitjean. All the variations: *mayhem, carnage, pandemonium.* The types of words that get turned in journalese to *incident* or *affair* or *conflict.* "There was nothing to find," Petitjean adds. "The dirty laundry and the usual. This phone is maybe bugged, though I've checked it three times."

"Unlikely. Not if you can't find it."

"So where are you?"

"In the city. Safe."

"That's good. I'm pleased."

A few seconds pass while Zane knows they are both listening for an echo or a ticking or that mosquito sound that signifies an eavesdropper.

"I have mail for you," Petitjean finally says. "From a friend of yours."

"I don't have any friends, Petitjean."

"He says he is only half of a friend."

He is reduced to a whisper. "Demi."

"There are two parts to the message. First, he says *light water details*. Second, *read the sports page at the Painted Bird*. Do you want me to repeat that?"

"Sports page," Zane echoes. "Painted Bird."

Demi's smile is a mass of diamonds and bone around the mouth while his eyes brood. He is both French and black Algerian and his Christian name is Jean-Abdul, which would be a joke if he could laugh at it. He lives his life on the Mediterranean fringe, bringing marijuana and hashish across Gibraltar into France or dealing smuggled African art to collectors along the Côte d'Azur. He has never mentioned family or friends and his raking has always been sporadic, a break from illicit commerce. There is often a hysterical edge to his banter and Zane has concluded that he must be intolerably lonely. He is the only raker who has never intimated why he does what he does. Perhaps, like Zane, he doesn't exactly know.

Though it is Sunday night and the streets are empty, the night air seems electrified and filled with tiny points of light. In the moonless dark streetlamps are like floodlights, but Zane reminds himself that the menace is mostly in the dark corners. He crosses the Seine to the Right Bank and realizes that without thinking he has begun to run, and immediately slows to a walk. The panic won't subside, so he conjures thoughts of water; tap water, flowing water, the brown Mississippi, the lake where the man called Jack taught him to keep the perch and throw back the bullheads. When this doesn't work he stops at the first bar he sees, orders a whisky, and changes his mind. Walking away from that whisky gives him a sense of purpose. Any small victory might change his luck.

At nine-thirty he crosses into a gritty *impasse*, a dead-end street in the ninth arrondissement. He is a mere half-mile from the ABRI offices. At the end of the *impasse*, partly obscured by a broken and sagging awning, is a brasserie named L'Oiseau Bariolé, the Painted Bird. There is a small dining room in the back, empty at this hour, and he is one of only three customers at the zinc-topped bar. To his right is a white man, approximately fifty years old, with white hair and a thick beard; despite the heat, he is dressed in thick blue slacks and a black wool jacket. He is holding a glass of mineral water in his long fingers and without glancing to either side he lifts it and tips it to his lips. Zane notices he is reading the newspaper. To Zane's left is a black man dressed in workman's blues. A cup of tea is at his elbow while he, too, reads the newspaper. For the second time in half an hour, Zane orders a whisky that he refuses to drink.

"You come for smoke?"

The bartender, a razor-thin Arab with black eyes, is leaning over the bar, his face close to Zane's. He has spoken in a half-whisper. Zane, surprised to be addressed in English, hesitates a moment and then shakes his head.

"Got black, got brown. Clean cut, like hard river mud."

Zane lifts the glass to his lips and then sets it down. He wonders for a moment if Petitjean got it right. Was he supposed to buy something first? The man to his left has finished his water and gone out the door, taking his newspaper with him. The bartender, suddenly angry, asks him what he wants, why he is there? "You want pills? Pills or sniff stuff?" He taps a nostril with his finger.

The front door, Zane measures, is too far away. He has come too far inside the bar to escape quickly and the white-haired man with the newspaper is between him and that door.

"Maybe," the bartender decides, "you are po-lice-man. White-face stupid fellow."

The white-haired man reaches a hand into his left pocket and leaves it there. He speaks to the bartender in Arabic. For a few moments the bartender glares at the two of them and then finally moves down his slot, away from the door, to a tubful of dirty dishes.

Zane is watching the man's hand, still in his pocket. When he lifts it out, there is only a cigarette in his fingers. After lighting the cigarette, he folds the paper and places it on the bar. Then, with a final glance in the direction of the bartender, he crosses to the door and goes out.

This is how his mother lived, he senses. Years and years of chewing on her own heart among strangers who might or might not be innocent.

The sports pages of *Le Figaro* are orange, so the red marks are more easily camouflaged. Words and numbers. Setting his glass to the zinc, Zane reaches for the paper and opens it before him. Tennis results, horse racing, golf scores from the Trophée Lancôme. He doesn't have to write down the letters or numbers as he finds them. Each burns its way past his eyes to the hardwood of memory.

The Paris metro smells of metal and body heat. The evening crowds are sparse and dotted with German and Dutch tourists. Zane takes line three from Pigalle to Anvers, Barbès-Rochechouart, Stalingrad, and Jaurès, where he has to change. While waiting for the next train, he memorizes the address and throws the paper onto the tracks. He is no longer in Paris. He is in Dakar and is surrounded by black faces and mothers dressed in bright colors with children on their backs. His face is painted a tourist color. He wears it as the badge of someone just passing through. A black man in working blues comes by with his broom, and Zane lifts his feet to let the man brush underneath him. A year ago, the metro cleaners went on strike and after ten days the underground was filthy with discarded tickets, Gauloise stubs, newspapers, and other urban jetsam. At the station at the Place de Clichy, a number of strikers played watchdog to make certain none of the citizens would take it upon themselves to clean the place up. One morning Zane took a plastic bag along and had begun filling it with litter when a pair of North Africans—Algerians? Tunisians?—came by and showed him a blade. When he failed to acknowledge them they ran the knife across his bag and scattered the garbage across the platform. "*C'est nous ou personne*," he was told. It's us or no one. An older man standing nearby muttered "Idiot" and Zane didn't know if he was referring to him or to the man with the knife.

The train arrives and he snaps open the door and steps inside. One stop later, at Laumière, he gets out and climbs the stairs toward the south side. After the underground, the stars overhead are a surprise and he stops for a moment to watch them. He walks seventy-five meters south and then turns left into an alley. Though the place he is looking for has no number, he finds the marking, three interlocked circles, carved into stone above a doorway, and he steps into it as into a deeper version of night. The paving stones are old and uneven and he stumbles twice as he advances down a corridor where the air is stale but cool. At its end is a tiny courtyard crowded with garbage canisters and a single, small door, of the sort from a hundred and fifty years ago, when everyone was the size of Napoleon.

He stands in front of the door for a long while. There is no bell, no way to announce himself other than to knock. But as he raises his fist, the door opens to the inside and a young woman looks out at him. For a brief and terrifying moment he thinks it is M'Khlea, then she steps into the light. Although she isn't M'Khlea, she could be her sister. The same long neck and polished beauty. He tells her his name and she says she knows. "Your friend called ahead."

He is led inside, through a room filled with African wood carvings in ebony and mahogany. He stops to look at one of them, a fertility icon of a woman with an enormous belly and long breasts, all in burnished black. He wants to touch it, to feel the smooth wood, but the woman frowns and beckons him to follow her. At the other end of a narrow hallway, two men are waiting for him in a makeshift office equipped with two desks, a telephone, a file cabinet, a telex, and a very old manual typewriter. The furniture looks as though it has been salvaged from some ancient bureau or junkyard, as though nothing in the room has been purchased with money. Both the men are tall and thin and neither moves to shake his hand. The one nearer to him gestures to a chair. Zane is instantly on edge and wants to light a cigarette but there isn't a single ashtray in sight.

The first man nods to the other, who then exits, leaving Zane sitting across from Ambrose Okimbo. He is even thinner than Zane remembered, or perhaps it is the dim light. His fingers are long and well manicured, the fingernails grown back. He sees Zane looking and says, "Arms and legs, even fingers won't grow back. But fingernails grow back stronger, thicker, much sharper."

After a moment, he says, "Why have you come here?"

"I was summoned."

"Don't toy with me. You were sending out feelers for days. I need guarantees."

"Of what?"

"Of your good faith. You have already proven to me once that you cannot be trusted."

He can only be referring to M'Khlea and Zane's part in hiding her with Street. "What guarantee can I offer?"

"Your address. Your mortality. So *we* know where to find *you*."

Zane writes his address, or what was his address, on the paper offered him, uncertain of the meaning of this contract.

But Okimbo is satisfied. He folds the paper in half and slips it into his pocket. Zane wonders how many other such contracts he is keeping in that file cabinet. Okimbo sits with hands folded on the desk before him. "You have told your first lie," he says. "You no longer live at this address." He has the smooth face of a diplomat with skin so black as to appear blue in indifferent light. "You were wanting?"

"Information," Zane tells him. He can see in Okimbo's eyes that he is the enemy. Or at best a hostage.

For the next half-hour Okimbo answers Zane's questions with insults or sarcasm. Sometimes his only reply is hostile silence. The other man, who Zane realizes is Okimbo's lieutenant, comes in and out of the room at various intervals, and at one point simply stands behind Zane and breathes down on his head. Zane is surrounded by rage, in the presence of men who have *turned*. He will never find out where they have come from or why they are here, never know what revulsion they have felt, or the source of their fury. They have the faces of men who have never slept and are dying for rest. Paris is full of these men, from every country in the world. They come because it is a city that lures exiles: assassins disguised as mid-level diplomats, phalangists, budding terrorists. When Khomeini left his exile in a southern suburb of Paris, Bani Sadr moved from Tehran to Neuilly. In Paris, consulates get torched and little murders in streets like this one are commonplace.

They want more than a token in return. Okimbo asks Zane about his rakers, about ABRI. He wants to know about methods for validating the data that comes over the lines and Zane explains the twin-angle approach, the kicker routine; no news is biblical until it comes from two different sources.

"How do you trace the transmission source?"

"Telematic footprints. There's always an octal signature at the beginning and end of a send."

"These can be counterfeited by children."

"Petitjean took care of that. If we smell a rat, he runs a tomcat into the multiplexor."

Okimbo lays his palms to the table and lifts them slightly. It is a gesture that he repeats more than once, as though the proximity of his hands to the wood is a barometer of Zane's credibility. "Explain," he says, his voice somehow softened.

"I don't know all the technical ins and outs. Petitjean's the artist here and I just dabble. He says the routine relies on an echo. If we think there's been a counterfeit, we return the message as though it never came through to us and request a retransmission. Like shouting into a canyon and waiting to hear your words come back at you. If nothing comes back the message was a dog and knife. . . ."

Okimbo's hands rise from the table.

"The dog licks the knife, tastes blood, licks again, bleeds to death. They sometimes try to get us to chase false information, something we can never catch up with, and the pursuit will exhaust us."

The hands remain suspended in mid-air for long seconds. Zane decides to skip over explanations of the language and to speak in as straight and narrow an English as he can muster.

Okimbo asks about a month-old operation in Ethiopia in which a fleet of Red Cross grain trucks made a risky night-crossing around rebel troops to get the food to a refugee camp in Wollayta. Zane recounts what he knows: grain quantities, storage and distribution methods, the make and range of the trucks utilized. But he doesn't mention names and Okimbo seems annoyed. He wants the identities of informants and when Zane refuses to give him any his eyes turn cold, moving slowly around the room as though he is considering how to reach Zane's open wounds, how best to finger the source of his pain. Until that moment Zane has fooled himself into thinking that they are negotiating something; but in fact he is Okimbo's prisoner until he purchases his way into sunlight.

"Give me a sign," Okimbo says at last, "that you have not come here to scrape my flesh. Offer me something besides these shiny little beads of useless information. I already know that you are Emelle's errand boy. I once knew you as something more."

For another hour he probes Zane's activities, and Zane tells him whatever he can, nearly always without mentioning names. Okimbo is a master of the stagecraft of interrogation, and his questions are purposefully varied; randomly, he skips from country to country as if they're of equal interest. But his questions inevitably return to the western belt, to Nigeria and its bordering countries. Not once has he betrayed his tribe or tipped his hand as to what side of the political polygon he is living in. Now and then he asks a question that he already has asked, tempting Zane into a different answer. When Zane lights a cigarette Okimbo asks if he's nervous and Zane says of course he is. "Aren't you?"

Okimbo ignores the question and pursues one of his own. Details about a covert printing operation in Port Harcourt. Only a half-dozen people outside of Nigeria know anything of substance about the operation, Zane among them. The group prints everything from poetry to plays to political and economic commentary and is steadfastly unaligned; in a circle, it is said, right and left are the same direction. For over a year these printers have provided Zane with data, details of operations that were otherwise vague, safe houses for rakers in distress. If he refuses to give him names, Okimbo says, can he at least offer him an address? "Here," he says, slipping Zane a sheet of blank paper and a pen. "You can write it if you prefer."

The printing operation is a floater and is moved every few months, so Zane considers giving him an old address. But even that might provide a lead to the new one.

"If you want something from me," Okimbo says, "this is my price. It is all you have that interests me."

There is no place to put out the cigarette, and Zane drops the butt to the floor. He takes a deep breath and within nanoseconds in the core of the human brain and heart, he decides to risk it. He stands, noting the surprise in Okimbo's eyes, and says, "It must be getting late."

"You refuse?"

Zane nods. "I know those people and they are not your targets—or they shouldn't be. Without their work the whole country could go dark for ten years."

Okimbo points abruptly for him to sit. "Do not lecture me on the fate of my birthplace!"

Zane waits only a few sullen seconds before returning to his chair.

Reaching into a drawer, Okimbo takes out an ashtray and places it on the table. "Smoke, if you like. I have no objections." He pauses. "Your agency is compromised. Emelle is untrustworthy. She is old and has become stupid. There is a serious lack of funding and she is stretched very thin."

Zane lights his cigarette and decides to only listen. To listen as though his screen is below his lids and the letters appear one after another.

"Vigilance," Okimbo says, "is very wearing. ABRI has become a hole in the net of worldwide amnesty. Emelle is tired. She is maybe in poor health. She is killing people without knowing it. Or I am exaggerating. The killing goes on despite her senile attempts to stop it. If ever you see her again, you should encourage her to close her doors before others come to burn them down. I am curious to know what your files say about me."

"That you're rabid. Gangrened. That your teeth have grown as sharp as your fingernails."

Okimbo smiles. "These are metaphors, Mr. Zane. Your point of view and not particularly factual. What have you in the way of serious information? The kind of news you pass on to the wire services."

"That you've linked up with the Touaregs and have your own private army. In exchange, you provide arms through a Syrian supplier whose only Koran is the U.S. dollar. No links to fundamentalist Islamic causes. That you recently arranged for the assassination of a diplomat in Niger."

"He was not a diplomat, he was a soldier. His troops were responsible for the massacre of great numbers of people. *Their deaths went unreported.*"

"Not by me."

"No. Your newsletter included half a column, if I remember, and you refer to the rumor of their death as though it were a gossip item."

"I didn't have a kicker. No confirmation."

"There is something else that you have not mentioned."

"It's a thick file. What did I miss?"

"My wife." Okimbo's eyes flash with hate, then soften instantly. Heat lightning, Zane is thinking; beneath his civility, the man is a bundle of raw nerve and crossed wires. "You have failed to mention that after you helped alienate her you also abandoned her. You left her exposed and she has been murdered."

"Who killed her?"

"Harry Street."

"That's impossible."

"Because he loved her? He did not love her. He wrote letters to her, he drew an arrow straight to her door for his enemies to follow. This is self-indulgence, not love."

"You abandoned her."

"I protected her! I kept her far from these killing chambers, and you betrayed me." His breath is suddenly short and for the first time he has trouble speaking. "Who are you to measure my love? And who is Harry Street? You betrayed me, Thomas Zane, and now my wife is dead."

Hearing the shouting, the lieutenant has come back into the room with his pistol drawn. Okimbo wearily waves him away. Zane lights another cigarette, but then he stubs it out. A plume of smoke rises from the ashtray as from a tiny campfire.

"When I was there," Okimbo says, his voice barely a whisper. "In Port Harcourt. I wore a halo and I saw clouds."

Zane is slow to realize that he is talking about his imprisonment.

"I no longer suffered," Okimbo continues. "I was asleep and I was awake. When I spoke I told many sweet lies. I heard myself in disbelief and yet I carried on. I told as many lies as I knew to tell. I am a writer and can lie with great elaboration. But I felt the halo around my head and after a time the lies were spent and I found myself telling the truth. Little circles of truth at first, mingled in with the fiction. I resisted but the halo was there and I had to speak. At the end I was worn down. I told truths as I knew them, truths that I had known all of my life. I told about my childhood and then the school in England. I remembered things I had long since forgotten. Standing on the edge of the green and watching white boys play rugby and wishing I were not so tall as to stand out amongst the others. The color and shape of my first pair of leather shoes. Do you remember your first pair of shoes?"

"What is the halo?"

"My crown. My remembrance. My crown of thorns." Okimbo lifts a forefinger to his head and leans forward. In the dim light Zane can see tiny white scars like X's across his forehead. He had noticed the scars the night they'd met and had assumed them to be tribal scarring, African flesh ornaments.

"Electrodes?"

"Laser probes. To the heart of the heart of my speech."

B. BX. Berne.

"I ran out of harmless memories. After days and days of reminiscing as though inebriated. I *was* given alcohol but not a brand of whisky that finds its way down your throat. And when there were no other memories to relate, no innocent pathways of nostalgia left to me, I betrayed my wife. I had been searching for memories that would resist his questions and those memories that were strongest and most resplendent were those of M'Khlea. I recounted all I knew of her, or felt. And he encouraged me to tell more, to tell everything, until all privacy and affection were gone from me. I had given them my wife and her love of me and I could no longer resist."

He is looking at his hands which are spread before him, as though they are instruments and not flesh. Then abruptly he turns his head in Zane's direction. Their eyes meet.

"I named names. When I heard myself saying those names, I tried to go back, to speak again of M'Khlea, but he wouldn't let me. 'M'Khlea is gone,' he told me. 'We are alone now.' And when the names were all used up, I gave away addresses, codes, the location of safe houses. I implicated my own brother and suggested where they might find him. I emptied myself of all I knew or had ever known. My brother is dead, his wife as well. A literature professor who once hid me in his home is dead. And after this, how was I to return to these people and be a part of their cause? To say that a mistake has been made, I have slipped up but will sin no more. There is no sufficient penance if people are dead because of your weakness."

"But you were tortured."

"Not that the world could see. Neither the world nor my wife. My fingernails were missing. A minor incident, from the first days I was taken in. Later, there were only the drugs. The drugs and the halo. When I was released, I found I had even gained weight while in their prison. I could not face my wife, knowing how I had recounted everything about her, her most private self, to my interrogators. That is why I brought her to you. I had hoped that with time I might forgive myself. That we could create a new privacy for ourselves, a history that I could not betray. That I might reclaim her as my wife."

Zane is unable to look into his eyes. He tries to imagine the loneliness that follows a recitation of your entire life and the subtraction implied in the telling.

"I came to ask if he is alive. Harry." His voice seems to have left his body. "And if so, where I can find him."

Okimbo stares at him for a moment, seeking to understand the question. When he does, his eyes regain their heat, at the center a familiar blackness.

"I already know that you met," Zane tells him. "In a field north of Gao."

Okimbo closes his eyes and opens them. "I had Harry Street in my sights," he says. "I had been following his movements for quite some time and I knew that he was trying to find me. Soon enough, I knew why. When he came too close to me, in Mali, I knew that it was time to drive him away. He was dangerous to me because he was so careless. I went to see him. We spoke on one occasion and then I left him. We all of us betrayed M'Khlea. Myself and then Street and then you. I could not have him killed. And once again, we found ourselves in the same camp. He was providing aid to my Touareg brothers."

"What happened to him?"

"I know you are thinking he is dead. If he is, it is not on my orders. After we met, he was safe. Some days later, we heard that he was taken from the house where he was staying."

"Taken by whom?"

"Mali soldiers. Although they weren't alone in wanting him."

"Who, then?"

"Their government's adviser. He has no specific title but he provides a service to the Nigerians, the Maliens, and others. I know this man like I know my mother and father. He is close to my soul."

"Who is he?"

"My tormentor. My physician and healer in the Port Harcourt prison. The man who placed the halo on my head and like a muse summoned from me my whole life. At the time I didn't know his name. He gave me medicine. He called it medicine and the word made me laugh and I felt stupid for laughing. He understood me, my pride. He had a way of making me feel ridiculous. I am ridiculous, am I not?"

"What is his name? This man."

"His name? Didn't Harry Street ever tell you? I thought you shared every secret. He spoke to me the night we met, when you were out of the room. He knew all about the man, it seemed. He had known of him for years."

"His name."

"Berne. Or Burn, with a u. I only heard it spoken and cannot vouch for the exact spelling."

Zane feels a hole widening where his heart should be. "Street was gathering evidence," he says, "to flush him into the open and put him out of business. For years he's been telling me as much. But I didn't believe him." He stops short of mentioning the letters.

Okimbo's voice and eyes are out of harmony. For the first time in their conversation he avoids Zane's gaze. "We want him, too. Not only for his crimes against myself and my Touareg brothers but also for his collaboration with the governments of the oppression. With the help of an informant, a Bambara, we were able to find where they were keeping Street. We had assumed he had been taken to Bamako, but we were wrong. In early April, we found that he was still up north. We organized a raid to free him. But during the battle, he escaped us all."

"Then he's alive."

"We have had no information since the raid and this is now four months in the past. He is either hiding or anonymously dead."

Once again the lieutenant enters the room and stands behind Zane's chair.

Zane asks Okimbo, "Why did you tell me these things? After I'd refused to give you the address of the printing press."

"I already know where the printers are," he says. "I am not as evil as you and your files imagine. It is my printing press."

Zane wants to ask another question, but Okimbo raises his palm to signal that he shouldn't. Then he stands and looks over Zane's shoulder to the door.

Zane knows better than to extend his hand. The lieutenant leads him down the corridor to where the woman is waiting, then turns and goes into the office. The door snaps shut behind him and Zane can hear the turning of the lock.

He again pauses to examine the art in the front room. Most of the pieces are from West Africa with only a few from the central republics. His guess is that they were smuggled in by Demi, and as such they may be filled with more than sawdust. Hard cash for a movement Zane has never documented.

The woman opens the door for him and, to Zane's surprise, extends her hand. Her fingers are thin and almost translucent in the sunlight. As he reaches for that hand, Okimbo suddenly steps into the room. He is holding a piece of paper and appears to be out of breath. Zane will wonder for a long time what has come over him, forgiveness or mercy or remembrance or compassion. It never occurs to him that he's being made into live bait. Okimbo passes the paper to the woman, looks long and hard at Zane, turns on his heel, and is gone.

Zane reaches outward and feels the paper in his palm and then her hand is withdrawn and she's closing the door. Zane has the sensation of seeing her face even once she is gone, as though in that single last gaze he has photographed her with his eyes. He waits until he is safely away from the building and certain that he hasn't been followed before unfolding his palm and reading the note. There are only three words and none of them have any meaning to him:

MOUROU KOUROU BOUGOU

A sentence, a phrase, an address? The name of a man who knows a man who knows an address?

He takes a taxi back to the club. It is Sunday and the jazz club is closed. He takes the phone out from behind the bar and dials Kirk's home number. After a dozen rings, Kirk answers with a curse.

"Zane here. I need some computer work and you're the only source I've got."

"Do you know what time it is?"

"Mercy never sleeps, Kirk. Rise and shine."

"I thought Petitjean was your sidekick."

"His phone has ants all over it. At least there's always a chance."

"In the morning, Zane. Office hours."

"Kirk, you sonofabitch. Do you think I don't know you were giving copies of my transmissions to the CIA? Whatever they asked for, am I right? I've known it for months and I fed you, you shit."

"You knew?"

"Everything you touch leaves fingerprints that read like the front page."

Kirk coughs into the phone. He hates confrontations. "I'm an American, Zane. Not like you."

"It was patriotism? Is that what you're trying to tell me?"

"There were pressures. Inducements. You wouldn't understand."

"No, but Emelle might."

There is a long pause. "How in hell did we ever get on opposite sides of the fence?"

"When you began believing in fences. I've given you the words. Figure out if it's language, an address, someone's name, whatever."

"That might take some time."

"Time is what it's always been. Now run the query before you bleed to death."

Kirk's apartment is fifteen minutes from the ABRI office. The query will have a word-link search through the encyclopedia and there is no guarantee that any answer will be forthcoming. After an hour, he calls Kirk's line at the office and is told that the job is running. "Where can I call you when it's finished?"

"I'll call you." Sitting at the bar, he waits another hour with full bottles of whisky at his back and in the shelf at his knees. The litany: Cutty Sark, J & B, White Horse, Glenfiddich. He wants to open all of them but keeps his hands to himself.

When he calls back, Kirk tells him to grab a pen and Zane copies what he hears:

MOUROU KOUROU BOUGOU. MALI. 50 KM NW OF BAMAKO.
POP 202.

"What's next?"

"You can log out and go home. Forget I called."

"There's more, Zane."

"Let's have it."

"Listen, Zane. Just so you know I'm not the complete shit you take me for. This is a freebie from my own paid line."

"Read it, Kirk."

"*National Geographic* is the source. It's 'Village of the Blind.'"

"Say it again."

"The blind, Zane. Sightless."

"How sure is this information?"

"I used five micros and every variance I could think of. Four of them came up with the same answer and the fifth was blank."

"Five micros?" Zane's breath is gone. "Which lines?"

"My own, Nadine's, the secretarial line, Petitjean's, and your old line."

"Christ, *no!*"

"What's the matter? You said you were in a hurry."

"In Petitjean's program library, the one named Ice. There's a program called Stalker. Start it up from his line. Now."

"What for?"

"An eavesdropper's been on my line. I've got to know if he was tuned in."

"Hold on a sec." Minutes later, Kirk is back. "There are six users on the network, Zane. Five of them that I can account for and the other one's attached to your line. Sorry."

Zane hangs up and stares for a long time at the letters that he's written onto the back of a matchbook. In his mind, he can see the same letters printed out in cathode green on Berne's black screen. Mourou Kourou Bougou. Village of the Blind.

Sunrise, sunset. Who finds Street finds Berne.

It is past two when he returns to the room. She's waiting for him and wants to know if he's drunk or sober. He says he doesn't know. She closes the curtains and then waits for him to move behind her. When his arms come around her he can see her face reflected in the mirror at their side, her surprise. Recognition and not gratitude. He moves his lips to her neck and her hands lift into the air and hang there. After a moment he steps back and undresses himself, then waits for her on the bed. The lamplight embarrasses her and she undresses slowly, button by button, with her back turned to him. When she is down to skin and trembling he pulls her to the bed. Her legs part and he puts his hand there as if into water. Her face seeks the hollow of his neck and her lips take his pulse. When he moves over she twines herself around him like roots around stone. Then all at once she slips away and rolls to her side. "I thought I wanted to," she says. "Now it's something else."

He knows. "I'll hold you," he offers, and circles her with a single arm, resting his hand above her breast. "Like this?"

"Oui."

He is exhausted, worn thin. His eyes follow the cracks on the ceiling and he sees the lines of a hand, the graph of a heartbeat, the River Niger.

"How long have I known you?" he asks.

"Three years," she says. "But in the first year we were never speaking but to exchange money for whisky. You were always polite."

"I was always drunk."

"You wanted ice. More ice. Even in winter."

"Ice heals me. The melting."

Later, she stands and his eyes follow her to the door. She is going down there, he thinks to himself. But it is Sunday night and the club is closed. He falls asleep against his will and when he awakens it is still night and she is sleeping at his side. He sits up and can feel the ice dried on his face and arms. He can only see her in fragments and his hand searches for the lamp. The shock of the light is like a picture-taking and the image of her burns behind his eyes. When her own eyes open she sees that they are naked and he is ready for her. She reaches to turn out the light and he turns it back on.

He is awake before sunup and she is already gone. He rises from the bed and crosses the dark room to the chair where he left his clothes. Patting pockets, he finds the letters and takes them to the bed. The last two letters. Switching on the lamp, he reads the first of them quickly. *When I leave your building I feel their eyes upon me and I know I am wearing your face on my own.* From the floor above he can hear footfalls and the sound of running water.

She is washing me from her skin.

He sits in front of the screen and finishes the entry of Street's letters. Those that he has already read and keyed in have only laid grief on grief. Street's accounts of mercy missions in Afghanistan, the Sudan, Ethiopia, Iraq, Mali, and Benin. The sound of Street's voice is in his writing, the black humor and the white anger. Zane has arranged them into a chronological order and until now has read only as far as last winter, when Street was back and forth between the north and south, frantic over something that remains unexpressed. He uses initials rather than actual names of places or people, as though he expected his mail to be intercepted. It had taken infinite guesswork to know precisely where Street was while writing; the postmarks alone were explicit and may have only signified the place from where the letters were mailed. When the text file is complete, he burns the remaining photocopies and returns to the screen. He runs a word count and finds forty-seven references to B or Bj. There is no reference to Mourou Kourou Bougou but he notes that, in later letters, references to Mali increase in number. Love and mercy. Mercy and love. The initial Z appears twenty-four times. And toward the bottom of the list, Zane finds that the word *blue* appears fourteen times. Setting the program to search out the word, he finds that six of these instances are "innocent" but that the other fourteen are a part of the phrase *gone to blue.*

Of course.

He resets the search program to isolate phrases containing the key words *blue, Z, light,* and *water.* As the first rays of dawn light appear in the window, the program kicks out the answers. Zane's name is clear enough in the letter Z that appears in the last sentences of the last letter. "If ever you receive those signals, you must avoid telling Z what you know." She pretended at first not to understand the message and then she pretended to deny its veracity. Eleven gone to blue. Light water. But she knew the words, knew them by heart. Not in his language but in hers and Street's, some spin they have put to the original Zanespeak. He has only been a message boy, an intermediary and not a translator. She was expecting Zane and he fulfilled his role.

And now he is in need of a translation of his own.

As always, I am writing this letter late at night but I have forsaken the bottle and am sticking to fresh river water that K has boiled and cooled. The rain is falling again and every few hours I go outside with him to check the drain gutters and spouts of his elaborate water catcher. K's personal reservoir already holds over three hundred gallons and he acts as if he's just won the lottery. But if this downpour lasts the night, the reservoir could overflow and flood the house, so we have to keep an eye on the operation. That is the continuing story of this town, either too little or too much. My shirt is soaking wet or my shirt is caked with white dust. And the drumming of that rain on a wooden roof has deafened me to anything but thoughts that are loud enough to rise above the din.

When the rain falls here, especially as now, at the beginning of the wet season, it seems to disappear into the earth. An hour later the topsoil is dry as if the rain were merely a dream. But I am atop the hill and down below are puddles and rivulets leading to the swollen river. Last week another UN team arrived with shovels and an American contraption called a ditch witch for digging irrigation canals. In the past few years, they tell me, they have reclaimed nearly five hundred hectares around Gao and to the west, which space does little to offset the hundreds of thousands of others that have been lost to erosion and overgrazing and the usual African bad luck. This past week, with time on my hands, I have joined a crew in the valley where the drainage is poor. The irrigation ditches were dug ten years ago but the land is mostly waterlogged and has become salinised. K tells me that the effect of the irrigation was negative, that a salt swamp has replaced the dry fields and nothing will grow there. The waters have to be leached and so we are digging drainage paths and planting saline-resistant trees along waterlines. Here the choice is acacia albida but nearer to the village is a young forest of eucalyptus which will be used for fuel. It is a new Brazilian strain and you can almost see it growing. K has been given the task of hiring rangers to prevent the local populace cutting these trees prematurely. Elsewhere our brethren steal cars or cattle; here they steal trees. As the ditches are completed, the workers are covering the topsoil with gypsum and pellets that look to be plastic but are polyachrylomide, a new and increasingly cheaper compound that will retain groundwater and reduce alkaline. It would take several million tons of the stuff to turn the sub-Saharan tide, but at least in this village the fifteen tons contributed by the UN will do wonders.

But now the rains have come early and all digging has been interrupted. My contribution as a ditch digger was, I imagine, largely symbolic but the ache in my shoulders and hands as I write this letter is comforting to me. When I am working with my hands I can usually manage to fend off despair. After three weeks here I am prone to melancholy and each day I have a choice between blisters or the bottle and I fear that I've drunk an ocean already.

I am no longer alone in my search. K's wife tells me that a man, Swedish or English, it is hard to tell, has been making the rounds of the villages in this sector and asking about your husband. Apparently, the man is well funded and is passing out CFR, the Malien currency, in fat bundles. No one is certain where he comes from but he is obviously neither a policeman nor a soldier. He was also asking about a man with a number for a name and it is evident he is looking for me as well. He has even bandied Z's name about and seems aware of a connection. Since I began my search, there have been others who have crossed my path but this is the first time I've heard of anyone searching the same area for your husband. As you might have guessed, Ambrose is close by. And now I have seen him.

Three days ago I was on the rooftop of K's house, giving him a hand with his drain spouts and gutters. Two men in a car approached from the town side of the road and I recognised him on the passenger side. The car stopped only for a moment and when I raised my hand in greeting they drove away. I was holding a hammer in that hand and they may have taken it for a gun. I didn't so much see your husband as sense his presence. I suppose that's a phenomenon of this long search, using the heart as antenna instead of simple eyesight.

Then yesterday I was walking the hills with K who wanted me to point out roots and tubers that might be used for medicines. The rainy season often brings disease as well as water, and shipments from the West have been slow this year. As we reached the summit where the trees and shrubs grow thicker and longer roots, two armed men in green uniforms stood in our path. One of them was your husband.

He was as thin as ever but has shaved his moustache and beard so he looks surprisingly young compared to the AP and Interpol photos. It may have been the sunlight or the peace of the morning hour that gave me the mistaken impression that he would be docile, reasonable. His uniform was torn and wrinkled and included a gold braid around his shoulder. His partner led K away at gunpoint so that we could be alone. I kept listening for the sound of gunfire and even asked Ambrose if he might spare K's life. He didn't answer me. He just kept his gun pointed at my head though it was obvious I wasn't armed and hadn't been followed. Then he led me further up the hill and gestured to a patch of ground where he wanted me to sit.

He trusted no one, he explained. His government, the Americans, the French, the English, the Organisation for African Unity, the South Africans, the ANC, soldiers from Mali, Niger, even the Red Cross. And now a roving pimp, yours truly, from the British Medical Company. I wanted to speak to him about you but as soon as I mentioned your name he was in a rage of pain and ordered me to shut up. I will not detail the hour that followed, his winding narrative or his accusations concerning the two of us. His speech had the same elegance as always, that hypnotic tone and poetic turn of a phrase that so impressed the journalists some years ago but now and then he would simply begin to curse in any of ten languages. He sat with his back to a tree and spoke as though he were drugged but his eyes were clear and the point of the gun never wavered. What he meant to do was to warn me off. He has an army in the hills, he says, and he is aware that the whole lot of them will die within the year. All the same, I am in his way. My presence in the village could lead others to his trail. One year, he kept saying. He wants one more year to finish his work. There is political surgery to be performed, scores to settle, villages to be salvaged. His motives are impossible to decipher. Does he mean to clear his name and reputation? Launch a revolution? Revenge his years of exile and flight? It is equally impossible to guess who his targets have become. His rhetoric contrived a bizarre history of the continent and included episodes that I am convinced he has merely imagined. Even his memories have blurred and he denied, for example, that he was ever educated in the United Kingdom. When I pointed out his perfection of the English language he simply shrugged and said all languages are the same, "a simple means of lying with tongue and teeth."

But he does not deny you, M'Khlea. There was a brief moment when he lowered the gun barrel to the ground and appeared to relax. I knew it was useless to remind him of his past, the compassion he once displayed for the humanity around him. Compassion is a bond that he has long since severed. So I simply mentioned the vows and my wish for you to live. I asked him to call off his men and to give you your freedom. As I spoke, it was difficult to look in his direction. I was looking at the sky as if I were speaking to the clouds or to the setting sun. His eyes were upon me and they felt more menacing than the gun. He let me speak until I was finished and then we sat there for a long time, each of us looking at the same rainclouds that approached from the distant hills.

I changed my approach and asked him about the interrogations when he was imprisoned. The night we met at the hotel he had told me about a doctor with blue eyes, the same man I now have been stalking for years. He stared across the distance to me and pointed a finger at his head. He said that the man was forever there, bidding him to speak. "Confession is a human reflex," he told me. "The words cannot live caged in memory. They need to be said."

I asked him if the man was still operating in West Africa and he nodded. Then he rose and holstered his gun and whistled for his companion. When I pressed for further information he simply turned his back and began to descend the hillside. I was prepared for any other response, but not that. A threat, a blow to the head, a bullet. Though I called after him, he continued down the hillside and disappeared in the bush. Some minutes later K appeared, unharmed.

He is still there and he will find me when he chooses. It is impossible to read what he meant by that silence. Or I am deluding myself into believing it signified doubt, the word *perhaps* drifting across these rainy hills. I am torn between staying here and awaiting him and rushing back to Paris to steal you away to some safe and secret place. His time is coming near. When the rainy season is finished, his enemies will reactivate. He and his weird army will almost certainly be forced out of the area and I will never be able to find him again.

K is convinced that Ambrose has thrown in his lot with the Touaregs. They have created a guerilla force to combat the soldiers from Mali and Niger who have been hunting them down and shooting them for some time. A Syrian arms merchant was spotted in Gao just before my arrival and last week the bodies of five Mali officers were found near Kidal. There are close to eight hundred thousand Touaregs in Mali alone, so you can imagine the consequences if they've taken Ambrose as their military counsel. The UN workers have requested a protective force and for the past week there has been a curfew in Gao for females and children.

I have received instructions from London to leave this place. They want me to go to a village southwest of here to supervise the distribution of ivermectin and mectizan, drugs that control the spread of river blindness. I had already sent a cable requesting a delay and received a stern denial. My dedication to the firm is increasingly under a cloud and I am told to return to London by the end of the month. But there is no question of my leaving here. There was nothing else to be done, so I tendered my resignation. After three years of searching the continent for Ambrose I am closer than I will ever be. All the same, I feel myself surrounded by menace. Dr. Renault has disappeared. You remember that he was holding my blood samples, those that I had hoped would reveal what has been done to the Touaregs. I have spoken twice to his wife and she will tell me only that he is alive. I suspect he has gone into hiding but cannot be sure. Through a diplomat I know in Abidjan, I have made enquiries about the location of the blood samples but nothing has been returned to me. I now have five eyewitnesses, four of them Touaregs and the fifth a Malien Bambara who was suspected of aiding the Touaregs. Each of them is prepared to identify the man that K and I refer to as Bearne. For lack of another name. Sky eyes, the Touaregs call him. And it is odd to note that none of them exhibit any loathing for the man. To the contrary, they have asked that he be spared death. The other captors, they say, are the evil men. Sky eyes, they insist, is not evil.

In haste. K has just come to tell me that a car and driver are waiting outside for me. Given the hour, it can only be your husband. We have things to say to each other and time is running out. I am giving this letter to K to be posted to you and have instructed him to send signals to Z if anything happens to Ambrose. I trust that you have not forgotten the cross-translations. If ever you receive those signals, you must avoid telling Z what you know. Your husband's reach and wrath are impossible to measure.

The rain just stopped and the silence is unsettling. In a few hours the sun will rise over the hills and the blue flies will be everywhere. I imagine that K's reservoir is now full and he will be pleased. I am surrounded by hope and the village is filled with rainwater. Fold your hands and pray with me. I send my love in its usual bright colours.

THE RAINY SEASON IS ENDED, THE TRAVEL AGENT tells him. The Niger waters are high and boats are running from Bamako to Gao. "There wasn't much of a downpour this year, so you might find that prices vary from the desperate to the hopeless. I suggest you not miss Bandiagari and the Dogon Escarpment."

"There must be a flight before Wednesday. I can't wait two days."

"That's all there is. Bamako isn't London or even Oslo. One flight from Paris per week, every week."

"What about out of Geneva or London?"

"Mali is a former French colony and the majority of people who go there are French. The only other European flight to Bamako leaves from Marseille on Wednesday."

"What about a flight to Abidjan first, or even Dakar, and then a transfer on to Bamako?"

The man doesn't give a damn whether or not he sells a ticket. He looks at his watch to measure the time between now and lunch hour. Then he reaches under the counter for his catalogue. "The African companies aren't on the same system," he explains. After several minutes' paging through the flight schedules, he concludes that the fastest possible flight to Bamako is the one that leaves on Wednesday night from Marseille. "Like I said."

After some hesitation, Zane refuses the connecting flight from Orly, takes the Marseille–Bamako ticket, and offers his last name as Dane. He can later claim a typo if during boarding they ask for his passport. He pays cash, pockets the ticket and his receipt, and goes out onto the street, where the sunlight is white and there is no breeze whatsoever. He already has a seven-day visa for Mali but has been told to immediately check in at a police station and have it renewed. With two days on his hands he still has time for his shots against yellow fever and cholera.

Bamako, Bandiagari, Gao. Places that oblige him to have antitoxins in his blood to save him from diseases that belong to other centuries. He once thought alcohol was a cure-all but here he is in need of immunity. Mali is landlocked and is the size of his thumb on a wall map. He breathes the concocted air of Paris on a hot September afternoon and feels he is already at the edge of that desert.

His guidebook has no mention of Mourou Kourou Bougou or any Village of the Blind. But the village itself is indirectly cited in Street's letters and a detail map of the country provides confirmation that it exists. A thin black line, either a dirt road or a misprint, leads from Bamako in the general direction of the village but the line disappears before arriving there.

In his archive of transmissions from Street, he found five messages that concerned Mali. Without detail or available corroboration, Street had a year before reported an escalation of tensions between the Mali military and the Touaregs, a vast tribe that inhabits the northeast corner of the country and spreads into Niger. The systematic killing of Touaregs by the ruling parties of Niger, Mali, and Nigeria had been a page-seven story for years; no one save the Touaregs gave a damn. And Street's messages offered nothing substantial for Zane to unravel and report. "Stars count ten Touareg pink slips. Fields of Gao." A week later, he dropped the language: "Alive, if slightly ill. Nothing in the papers anywhere about the killings near Gao. Am I the only one who noticed?" This transmission had come from Abidjan, to where he had fled.

And in March, a single transmission: "Have found my doctor. Evidence imminent."

Evidence imminent. Zane stands at a red light at the Place de Clichy and wonders about what it actually means. As a mere amnesty agent, he has only seen the evidence of crimes, never the crime and never the criminal. He is the master listener, the voyeur. The players, like Demi, think of him as a bystander or a witness. Neither victim nor victimizer, a human version of smug Switzerland. A man he knew who worked for the Red Cross once admitted to Zane his loathing for a number of the sponsors he came across, check writers and fundraisers, the kinds of people who give dinner parties to raise money for famine victims. He acknowledged a certain self-righteousness in his loathing. "It's just that I always imagine them folding the lobster and asparagus tips and Béarnaise sauce into an envelope and mailing it to the Sudan. Licking the stamp with champagne-wetted tongues. At least they're reacting to their better instincts. It's the comfort of it all that drives me mad. The good works emanating from poolside with a telephone in one hand and a Mai Tai in the other. But I'm the perverse one. I feel most alive when I'm out with mosquitoes and the beggars' outstretched palms."

Zane knows that he has taken himself seriously only when he has exhausted himself, when he has spent nights on the mattress and pulled himself through crises with coffee, Dexedrine, and the illusion of his own utility. He can speak only two languages, English and French, and three if he counts Zanespeak; but this is a limited language, reserved for skulduggery and calamity. In his work he is often in the presence of people who possess four, five, or six languages, whose lives are webbed and lined from famine operations and refugee camps, the art and practice of mercy and alien discourse. Who only carry cameras to take pictures of others. Tourists seem to photograph *themselves* with symbols of place in the background as evidence that they were there. But these people in the field are not tourists. Zane doesn't know for certain what he is, but knows he is somewhere between the two.

At twelve-thirty he climbs the high hill of Montmartre and sits on the steps of the Sacré-Coeur, high above Paris. He considers whisky but decides instead on a bottle of Alsatian beer. He lights a cigarette and takes long pulls from the bottle until the taste of pennies has left his mouth. The sky has that watercolor look of fading light and chemicals and the city before him is flat and tan and covered in its own dust. He remembers he had his first Paris haircut not far from here, on the rue de la Goutte d'Or. In Zola's time it was a grimy, working-class district where the laundry-women gossiped about husbands and prostitutes and everyone descended into absinthe stupors of a Saturday night. Today that street is crowded with North Africans and still is only partly paved. His barber asked him, "Not too short, not too long?" and Zane answered, "Just do your stuff," and emerged looking distinctly Moroccan.

The thought of his leavetaking calms him and he finishes the beer and tosses the empty into a nearby bin. Not far away, a Vietnamese guitar player starts in on a Neil Young song and is instantly surrounded by young travelers with backpacks. Zane steps into a phone booth and dials the number Petitjean gave him. For a moment he thinks he hears drumbeats, though it is only a small boy banging his plastic bottle against the pavement.

THE ABRI OPERATIONS ARE BEGINNING TO UNRAVEL. The harmony is gone, and Petitjean wonders how much they ever truly had. Messages are missed, lines are crossed or have gone down. For two days running the telefax has issued smudges and blurs that were supposed to be photographs. Three of the sixteen print pins on his matrix printer are broken and the letters he issues look like pencil scratches rather than serious correspondence. He has seen the expense sheet of one of Emelle's observers, currently in South America, and finds an item clearly marked *Sexual favors: 12,500 bolivars.* And Emelle's approving initials at the bottom.

The office is quiet and each of them remains in a private space. Petitjean can see it in their eyes, their anxiety. It is as though they have all slept badly and awakened to a continuing exhaustion. They are reluctant to look at their screens or at each other. Nguyen unfolds a newspaper and lays it across her desk. Nadine arranges paperclips, pencils, stapler, Scotch tape while Kirk spends more and more of his time boning up on Portuguese rather than tending to business. He has been relieved of Africa. Emelle says she'll go it alone until a replacement can be named. But she is too seldom in her office and the messages that come across Zane's old line go unread and unanswered.

Emelle has called a morning staff meeting to review current priorities. They gather in the windowless conference room in the back and arrange coffee cups, pens, notepads, and ashtrays, then take their usual places at the oval table. Despite the heat, Emelle is wearing a long-sleeved blouse with a collar that buttons to her chin, a black brooch in the form of a ladybug, a strand of pearls. She has a photocopied agenda for each of them but only Raymond Li, Petitjean observes, is taking any notes. While Emelle reads aloud what she has written, the others stare at the memo as if it's a placemat. The first line, highest priority, reads: "Renew contacts with the press." She knows that of late they are friendless; invitations to conferences are not forthcoming and her incoming mail is thin. "It will take a bit of honey to attract the bees, but the entertainment budget has already been exhausted. We will have to use our imaginations. And the sweetest honey is results. Data. Visibility."

Zane's chair is unoccupied but the new English secretary has forgotten and left a copy of the list in his place. Nguyen is looking at the chair, and when she feels Petitjean's eyes on her, she looks away.

He searches for the English word for this feeling. Corrupt. That will do. The boredom is painful. Emelle drones on, her voice muted in the airless room. Priority seven: reduce paper costs. Still speaking, she glances his way and he bows his head to the list, lifts his pen, and checks off the first six priorities. Then he writes "Eleven." He draws a circle and a circle around it, and another circle. Emelle is asking if anyone can offer suggestions for reducing, streamlining, belt tightening. There is no reply. When the entire list has been covered, no one besides Emelle has spoken a word. She asks Kirk when he expects to complete his article for the newsletter and he replies that it has been on her desk for three days. Then he asks when they might expect a replacement for Zane. Someone to fill the African desk.

"The African desk," Emelle replies. She stares for a long moment at the stack of papers before her. "The sector may be discontinued. For the moment, we are in no financial position to continue to cover the globe. We will have to count on the circle to fill our absences."

The meeting doesn't end, it melts away. As Petitjean returns to his office, Emelle approaches from behind and touches his elbow. "In my office? Five minutes?"

He leaves his coffee cup and cigarettes at his desk, slips his speaking stones into his mouth, and follows her into the glass room. But instead of sitting, she leans her weight backward against her desk. Petitjean stands with his back to the closed door.

"You are angry with me," she says. "And to punish me you are working fewer hours."

He replies that the lines are unusually quiet. The summer heat, perhaps.

"This is a crucial time for your sector. Glasnost, perestroika. Hungary is bursting at the seams and Poland has become fairly translucent. The news from Prague is like a breath of fresh air. As the Soviet Union is liberalizing, the ethnic questions are being unearthed all over again. Your data flow should be rising to flood level by now and yet only trickles reach my desk. Do you miss him that badly?"

The question revives him. His boredom dissolves.

She continues, "I know that the two of you were very close."

He tells her that no one is close to Zane. "He lives *his* secrets."

"Precisely. And you, Alain, what secrets are you living?"

Stolen cars. A blinded policeman. Love of a windblown soul. "I have a doctor in Romania," he says.

It is not the answer she had hoped for but she plays along. "Yes, him. He's out, is he?"

This is his first success in weeks, the only news on his screen that has lifted his spirits. The Romanian authorities have granted a travel visa to his besieged doctor, who will attend a conference in Trieste, and from there a boat will spirit him across the Adriatic Sea to Italy. The funds for that journey—boat, pilot, food, bribes—have been supplied by ABRI. The classic approach has paid off; petitions, floods of letters, articles in the French and English press, and harassment of front-line diplomats have lifted the man's plight out of the corridors of Bucharest into the courtyard of the continent. The doctor has become an embarrassment to the government, and although they are aware of the defection, they will kick up an official fuss when the deed is done.

"Amnesty is taking the credit," he tells her. "You will have to negotiate the press announcement with your English friends."

"We have no friends," she says. "We are as alone as we have ever been. Zane's defection has cost us dearly."

The stones rattle his teeth. "You are fucked up, Emelle. Pardon my French. He's as clean as Ajax."

She doesn't know the term. Neither did Petitjean, once.

"Sweetheart," he continues. "For a long time. He called you Sweetheart and he licked the floors of this place to keep it clean."

Her eyes flicker. There is a mist of perspiration covering her face. Her make-up has dissolved and her face is distorted. Her phone rings and she signals to her secretary through the glass to take a message. "Did he tell you anything, Alain? Did he ever confide in you about these rakers of his?"

"Never."

"And you do not feel betrayed?"

He has only the semblance of a career and Emelle doesn't ever give pay raises that exceed the cost of living. He wants to slap her face, pinch her breasts, lift her skirt and shout between her thighs that she has betrayed him, she has exiled the guardian of the language and shelter and foreverafter there will be only static or silence. He rolls the stones from one side of his mouth to the other. And then, deliberately this time, he swallows them.

"He taught me the meaning of one of his phrases. 'The moon is down.' It means total darkness, absolute silence. He did everything you asked to hold that moon up high. Moonlight, he said, would be the best we could hope for."

"But here, amongst ourselves. Surely we must be transparent to each other."

He shrugs. "You should have thanked him for exposing Bartholomew. Instead you whipped him."

"Why? Why did I whip him, Alain?"

The word is nearly the same in both French and English. He has his choice. "Vanity," he says. "Vanité."

Liberated from Emelle's embrace, Petitjean spends the remainder of the morning filling a dossier with updated case histories of detainees in Prague and then skips out for a sack lunch on the steps of Notre-Dame de Lorette. It was Catherine who packed the lunch and he silently pardons her for forgetting the bread that is usually essential to a ham sandwich. The ham is abundant, however, and the lone lettuce leaf is fresh. Though he cannot feel the stones in his stomach, he knows they are there. He devours his apple and throws the empty lunch bag into a nearby can, then lights a cigarette. The sun is full in his face and reminds him of Normandy. Now that August has ended, the traffic has picked up and Paris is beginning to look like its crowded old self. He decides that without Zane there is little reason for him to stay on at ABRI. There is work to be done everywhere, he figures, beginning with his own neighborhood, where more and more *clodos* are sleeping in cardboard. Instead of babysitting rabble-rousers on the other side of Europe he could sow some brotherly love in the tenth arrondissement. He could open a soup kitchen in an abandoned warehouse, provide mattresses in place of cardboard. The operation would be funded by the cars he would steal from the rich. A Mercedes a week should do the trick. With one hand on the steering wheel he would offer the other to Catherine. Look at this hand. Life line, love line, anonymous wrinkles. Trace them to the end, he will ask her, and tell me what is there.

At five minutes to one he steps into the corner brasserie and leans against the bar nearest the telephone. At precisely one minute after one, the phone rings and he takes the receiver from the barman.

"'Renault is dead,'" he says, "'and no records you asked for have been located.'"

"What's the signature?"

"Mozart."

"Nothing more?"

"Your line is now dead. I disconnected it at noon. You don't exist."

"No," Zane agrees. "I don't."

"The other matter. I queried all of my best travel sources and your man didn't lie. From any point in Europe, the soonest flight to Bamako is on Wednesday."

"Including transit from other African capitals?"

"It's a backwater, Zane. Page seven, like you say. There aren't even any train connections that could get you there faster. I'm assuming that you're the passenger in question."

"I've always trusted you, Petitjean."

"I never knew. I wanted you to." There is a pause and the usual sound of electricity, though this time it is benign, the fuzzwah of an innocent public line. "Stay in touch," Petitjean says.

"Sure thing. We'll use the dedicated line. A Dick and Jane. Look and see. Do you remember?"

"See Dick run. Run run run."

"I'm Jane, Petitjean."

"We don't have to sign anything. If it's baby talk, I'll know it's you."

For two days he remains hidden in that room, awaiting his rescheduled flight to Mali. At night he can hear voices, clash of bottles, and music coming through the floor. They've been playing a new set since the end of August. If he leaves the door open, the music rumbles and soars, an excavation of the heart, and the keyboard sounds like bullets that strike their targets. But if he closes the door he hears a hollowness of bass and cymbals and only the faintest tones of piano, like the sound from a cheap radio tuned to a station far away. Now he knows what it is to have a safe house, to live concealed in a friendly cage. While listening to the music he lies with his head at the foot of the bed and gazes at those photographs on the wall, the sepia of Fingers' youth, the black and white of his middle age, and the Kodachrome of his old age. Fingers with his woolly cap and goatee, Fingers with his shining forehead. Zane in the crowd with his shabby smile and upraised glass. Though at first he expected visitors, no one has come asking him. He is not what they want anymore; he is a dead wire leading to a frayed end. With that intercept they already know, as he does, where to find Street.

On Tuesday night he dials Emelle's home number and is surprised when she answers. For long seconds he says nothing, but she doesn't hang up. She waits as if she knows it is Zane who is calling.

"Is it true that Zanespeak is a dying language?" he asks her. "Or is it only a tongue spoken by those soon to be dead?"

"Come in, Thomas. Come back. Your life's in danger."

"It's not me they want, Emelle. Only my tongue. Which with your help has been torn from the root."

"Petitjean has resigned. He came in late this afternoon and left a letter on my desk. When I read that letter I thought he was merely distraught. His Romanian doctor was arrested and killed. But in the packet with his letter were photos he had taken of your apartment after . . . Thomas, I had no idea."

"Tell me about the man you hired to watch me."

"I've made inquiries. Through the back channels. I have been a fool, Thomas. He was not who he said he was. It's your Eleven he was after and he used me to flush you out."

"Where did you find him?"

"He found me. We met at that conference on amnesty surveillance—you know, methods and practices—in Copenhagen last March. He offered security screening of the staff and after Bartholomew I felt I should listen to him."

"What does he look like?"

"No taller than you. Blond hair with some gray in it. He's European, but I had trouble placing his accent. Northern Europe. German or Dutch."

"Swedish. And his eyes are blue. I don't suppose he told you his name."

"I only had a business card with the name of the agency. He insisted on discretion."

"Berne? Bearne? Anything like that?"

"No, I never knew his name."

"Do you know who he's working for?"

"I thought he was working for me. Listen to me, Thomas. I have put out an SOS to the circle and to my last friends at Interpol. You can come in. You will be protected."

"My friend tried to tell me that he existed. I didn't believe him."

"Speak to me, Thomas, come back into the circle. Where you belong."

For a moment he thinks he hears a ticking on the line, that mosquito sound. "Your phone is jacked, Emelle. We're on a party line here. Petitjean could have swept it for you if you'd asked."

"Thomas, listen to me—"

"The moon is down. Molly's soliloquy. Send juice. Pink slips. Skin on skin."

"I don't speak the language, Thomas."

"I am speaking to Berne, or Bearne—whatever. *He* knows the language, Emelle. Now that you've so kindly introduced us. He could teach you the whole thing. He understands every dying word."

He leaves the room only after the club is closed and the shades are pulled down over the windows high up on the wall and the doors double-locked. Marie comes up the stairs to knock on his door and to tell him it is safe to come out. A whisky is waiting for him on the bar and he sits with Fingers, who drinks mint tea and tells Zane it was a good crowd, the truest of the faithful, they all come back when summer's over. He is breathing hard as if he's been running, and his forehead is shiny with sweat. Zane searches his eyes for anger but sees only an after-jazz glow that doesn't necessarily spell tranquillity. Fingers says that Marie could use a hand with the ice buckets and then, when Zane rises, he reaches for his arm. "That's okay. I just like to see men jump in the presence of a lady. Sit back down here and don't give me those eyes. I am approvin, if you haven't got the drift."

When the club is swept and closed down, he climbs the stairs again and moments later Marie is there with him. She looks at him in disbelief, as though he was meant to vanish, but the flesh and blood of him is still there. They make love with the lights on while he props himself on his elbows and takes inventory of the joining. A hundred photographs of Fingers and his world look on.

Wednesday dawn. The club smells of coffee and ash and the floor is slick under his feet. From the door she tells him that the street is empty. "*Pas un chat.*" The taxi arrives and he bends to his travel bag. Map of France, map of Mali, toiletry kit purchased in a discount store, pellets for purifying water, leather walking shoes with tire-tread soles, socks, salt pills, pen and paper, light and medium clothing, shirts, jeans, passport, blade and foam.

She is standing off to the side, but as he crosses the threshold, she presses his hand with her own and it is wet with ice.

He descends to the south in an odd fashion, taking the taxi to the Gare de Lyon, then a train to Chilly, Nemours, Beaune. He is avoiding the obvious paths and assumes that once he is cleanly out of Paris he will be able to catch his breath. After an hour's wait in Beaune, he boards a local train to Lyon and arrives with an hour to spare for the ten o'clock to Marseille. There are express trains, but he has chosen a slower and more discreet local. Throughout the day there are several stops that are never announced, the train pausing for a minute or two in stations that look to be abandoned. He is the only one awake in the second-class compartment. The car is filled with a haze of yellow light. To his left is a window that shows only growing darkness and to his right an old woman who occasionally leans into him, her gray head falling against his shoulder as if she were about to tell him a secret. The first few times he nudges her away, but then ho lets it go and she burrows her head close to his chin. Just before Avignon she awakens suddenly and finds her head in his lap. Unimpressed, she sits up, lifts her hands to her hair to pat it into place, then stands and reaches to the overhead bin for her bag. As the train pulls into the station, she leans in his direction. "Vous avez les genoux d'un prêtre," she tells him. You have the knees of a priest. And then she turns and struggles out the door.

In years past, when he traveled for ABRI, he learned his way around the airports and was comfortable even during flight delays or while standing in long ticket lines. He enjoyed the routines of the seat assignment, bag checking, passport stamping, smoking/ no smoking, classe affaires or classe économique. He was comfortable because he was at home. He was neither in France nor in England nor in Denmark nor in America. Airports are the universal country. When he crossed the passport control he was in the nation of the transient, where no one is foreign. Orly, Schipol, Charles de Gaulle, Kastrup, Leonardo da Vinci, Fornebu, Heathrow, Gatwick, once he had his passport stamp and boarding pass he was in limbo and among his peers. He always made it early to the airport, even if it meant walking out of a conference or a meeting with ABRI's financial backers. He did not want to miss his flight, he explained, citing the perils of rush-hour traffic, though in his heart he was always eager for an hour in the airport and was disappointed if his time came to anything less. He learned which bars were the least frequented, hidden away in upper stories where tourists never wandered. He knew which newspaper stands carried hard-to-find American magazines or political journals and which duty-free shops sold his brand of cigarettes. He memorized the paths to follow from passport control to the newsstand to the bar to the men's room to the plane. He seldom had to sit or stand in crowded waiting areas while the plane was being loaded. He would wait until final call and then would be the last on board. Which meant that the overhead racks were already stuffed with backpacks and briefcases, shopping bags and vanity cases. It was no matter. All he carried onto a plane was himself, a book or newspaper, and cigarettes to last the flight.

At Marignane Airport in Marseille he has more than an hour before his flight is to take off. This airport is new to him and it is too early to check his suitcase, so he carries it with him to the first brasserie in sight.

He intended to remain sober, shiny-eyed, and in possession of his senses. He hadn't expected to be overcome by a terror that only alcohol could distill into anxiety. He is not going home for Thanksgiving. He is going the other way, to a black-and-brown land of stone and dust and flies where everyone is said to be sightless. And until he has finished his first drink he thinks wistfully about turning one hundred and eighty degrees and fashioning a straight line, as the crow flies, back to Marie and to Fingers and to that wall of photographs. He spends forty-five minutes in that brasserie. He folds and unfolds his Mali maps, writes notes in the margins, and reads the *International Herald Tribune*, all of it, including the stock and bond reports, twice, but there are no red dots to decipher, no mail addressed to Thomas Zane. Only the news of the world. Little by little, he is calmed by the whisky and the amnesia of newsprint. Fifteen minutes before his flight, he stands and carries his slim suitcase to the ticket counter. He orders a smoking seat on the aisle and then proceeds to passport control. For ten minutes, he stands well away from the doorway and watches the passengers as they cross. None of them fit Berne's description and he finally decides it is safe to board. He is held up for a few minutes by a Lebanese family ahead of him. Dark faces pass slowly through the portals of France. His pale skin and U.S. passport produce only a nod and a wave of the hand.

Once on the other side, he forgets about the newsstand and the duty-free and heads straight for an American-style bar with a zinc-and-brass counter and leather seats. He hasn't slept in nearly two days and his thoughts circle without landing. The letter is in his shirt pocket and he reads it again. He has been reading the letter for three weeks and can see the words with his eyes closed. *I trust that you have not forgotten the cross-translations.*

She wasn't alone when the window opened to the sky. Whoever was with her had waited for him to walk away and then climbed the stairs on cat's feet. He remembers the man he bumped on the first-floor landing. The man had said "Sorry," in English. Her door was already open. She had given away the letters and was thrown from the window into the Paris sky. Street is alive or dead in the Village of the Blind, having breathed his language back onto Zane as onto a mirror. A gauze covers his eyes and he closes them and then snaps awake, his heart beating fast. He checks his watch and sees that he has dozed for five minutes. His hand is still curled into a claw around his drink.

Later, when he is seated in 7C, he closes his eyes but fails to sleep. His thoughts drift to his mother. Her husband died in Korea while she was in the arms of the man who would become Zane's father, a man she would abandon before Zane was old enough to talk. When he was born, there were some early doubts as to his bloodlines, but soon he grew into his father's face. There are motives that move people to violence and he supposes his mother's had to do with both love and shame and a piece of Chinese shrapnel in a man's heart. The man had gone to war against her wishes and she came to believe her instincts were infallible; he went to war and he died of war, not of her infidelity. She didn't marry again, because she had long since hopped on the bus of revolution and what validity was there in a piece of paper from the state of Minnesota? She has been a widow the entirety of Zane's life.

The stewardess bends to ask him what he would like and he hears himself describing an ocean of Scotch whisky, a golden sea dotted with blue icebergs, and a melting ball of sun. When she has answered his prayers and brought him a glass, he lifts it to his face but does not drink. The floating ice turns from white to clear and as the plane banks left across the Mediterranean Sea, he gazes into that ice as into a crystal ball.

The contour of a country, the shape of a remembered face. A gold chain hangs to between her breasts, bearing a black stone teardrop. Light water.

Midnight comes to Africa and Zane is shaken awake by the sound of the landing gears. There is a single scream of rubber as the plane touches down in Bamako, in Mali.

LIGHT WATER

IT IS THE SUNLIGHT THAT AWAKENS HIM RATHER THAN the noise in the street. When he opens his eyes, he can feel the thorns behind them. Dear God, this morning prayer.

.The night before, he had panicked at the airport, thinking that he would be denied entry and, once in, fearful that he would never be allowed to leave. But his passport was examined and stamped without incident. As he approached customs, he swore off liquor once and for all, but the *douanier* waved him through after only a cursory glance inside his single suitcase. There is nothing more guilty-looking, he reflected, than a man unable to prove his innocence. His fear subsided for less than five minutes. On the other side of customs, he lit a cigarette and smoked it down while he glanced around the airport in search of watchful eyes. But his was the last arriving flight of the evening, and except for the inevitable soldiers in khaki and camouflage fatigues the hall was nearly vacant. Satisfied that no one was waiting to intercept him, he climbed into a taxi and felt a wave of alcohol sickness as the driver swung onto the road. The night was black and in that blackness his fear returned and overwhelmed his good sense. He directed the driver to the nearest bar, where he purchased two bottles at cutthroat rates before continuing on to the hotel.

While he registered, the young clerk at reception politely listed the attributes of the room: private bed, clean linen, washing sink with hot and cold running water, window with view of street, clean floor of stone tiles cool to the feet, nightstand with working lamp, electric fan, high low medium; toilet two doors down the hall, shower three doors down. As Zane signed his name, the man added, with the same politeness but in a distinctly softer voice, that he could supply amusements, distractions, escort or tourist guide, "and if Monsieur desires, a telling of his fortune."

Zane climbed the stairs and locked his door against visions of his future. Then he closed the curtains and left a lamp burning by his bed. He uncapped and drained half of the first bottle in a quarter of an hour as he watched twenty different species of moth at play around that lamp. Insects clung to the walls or flitted from the ceiling to the light. The more he drank, the larger the insects became. By the time the bottle was empty he was surrounded by dragons in full flight.

In the morning light, he attempts to dissemble that fear, to break it into small pieces that might be examined. But fear is not a telex or telefax to be deciphered. He fears for his life and wonders why. Do I value this life? Am I *enjoying* myself? He fears not finding Street. He fears he will find Street. He dreads the moment when he will enter the Village of the Blind. The black joke: If no one can see me, how certain is my existence?

His breath is stale and he needs a shave. The bottom of his whisky glass is filled with drowned moths. And with the dawn's early light, his dread has dispersed and all he truly needs, he tells himself, is aspirin and fresh water and a change of clothes. He takes off his stinking shirt and, once he is naked, thinks of Marie. There is a rusted sink against the wall and he washes his face and torso with tepid water and soap, but the smell of whisky remains until he's scrubbed it from his mouth. Then he reaches for his small suitcase and soon begins to feel reassembled, clothed in jeans and work shirt and walking boots. There are no aspirin in his bag but already the headache has begun to withdraw.

He has been strongly advised to extend his visa beyond the customary six days already granted. Mali officials, according to the rakers, are known to shake down tourists beyond the limit. When he leaves the hotel, he therefore goes first to the police station to pay for an extension. Street once told him it was a custom in former colonies to stand in line for papers or stamps or signatures or countersignatures. *Préfet, sous-préfet, commissaire, conseil d'administration, notaire, chef et sous-chef de service.* The Maliens have apparently inherited their bad bureaucratic habits from the French and Zane frets over lost time while this simple exercise takes most of the morning.

Across from the train station, on the rue Bara Diarra, is the American Center. When he first stops there he finds a sign, CLOSED FOR THREE HOURS. It is of the type he has sometimes seen in Paris, with its inherent riddle. Which three hours? He glances at his watch and finds that the second hand has stopped dead. Another moment of disinformation: it couldn't possibly be 6:47, a.m. or p.m. The noonday sun offers no shade, so he returns to the train station for a lunch of chicken and steamed rice and a quarter *pichet* of room-temperature rosé that tastes of warm water mixed with tanning lotion. From where he sits he can see across the road to the American Center. He waits, hoping to measure the lengthening shadows, but it is hopeless. If he has to read the sky to know the time, he is limited to sunrise, noon, and sunset.

Throughout his lunch, he is approached by children selling bone jewelry, wood carvings, maps, or sweets. In his weakened state, he is tempted to buy it all, to drain his pockets of the last of his CFR, his francs, his dollars. Money weighs so heavily in your pockets when you are face to face with the penniless. Give it away, join them. Setting aside his fork, he purchases a map of Bamako, a wooden comb, and a bone necklace. He wonders briefly if Marie would wear it. He imagines her wearing nothing except that necklace against her pale skin. His buying spree has encouraged other children and he finds himself surrounded by outstretched hands bearing earrings, bracelets, brooches, hair-pins. He doesn't know a word of Bambara and says "Thank you" over and over until at last an enormous man in immaculate white, evidently an officer of some sort, comes by and scatters them with the wave of a hand.

At last he sees the door of the center swing open from the inside. He pays his bill and leaves a tip that is so ridiculous that the waiter corrects him and gives half of it back. I'm doing this badly, he considers. Everyone will take notice of me, a stupid American throwing money around like autumn leaves.

A clock on the wall at the American Center reads 3:20, though he decides not to trust it. He is greeted by a polite young receptionist in a white blouse.

"Passport?" she asks.

He places it on the counter but she doesn't bother to open it. "Pointless routine," she explains. "My duty. Where do you live in America?"

"Paris."

"I see. Tourist?"

He explains he is in need of a guide and driver to Mourou Kourou Bougou, and he expects her to ask him why. But she merely hands him a mimeographed list of names. "Behind the station," she tells him, "there is a parking place. Ask first for these men." With a pen she checks off a half-dozen of the fifty names. "They are the most reliable."

"How much should I pay?"

"Whatever they ask, offer half. Don't argue needlessly. Just pay what you want, within reason. Where you are going is not far."

"Is there any danger? I mean, along the road?"

"What kind of danger?"

"Touaregs or soldiers. People with guns and bad manners."

Her smile is brief and stunted, as though she has long since learned to wear a face like blank paper. "There are no hostilities close to Bamako. And very few Touaregs. But why would a tourist want to see a village filled with blind people?"

"Can you keep a secret? There are secrets in Mali?"

"Mali is a secret. The entire country and everyone in it. We are never mentioned in *The New York Times* or on CNN. Perhaps when the war erupts, we will be noticed. What is your secret?"

"I am looking for a friend."

"That is no secret to anyone who isn't blind."

He crosses the street and walks to the north end of the station. His shirt is already damp and white dust has gathered on the backs of his hands. To his left is a small square where people are selling clothing and brightly colored fabrics. At one end, beneath a massive hand-painted Sony poster stretched across the station wall, a group of men is standing before a row of cars that look like roadside salvage. As Zane approaches, they take note of him and two of them advance slightly and gesture toward their cars. When Zane is surrounded by upturned faces, he reads aloud the first name marked on the list but there is no response, nor to the second. He begins to wonder if he's pronouncing the names correctly, but when he calls out the third he is answered with a shout and within seconds a man is standing before him. He is Falaye, he says immediately, twenty-five and very strong; he is reliable and prudent, a driver who knows the city like the smile on his mother's face. He is wearing a short-sleeved white shirt with a blue packet of Gitanes showing through the front pocket. His feet are bare and covered with white dust. The sun is in his face and he smiles into it.

Zane offers his name and explains that he needs a driver to take him to Mourou Kourou Bougou.

"I have a jeep," Falaye says. "Michelin tires, best." He has been to Mourou Kourou Bougou many times. "For Yusaid, Yunido, CARE. Why do you want to go there? Are you who?"

Zane repeats his name before realizing Falaye is asking if he is from the World Health Organization. "No. I am unemployed."

"Not a doctor? Not from the UN?"

"No, not a doctor. I can only cure hangovers."

Falaye wants five thousand CFR, about fifteen U.S. dollars. He explains that they can leave in two days. Ignoring the advice he's been given, Zane tells him he'll pay him double if they leave right away, but Falaye shakes his head. "The roads are bad with rain and the sun is go down fast. I have no lights and the drive is two hours, maybe three."

"But it's only fifty kilometers."

Again Falaye shakes his head, though his smile is intact. "Pretty bad road," he says.

Zane gets the drift that Falaye needs further convincing in monetary terms. "Triple," Zane tells him. "Fifteen thousand if we leave in ten minutes."

Falaye holds out his hand. "Pay now."

Zane counts out the bills and Falaye folds them once and stuffs them into his shirt pocket behind the Gitanes.

"Smart man not a doctor. Time is time. No sweat."

His jeep is nearby, he says. Zane should wait for him while he fills it with gasoline. They settle on a meeting point and Zane returns to the hotel for his suitcase and comes back to the square, where he drinks bottled French water and debates the wisdom of a whisky. Half an hour later Falaye drives up in a battered Renault 4, what they call a *quatrelle*, with the top stripped away. But the tires are oversized and in good condition and Falaye says he can drive through mud as high as his knees. He also shows him how they can erect a small tent over their heads if the rains come. He packs Zane's suitcase into the rear seat, which already holds a spare tire, tools, blankets, a barrel of fresh water, and a drum of petrol. Zane sees Falaye pack a pistol among the maps in the glove compartment. "Is it loaded?" he asks.

Falaye ignores him. "We go now." He points to the sun. "We go fast."

They inch out of the square and Falaye turns onto the rue Bara Diarra and continues to a large avenue, where he turns right. "Kasse Keita," he says and, a half-mile later, Zane sees the street sign for the Avenue Kasse Keita.

Falaye drives parallel to the train tracks toward the edge of town. The avenue is swollen with the traffic of cars and wagons and pushcarts. The cars are an unbelievable collection of old French models and hybrids with mismatched fenders and tires or missing doors. The traffic thins out gradually and within fifteen minutes they are on the open road, a thin blacktop surface with a worn divider stripe. Falaye looks at his watch. "Five o'clock," he says. "Very fast. No sweat." He fiddles with the radio and can produce only parasitic news from a Bamako station, so he switches it off. He speaks in either French or English, depending upon the words he wants to use, though occasionally he throws in a phrase or two of Bambara. To show off his culture, he sings bits of rock songs he's learned from listening to a station in Abidjan. The lyrics are so mangled it takes Zane a while to realize he is singing "Hotel California":

"Livin a tup a la Hotel California. Sum a rummy pray, sum a rummy pray."

Such a lovely place. Such a lovely place.

Falaye offers Zane a Gitane. He doesn't refuse, though the dark-brown tobacco never fails to give him a headache. His acceptance puts them on good terms and Falaye urges the car to fifty kilometers an hour and they have to shout above the noise of the engine.

"Tell me about the village."

"Bad place, very popular with UN. *Mara*, everybody blind."

"But why?"

"I just say you. *Mara*."

"What is *mara?*"

"Bad business. Spirits. *A mandi.*"

This doesn't make any sense but when Zane asks for an explanation, Falaye merely repeats himself. "Spirits. Badness." The road begins to revert to nature and Falaye swerves regularly to avoid sudden holes or bumps. "The rains make this," he says. "Every year is worse. Mud is better." After half an hour he turns off the tarred surface and steers the car onto a dirt road that leads into the bush. The rains have only recently ended and the road is uneven, ridged with tire marks and pitted with small or large puddles that Falaye ignores, pushing the car through them with occasional bursts of speed.

For the next hour, the drive takes them on a semicircular route north by northwest. Though the odometer is broken, Zane could swear they have come seventy or eighty kilometers from Bamako. This is a road that has been maintained almost solely by rain, wind, haphazard undergrowth, and the ruts of tires through deep mud. No road crew ever passed this way. The sun has begun to dip below the treeline when Falaye makes a last turn onto a bush-lined path that is barely wide enough to allow access. Then he abruptly brakes and turns off the engine.

"Where are we?"

"The village," Falaye points to a ridge up ahead, "is there. I go ahead, speak Bambara. *I-ni-sogoma.* Talk to chief. You stay here."

Zane steps out of the car to stretch and get a fix on where he is. The land is mostly flat, rising occasionally into gentle, bush-covered slopes. The daylight is fading quickly and the sunward slopes, which were white during the afternoon, have suddenly fanned into different shades: black to the distant east, blue in the near distance, white and gold to the south, coral and pink to the west. There are few trees and no birds that he can see or hear. He lights a cigarette and gazes toward the ridge beyond which Falaye has vanished. He wonders if he could find his way back to Bamako alone and he decides not. Darkness gathers and his shadow lengthens across the grassy field. He is watching that shadow when a fly begins to circle his head. Then there are two, and then more; a cloud surrounds his face and he waves his hand in front of his eyes but one of the flies lands and bites before he can slap it. He begins to run down the road, still swarmed, so he returns to the car and reaches into the back seat where an old newspaper lies amid Falaye's tools. Folding it once, he lights it on fire and swats the air around him with the flame until at last the flies disperse.

The bite, at the corner of his eyelid, is painful. He examines it in the rearview mirror of the car and finds a pink swelling that is worse when he scratches at it. Looking at that eye, he can't help laughing. Less than twenty-four hours on a continent he has never seen and already he's a victim of the wildlife. He sits in the car and lights another cigarette, hoping the smoke will keep the flies at bay.

Half an hour later Falaye appears on the ridge, his face lit with a grin. He bears on his shoulder what looks to be a blanket. "You are welcome," he announces. "*Demain*. Tomorrow. Now is late for visit. Tonight we stay here."

"We sleep in the car?"

"No," Falaye says. "In tent." He drops the bundle from his shoulder and unfolds it. Zane bends to give him a hand but Falaye gestures him away. "I am *barakèla*," he explains. "Manservant. Same price, no more."

When the tiny tent is erected, Falaye lights a small twig fire and bids Zane sit. Then he takes a sack from his jeep and prepares a meal of crushed corn, rice, and water sweetened with mango. The sun goes down behind his back and he tosses more twigs onto the fire as well as dry grasses that make a thick smoke. "*Les mouches*," he explains. The flies.

After they've eaten, Zane allows himself a few swallows of whisky. Falaye declines to join him and carefully repacks his remaining food and stows it in the jeep, then offers Zane another of his Gitanes. They both light up with a burning stick and smoke in silence. When his cigarette is down to its last quarter-inch, Falaye throws it into the fire, then once again adds dry grasses.

"We sleep," he says.

The tent is meant to cover only their heads and they recline on Falaye's blankets while the fire smolders at their feet. Falaye's face is inches from Zane's. Before sleeping, Zane asks him, "In the village. Did you see a white man there?"

"No," he answers. "But there are always white men there."

"Which white men?"

"Yunido, Who."

At length Zane understands him. UNIDO, the United Nations International Development Organization; WHO, the World Health Organization. "Why do they come here?"

"I already tell you. *Mara.* They come to see *mara.*"

Sun, moon. What Paris will seldom reveal to you. Sunset, moonrise. The slant of a tree and the branch that sags with dark fruit. Zane awakens with his cheek resting on bare earth. The earth, to his surprise and pleasure, is warm and smells of onion and clover.

Falaye rouses him and grimaces at the sight of his face. The previous night, in darkness, he had not noticed the fly bite. He hurries to the car and returns with his knife, then bends over Zane and presses the blade close to his eye. "Be all shut up and still," he says. And he scrapes around the sore spot, drawing blood.

"It's only a bite," Zane tells him.

"Not bite, eggs. Now blood and no more eggs."

"Who taught you this?"

"Yunido."

Zane stands and washes with water from Falaye's plastic barrel. The water is cold on his hands and forearms and he can feel a breeze at his back. He dons a clean shirt and replaces his dusty socks with a clean pair. Falaye tells him that they should hurry. There will be food for them in the village but first they must be at the trees to meet the chief. "Look at the sun. He is waiting."

When Zane is in the passenger seat, Falaye presents him with a paper bag. Inside is a bone necklace flaked with glitter, a net sack filled with onions, and two bags of rice.

"*Cadeau*," he says, "for the chief."

Zane confesses that he hadn't thought about it.

Falaye says he knows. "Same price," he says. "No sweat." He starts up the engine, presses it to full throttle, and jerks the car backward into the field, and then drives slowly and cautiously up a sloping path intended for men on foot. As they come to the top of the ridge, Zane looks down upon the village of Mourou Kourou Bougou. There are perhaps fifty round mud huts with thatched roofs, scattered pens and shelters, and three footpaths leading off to the Koba River a half-mile further on. Falaye parks twenty yards in front of a pair of trees that bend toward each other to form an archway. A man and two children are standing by that gate.

"He is Doukla Diarra," Falaye explains. "The chief of this village."

Zane slowly approaches the man while Falaye remains a half-step behind him. The chief has a faraway look and his eyelids flutter. When he is still twenty feet away, Zane realizes he's blind. All the same, his eyes are turned toward Zane's face. There is oil in his hair and his arms are white with dust. It is impossible to guess his age. Stepping close to him, Zane presents the gifts that Falaye has provided him and the man touches them briefly, one after another, and then hands them to one of the children at his side. The other child lifts a gourd in their direction. It is filled with water and he offers it first to Zane and then to Falaye. They drink and the chief motions for them to enter. When he turns, the children to either side of him take a hand and lead him through the archway of the trees, across the village in the direction of his hut.

Falaye and Zane follow, and once they are seated before the hut, a woman brings them millet in peanut sauce, maize porridge, and rice. Zane tells Falaye to translate for him and asks if there is a white man in the village.

Falaye speaks for three long minutes, then turns to tell Zane that first he is making conversation. "For nice talk, friend things. Now I will ask your question."

In reply, the chief only stares straight ahead.

"Street," Zane continues. "An Englishman."

This time the chief responds and Falaye translates: "There have been many visitors. English, French, American. You look for your friend with your eyes." He adds that at this hour most of the people are in the fields.

When the chief has finished eating, he rises and is again led by the children, this time in the direction of rolling hills to the north. Falaye tells Zane they are free to move about, and so they wander the village, from hut to hut and fire to fire. There are mostly older adults and very young children. Zane sees a pair of blind lepers dressed in homespun cotton shirts being led by a child. A dozen women sit in a ragged circle and make rope while here and there groups of children are hauling wood or water or bending to small garden plots behind their huts. All of the adults are in some state of blindness. Even those unaccompanied by children tend to stumble and meander, their hands held before them as they walk. Cooking fires are tended by women with staring eyes that from a short distance seem unusually large and white.

In less than an hour they have circled the village twice without seeing any trace of Street. For the first time, Zane doubts Okimbo's message. Perhaps it was a ruse, a joke to play on Emelle's office boy.

Falaye asks, "What now?"

"We sit tight. Wait. Pray."

"I am not a Christian," Falaye says. "My friends, many others are Moslem. Almost everyone in Mali."

"And you, Falaye?"

"Je suis un ombre, a shadow. My father, Bambara, and mother, Touareg. I pray to ancestors who murdered each other. To who go your prayers?"

Zane reflects for a moment, remembering the candles he never lit in Notre-Dame. "I don't really know, Falaye. But I can promise you I don't pray to my parents."

Throughout the remainder of the day, Falaye and Zane join in with the rope makers, one of whom, though blind, teaches Zane by example the weaves and knots. She is a woman about his own age and she stops working now and then to scratch her hands

and legs, which are mottled pink and white in at least a dozen
places. She neither smiles nor frowns, nor does she blink when
a fly circles near to her face. Her hands lift, separate, cross, rotate,
and join as she holds the threads between her fingers. By the end
of the afternoon, Zane manages to fashion a length of rope twice
his height, but the cord is uneven and woven too loosely. The
woman runs the rope through her fingers and smiles for the first
time. When she thinks he isn't looking, she slips two fingers into
the end knot and in seconds has unraveled the entire length. To
cover his embarrassment, Zane follows a young girl out of the
village to a place where there is dry wood and helps her to carry
it back to the fire. As the sun goes down he is sitting unhappily
before that fire and watching the girl, who cannot yet be five years
old, gathering dry grasses and twigs to his side.

The flies are out in force and he is reaching to put grass onto
the flame when Falaye touches his arm. "Look," he says, "they
are coming home."

Beyond the huts, a large group of children in dusty clothing
approach the village. Behind them is a row of men holding a long
stick borne like a leash by a young girl. As they enter the village,
Zane can see them clearly in the fading light. The men are wearing skirts or short pants and their legs are bare. Their faces,
hands, and feet are covered with white dust. Some of the children are carrying baskets with grain and the adults are hauling
wooden hoes and pitchforks. Within half an hour the village is
filled with people and cooking fires are burning before each of
the huts. Zane stands on weak legs and walks to the eastern
perimeter to watch the last arrivals from the fields. After a day
of bright sun, he confuses the long shadows with men and has
difficulty fixing his gaze. Twenty yards away, he spies a tall man
being led by a young boy. The man is wearing brown cotton pants
and what looks to be a pajama top. He holds the boy's stick with
one hand and in the other he carries a hoe. The boy leads him
slowly across a patch where the soil has turned to powder and
then turns directly toward Zane.

The sun is almost down and in the firelight the shadows flicker
and fade. Zane gestures for the boy to stop and, when he does,
the man stops behind him. His head is wrapped in a print scarf

which, like his face, is covered with white dust. Beneath that dust is Harry Street.

"Eleven," Zane says. "Light water."

Street turns his head in Zane's direction. His mouth opens but he doesn't speak. Tears form in his eyes and turn to mud. "Zane?" he says. And though directed at Zane, his gaze is neither fixed nor certain. Street is looking beyond him, to somewhere distant. Toward the fires, where there is light.

They sit next to the fire in front of a hut that Street says the villagers have given him. He lives alone but is attended day and night by the boy, Camara, who brought him in, a nephew of the chief.

Camara arrives with millet in peanut sauce and then dips a gourd into a steel pail of water. He reaches to touch Street's hand and passes him the gourd, moving to sit a few feet from the fire. All the while, his eyes are on Street.

Zane is afraid to speak. Street's open eyes stare across the rim of fire while his fingers lift the food to his mouth. Camara has washed away the dust to reveal deeply tanned skin and a beard that adds years to Street's face. His eyes are mottled pink and white, and there are flecks of gray where his hair has thinned at the temples.

When he has finished his meal, Street holds the bowl outward and Camara jumps to take it from him. "Did you bring any whisky?" he asks.

"A full bottle in the bag. There, in front of you."

Street leans forward and slaps at the bag until he feels the familiar glass shape. "Moro me-mi yorodoumó," he says. "An important phrase. It means, Where can one drink?"

Camara produces three cups but Falaye says Ai, which Zane takes for a refusal, and so pours only for Street and for himself. Street sips the whisky slowly and swallows with pleasure, then holds out his cup for more.

They drink in silence while Camara and Falaye look on. All around them, other fires are burning as the villagers eat and drink. Not far away, a pair of blind men begin to tap on log drums and Falaye reaches into the fire for a stick that he claps against a stone.

"How did you find me?" Street asks suddenly. There is a trace of anger in his voice that puts Zane on the defensive.

"A message on the public line and a kicker on the dedicated line. Telling me you were dead."

"I'd assumed that I'd disappeared quite completely. Does Abby know that I am still amongst the living?"

"I didn't know myself until now."

"Then she must've thought I was dead. Getting on with her life. The rest of it to be lived."

"The message was unclear. Our language is flawed. Gone to blue's supposed to mean dead."

"It has multiple meanings."

"Tell me the others."

"Is that what you came for? To brush up on our codes?"

"I came because I couldn't accept the translation."

"And who told you where to find me?"

"Ambrose Okimbo."

Street is silent for a long moment. "I sensed he was still alive. As if he will never die, whereas for so long I thought he could be dead at any given moment. Where did you see him?"

"In Paris."

"Paris," he says.

Both of them are thinking of M'Khlea, but Zane can imagine nothing to say about her. Instead, he says, "We must leave the village. As soon as possible."

Street shakes his head. "This is my home now. Have you come to save me, Zane? Or is Emelle offering sanctuary?"

"I wasn't the only one looking for you. We're in danger here."

"Danger from what?"

"From Berne."

The name falls from Zane's lips like a stone and Street again falls silent. Then he lifts his head and tries to focus on Zane's face. "He has followed you?"

"Almost certainly."

The drumbeats quicken and Zane notices that nearby several women have begun to dance. They skip and leap to the drumbeats and children joined in. A number of them are blind, and stand and stumble awkwardly in an imitation of dance. A young boy holding a stick leads the lepers in a swirling pattern around a fire.

"The end of the rains," Street explains. "We dance every night since the rains have ceased. I don't know when it will end." He is then led by Camara to take part and his movements are wooden and uncertain, what one would expect of a blind Englishman.

"I'm not leaving, Zane!" he shouts in the general direction of the fire. "I want him to come. Light water! I want to see his *face!*"

The drumbeats wax and wane and wax again and Zane sees the chief from across the fire lifting his arms to the sky. Then Falaye stands to dance and, glancing around, Zane finds that he is the only one who isn't. Men, women, children, blind and half blind, all leap and stumble to the drumbeats that signal the end of the rain and the beginning of the planting season. Zane feels arms lifting him upward, but when he looks no one is there. He is standing of his own volition and his feet lift from the dust and he is dancing. In his entire life he has never danced. His partners are blind and their gestures are clumsy, like his own. Only the music is pure and certain, those drumbeats and the clacking of sticks. The fires burn and Street shuffles past him into a knot of adoring children. Looking upward, Zane sees that the sky has been overrun with stars. He has come to the other side of the language, the other side of the screen. As the pounding grows louder and the blind men begin to chant and scream, Falaye is at his side, pulling him away from a human oval that is forming in the center. Street is a part of that oval and he is held up by Camara and another boy. His sightless eyes are raised to the heavens and Zane is aware that he has danced this dance before; he knows the steps and the rhythm as the oval closes and reopens and then closes again until the dancers are knotted and confused and begin to flail blindly against one another. Fear dissolves Zane's sense of awe when suddenly the drumbeats end. Street lets loose of the children at his side and falls gently to the dust, his face haloed in firelight and with a weird smile of joy and satisfaction and confusion.

Night. Falaye and Camara are stretched out on straw mats nearby and the villagers sleep while Street and Zane remain by the fire.

"The rainy season is ended," Street tells him, "but twice now we have had sudden downpours that swell the riverbanks on a moment's notice and just last week a child was drowned. I feel I should warn you. Do not go to the river at night."

"No chance of that, Harry. I'm not much of a swimmer."

"Where have you put the bottle?" Street asks.

"At your feet."

"One bottle. I imagine you expected a short visit."

"We're leaving in the morning. There's room in Falaye's jeep. We can get you to a hospital."

Street shakes his head. "I remember reading a story when I was a child," he says. "About a man lost in the American wilderness. He was starving and without a gun to hunt with. After setting a trap for small game, he realized he had no bait so he cut off his own hand and strung it over the trap."

He reaches his hand downward until his fingers rest on the neck of the bottle. After prying loose the cap, he pours the whisky, keeping a finger over the lip of his cup to know when it is filled.

"I have no more witnesses," he continues. "The Touaregs I had have scattered and the blood samples have disappeared with my doctor in Abidjan. You have admitted to me that Okimbo named him, so you believe me now. That he exists. And if I leave here, I will lose my best chance of finding him." His smile in the firelight is like a grimace. "The desperate hunter uses himself as bait."

"And when he comes. Then what?"

"I don't know. Kill him?" The cup trembles in his hand and he sets it to the ground. "A test of my pacifism, Zane. One that I cannot pass without also failing. Do you understand me?"

"Killing the wolf to save the sheep. Like my mother."

"No. Your mother wanted the world to dance to a new music. I don't want to call the tune. I want to kill a single man, still his heartbeat once and forever. One heart, Zane, not billions."

"Why does he want you, Harry? You're not a player."

"I never was—until we did our part in letting Okimbo out of the bottle. Circumstances have changed, no? Hiding M'Khlea. Loving M'Khlea. Hiding her from her husband."

Falaye stirs in his sleep, one hand reaching for a stick that he keeps nearby. Street's eyes are turned toward that stick and for a moment Zane could swear he is staring at it.

"Berne must have got wind that I was gathering evidence. To expose a man who has lived in veils and shadows for the past twenty-five years. He slipped up in Nigeria. Okimbo has a world-class memory and his erasures did not take."

"But all you could hope for was to expose his existence. How would that have stopped him?"

"He has worked mostly for governments. Not insurgents or revolutionaries. Once exposed, he would have difficulty finding employment or safe haven. He could be flushed into the open. At any rate, my witnesses are gone. Now I will deal with him on my own."

Again he reaches for his cup and pours. To Zane, the night has grown even darker than it was, the sky changing from blue to purple. The thin trees at the edge of the camp are black and in the changing firelight seem to be constantly moving. He keeps thinking he sees soldiers on the perimeter. When the embers have burned so low that he can barely see Street's face, he reaches for more wood and dried grasses.

"Go gentle with the grasses," Street says. "You can grow dizzy from the smoke."

"I need to know what happened," Zane answers. "This spring and summer."

"What happened?"

"Your eyes, to begin with."

"I can still see shadows and light, like many of the others. There are more than two hundred people in this village and only twenty are totally blind. But nearly all of the adults are affected in one way or another. That is where the children are saviors. They do our seeing for us."

"Falaye used the word *mara*."

"It means possession. These people are animists, great believers in spirits. They consider this blindness a curse on the village."

"What *is* the curse?"

"Onchocerciasis. River blindness. The black flies are the carriers. To be precise, the females. When they bite, they leave parasites, worms, beneath the skin. No doubt you have seen these people scratching pink sores."

"Yes."

"These parasites reproduce and eventually they attack the optic nerve. As time passes, the nerve weakens and eyesight diminishes accordingly. You are less sensitive to light and color, and objects take on a blurry outline. Then there is no focus whatsoever, just obscurity, a beclouding. At the extreme end is total blindness. Some of the older men have what they call 'the lion's stare' and can sleep without closing their lids."

The chief, the leper, the woman who makes rope. "Can it be cured?"

"No." Street pauses to drink from his cup. "But it can be prevented."

"Then how—"

Street holds up a hand. "Then how it is that I'm afflicted? We'll come to that," he says, "when the bottle is closer to empty."

Zane, impatient, pours for himself and then for Street.

"The land is richest near the rivers," Street continues, "so that's where the people live. But that is also where the flies proliferate. Years ago, this village was on the banks of the Koba and there were many more people. But the flies were so terrible that they moved upland, to this spot. Apparently they didn't go far enough."

"You said there was a way to prevent it."

"New drugs, ivermectin and mectizan. For the past year my company has been distributing both all across the western savanna. There are villages like this one from Senegal to Ethiopia. The drug doesn't kill the parasites but it does stop them from reproducing. This generation may be the last to suffer from river blindness."

"Then why you? Why didn't you have the drug?"

Street lifts the whisky bottle and shakes it. "Just enough," he says, "for a last nightcap. You have come a long way to find me and I still find it hard to believe you're here. I hadn't realized

how much I'd missed some things. Like Scotch whisky and listening to spoken English. Even your American English."

"If you're too tired, we—"

"No, not at all. The whisky relaxes me. I can feel a heat in my
blood, is all. My tolerance is down."

Camara murmurs but he is talking in his sleep.

"He's dreaming," Street says. "To the Bambara, dreams are a
means of communicating with their ancestors. Camara is adept
at conjuring dream states. It was an honor for me when he was
made my *barakèla*."

"Who are you to these people?"

"A field hand. A scarecrow. A man. With everyone being blind
in one way or another, we're all of us equal. And no one here has
ever heard of England. No one knows where it is."

Falaye stirs beneath his blanket and opens his eyes. "Is it
time?"

"No," Zane tells him, "it is nighttime still," and he falls back
to sleep.

The silence is filled only with the wind and the crackling of
the fire. Then Street, at last, begins his story.

"As you already know, I had been searching for Ambrose
Okimbo for three years. After we met him, I found it hard to
believe that he was killing people, but M'Khlea seemed to feel he
was lost the moment he was released from prison. He had chosen
his mountain, she said, and would not come down. But it wasn't
until he began organizing his army that we became seriously
alarmed. His people in Paris had located us once again and in
self protection we decided to rely on our own devices. We even
kept the truth from you, to spare ourselves from unanswerable
questions."

"What questions could I have asked?"

Street shrugs. "We needed to encrypt our communications. You
were in the business of seeking information. Okimbo was big
game."

"You didn't trust me."

"No. You were too close to Emelle, ABRI. It was never an organization that inspired confidence, though you were always reliable when it came to the language."

After a brief hesitation, Zane says, "I've read the letters. M'Khlea gave them to me."

"M'Khlea," he says and his eyes stare straight into the fire. "Tell me how she died."

By now Zane can tell this story almost without thinking; a blessed relief. "She pretended to disbelieve me, claiming there'd been some mistake or misinterpretation. She gave me your letters and told me that I would understand only after reading them."

"And then?"

"And then I left. I was across the street reading the first of the letters when she jumped."

"Are you sure she jumped?"

"At the time I didn't question it. She thought you were dead. So did I. Because of the message."

"Who sent it?"

"It was signed by Demi, one of his name codes. But he isn't the one who sent it."

"Then who?"

"It took me a while to know for certain. But whoever sent it knew that I would take it to M'Khlea."

"Berne. In search of me."

"Emelle hired him. Stupid of her, I know. She thought he would be a security against leaks."

"That isn't all of it. Christ, Zane. That language isn't perfect. Meanings stick out from behind the curtain. We should have overhauled the verbs a long time ago."

"The way you and M'Khlea did?"

"Precisely. Same words, new meaning. Do you blame me?"

"No." Zane reaches for his whisky and finds that the taste is mingled with the odor of burning wood. "No, I don't." He has yet to fully recognize that the man across from him is Harry Street. He reaches for more wood to add light but only twigs and sticks and a handful of dry grass remain.

"If you've read the letters," Street says, "then you know that I found her husband."

"In Gao. But I know precious little beyond that."

"He was obsessed with his sense of immortality, his soul, what he referred to as *tunzi*. It's a Zulu word that applies to spirits but also refers to the soul leaving the body. When he and M'Khlea were married, their souls became inseparable. If he were to die, she would have to follow him. And he clung to that idea even after she left him. To not go into the realm of death without her. Until he was released from prison I admired him totally. He seemed to be the alternative, unpolluted version of myself. I lose hope so easily and Ambrose seemed to be a composite of all the attributes, words that come to my lips with difficulty: forbearance, steadfastness, vision. I am closer in spirit to you, a cynical, quasi-alcoholic humanist continually on the verge of irrational tears. Understand, I don't mean to belittle either of us. I have not lived my life any better or worse than you. We have our honor, as derelict as it may sometimes be—the schemes and blueprints, the lifeboats we toss willy-nilly round the continent. But ours is a shabby honor, Zano, by comparison to what once was his. And I was convinced that he would listen to me, that he would hear out my confession and release M'Khlea from that vow. Considering the danger in which he lived, he could have died at any time. And when I held M'Khlea in my arms, it was always with that thought of her mortality in mind."

"And that's why you were looking for him."

Street nods. "M'Khlea, and the possibility that he could lead me to Berne. He was being hunted by the Nigerian government, by the CIA, Interpol, and by the Bambara—the ruling half of Mali. His ragtag Touareg army was on its last legs. He knew he couldn't survive for long. I felt that time was running out and I had to find him soon."

"Your last letter says you did."

"I was walking with my friend Kevin Dioulasse. We were in the northern hills looking for roots that could be used to make medicines when we were intercepted by Okimbo and his men. Kevin was led down the hillside and I was certain he would be shot. My nerves were gone, and over the years of hiding M'Khlea from him I'd developed a vision of Okimbo that was less than accurate. I thought he was a killer and nothing more. But that afternoon he was just as calm on the outside as he was the night we met him. And despite the uniform he still had the look of a gentleman. Does this make any sense to you?"

Remembering their meeting in Paris, Okimbo's measured gestures, Zane nods. "Yes, it does."

"At first I tried reasoning with him. I made a brief appeal to his past, to the humanity of his own poetry. That resulted only in stony silence. A few of his men were within earshot, men he had every intention of leading into death. Many of them were boys, Touaregs who didn't give a toss about pan-Africanism, they just wanted the soldiers to stop shooting at them. So that afternoon, surrounded by his lieutenants, I insulted him, mocked his accomplishments, and ridiculed his recent poetry, which even he had rejected as rhetoric. I pointed out to him that his efforts had been ruinous to the cause of African unity, that he had put an ugly face on the whole affair with his killings and bombings. It was all quite pointless and futile, more people dead for no gain whatsoever. I wanted him to answer me, to provide a clue, however thin, as to why he was comporting himself like some black messianic Nazi. But he refused my provocations and said only that his accomplishments had been exaggerated. 'I am not half the hero you took me for,' he told me. 'Nor half the villain.' He had the look of a man prepared to die, or of a man already dead. The knowledge that he was at his end. I kept up the tirade long after my fury was exhausted, certain he would kill me as soon as I'd finished. But as the sun went down he merely rose and ordered his men to escort me back to the house in Gao. I asked him about Berne and he told me I was close. The other side of the hill, he said, and I took this as more of his poetry. 'If you come any closer, he will kill you.' Those were Okimbo's final words.

"I returned to Gao and waited, certain that he would come back for me. Kevin begged me to run. I couldn't, though. I was still clinging to a scant hope that he would release M'Khlea from that Zulu pledge. This was early in March and my time was running short on all ends. Kevin had helped me locate and examine half a dozen Touaregs who had been arrested and released by the government. Four of them were confident they could identify Berne. Three of these witnesses had been freed months before, and their blood samples showed nothing that could be used as evidence. But you've read the letters, you know these things."

"Dr. Renault is dead. Mozart reported it."

"I had assumed as much when I heard he'd disappeared. That same month, I was receiving daily messages from my company superiors. For weeks I'd been giving them the impression that I was elsewhere. I couldn't have Berne finding me simply by calling my employers. They wanted me back in London, so I resigned. The two men I'd searched the whole bloody continent for were too close to me."

"At the end of your last letter, you said you were meeting with Okimbo again."

"So I imagined. He had a place in the hills and late one night a car arrived. I thought it was Okimbo's men and was so eager I nearly leapt into that car. It *was* filled with soldiers, though none of them were in business with Ambrose Okimbo. I was bound and stuffed into the trunk. It seemed that we drove all night and then, for two days, I was held in a cement-block basement. I didn't know until much later that I was in the hands of the Malien army. Not a regular corps, though. These men were working for Berne and I gather they were acting under his orders. I was moved twice more before they stuck me in that hut."

He sips at his whisky, holds it on his tongue before swallowing. "It was a hut like this one, with mud walls and a thatched roof. These people can survive the worst of the heat but are obsessed with the rain. They often build huts with no aeration to speak of, just mud and sticks and straw and no way to bloody breathe if you're inside during the hot months. The hut they put me in was just such a place and they even sealed the fire hole in the center of the roof. The rains were falling daily and I lost track of time. I was fed and given water but they refused my requests for a walk in the open air. To keep myself occupied, I practiced self-preservation routines I'd heard and read about. I did jumping jacks, push-ups, and isometrics. I told myself the history of the world, from Babylon to Napoleon to the present day, with special emphasis on the decline of the British Empire. When I grew bored with that I recounted to myself, one by one, all of the sexual encounters I could dredge up. With bits of straw I built a tiny but elaborate metropolis and encouraged the ants to wander through its mazes. In short, I was half mad before the week was out.

"At some point I was expecting to be tortured and was surprised that the prospect didn't fill me with terror. In fact, I felt oddly curious as to what method they'd employ. You've handled enough cases, you probably know the encyclopedia by heart.

"One evening I dozed off and was awakened by the flies. I was bitten on the hand and then on the neck. In the darkness I couldn't see them and at first I assumed that there were three or four. Whenever one landed I would swat it away and I must've killed dozens. But there were always more. You've been bitten by now, I imagine, so you know how painful it can be. Each bite leaves a reddish welt that itches terribly. But by scratching, you scatter the parasites into your bloodstream. You don't worry about that at the moment, of course, all you can think of is that terrible itch. I began to lose my mind and started screaming. What seemed hours later, the door opened slightly. I thought that they were going to let me out but then I saw a hand opening a jar and more of those flies streamed inside. Berne's men were gathering new flies every day and loosing them into my hut. There was nothing to feed on but me. I waved and slapped and swatted until I no longer could move my arms. And after a time I had to sleep. Whenever I awoke the itching was terrible. My hands and legs and around the eyes. They are attracted to the salt of tears and to dried blood. This went on for days, I don't know how many. In normal circumstances it takes years of exposure for river blindness to develop but I was being bitten a hundred times a day. I can't say when my sight began to fade, because the hut was always dark. When I was rescued, I could only see what I see today, shadows and light, everything the shape of this fire."

"But how did you get here? Okimbo only mentioned a failed rescue."

"I didn't know who it was at the time. I still can't swear they were his men, but I know it was night when there were gunshots. After the first shots, I was taken from the hut and thrown into a car. We drove cross-country and then along a road. As we were being pursued, my captors were firing automatic rifles from the car. Then, abruptly, we stopped and a body was thrown over my face. My first thought was that we were in water. The man's blood covered me and when I finally pushed him away I found that the car had tipped on its side and I had to climb out a window. Shots were still being fired, but from far away. I don't really know how far. Blind men at night make poor witnesses. I was slightly insane but at least I was free of the flies and I had the good sense to wander downhill, certain that I would eventually come to water. Camara and his mother found me stumbling around the river's edge and brought me here. I was covered in blood and filth and they must have known I was being hunted. The fact that I was blind, it seems, made me one of theirs and they have allowed me to stay with them. This village has been a perfect hiding place. The soldiers steer clear of it. They believe in the curse."

"How long have you been here?"

"Weeks. I don't know how many. Until you found me, the only one who knew I was here was Kevin Dioulasse. Camara's mother found him in Gao and he came to take me away. My recovery was slow and I couldn't travel. I was undernourished and extremely weak. Kevin sent word to M'Khlea that I was well but he didn't tell her where I could be found. Four days ago he came back, hoping to take me north to Chad in his truck. From there I could make my way back to Paris. But he brought the news of M'Khlea and my darkness was complete. As though life has ended. So I have stayed. Since I came here, I have my own supply of mectizan, like everyone else in the village, and my sight will stabilize. I never will be totally blind."

The bottle is empty and the fire is almost out. Zane reaches for more wood but now even the twigs and grass are gone. He thinks of the night he spent at ABRI waiting for the kicker. His mouth is dry and a cigarette burns its way like a fuse to his fingers. The words appear on the screen and fall through his eyes to his brain.

A blue light appears across the eastern horizon. Camara awakens and stretches his body across the blanket. Then he rises and removes his shirt, shakes the dust from it, and sets it near the fire. Reaching his hands into the water bucket, he rinses his face and hands, and then puts the shirt back on. He goes into the hut and moments later reappears with pots of rice and maize. Stirring the fire to life, he sets the pots onto the embers and then bends to wash Street's face and shoulders with a wet cloth. Around them, other villagers are awakening and tending to their cooking fires. Street eats sparingly and passes the bowl to Camara, who finishes what's left before rinsing the bowl and returning it to the hut. The others are assembling at the eastern edge of the village and Camara leads Street among them. Before the sun has risen, they begin to walk in its direction, carrying hoes and forks and bags of seed while the elders, the blind, hold the hands of their children, who guide them across the dusty paths to the waiting fields.

Through the remainder of the morning, Zane dozes in the shade near to the hut. Falaye has once again joined the rope makers and Zane is free to sweat his hangover into submission. He is awakened near noon by Falaye, who tells him that dust has been seen in the south.

"Meaning what?"

"Trucks. Soldiers."

"Which soldiers? Malien or Touaregs?"

Falaye shrugs. "Soldiers."

The village is alive. Women and children are leading the blind with their sticks in the direction of the river and the cooking fires have all been extinguished. The dust on the horizon is in the same direction as the road that Zane took from Bamako. Even as he stares, a long jeep appears at the crest in the rise and stops. A few moments later, it begins moving again, descending the slope toward the trees that mark the village gates.

"Not Bambara," Falaye says. "Lepers here and bad spirits. Bambara soldiers never come." He instructs Zane to go inside his hut and wait, then heads off toward the trees. In the stifling half-darkness of the hut, Zane falls to his knees; he peers out a gap in the woven branches, and tries to measure the distance between the village and the river. There are at least a hundred yards and nothing to hide him if he runs. He wonders briefly if this is where he will die. He could soon become one of his own statistics. That's what it's come to. You can't drink your life away, Marie told him—or you can, he thought to himself. You can drink in the river, this river, and it will flow through you until you drown.

Several minutes later, Falaye returns to the hut. Another white

man has arrived, unannounced and without a guard. The chief
wants to send him away because of the soldiers. "He is like you.
Not Yunido or who. He comes with soldiers but says he is a
doctor."

Zane stands on stiff legs and follows Falaye across the village
to the trees that represent the door to Mourou Kourou Bougou.
The chief is there with his accompanying children and beyond
them is a tall man in khakis. He wears a wide belt with an empty
holster and carries a knapsack. Beneath his hat his hair is blond
and white.

Zane quietly tells Falaye to ask the chief to let him pass.

The man strolls between the trees and into the village, one
hand resting on the empty holster. He recognizes Zane from a
distance and stops for a second before continuing in his direction. Three trucks and a second jeep appear on the rise to the
south, and over the man's shoulder Zane can see soldiers getting
out. A breeze blows dust into the air and the two men face each
other through a small cloud. Zane feels a sickening urge to rush
forward and squeeze the life from him. When they are separated
by only a few yards, Berne stops. Zane is amazed to see that he
is smiling. "You should not have come here," he says. "There is
leprosy in this village and the flies carry disease."

His accent is impossible to place. There is a clipped British
tone alongside a dispassionate Nordic precision, each word equal
to the others. No italics, no spice.

Upon hearing his voice, Zane feels his murderous urge subside.
His mouth is arid and his tongue is stuck to his teeth. "Who have
you come for?" he asks.

"I've come for no one."

"You've been trying to kill me."

Berne only smiles. "To kill you? I could have killed you at any
time. But you were more valuable to me alive. Don't you recognize me?"

"We've never met."

"I have white hair and a beard. I read the sports pages in Le
Figaro."

Zane feels a chill. "At the Painted Bird. You led me to Okimbo."

"You were too helpless," Berne says, "to find him yourself."

"And Okimbo knew about this village."

"I've come to treat the lepers," Berne says, lifting his bag.

"Then why the escort?" Zane points toward the soldiers waiting in the distance.

"My fellow travelers. Shall I send them away? As an act of faith?"

Zane nods and Berne, turning round, raises both arms into the air and crosses them. After a moment's hesitation, one of the figures on the hill returns the signal. Then the men shoulder their rifles and climb back into the trucks. A minute later, there is only dust in their wake.

"Where will they go?" Zane asks.

"Not far. To the other side of the hill. But they will not disobey me. No one will come into this village unless I tell them to."

He notices Zane staring at his holster.

"As you can see," he says, "I am unarmed. This holster is forever empty. So that everyone can see I am a civilian, a country doctor. Now, if you will excuse me, I have my rounds to make."

When he attempts to cross into the circle of huts, Zane blocks his path. Their faces are nearly touching. "He isn't here."

"Who, Mr. Zane?"

"Harry Street."

"Of course he's here. That is why you have come out from behind your screens and your fax machines."

"Who do you work for?"

"For the same outfit that you do. The suffering citizens of Africa. Now, if you don't mind . . ."

But Zane still blocks his way, uncertain to what lengths he will go. Berne is taller but much older, at least sixty. The sun is in his eyes and he has to squint to look at Zane. "I promise you, I have my rounds to make. The lepers here know me. I have come before."

Zane still stands there.

"You are alone here," Berne says. "You spent one night in the Hôtel France. You had no visitors and you made no phone calls. The next day you made a brief visit to the American Center and then you hired a guide and driver from the central square. No one on earth knows where you are, and you *are* exposed. Now let me pass or I will see to it that you are not allowed ever to leave this country."

His hand rests on the empty holster and, after a moment's hesitation, Zane steps aside. But when Berne has turned his back and headed into the village, he calls after him. "How did you learn the language?"

Berne turns and now Zane has the sun in his eyes. "Semantics. Your cables and transmissions were so numerous that I had an abundance of raw materials for decoding. I studied the redundancies and repetitions as though they were poems written in a foreign language, then compared them to African events. Stars being soldiers, for example. The moon is down. I had great difficulties with the term *light water* but in the end you might as well have communicated in English. If you have a secret, everyone will want to know it, won't they? I wasn't alone. There was even a minor glossary available in a CIA data bank. Courtesy of Mr. Kirk."

"How long have you been shadowing me?"

Berne ceases to smile. "Ever since your efforts to liberate Ambrose Okimbo, I have been aware of you. I admired you at the time. I assumed you had vision and passion. But in these weeks of observation, I have my doubts. Perhaps you are only another petty spy like these men you call rakers. A typist, a list maker. Be careful, Mr. Zane. With time and alcohol and your illusions of usefulness, you might someday become Emelle."

He turns and heads for the huts, where once again the cooking fires are lit. Smoke rises toward a sky grown white from the sun.

Throughout the afternoon, both Falaye and Zane watch over him as he moves from hut to hut. He treats the lepers and those with fly bites. Seeing him with the lepers, Zane momentarily feels a diminishing of his hatred and then remembers that even the worst of criminals has the capacity to exhibit kindness. The love of dogs and children, a knife in one hand and chocolates in the other. Twice Berne returns to his jeep for medicine or bandages, and although Zane is breathing down his neck on both occasions, he ignores him.

Near sundown, Zane leaves Falaye to keep watch and crosses the village toward the river. He finds Harry Street standing in a cornfield with a child to either side of him.

"He's here, isn't he?"

"Yes."

Street closes his eyes and opens them. "How much sunlight is left?"

"A few minutes."

"Take me to him quickly. I see so little in sunlight but in darkness I see nothing at all."

The children precede them out of the field and onto the path to the village. "Rain," Street remarks. "I can smell rain."

Zane tells him there isn't a cloud in the sky.

"Then what am I smelling?"

When they arrive at their hut, Berne is already seated in front of the fire. He is surrounded by children and a woman, a leper, sits close by his side. He has obviously awaited them. Street stares in the direction of the fire. "Where is the bastard?" he whispers to Zane.

"In front of you."

The black hands of children fill bowls with maize and millet. A breeze stirs white dust, and the grasses in the fires burn blue and yellow and leave a pearly smoke in the air. Camara brings a gourd of water and an empty bowl. Sitting next to Street, he rinses the dust from his face and shoulders. Across the low flames from Street, the leper woman washes Berne with a sponge of moist leaves. Once the sun is down, Berne gestures for her to withdraw, but she remains seated close to his back. Zane stands behind both of them and watches.

"I am sorry about your eyes," Berne says. "I did not know about the flies and the hut. This was not done on my orders. Please believe me."

Street is silent. When Camara places a bowl of millet in his hands, he sets it to the ground.

"Is there any sight left to you? Shadows or sensitivity to light?"

"I can see you," Street says. "I can see right through you."

"You were to have been treated with humanity. With the same mercy you have dispensed to the Touaregs. But the soldiers wanted to punish you. It is their business to punish."

"As it is yours."

"No, Mr. Street. You are wrong. You have misread me and have hunted me in error."

"You weren't in Wollayta in 1984? In Algiers? Who was it who arranged for the torture of Ambrose Okimbo and, more recently, countless Touaregs?"

"I have been many places where torture has been rampant. As have you. But no one accuses you of having tortured. Why do you assume that I am less innocent than you?"

"There are witnesses. They call you Sky Eyes."

"Witnesses who have placed me at the scene of their torment. But did they not tell you that I comforted them? For years I have been amongst them, closer than you have been. You always came afterwards, but I was there when it happened. For years and years."

Falaye has posted two young boys at the edge of the village and one of them has returned. He speaks into Falaye's ear and Zane strains to hear. Berne takes no notice while Falaye relays to Zane the news that the soldiers are still on the other side of the hill. There are three campfires, twenty-one men.

Berne is still speaking. "I was a doctor in Algiers in 1961, a volunteer intern from a neutral country. The French were losing the war and becoming hysterical. As a neutral I was assigned to civilian wounded, but one day I was taken by the French soldiers to a place outside of the city. They brought victims to me and asked me to heal them. I had bandages and disinfectants, plasma, salves for cigarettes burns, and a limited supply of morphine. The first man I treated took two weeks to recover from his beatings. I released him to the French and a month later he was brought back to me. Le gégène, they called it. Electrodes to the gonads. His legs and buttocks were swollen from broken blood vessels and he had suffered a heart attack. I gave him the last of the morphine and he smiled at me through an entire night before dying."

Street is silent but Zane can see he is still trying to focus through the firelight in a vain attempt to see Berne's face. "You were in Vientiane, in Phnom Penh. Uganda and Benin and Nigeria."

"You exaggerate my influence and my scope. I have been in some of these places, but not all of them by any means."

"In Wollayta," Street says. "You were there. I have evidence."

"Yes," Berne says. "I was in Wollayta. I studied the pain of the tortured and as a doctor my role was to eradicate it. This I have done, through the development of medicines and various treatments. The wars in Ethiopia are amongst the cruelest in the history of the planet. I went there as into a sea of misery, and there was nothing I could do to ease it."

"Euthanasia."

"I thought of it as mercy."

"A dozen people put to sleep and buried."

"The soldiers wanted to tear their limbs away and I interceded. I did not bury them. I closed their eyes." Berne holds his fingers to his head and massages his own temples. "We are both doctors, Mr. Street, and—"

"I never finished school," Street corrects him.

"Nevertheless, you provide what a doctor provides and we are working toward the same end: the eradication of pain. The difference is that you assume you can stop the torturer by exposing him to public view. Amnesty and human rights and all the self-righteousness of letter-writing and petitions and rallies in the park on Sunday. *We shall overcome.*" He smiles and in the firelight Zane sees his teeth. "I walked with the killers. I ate at their table and drank their wine. There was a colonel in a roving outfit whom I knew to be a mad dog. There was no reasoning with him, as vicious a man as God ever put on this earth. He wanted nothing of me or of my methods. You think it's all politics and ambition and then you see a man who kills for pleasure or simple profit. In a village not far from here I saw him shoot a child between the eyes, a boy of ten who was meant to carry water for the men. I was tempted to make it painful, to offer him agonies that would even some universal score. But that was against my nature. I cannot inflict pain. So I induced fatigue. He drank his whisky and had to lie down. To his lieutenants, he had a fever, perhaps from a fly bite. They came to me and asked me to tend to him. I did what I could but the next day he slipped into a coma. This happens often in the rainy season. Men go to sleep and never awaken."

The wind is blowing in from the south. It is warm and smells of the earth. Street had smelled rain, but the clouding sky is littered with long stars.

"So you *worked* with them," Street says. "In their horror galleries."

"I was present when men were tortured. I offered the torturers a different set of methods. There are two activities that distinguish us from animals. We torture and we keep secrets. I taught, in secret, humane torture. The words cancel each other out, I know. But consider that the motives for torture are always the same: to break the will of the individual and thus his resistance, or to elicit information. Electrodes and razor blades inflict pain to arrive at the desired result. My methods do not. I have reduced human suffering wherever I have gone. I have dealt, as have you, in mercy."

"With surgical haloes and brain scans. Intravenous drugs that squeeze memories from men like juice from an orange."

"Torture gives voice to a language of pain, human pain: syllables and grunts and screams that contain little of the information the torturer wants. *If* the torture is political rather than personal. There are also the confessions that are only, in truth, screams for mercy, what you called in your language Molly's soliloquy. I spared them suffering."

"*Physical* suffering. I've seen your happy specimens, Berne, and they are now suffering through the personal hell of having betrayed friends and family."

"The betrayal was inevitable, either through torture or my methods. Once captured, they could only speak or die."

"You removed the option of death and dignity."

"What would you have me do? Yours is a shabby mercy, Mr. Street. Bandages after the fact. I *prevented* the bleeding. I have seen suffering that transcends the worst nightmares. Fingers torn from hands with pliers, eyeballs crushed, open mouths filled with kerosene and lit with matches. I have heard screams that could awaken the dead. There is no forgiveness, there is only mercy."

"You opened the door to the human heart and dragged secrets from men. Your employers profited when your patients pointed a finger in the direction of their comrades. After your mercy there was endless slaughter."

Zane notices that Falaye is no longer among them. The leper woman leans forward to put more wood on the fire, and as the flames grow Berne pushes backward to avoid the heat.

"People sometimes choose to die to protect those they love." Street is leaning too close to the fire and a tongue of flame rises close to his eyes. Camara touches his shoulder to steady him. "Ambrose Okimbo was prepared to die. As were those poor Touaregs. And now they are worse than dead."

Someone approaches Zane from behind and when he turns Falaye is holding a small pistol. He remains beyond the firelight, in the moonshade of the hut. Glancing at Zane, he offers the gun.

Zane takes it into his hand and feels its weight. He is only ten feet from Berne. The man's light hair presents a target that fairly glows in the dark night. He aims and Berne turns to face him.

"Come into the light, Mr. Zane, where we can see each other."

Zane steps forward toward the fire, still training the gun on Berne.

"If you are going to shoot," he says calmly, "do it now. Later you may not have the chance."

"You sent the message," Zane says. "Eleven gone to blue. Light water."

"And followed you when you carried it to the woman. You don't remember me? We bumped each other on the stairway and I failed to notice you were carrying the letters."

"Shoot him, Zane. Pull the bloody trigger."

"It was a message that you couldn't fail to take to her. I was only afraid that you would be too drunk to remember her address."

"And when I was gone you entered her apartment."

"She didn't even lock the door."

Berne stands and holds his arms outward. "I told her that all I wanted were the letters. She said she had burnt them, but I didn't believe her. I asked her where I could find Harry Street and she lied, which I expected. You were always so careless with your language and your codes."

"She didn't *know*, Berne! She only knew I was alive!"

For a moment Berne is silent. "She was not afraid of me," he says. "That was a surprise. I have a great capacity to inspire fear, and I needed her to be afraid, so I opened the windows wide."

"Aim for his head. The eyes."

"'Do you know my name?' I asked her. She moved away from me. I circled her, astonished at her beauty. I had only seen photographs before that day, newsprint photos that did her no justice. Okimbo had spoken of her during interrogation. His poetry. Her eyes, her long neck. She stood only a few feet from me and the breeze from the open window carried her scent. When we questioned Okimbo, he resisted us with thoughts of her. He told us everything about her, the feel of her, what she said to him while making love, the way her back arched."

Street cries out but Zane doesn't take his eyes from Berne.

"When we asked where his comrades were hiding, he told us instead about his wife, all that he could remember of her, their every intimacy. Days and nights I listened to him. I encouraged him to tell me more. His confession of love became my own."

Zane lifts the gun a notch higher until it is pointing at Berne's head.

"I was weakened in her presence. But I couldn't have you exposing me, Mr. Street. You understand so little. It's evident I was right. She wouldn't speak to me. Not in any of her many tongues."

"So you pushed her."

"No!" He shouts. "I moved closer to her. I wanted to touch her, you understand. I knew that after that day I would never see her again. I remembered all of Okimbo's words. The way he loved her. I had never heard of such love. In my life there has never been time. 'He is alive,' I said to her. 'Your precious Harry is alive.' I thought she was about to speak, so I reached out my hand to her. Just my hand. But she withdrew and when I followed her toward the—"

"Do it, Zane!"

"I *can't*, Harry."

"Then give me the gun and I'll do it."

"Do what he says, Mr. Zane. You know he's right. One of us will have to die."

"Shoot him!" Street leaps to his feet. "Pull the bloody trigger!" Camara grabs his shoulders but he stumbles and falls face forward into the fire. He is up instantly and his hair and shirt are alive with flames. He lurches toward Berne, who sidesteps him, and tumbles to the dust. Zane drops the gun and falls to his knees at Street's side. With both hands he pours dust over his head and arms. Smoke and dust rise from his body and his hands and face are blistered.

Zane leans to his face and finds it wet with tears. "Kill him," Street says. "Kill him, kill him."

Falaye bends down and hands the gun to Zane, who stands and looks around him. The trampled fire has gone out and Camara has arrived with water and grasses and kneels to tend to Street. The wind blows stronger and smells of dead leaves. The leper woman is gone. As is Berne.

When the rain begins to fall, Zane is again holding the pistol in both hands. He steps backward into the thin shelter at the edge of Street's hut. Camara is inside watching over him. The burns are superficial but Street is in extreme pain and now and then Zane can hear him cry out. Falaye has been gone for what seems a very long time. The downpour increases and makes it impossible to see more than twenty feet around the hut, or to hear anything above the din.

A figure approaches from the other side of the swamped fire circle. Zane crouches and strains to see through the rain, which is silver and falls in great slants. He hears a sound like snapped sticks and gradually he realizes bullets are flying around him. He collapses to the mud and aims the pistol at the figure. To his surprise, the gun fires; he hadn't even felt his finger on the trigger. Berne appears through the rain—the bullet missed him—and stands ten feet from the door of the hut. Zane rises to his knees and the two men face each other with upraised pistols. Zane's is trained on Berne's chest, and Berne aims for the head.

"Shoot first, Mr. Zane."

In his eyes, there is an immense sadness, or is it only the rain between them? Zane wonders fleetingly if Berne has a death wish. Euthanasia. A bullet to the heart.

Street asked this question many times. Could you kill a killer? To cancel out murders of the future. Kill the wolf to save the sheep. Even if you die doing it. Answer me, Zane.

He can hear the sound of gunfire and he is still alive. Berne lowers his hand and turns his face toward the hills. There is more shooting and through the noise of the rain Zane can hear the ripping sounds of truck engines. Over Berne's shoulder, lights appear like weaving fireflies and Zane slowly concludes they are the headlights of trucks descending the slope. Berne's army.

But when Berne sees those headlights, he suddenly rushes away. Rising, Zane runs forward and can see Berne's back as he runs into the near cornfield. The stalks are only knee high, and though Berne is crouching, Zane can pick out his profile moving across the rows. On the other side of the field is the path that leads to the river. Emerging onto it, Zane sees that the village has been overrun with soldiers, but after a moment he spins and races after Berne.

When he comes to the river, Berne is just ahead of him. He steps into shallow water that reaches only to his waist, but the current is strong and he fights to remain upright. In the light of a half moon, Zane sees Berne go down. Then he can't see anything. He creeps to the edge of the water and sees a dark swirling. Berne's head emerges from a point where the water is deeper and he struggles to stand. He sees Zane on the shore, twenty feet away. "My boots are filling," he shouts. Zane looks around for a tree branch, a stick. Finding none, he wades into the water toward Berne, who just shakes his head. The water is up to his neck. When Zane gets to within five feet, he reaches a hand, but Berne doesn't move to take it. He is looking past Zane, beyond him. There is someone else in the water. Zane can't see anything but can hear the sounds of swimming. Again he reaches out his hand and this time Berne tries to take it; their fingers touch briefly, but suddenly Zane is pulled under by the weight of a man. He struggles upward and as his head emerges from the water he can see

Berne's head disappear. Zane dives but the water is black. He is in a warm black emptiness, pushing and gliding. He rises to the surface to catch his breath, dives again, gropes blindly, and finds only river mud. Then arms encircle him and drag him backward toward the shore. His head goes under the water and he kicks upward, freeing his arms. His hands close around the man's neck until his lungs burn. One of his feet is buried in river mud and it feels as if he's being sucked back in. With his free leg he pushes himself upward, gripping the man's neck, until his feet find rock. Then he lunges to the surface, his fingers still around that throat like a necklace.

It is Ambrose Okimbo.

He relaxes his grip but leaves his hands there and his head tips forward until his skull is touching Okimbo's. At last he lets go and together they collapse to the muddy shore, gasping for breath. Zane rolls to his side and vomits black water. I am not drowned. Turning, he finds Okimbo staring upward while the rain falls into his open mouth.

"Why?" Zane asks. "Why?"

"You were going to save him. And he desperately needed to be dead."

The rainfall lessens as the winds die down. Zane swears he can hear his own heartbeat but almost certainly it is the rain drumming on a hollow log. His legs are still in river water and finally he pulls them free and rises to his knees. Okimbo stands over him and offers a hand as two men hurry down the bank to help them up. Zane recognizes the lieutenant who was with Okimbo in Paris. They move slowly through the cornfield to the village, which is now surrounded by Okimbo's Touaregs.

Street is standing near his hut with one hand on Camara's shoulder and with soldiers on either side of him.

Okimbo stops before Street. "Have you been harmed?" he asks.

"Ambrose?"

Okimbo doesn't answer, just stands a few feet away and stares at Street's face. Zane expects him to say something, to offer a curse or a blessing or a fragment of forgiveness. But then he turns toward his men and gestures for them to return to the trucks. He tells Zane, "The road to Bamako will be clear only for another two days. After that, you would need to be armed to find your way home." He looks again at Harry Street but his gaze is cold. He is a soldier, no longer a poet. He turns his back and heads toward the gate of the two trees.

"Ambrose!" Street calls. "Zane, call him back!"

The Touaregs climb into their three trucks and Okimbo takes his place in a lead jeep. The driver hands him a beret, which he fits over his head. He does not look back as the jeep pulls away. The trucks follow without headlights and they drive up the slope and disappear into the darkness.

THE NEXT MORNING, STREET IS TOO WEAK TO GO INTO
the fields. He sleeps on a pallet in front of his hut, his burns
covered in ointments and river mud. Camara sits nearby to shade
him and wave the flies away. Accompanied by Falaye, Zane climbs
the slope on foot and, at the top of the rise, he searches the ho-
rizons for signs of soldiers. Three men lie dead at the edge of the
road. They are Bambara, Falaye says, and should be buried. The
high ground is already dry and it takes most of the morning to
dig the graves. When they are finished, Zane leaves Falaye alone
to pray over the souls, which he says linger in the vicinity. To the
animist, he realizes, it is as though they are planting seeds with
those corpses and the soldiers will grow from the soil into other
creatures, serpents or butterflies or jackals. Out in the open, as
they walk back to the village, there are no flies and the sunlight
is blinding. Falaye is somber, but when birds fly overhead he stops
suddenly and points them out to Zane as if to say these are souls
reincarnate; the eternal circles of an earth that will last forever.

Back at the village, Street is still asleep. After washing, Zane
and Falaye follow the river downstream for the remainder of the
afternoon, but there is no sign of Berne's body. The river is over
its banks by twenty feet. The current was strong, Falaye says. It
may have carried him further down, to where the river is wider
and forms a small lake. Or the body is buried in the deep mud
along the banks.

"Could he have survived?" Zane asks.

"Children die in those waters," Falaye says. "Sometimes men."

So he returns to the village without evidence either way. Gone to blue, as the language would have it. Light water pending.

At nightfall, Zane leads Street to the river and they shed their clothes before wading into the water. Camara and Falaye wait onshore.

"Are there any fish?" Zane asks.

"A few. None of them the size of men."

When they have finished bathing, they put on the same clothes and sit on the bank while an alabaster moon rises slowly above the treeline.

"That man," Street asks. "You tried to save him."

"I stuck a hand in his direction. The first time he refused to take it."

"But you tried again."

"Okimbo stopped me."

"If he hadn't . . ." Street waves at a fly that is circling him. "If he hadn't, would you have gripped that hand? Pulled a dying man from the water?"

"I thought I had him in my hands. That I was strangling him."

"To save the sheep?"

"To save myself. Anyone can kill. The rain was blinding." The river has already receded and flows more slowly. From where he sits, Zane can see the spot where Berne went under. The water there is now only knee deep. Children could swim there and no harm would befall them.

"What are your plans?" Street says. "Now that you're out of a job."

"Something will turn up."

"The amnesty business?"

"Whatever comes along."

"What happens to the rakers?"

"They're scattered to the winds. I wasn't the only one they were talking to. The juice is still flowing somewhere."

"There are many kinds of mercy," Street says. "Unless you've had enough of this life."

"Falaye is getting anxious," Zane tells him. "He wanted to know when we're leaving and I told him tomorrow."

"That's fine. Tomorrow, then."

"Will you be coming with us?"

Street takes a long time before answering. It is a question that he must have been asking himself since he first heard Zane's voice in the village.

"No," he says, his voice barely a whisper. "I will stay on here."

"Come with me, Harry," Zane insists. "To Paris at least."

"I'm blind. Unfit for work. I'll never be a doctor and my children in England have little need of me. Tell me, Zane. What would I become back there that I am not here in this village?"

Zane can't answer that. He never has an answer to such questions, what a man can be in one place or another, what a man can be to other men.

"Camara takes care of me and in time I can even take a wife, if so inclined. I have food and shelter and will retain what little eyesight is left to me. Though this blindness is almost a relief. The things I no longer have to see."

"But there's no need to hide, Harry. You could—"

"I'm not hiding! In London or Paris I would be an invalid. I would sit in a chair and let my fingers trail over the sheets of Braille. It's what we do in the Western world if we're missing a limb or our eyes or our ears. We rot. There is no Braille here, there is no writing whatsoever—only spoken words which I can bloody well hear. I have a language to learn, Bambara. *Kongo béna*, I'm hungry. *I kakène*, How are you? As time goes by I will learn other words and grow old with them still on my tongue. An Englishman, a Bambara, what's the difference? I work the fields, Zane. I'm part of this tribe now, a scarecrow. It is no different in its way than what you have been doing for years, scaring away predators and intruders. I wave my arms and the fields are safe. I can feel the sun in my face and I can sense the presence of children at my side, and at night when I close my eyes to sleep I am too weary to dream or to ponder what might have been."

When Zane reaches a hand toward him, he senses it and takes it into his own. "I am shedding my Englishness already," he says. "I eat with my fingers, I dance around the fire, and now I am *holding hands* with a man. Fucking hell." He turns toward Zane, trying to focus on his face, and as he does his eyes turn from gray to green.

"Which isn't to say," he says at last, a smile spreading over his face, "when all is said and done, that I might not someday get tired of the whole affair and send you a telefax asking for an Air France ticket out of here. *Classe affaires*, of course. We can use the same code as before. Trouble is, I'm not sure I remember them."

"High five."

"Another of your damned Americanisms. How could I have forgotten?"

As they return to the village Zane tells him that he once loved M'Khlea, too.

"I knew," Street replies. "And M'Khlea knew, of course."

Zane is awakened before dawn by Falaye and they pack up his Renault 4 for the drive back to Bamako. Zane pauses at the arched trees to watch the field hands assemble at the eastern edge. Street is clearly the tallest among them and Zane can see him follow Camara's lead down the path and beyond.

"Wait for me," he instructs Falaye. Then he hurries back to the village and down the same path.

The fields are strung along the riverbank. Rice paddies, sorghum, corn, and peanuts. The villagers are already scattered across the distance and he finally sees Street heading into a field of corn that doesn't yet come to his knees. In his red shirt he is the only thing in that field that is not green or brown. Camara hands him the stick and leaves him there and for a long while he stands calmly among the low stalks, balancing his weight against the stick. When the sun is fully risen and the field is bathed in light, his long shadow precedes him as he walks the rows up and down. Suddenly he stops still as a troop of crows approach at his back. They circle him for a moment, then descend toward the corn, and at that moment Street lifts his stick and swings it round and round, driving them back into the sky.

THE BOOKSTORE DEALS IN FOREIGN TITLES: ENGLISH, Italian, Russian, Hungarian, Turkish, German, Polish. The clients are usually immigrants or exiles, most of them elderly, for whom the bookstore is one of the few links to their pasts. When they stop in, it is more often than not to browse the titles, scan the pages, and finger the worn covers. They seldom have the money for a purchase. It is enough for them to cast eyes upon written versions of their own languages. Often, they seek to engage Petitjean in conversation, and he offers what he can manage in French or English or German, but these conversations are clumsy and unsatisfying. Once a week a man from Budapest comes into the shop and speaks Hungarian to Petitjean, who doesn't understand a word but nevertheless will answer in German, which his visitor seems to respond to. Though their discourse is meaningless, the sound of his own voice seems to comfort the man as he describes, complains, confesses, relates, and informs in the language of his childhood. An hour after arriving, he will abruptly cease talking, choose a book from the Hungarian shelves, pay for it with a combination of tattered bills and small coins, shake hands, and depart.

The bookstore loses money but the owners, a cooperative of exiled East European families, are unconcerned. Petitjean's pay is delivered in cash at the end of each month, and new sets of books, donated by other exiles or purchased in bulk from various corners of the continent, arrive on the first Monday of every month.

There are two back rooms, one of them a waiting room. Sometimes, Petitjean receives a phone call or a message through the mail and, shortly thereafter, a man or a woman is delivered to him. *Letters*, they are called, when they come to him on their way to somewhere else. No one ever stays longer than five or six hours. The bookstore only serves to keep them off the street.

As winter approaches, he installs a hot plate and provides coffee and tea to the customers who come to visit him. Poetry readings take place in the larger of the spare rooms. On occasion the readings are held while a refugee or escaped prisoner hides on the other side of the wall. Various East European newspapers and magazines are stocked on a free reading shelf. One rainy afternoon, with nothing to occupy his mind, Petitjean takes a faded grammar from the shelves and, between visits from customers, he begins to unravel the vocabulary and syntax of the Hungarian tongue. The verb conjugations are baffling, and the accents impossible, but he persists until he can say a hundred words and understand an occasional phrase or two. After a visit from a Romanian woman, he resolves to study her language as well. Then Polish, Serbo-Croatian, Greek. In time, he decides, he will speak all of their languages, one after another. He has years ahead of him, a lifetime to learn the words. So that when they come to the bookstore to visit him, these exiles and refugees, he can offer them, along with coffee or tea, a moment's amnesty from human silence.

At six in the evening, his most recent letter delivered and the sky growing purple with darkness, he pulls the blinds and locks the front door. He is already late so he takes a taxi and tells the driver to wait outside for him. Cathcrine is sitting on the couch in her go-see-the-doctor clothes, white blouse and blue skirt and a string of fake pearls around her throat. This will be their third visit and she is still terrified and wonders why she has to go to the office. Why can't the doctor come here instead?

"He needs his equipment, Catherine. Those machines he used last time."

The office is on the rue de Paradis, not far from the Hôpital

Saint-Lazare. During the first visit, the doctor had taken blood tests, X-rays of her torso, had told her to stand, close her eyes, lift one foot. She had read small and large letters from a distance, and he examined her ears and throat and asked her to blow up a balloon. Then he had put her into a quiet room with blocks and balls that had to be fitted into their slots. He gave her a pen and told her to trace her way out of the maze. The first time she came back with a maze that had been colored in and he had to repeat his instructions. "Start here and imagine you are walking. Draw a path from here to there without crossing the lines. Can you do that?"

On their second visit, the doctor asked Catherine to sit in a comfortable chair and relax. He gave her a set of earphones and told her to press a button whenever she heard a sound, and to hold that button down until the sound went away. The button was attached to a red light so he could gauge the precision of her hearing. Petitjean sat across from her and she reached out her free hand and gripped his knee. The doctor turned knobs and lifted levers. After a few moments, Petitjean saw the red light come on and then go out again. It seemed that most of the time the light was off and he took this for a bad sign. The doctor continued this routine for twenty minutes and occasionally wrote notes on his clipboard.

After a time he turned to Petitjean and asked him to leave the room. "She isn't concentrating," he said. "You are distracting her."

So Petitjean waited in the lobby with its Louis XIII furnishings and not a single ashtray and leafed through old issues of *Paris Match* for over half an hour.

Then the doctor called him into his office. "You are her brother?" he asked.

"Friend," Petitjean said. "And guardian."

"This woman is a curiosity but her health is generally sound. Good wind, healthy blood, though lacking in iron and magnesium. A bit of fresh air would do her good. As for her intelligence tests, she scores out nicely. She is not in the least retarded."

"What, then?"

"She is simply clinically deaf."

"Stone deaf?"

"She can hear many sounds but only of a certain pitch. She is obviously skilled at lip reading. You notice when you speak to her that she is watching your mouth and not your eyes. And when she speaks, her words come out without definition because she can barely hear herself. Lip reading normally has to be taught and my guess is that her hearing was better when she was young and then deteriorated over time. She should have been brought to me years ago."

Petitjean was tempted to tell him about the years. Either that or murder her mother. Then the doctor told him to come again in three days. "That's how long it will take to deliver the device."

"What device?"

"A hearing aid, of course. Marvelous what you can do with thom these days. Even so far as adjusting them for pitch sensitivity. I can do that part on my own. As for the moaning at night, it is most probably her thinking aloud. She can't hear herself but must feel the vibrations of her voice."

When Petitjean faced Sylvie with the news she wept and claimed innocence, ignorance, sorrow. "They told me she was an idiot. When she was a little girl I took her to a doctor. What could I do but believe him? She just sat there with that blank look on her face. You've seen her. She can't even button her shirt correctly."

"She has never been taught."

"I did what I could for her."

"Which was nothing whatsoever."

"I kept a roof over her head. I fed her and clothed her."

"Eighteen years indoors. Eighteen years with no one to talk to. Learning everything she knows from pictures in magazines."

That night Sylvie packed a small suitcase and disappeared. Catherine joined him in the bed with the broken springs. Neutral territory, a mattress without history. When she moved her legs for him, he edged himself forward. What she heard as a whisper he heard as a scream.

They are late for the appointment and will have to wait for a full hour. Petitjean stands near an open window and blows cigarette smoke to the wind while Catherine sits calmly in an enormous chair and watches him. Twice the nurse comes in to tell them that the doctor will be with them shortly.

It is nearly seven in the evening when at last they are called into his office. The apparatus is in a steel case and looks like a set of pearl earrings. Catherine is directed to recline on a high table and the doctor speaks into her right ear, telling her to be calm, that she will not feel anything except the cold of the metal.

"The right ear is stronger than the left," he tells Petitjean. "You will have to come back in a few weeks so that I can check the balance between the two devices. Now please do not speak until I have finished."

Five minutes later the hearing aids are in place. With his hands, the doctor gestures for Catherine to sit up. She reaches her fingers to her ears but does not touch them.

"Catherine," the doctor says with a quiet voice, "can you hear me?"

It is as though he has slapped her face. Her eyes widen and then fill with tears. When she hears herself crying she cries harder. The crying goes on for a long time.

"She is attuned to softer tones," the doctor says. "She will have headaches for a time. Be sure that she removes the device like I showed you before she goes to sleep. And remember, for the next week she will have the impression that we are shouting. Silence will never be the same to her again."

WHEN THE GUEST HAS RISEN AND GONE DOWNSTAIRS to breakfast, she goes into the room to make up the bed. The curtains are open and she thinks to herself that she should remind him of the rules, but she understands how they must crave sunlight, these guests; sunlight and an open window. With the curtains closed, the room is like a prison, despite the new paint and the prints that she has framed and hung, despite the paper flowers in the vase and the row of books on the nightstand. A room is a room; the prison is in the mind of the prisoner.

Thomas tells her it is this man's last day with them. At midnight, a black man wearing a blue suit and silver tie will come into the club and order a Manhattan. She is to answer, "Manhattan is an island," and if he pays with a two-hundred-franc note, she will return his change with a slip of paper denoting where the guest can be found. A waiting room, they call this address. Chez Fingers is referred to as a safe house.

The two remaining bedrooms are unoccupied, though they expect another visitor, if not several, near the end of the month. They are sent by Mozart or by Demi, or by friends she never knew Thomas had. They come from Africa or from Eastern Europe, mostly, though once there was a writer from China who was convinced he was being tracked by agents from Beijing. He had occupied this same room for three weeks while Thomas organized passage on a flight from Brussels to Montreal. Marie could only guess at what the writer would find in Montreal. Thomas seldom even confides to her the destinations of those who have come and gone. It is better that way, he says. The less one knows.

When the sheets have been changed and the curtains pulled tight, she closes the door behind her and returns to her own apartment, the two rooms she shares with Thomas. The bed is still unmade and there is a half-empty bottle of Scotch on the nightstand; next to it, a glass filled with melted ice. He swears to her that he is drinking less than before and she can only wonder how he has managed up to now. He drinks before sleeping, alone with her in the dark, but when he makes love to her he is always sober and gentle, careful with her as though she might break in his hands.

As the weeks have passed, their possessions have begun to merge and the bedroom has lost its aspect of a hotel chamber. Their books and records are arranged haphazardly in the same shelves and there is a tangle of common laundry in the hamper, his shirts and her underthings, his handkerchief and her blouse. She has changed the curtains from dark blue to white and he has hung a single photograph on the wall, a picture that he took himself with a borrowed camera and had developed and put into a silver frame. Before taking the picture, he admitted to her that her face had taken some getting used to. "Like someone with an eye patch or a scar," he said. "Something foreign in your eyes. And then it was only your face." And with the camera he took a close-up and told her to smile.

The jazz club is still open, though business has fallen off and now Smith-y-Vega says he'll be leaving in the summer to take part in the Côte d'Azur festivals. July has been let go but Leon and Darren L. are still with them, along with a piano player hired in November, a young Frenchman named René who offered to play for free just for the experience of playing with professionals. Darren L. suggested that Marie take on the ivories but she knows nothing about how to play the music, only how to listen to it. Breaking Fingers' oldest rule, she has added a five-franc cover charge, which brings in close to a thousand extra francs a week, and so far she hasn't noticed any of the customers complaining. There is enough to pay the musicians, René included, and to feed the guests who pass through the safe house on their way to another life.

When she has finished cleaning the rooms and sweeping the hallway, she checks her face in the mirror, takes her purse, and walks in the rain down the rue de la Montagne Sainte-Geneviève to the metro station. It is three stops to the Gare d'Austerlitz where she changes trains, and then six more stations to République and another change. Fifteen minutes later she gets off the train at Gambetta, climbs the stairs, and crosses the square to the south gate of Père Lachaise Cemetery.

The rain has ended and the sky has been erased. There is an emptiness to the air and the black trees are framed in gray and white. Turning down a narrow alley, she walks south until she comes to the middle of lot 96. The ground is wet and strewn with rotted flower petals and the gravestone, a massive block of pure black marble, is beaded white with rain. She is not religious and does not kneel. Instead she bends to touch the letters that have been carved from the stone, to read them with her skin, like Braille.

LESTER "FINGERS" MINK

1900–1988

JAZZ LEGEND

STARS ALL AROUND AND SAM ON THE RUN.
HANGING MY HEAD. DEMI

The words are green on a black background, the colors of his
new screen. Zane cuts a print and addresses a return to the Tan-
giers address that should relay it to the safe house in Tripoli.

SAM IS BOGUS. RUN TO LIMBO.
JOHNNY'S LIGHTHOUSE.

Demi has his ass in deep grass in the wilds of Qaddafi's mad-
house. Against Zane's coded judgment, he has placed his faith
in a man he thought to be a friend while attempting to liberate a
dissident poet. The word from Mozart is that the American is a
mercenary and gunrunner and Demi's cover is blown. If he makes
it to limbo, in Malta, he will have an easy passage home, aided
by friends with no names. But first he has to make it out of Tripoli
with his face intact.

There is no other mail tonight. The lines are tranquil, the season uneventful. Marie informs him that their last guest has made
contact in the waiting room and for the moment the house is
empty. As he switches the screen to *Receive Only* he can hear the
music from beneath the floor, the new piano player, René, working up a respectful sweat on an old Fingers number. He descends
the stairs to give Marie a hand at the bar. The place is surprisingly

packed and he counts the heads for the sake of record keeping, although all he has to do is divide the take from the cover charge by five to know that there are fifty-one of the true faithful who have come in from the rain to drink and to listen. While Smith-y-Vega takes a break, Zane admits to him that he's fond of the new boy's touch.

"René?" he says. "He just might be the real thing. Cross your fingers, hope to die."

Zane jumps to serve a round of beers to the party against the front wall, but then a Belgian in a three-piece suit wants a gin and tonic and he has to call Marie over to make it for him. Zane can handle only beer or soft drinks or whisky in all its tan shades, whisky water, whisky soda, whisky on the rocks, or neat. Anything else, from strawberry daiquiris to Singapore slings, he leaves to Marie.

At midnight he climbs back up the stairs to their room. He removes his shirt and bends over the sink to wash his hands and face. He can see that face in the mirror. The same forehead, the same thinning hair. His mother's gaze, the eyes that haven't yet seen God. A lamp is lit next to the bed, as always. They turn out that lamp only to sleep. When they make love he leaves it burning so that he can see her, all of her.

When he returned from Africa, she was not at all surprised to find him at her door. The rain had come to Paris, a furious rain the color of steel that hammered the gray rooftops and flooded the gutters. They spent most of the first week in or near the bed. I'm insane, he thought to himself. And she is, too. When the rain stopped falling he was afraid for reasons he could not place.

Early one evening she climbed the stairs to join him in their room. They exchanged dry kisses, undressed, began again. But that evening he felt in himself a laziness, a reluctance that was new; she was like a shadow in his arms, cool, unmoving, indifferent. They both stopped at the same time. He moved away from her but she clung to his hand. Then she rose from the bed and went into the tiny kitchen. Moments later she returned with bread, cheese, Burgundy, a pair of wine glasses. They ate and drank and talked. It was the first time they had done anything together other than make love. The rain lessened. Neither of them had to say the words.

So he has stayed with her. Her plainness soothes him. Beautiful women's faces need deciphering, elaboration; Marie's is opaque, transparent. And in the light of their room, in daylight, he is hard pressed to take inventory of the rest of her. Or of himself.

While he was in Africa, Marie went to his old address to move his things. The concierge gave her his mail, including a letter from the prison. His mother's parole has been denied but her privileges have been reinstated. The letter adds that her lawyer's ancient and long-standing request for pardon gathers dust. Zane has already reserved a flight for the following week. From Paris to Chicago, Chicago to Minneapolis. A rental car will be waiting for him. Everything is arranged except the words he will use to break the silence of seven years.

He pours a glass of J & B and turns down the bed. He is about to lie down when he notices the incoming filtering across the screen on the desk nearby. Taking up his glass, he drains it slowly and walks around the bed to read the message. It is a relay from the Abidjan multiplexor and the first letters are a scramble of date, hour, minute, and second. There is an electronic pause during which the cursor blinks like a wished-upon star and then the message rolls across that screen a green letter at a time:

THE CROWS WILL KNOW BETTER FROM HERE ON IN.
SEND JUICE AND A HIGH FIVE. ELEVEN.

Zane taps for a screen print and switches the mode to *Send*, acknowledges receipt, and provides a confirmation of the drop address. Then he switches the screen back to *Receive Only*, takes up his whisky, and sets it down again.

They will need a new railing on the stairway and a buzzer system so he can find them when he needs them. Zane has recently read of a news service in Braille and of a surgical method for resuscitating damaged optical nerves. There are exercises that entail blinking and squinting that may leave him able to read headlines at the least. They will begin with his shadows and his light. And after that they will move on to the italicized print of human events.

He slips into the bed and can hear the music through the floorboards. The sound is muffled and distorted and he cannot sleep.

It will be hours until Marie comes to join him, so he rises and opens the door and can hear it loud and clear, every note of Fingers' music and the applause of the faithful. He leans back against the pillow, bathed in the light of that lamp, and nods his head to the rhythm while beside him the screen is set for incoming from men and women in the faraway fields.